The Mystery at Black Partridge Woods

THE
Mystery
at BLACK
Partridge
Woods

Pat Camalliere

First Edition   ISBN 13: 978-1-937484-44-6

AMIKA PRESS   466 Central AVE #23 Northfield IL 60093   847 920 8084
info@amikapress.com   Available for purchase on amikapress.com

Edited by John Manos and Ann Wambach. Photography by Richard Hoyt Lee. Map illustration by Ingrid Kallick. Designed and typeset by Sarah Koz. Body in Janson Text, designed by Miklós Tótfalusi Kis in the 1690s, revived for Mergenthaler Linotype by Chauncey H. Griffith in 1937, digitized by Adrian Frutiger in 1985.Titles in Dwiggins Uncial, designed by William Addison Dwiggins in 1935, digitized by Richard Kegler in 2001. Thanks to Nathan Matteson.

~ ~ ~

For the best family a woman could hope for:

Chris, John, Bob, Clare, Dolly, Collin, Aidan, and Mia.

You inspire and support me—I love you above all else.

To Portage and Fort Dearborn →

Des Plaines River

Black Partridge's Village

Noah Injured

Lemont

To Illinois River and Fort Clark

W   E
S

KEY

Bluffs

Marsh

Forest

River

Wawetseka's Route - - - - - -

Or, as some said, maybe she was not an ordinary wolf.
   —Wawetseka

Cora

2013

Chapter 1

Cora hadn't planned to write the book. She didn't even know the story existed. It all began when Nick walked in on Cora that morning. A young man, a stranger with dark hair pulled into a ponytail, he startled her with his unforeseen entrance. She had no way of knowing she would come to share his ambitions—ambitions that would lead them all into danger. Nick would probably say it was the Trickster, throwing one of life's surprises at her.

Cora had been standing beside a large library table in the choir loft of the Old Stone Church that now housed the Lemont Area Historical Society, known locally as LAHS. She gazed at stacks of partially sorted books, files, and documents scattered over the table. She had been in a good mood when she woke that morning *and* had a clear head, not always a given for a woman moving into her seventies. She was determined to make serious inroads to clear that table and get every item inventoried and into a permanent home—taking a bite of the elephant, she called it. Then one by one the volunteers that helped her make organization out of chaos called to say they couldn't make it in. That was a difficulty with volunteers in general, but these women were usually dependable, and it was rare that she worked alone. But there she was.

And it was hot! She hated to be hot—it was only early June. *And* this spooky old building was said to be haunted. Some of the members had had "experiences," but Cora never had. Still…

Staring at piles that never seemed to go down, deserted by her team, alone, hot, ears on alert for strange noises, her positive mood was rapidly deteriorating.

She picked up an item at random from the top of a pile, trying to decide where to begin. A ledger from a polling place, 1945, listing voters. People came to the historical society to look up evidence of ancestors and relatives and to find addresses. But where should she place it? With genealogy materials? Village records? No, it was a county election. She'd assign it to county materials. But then, the county kept its own records… should she keep it at all?

She was startled to hear the clang of the panic bar ring out from below, alerting her that someone was opening the front door on the ground floor. She jumped, dropped the ledger on the table, spun around, and banged her knee on a table leg. *Damn it! My bad knee!* She rubbed it and limped toward the staircase, heart pounding.

It wasn't possible for anyone to *sneak* in; the warped door announced visitors with a sound that reverberated through the sanctuary as the heavy, metal lock released, followed by the squeal of worn hinges that no one ever seemed to get around to oiling. She wasn't expecting anyone this morning, but unexpected visitors weren't entirely unusual.

Cora stood at the top of the staircase and called down, "Hello? Can we help you?" Didn't hurt to imply more people were present.

"Uh…yes…," a bright male voice replied. "I'm looking for Cora Tozzi?"

Cora didn't recognize the voice. She started down cautiously, clutching the railing to support her throbbing knee. She couldn't see anyone below. "I'm sorry, and you are…?"

A man appeared in the doorway at the bottom of the stairs. He was young and handsome, of average height, with a dark complexion and broad shoulders, his shirt tight against muscular arms, his long, black hair gathered neatly at the back of his neck.

"No, *I'm* sorry—for showing up this way." He smiled at her. "When I called, the secretary told me Cora Tozzi worked here Wednesday mornings. I thought I'd just stop in and try to catch her. Is she here?"

Cora closed her eyes for a moment, cursing Maureen for giving out that information. She hated interruptions. *So much to do and so little time.* She opened her eyes and forced a smile as she arrived at the bottom of the stairs, where the man stood in the building's small gathering area.

"I'm Cora." She waited for him tell her what he wanted.

His grin widened. "Cora Tozzi!" he said. "Wow!"

Despite her trepidation, Cora laughed and ran a hand through her thinning white hair. "I have no idea what I've done to deserve that!"

"No—I mean, yes, you have!" he said, thrusting out a hand for her to shake. "We just moved here—I'm a new fellow at Argonne." This man did not match her image of a typical scientist from Argonne, the national research facility about a mile away on the other side of the Des Plaines River Valley.

His hand was warm and smooth, and as Cora shook it she could sense the man's energy.

"I read about that old mystery you solved last year, about Sag Bridge and the murders? I just had to look you up. I'm Nick, by the way—Nick Pokagon."

He seemed friendly, and such obvious enthusiasm made a favorable impression, but Cora turned and called up the stairs to imaginary coworkers. "I'll be downstairs a few minutes." She pointed to the secretary's office.

The Old Stone Church dated from the 1860s and was never meant to house a modern office. The small room doubled as a bride's dressing room when the charming old building was rented for weddings, a necessary source of income for the historical society. A computer and printer took up most of a small desk. The rest of the room held a file cabinet and a pile of assorted items in a corner; a dressing table with a tall mirror for brides on one wall; and a church pew, now piled with boxes and stacks of paper, against another wall for guests. Cora cleared a space on the pew, gestured for the man to be seated, and moved to a chair behind the desk.

The Sag Bridge murders Nick mentioned involved a mystery she had been instrumental in solving the previous fall. The whole story was never revealed to the general public. Secrets only she and a few close friends knew had touched Cora's life personally and left her with a sense of loss that was still painful if she allowed herself to dwell on it. Her visitor could not know that, of course.

She sat tall in her chair, as tall as her diminutive stature allowed, and looked Nick in the eye. "Why did you want to see me?"

He flashed a magnetic grin again, and Cora could not help but be charmed. She struggled to keep her face from revealing the effect the charismatic young man had, but she feared her eyes gave her away. She found herself wishing she were forty years younger and forty pounds lighter, despite being happily married to Cisco.

Silly old woman, she chastised herself.

"When I found out I received a fellowship, I was excited about coming to Lemont because my ancestors lived here—back around the War of 1812. Now I'll have a chance to learn more about them."

"Mostly Indians lived here then," Cora informed him.

"Yes," he chuckled. "Like me. I'm Potawatomi. Pokagon Band, from Michigan. But some of us lived here once."

That explained the dark complexion, the ponytail. *Now, don't be type-casting!*

"There's one ancestor in particular. I thought a local historian could show me where she lived...answer some questions. When I read about you and Sag Bridge, I...well, I hoped you'd help me." He held both palms up in a pleading gesture.

Cora placed an elbow on the desk and rested her chin on her fist. "I don't have any information about any *particular* Indians, just general information available to anyone. I'm not sure how much help I can be. Documentation from that time is pretty sketchy. There weren't many settlers—mostly explorers, people passing through. The local Native Americans didn't leave any written documents, you understand."

"Actually, there *is* a written document," he said, eyes twinkling. "That's why I'm here." He leaned forward, watching her face as he explained. "My ancestor was educated at a mission and then lived with a voyageur family at an outpost. She left a written memoir. I can show it to you. Maybe we can visit some of the places she lived."

Cora smiled but tried to hide the sudden thrill tingling inside her.

A document written by an Indian, a Native American woman, *no less! During the pre-removal period!*

"It's all different now, of course...if she was around here, the village would have been along the river, and it was moved in the 1890s...." Cora realized she was babbling and trailed off. *What a find, if true!*

"You mean the village was moved, not the river, right?" he chuckled.

"No, the river was moved."

He opened his eyes wide, and Cora laughed at the expression on his face.

"Yes—to build the Sanitary Canal the engineers moved the river and ran the canal through the original riverbed." She launched into a favorite topic. "It changed the topography significantly—islands disappeared, swampy areas developed or filled in, things like that."

He grinned again and relaxed against the back of the pew. "See? That's the kind of stuff I want to know. Even if it's changed, I want to go there, walk where she lived, get some sense of her surroundings. Can you show me?"

Cora laughed. "Well, not now, certainly. But I could point out where you should go and what you should look for. Don't you need to be at Argonne during the day?"

He rolled his eyes in the direction of the ceiling. "I have some—flexibility."

Cora leaned back in her chair, crossed her arms, and grinned. "Well, Mr. Nick Pokagon, it seems we might spend some time together. You've certainly got my attention. But nothing's going to happen this morning—I have things to finish upstairs."

As they stood up Cora had a sudden impulse. "Are you free for lunch, by any chance?" she asked. "I'm meeting a friend, but you're welcome to join us. I'm sure you'll like her. Maybe we can make some plans."

As she said this, Cora bit her tongue. She had just met this man—she knew nothing about him except what he told her. What was she getting herself into? Was she misled by his charm? He seemed harmless, but the places he wanted to visit were desolate, and she'd be alone with him. Cisco would throw a fit when she told him.

Chapter 2

As Cora locked the front door of the Old Stone Church, she half-hoped Nick would decide not to show up for lunch. Why had she been so hasty? She walked around the building and down an alley where three parking spots were reserved for LAHS. She was irritated to find a dark-blue pickup truck that had seen better days parked near her car. She glanced in the cab, thinking she would give the driver a lecture or at least a dirty look, but didn't see anyone inside.

She backed out and drove to the street, shaking her head and wondering once again why people failed to heed the reserved parking sign for the few spaces at LAHS but obeyed a similar sign for the larger, adjacent area of empty church parking spaces. She was surprised to hear the truck's engine clatter to life and watched in the side mirror as the truck backed into the alley. She had thought it was unoccupied.

The truck stayed behind her. When she turned left off Illinois Street and onto Stephen Street, it darted in front of an oncoming car, forcing the car's driver to brake and sound his horn. She arrived at Smokey Row Pub and parked in the lot behind the building. The truck pulled into the lot, passed her, and stopped a short distance away. When Cora exited her car, the truck raced off. She never got a look at the driver. Perhaps Nick had followed her and then decided to park in a different spot, she thought.

A few minutes later, Nick came striding up Stephen Street where she waited near the entrance to the restaurant. His head turned from side to side as he studied the historic buildings that lined the street, until his attention was caught by the Illinois and Michigan Canal, a short distance from where she stood.

Cora greeted him with a nod and a weak smile. "Do you drive a dark-blue truck?" she asked.

"No, a silver SUV," he said. "Why?"

"Nothing. I mistook the driver for you, I guess," she said. Although she thought the incident somewhat alarming, she pushed it from her mind, assuming she had overreacted.

Seeming not to notice Cora's cool greeting and distraction, Nick waved an arm in the direction of the canal. "So this is what started it all? Chicago and everything around here?"

Cora felt herself succumbing to Nick's boyish enthusiasm once again, and whatever doubts she had quickly dissipated. "Yes. This is the transportation link that connected the Great Lakes to the Mississippi River. It's unlikely Chicago would ever have grown without it." She turned from the canal to the surrounding buildings and Nick followed her gaze. "Some of these buildings have been here 150 years," she added. She caught his eye. "Let's go in."

Cora immediately spotted Frannie, a sixtyish, African-American woman, seated at a table against the far wall. She waved off a waitress who was heading in their direction and pointed Nick toward Frannie's table. Frannie watched as they approached, her eyes narrowing, obviously checking out Cora's companion. Despite her inviting words to Nick, Cora wasn't sure how he and Frannie were going to hit it off, but she had an idea she was about to be entertained.

Cora was amused by Nick's struggle to avoid staring at Frannie's most prominent features: her odd hairstyle—bunches of graying hair poking out at angles—and her chest, which was not merely large but astonishing. She'd seen other people react this way when meeting Frannie, but Frannie never seemed to notice.

"Who's the hunk with you, Cora? More important, is he buying?" Frannie greeted them with her usual bluntness, ignoring Nick's gaze. Cora bit her cheeks to hide a relieved smile; Frannie's remarks told Cora a snap judgment had been made to approve of Nick.

As they seated themselves, Cora nudged Nick. "I should have warned you. Frannie can be outspoken, if not downright outrageous." She winked at Frannie.

Nick leveled a serious look at Frannie and countered, "I can buy. Or we could trade. How are your negotiation skills?"

"Uh, huh—" Frannie shifted her eyes toward Cora, looking baffled. "What's that mean?"

"He's Potawatomi Indian, Frannie. It seems he's also a bit of a joker."

Nick flashed a wide grin at Frannie, leaned back in his chair, and crossed his arms.

"Oh, man, look at that smile! Well, he's a major sexy joker. I can get used to that."

"This is Nick Pokagon, Frannie. He's from Argonne, their new fellow."

"A scientist, huh? A major smart, major hot, joker. This gets better and better."

Nick studied the menu board. He appeared to be enjoying himself.

"I'm going to help him get information on one of his ancestors. She used to live near here. Think you'd want to help?"

"Well, I don't know…," Frannie hesitated. "He brought up about the trading thing—what's *he* got to trade? It's summer now, but I been saving for a fur coat. He can see my negotiation skills for himself if he's got any furs out in his car."

Nick elbowed Cora, jostling the glass of water she was lifting toward her mouth. "I'll have to stay on my toes to top your friend. This is going to be fun."

"I never knew any Native Americans before. I expect you to be all somber and shit, but you're nothing like that," Frannie said, pointing a finger at him.

"Not at all," said Nick, taking a roll from a basket and buttering it. "Nothing unusual about me there. The somber stuff's part of the stereotype. Most Native Americans have a very keen sense of humor. Ever hear of the Trickster?"

Cora and Frannie exchanged blank expressions.

"Who's that?" Frannie asked.

"The Trickster's a spiritual leader, a highly intelligent guy who uses cunning, magic, and tricks to make his point." He took a large bite from his roll and then waved the fingers of both hands in the air. "We believe life gives us surprises, disappointments, reversals, and the Trickster trains us to prepare for that. Humor is very important. We say we can't pray until we've laughed."

"Bet that training and praying comes in handy at all them casinos," Frannie said.

Cora sputtered, the comment catching her with a mouth full of water. She wiped her chin on a napkin and looked at Nick. He was laughing. "How did you wind up at Argonne, Nick?"

"After I got my doctorate at the University of Michigan, I applied for a postdoctoral fellowship and was fortunate enough to get it. It'll be a real kick-start to my career, and my wife is happy since it's not far from home, Dowagiac, and near our families."

"Married?" Frannie commented, faking a dejected expression. "Huh—just my luck."

The server came to the table and took their drink orders. "Sorry for the wait, but we're a bit backed up," she said, glancing around the crowded room. "Are you folks in a hurry?" Cora told her to take her time.

"You shouldn't have said that," Frannie said when the woman left. "She may not come back."

However, the server reappeared almost immediately, set down a fresh glass of water for Cora and Cokes for Frannie and Nick, but then disappeared without taking their lunch order.

Nick sipped his Coke. "Dawn, my wife, is a research assistant. She's doing some proofreading at home right now, while our baby's so young. Rose's first birthday is next month."

"You're not from a reservation or anything like that?" Frannie asked.

"Well, yes, we live on tribal land."

"In Michigan? I didn't know there was any reservations in Michigan, not Southern Michigan. Dowagiac is just, what, about a hundred miles from here?" Frannie seemed doubtful.

"About two hours, 125 miles, that's right. You've heard of the Four Winds Casino, haven't you? That's ours."

Although Nick didn't seem touchy about ethnic matters, Cora steered the conversation in another direction. "What are you working on at Argonne?"

"Aquatic Invasive Species Transfer."

"What's that in English?" Frannie asked around her straw.

"You've heard of Asian carp?"

"Those crazy jumping fish?"

"That's them. Lemont's right in the middle of the most likely pathway to spread them into other waterways. If we don't get a handle on a way to stop them," he said, pointing out the window at a long bridge spanning the valley, "you'll be able to look from that bridge in a couple of years and see the Sanitary Canal shimmering with jumping fish."

"I saw it on *YouTube*—those things jump right in people's boats. Big, ugly old things. Hurl themselves at people too. Some get hurt." Frannie knocked her straw to the table. She ignored it and picked up her glass.

Nick nodded. "Yes. It's important and interesting work until I can find someone to sponsor the project I'm *really* interested in."

"And that would be…?" Cora inquired.

"Repopulation of predators in urban areas," Nick said.

Cora threw a meaningful look at Frannie, but Frannie missed it and the words were already out. "Predators? You mean like coyotes and wolves moving back in here? Cora and I know all about wolves, from the Sag Bridge goings-on last year. We can help you there," she boasted.

Nick raised his eyebrows in surprise. "You two know about wolves? Why's that? I didn't see anything about wolves when I read about you."

Cora wished Frannie hadn't brought up the subject, and she averted her eyes. "Where's that server?" she asked, looking around the room. When Nick's eyes remained on her, she said, "We ran into what we thought was a wolf when we were investigating the Sag Bridge murders."

"That old wolf still visits Cora, time to time. Tell him, Cora," Frannie prompted.

"Oh, it's nothing," Cora said, giving Frannie a light kick under the table. Frannie dropped her eyes, apparently finally noticing Cora's intent look that clearly said: *Shut up.*

"Just sounds in the night, maybe dreams, who knows. It was all pretty bizarre, so we didn't mention it when we told people about the murders. But at the time we did a lot of reading about wolf behavior, trying to find out what was going on."

"What *was* going on?" Nick was clearly interested.

"Please, it's a complicated story. I'd rather not go into it now—maybe another time. Tell us more about your ancestor."

"Sure." He put his elbows on the table. "Her name was Wawetseka. She wrote a memoir in French, the non-native language she knew best. She learned to read and write at a mission and then lived with a French-Indian family when she was young. She was invaluable when white people started moving through the area, sort of like Sacagawea." He put the remainder of a roll in his mouth and reached for another.

"In her memoir she tells about bringing in the killer of a white man." He spread his roll thickly with butter.

"Do you know French?" Frannie interrupted.

"Just a little. The Potawatomi are a matriarchal society, you know? Each woman passed the memoir to her oldest daughter, generation after generation. When it got to my mother, I was an only child, so I wound up with it. The stories about Wawetseka always fascinated me, and I had a friend at U of M who spoke French and translated it in exchange for some extra spending money."

"A trade?" Frannie asked, winking.

"You got me!" Nick said good-naturedly.

"It sounds like quite a story," Cora said.

"Yes. Wawetseka was an extraordinary woman, more than just an Indian woman with some education and interpreting skills. Her son was accused of killing a white man, and he was to be executed under territorial law. She believed he didn't do it, and, when no one would look for the real killer, she tracked him down herself and brought him to justice, to free her son. That was not a role Indian women played in those days."

"When was that? Do you know the year?" Cora asked.

"I do. It was 1817."

"When I read about that time period, I was surprised how many people passed down the Des Plaines River. White settlers didn't arrive until about 1830, but people moved up and down the river, and the Indians traded with them. Most people think there were Indians, then traders, then settlers, and that's it. But tradesmen, merchants, missionaries, military, even bandits, traveled through before the frontier arrived." Cora leaned forward and moved her hands energetically, a habit she had picked up from her husband, Cisco, who characteristically used wild gestures, jokingly attributed to his Sicilian heritage.

Frannie nudged Nick. "You turned her on," she said. "You're stuck listening now unless you can find a way to turn her off."

Nick smiled at Frannie but held up a hand and turned to Cora. "That's true. History textbooks are awful, so how's anyone supposed to get the true picture? Some research is even based on lies. When our elders were interviewed for 'the truth,' some of them amused themselves by making things up. The history of that time period is—well—inaccurate isn't strong enough. Sad."

Frannie leaned back in her chair and narrowed her eyes at Nick. "You're leading up to something, aren't you?"

Cora examined their faces. "What's going on?" she asked.

He sighed. "Wawetseka's story should be known by people outside our band. It's not just entertaining, it's important, don't you think? Wouldn't it be great to publish her memoir? To set some history straight, let people know what it was like in her time and place? What *she* was like?" Nick frowned. "I'd really like to do that, but with the new job and baby, I don't have much time. There must be a way, though—if it's research— if it's important?"

Cora shifted her eyes and searched the room to see whether the server, absent far too long, was anywhere on the floor, but she seemed to have disappeared.

"You hinting about you got any *friends*, be interested in helping you?" Frannie asked with a sideways glance at Nick.

"You mean *new* friends?" Nick grinned and leaned his shoulder toward her. "New friends with historical knowledge, writing skills, and time on their hands? Those kind of friends? Do I?"

Frannie beamed and wiggled in her seat. "Oh man! We're all gonna be famous, write a best-selling book, based on a *true* story written by an Indian *woman?* Whoever heard of such a thing! Cora, how lucky is that—fall right in our laps?"

"Wait a minute, you two," Cora said. She held up her hands, palms forward and shook her head vigorously. "I promised Cisco I'd find a way to do less, not more. Don't go involving me in another project—I don't have time. Cisco will throw a fit, and he'll be right. Something like this will take months! We wanted to spend more time with the grandkids— do some traveling this summer."

Frannie ignored her. Her eyes gleamed and she squirmed with excitement. "A mystery!" she said. "That's how we sell this. We write it as a mystery. People love mysteries!"

"They'll love it even more if we tell them about the curse," Nick said.

The women froze. "The curse?" Cora asked, frowning.

"'Gémojshket, beware the curse of Mishipeshu,'" Nick quoted with a chuckle. He didn't seem to have noticed the women's reaction.

Frannie blinked. "What's that about?"

Nick rubbed his nose. "Gémojshket is Potawatomi for thief. I think Wawetseka wanted to be sure the manuscript stayed with her descendants and wasn't stolen, so she had a curse put on it. I don't get the impression she was much into curses or magic, but as a precaution she may have used a shaman. Mishipeshu is an Indian manitou, or spirit, also called the Water Panther, a half-cat, half-serpent, that lived at the bottom of lakes and rivers and protected treasures located there."

"Wait, now," said Frannie, frowning and shaking her head. "I don't know about getting involved with this after all. I'm not sure I'm up for any more crazy stuff—not sure I even recovered from last year." She glanced at Cora.

Nick's face fell. Cora suspected he regretted bringing up the curse. "I'm the Indian here, and I don't regard the curse seriously," he said. "Nor have I ever heard of anyone running into the Water Panther. I don't even think Wawetseka thought much of this particular legend, but back then many thought it was real, and maybe some still do. It still wouldn't apply to us, because we didn't *steal* the memoir—it's mine."

"Well...I was pretty excited until you mentioned this monster-panther thing. If I'm gonna get involved then, here's my condition: I'm not going out on any rivers or lakes where this guy hangs out. What d'you think, Cora?"

"I think this Mishipeshu," Cora said, stumbling over the word, "curse business is superstition, but I still don't know about the time commitment to writing a book. I'm sure it's going to be more involved than it looks."

"Come on, Cora," Frannie pleaded. "Without you it'll take too long, and I know you want to—I can see it in your face, the way you're holding back a smile, and you're bouncing your leg."

"Besides," Nick said, "there's a beautiful little one-year-old girl count-ing on you to pass on the family story." He stuck his lower lip out in a pout, which made Cora laugh, as it looked so unexpected on his rough masculine face.

She looked down at the table to gather her thoughts.

What am I getting myself into?

A few hours ago she hadn't met this man, and now she was on the verge of signing onto a long-term project on his behalf. Was it his charm and good looks? Was it because he and Frannie took to each other so quick-ly? The exciting nature of the project? Boredom? Or simply because for some reason it seemed the right thing to do.

It was all happening too fast! Could she trust her instincts, or was she being swept away? How could she explain this to Cisco when she didn't understand herself?

"Okay, okay—I'll *think* about it, along with keeping peace in my happy home. No promises now!" She spotted the server and stood up to wave at her so she couldn't miss the gesture. "Well, as circumstance would have it, we *could* do something right away. What are you two doing Sat-urday? Rendezvous is this weekend and we'll have to wait a whole year for it to come again."

"Rendezvous?" Nick and Frannie asked in unison.

Chapter 3

Carrying a gallon of paint and a bag filled with an assortment of items the man at the paint counter said he'd need to paint Rose's room, Nick walked out of the Ace Hardware on State Street. He supposed his face didn't reflect his usual confidence but something more akin to bewilderment. He had to admit the experience had been somewhat humbling.

"Pick out a nice color, something neutral, but something a girl would like. Not blue," Dawn said. How was he supposed to know what that might be? He was a scientist, not a painter. He'd spent all his time earning top grades—never lifted a paintbrush in his life. But Dawn asked, so he would do his best.

One of the problems in owning only one car was that he got stuck with errands. Rose's first room of her own had just been furnished, and the owner of the small, two-story home they rented was happy to have them paint its walls. Nick supposed it saved the man the trouble of doing it himself.

He placed the purchases on the floor behind the front seat and slid behind the wheel of his 2008 metallic-silver Mercury Mountaineer. He slid the key into the ignition but leaned back without starting the car. Before he went home and got busy there, he wanted to savor the very satisfactory outcome of his luncheon meeting with Cora and Frannie. He wondered how long it would take them to catch on that they'd been manipulated, if they didn't realize it already. The women would figure out they'd been conned, he had no doubt. Cora was a more trusting soul, and although she appeared reluctant now, she'd come around—she was thrilled about the memoir and wouldn't want to be left out. Frannie, though, probably had him figured before he even sat down. Thank God she was hooked by the concept.

He had visited Cora to learn more about Wawetseka, but from the beginning he hoped she would be interested in helping him turn the story into a book. He had no interest in a mystery or adventure story, only in a scholarly work of historic value. If he had to let them think they were writing a mystery to get them involved, so be it—he was sure they'd see his logic when they got started. It was probably a mistake to mention the curse though, which almost lost them. He thought a touch of the paranormal would entice people interested in mysteries and didn't expect it when for some reason Frannie was alarmed by the idea.

Stringing them along instead of being forthright was a bit underhanded, but he didn't feel guilty—he had to get them excited first. It was clear they *did* like the idea. Frannie was a bonus—a very welcome bonus indeed, and they hit it off instantly. They were not only going to get the book written but it was going to be fun.

Wawetseka's story had touched Nick since early childhood when his mother first showed him the memoir and told him the tale. As long as he could remember, he had begged her to let him hold and turn the pages. "She is my ancestor," he would say with awe, even though he could not read the French words. "She touched this. We share blood. A part of her is in me."

Although the number of citizens who lived on tribal land diminished each year, Nick remained proud of his heritage and close to his family and Indian community. He took advantage of educational funding and opportunities offered by the tribal council. It had been hard work, but he emerged well respected with a promising career ahead.

Wawetseka still spoke to his sensitive side, to everything he valued about being Native American. He was not about to let this opportunity to share her story with the world escape. The time to do it was now, while he lived in the same place Wawetseka had lived, but could he spare enough time on top of the crucial fellowship and his young family? He needed help, and, fortunately, help seemed to have been found rather easily in the form of Cora and Frannie.

Through his side mirror Nick saw a rather beat-up, dark-blue pickup truck park a number of rows away. The truck looked familiar. Nick watched the driver get out and head toward the hardware store. Billy! Although he could only see his back, he immediately recognized the man as well as his swagger—a swagger Billy affected recently to cover his hurt and insecurity, which Nick was at least partly responsible for.

Billy hadn't approached him, so he probably hadn't noticed Nick sitting in his car. Before Billy returned, to prevent possible confrontation, Nick started the car and drove to a grocery store at the next shopping strip to pick up a few other items Dawn had requested.

As he shopped and then waited in the checkout lane, he couldn't stop thinking about Billy. What was he doing here? Nick thought he had left any unpleasantness behind when they moved from Dowagiac. He hadn't seen Billy for—was it a year? But he was sure he wasn't mistaken. Had Billy followed them here? They hadn't made their new home a secret— it never entered their minds that Billy might come after them.

Dawn would be really upset. She'd want to lock herself in the house and would be looking over her shoulder, jumping at imagined sounds, and watching out the window. Unlikely as it seemed, maybe it was just a coincidence and Billy was here for some reason that had nothing to do with them, or was just passing through. Nick decided to assume that. Perhaps he wouldn't tell Dawn he saw Billy at all. That might be better.

Nick almost missed it as he struggled with his bags of groceries and his car door. In large letters printed in the dust of the driver's-side door were the words: NOT YOURS!!!!!!!!!!

Chapter 4

Each summer the Will County Forest Preserve District staged "Island Rendezvous" at Isle a la Cache, a small museum it operated to educate the community about the period when French voyageurs and Potawatomi Indians regularly traversed the Des Plaines River. The event attracted crowds who wanted to see what it was like to live in the 1700s and early 1800s in the Northwest Territory. Cora did research at the museum and knew the staff well.

Today the grounds were covered with white canvas tents lining the island's wide path. The sites were occupied by reenactors who assumed the identities of individuals from the past and dressed as those people would have dressed, surrounded by articles authentic to the period. Some cooked meals or performed other routine tasks the way they were done in the 18th and early 19th centuries.

Cora pointed out child reenactors to Nick and Frannie. "Look at that little boy—isn't he cute? You see," she said, gesturing around the grounds, "more people were here in those days than one might think."

"Yes. I didn't expect Europeans as early as the 1750s. I thought there would only be voyageurs and settlers from the east," Nick said, looking around.

They entered a cabin that was built in the French style, the logs placed vertically, unlike most pioneer cabins. Visitors stood beside tables and handled authentic articles from the period, such as fire-making kits, traps and snares, axes, knives, pots, smoking pipes, wooden scoops, powder horns, trade beads, and more. Reenactors in costume could be heard answering questions about the use of each item.

"I came from France in 1756," a woman said, in a soft French accent. She wore a patterned skirt with a striped vest laced across the front of her blouse, sleeves tied to it with thin strips of cloth. At her neck a Cross of Lorraine hung from a ribbon. A belt at her waist held a utility knife in a leather sheath.

"Only nobility can own land in France, but the king wants to establish this country as his, so he grants parcels to commoners who will settle the land in the name of France. If we work this farm for seven years, we will own it."

"Do you live alone out here?" asked Cora, speaking to the character, not the reenactor, getting into the spirit of the event.

"Oh, no, we are not alone. My husband was sent to conduct an investigation. The king wants to know why more furs aren't coming from this area, and he paid our way to find out. We came with another family, overland, not by boat, so we could bring a horse and plow, cattle, sheep, and pigs. We will clear the land this summer and build a barn. We will live in the barn this winter, on the side away from the animals, and next year we will build a house. Our son and daughter are young, but they will help."

"Why are the furs missing?" Frannie asked.

"Not so much missing as the men are not working hard enough."

"Aren't you lonely out here?" Frannie gazed around the cabin.

"Oh, well...it is lonesome, yes, but others pass by now and then. Other settlers, soldiers, or traders. Sometimes we see Indians. Some are helpful, and some are not friendly, but they have not made trouble. A few times a year we go to the trading post, and they hold mail for us. Right now we are lonely because our men are away in the French Marine, called to a battle."

With her cell phone, Cora took a photo of the woman, and then Cora, Nick, and Frannie left the cabin, stepping into bright sunlight.

At the next tent they visited a tall young woman who appeared to be in her twenties. Large and strong-looking, her braided hair was covered with a white bonnet tied under her chin, and she wore a long apron layered over a peplum. "I live with my father, since he is getting too old to care for himself," she said. "Pa was a trader, but he is not strong enough now. Fur bundles weigh ninety pounds, and he can no longer carry them.

He does a little trapping instead and trades with his Indian family, and I take care of the cabin and garden and cook for him."

"Indian family? Your father is Indian?" asked Nick.

"No, no. Pa is English. He used to acquire furs from the Indians for the North West Company. Now, in 1810, Englishmen cannot get trading licenses anymore, only Americans. But we have been here all our lives, and we find ways around the regulations. My mother was French and Potawatomi, a métis. Her father was a French *hivernant* who lived in the backcountry and married a Potawatomi Indian woman. That made Pa Potawatomi kin. Traders have a lonely life, but if married to an Indian woman her tribe adopts him and trades with him. It is good business and not so lonely. The whites call us métis, no matter how little Indian blood we have. Ma is gone—there is only Pa and me. We have been squatting here for many years, and we will settle when the land office opens. Others are doing the same."

Nick and Cora knew most of this, but it was all new to Frannie, so they let the woman talk.

"Pa taught me to read and write and figure and how to keep accounts in both English and French. I learned homemaking skills from my mother, both white and Indian ways. It is helpful to know many ways. I can pick the best of each."

Frannie started to move away, her attention caught by something at the next tent. Nick and Cora said goodbye to the reenactor and hurried to follow Frannie.

"Furs!" said Frannie, sweeping her arm over an assortment of animal skins spread out on the ground. A sign in front of the tent said, "James Paul Smith, Excellent Tanning."

"I knew it! There had to be furs here, all these trappers and traders. What's this dark, little, silky-looking fur?" Frannie asked a man who stood beside the skins, a leather apron tied around his waist.

"A mink," the tanner replied. "But beaver was used to make fashionable hats in Europe and was the heart of the fur trade."

Frannie smiled, picked up the mink skin, and stroked it, closing her eyes as she did so.

"Would you like to know more about the process?" the tanner asked.

"I'd like to know *all* about minks. I like mink," said Frannie. Nick and Cora decided to move on while Frannie stayed behind.

Nick seemed less enthusiastic than the day they met and frequently shifted his eyes as if watching for something. "Is everything okay?" Cora asked. "You look distracted, or nervous."

"Oh, no," he denied. "Just trying to take it all in."

They crossed a small bridge over a creek. A man sat on a stump of wood in front of his tent, performing card tricks on a small table. He wore tall black boots to above his knees and a scarf was tied over his hair. A thick-bladed knife fit into a scabbard that was attached to a wide strap across his chest. Cora recognized Josh, one of the museum's employees, dressed as a river pirate. She caught his eye, and he said, "I'll join you in a few minutes. Talk to my wife in the tent until I finish the tricks I promised."

Inside the tent was Pam, another member of the museum staff. Her tight, low-cut blouse revealed much of her breasts, and her bright red hair tumbled around her shoulders. She was heavily made up, and she smiled at them in an overly friendly way.

"Do you like my pottery?" she breathed in a husky voice, moving close to Nick. "There is none better. Perhaps yours did not survive the trip?"

Cora looked at the colorful creations on the tables under the tent. "These are lovely. Are they for sale?"

"Oh yes," said Pam, who rolled her eyes and emitted a harsh laugh. "Everything is for sale, even me!" She swept an arm toward her chest in a suggestive manner.

Nick appeared embarrassed. Pam laughed again. "The pots *are* for sale. My husband and I are river pirates. The business gives us a reason to travel on the river and encourages people to be friendly—to lure them. I make pottery, and he is a magician. But I am also a harlot, and my husband a counterfeiter and a con man. There are others. Some were once doctors, lawyers, tradesmen, merchants or bankers. Others are criminals escaping punishment. Some are hiding or in disguise. *All* are swindlers and thieves, and some are murderers." She winked. "Not everyone is here. It is not good to be seen together."

"What is there to rob way out here?" Cora asked.

"This is the *perfect* place. True, not so many people are here, but that is an advantage, as fewer will tell about us. Since there are only a few navigable river and land routes, everyone must take them, and they bring everything they own with them, so anyone we stop has some valuables. The chance of getting caught is less since lawmen are scarce. We don't go near forts or settlements—we wait for people traveling alone or in small groups." She leaned close to Nick and lowered her voice. "It is not unusual for travelers never to be seen again. Who is to say they did not have an accident or encounter unfriendly Indians? You see—perfect?" She crossed her arms over her chest, threw her head back, and laughed.

"I see," laughed Cora, who was wondering how Nick liked that comment and whether or not Wawetseka would have encountered such people.

"Hey," said Josh, coming up behind them, and putting a friendly hand on Nick's shoulder. "Who's your friend, Cora?"

"This is Nick. We're doing research for a book, trying to get a handle on how it all looked and worked in the early 1800s."

"Your wife said you were a counterfeiter," Nick said. "What was the currency back then? How did that work?"

Josh answered in a stage voice. "You are right—banks are not to be trusted. Each bank issues notes at whatever value they like, and the only standard is the Spanish doubloon. Although most Spanish left the area when they sold Louisiana, the doubloon remains the standard." He struck a dramatic pose and swept a hand down his body. "We trick people to trust *us* instead—we counterfeit doubloons, swindle, and sometimes stab them. We take their possessions and throw them in the river."

Nick looked around nervously, pulled out his cell phone, glanced at it, and turned to Cora. "It's almost time for Dawn to meet us—Rose should have finished her nap," he said. "Maybe we should head back so we can catch her when she gets here. When you picked me up I didn't realize—she'll never find us in this crowd."

"Sorry, Josh. I guess we'd better go," Cora said.

Josh made a theatrical sweep of his hand and said, "I bid you good day then, ma'am, sir."

Cora laughed and made a mock bow. "And farewell to you. I think we're going to be seeing more of each other soon."

Chapter 5

"It couldn't be a nicer day for an event like this," Nick commented, as they strolled back to the parking lot. "You were right to bring us here. It's much easier to see it as living history, rather than a picture in a book or online. Such a variety of reenactors saves time." Nick held a hand to his ear. "Listen, they're playing music somewhere. Is that a fiddle? And something twanging?"

"Voyageurs loved to sing as they paddled or in the evenings or at rendezvous. I don't know much about their instruments though."

"We came here to see voyageurs and Indians, and we haven't seen either."

"I'm sure they're here somewhere," Cora said. Frannie was still talking with the tanner as they walked by. Cora told her where they would be.

"What did your husband think when you told him what we were doing today? I thought maybe he'd come and I'd get a chance to meet him," Nick said.

Cora forced a chuckle. "Oh, he's not a history fanatic like me," she said. "He tags along when I ask him to and tries not to look bored. He was relieved I had other people to come with me, so he could stay home and watch golf on TV."

When they neared the parking lot, Cora sat in the shade while Nick went to watch for Dawn. Cora had been embarrassed to tell Nick Cisco's reaction.

As she expected, Cisco had not been happy when Cora told him about her new friend and their plans. *"Every* Saturday? You're committing yourself to meeting every Saturday? For how long?" Cisco passed a hand over the top of his head and awaited Cora's response.

Cora shifted her eyes away from him. "It's only for an hour or two."

"It's not just the Saturdays. How much *other* time are you going to spend? A book's a huge project!" He waved an arm. Cisco was noted for his enthusiastic gesticulations; he used his entire body when speaking—swaying, turning, waving, dodging, moving his hips and arms, not just his hands.

"You'll be sitting at your computer all day long. When do you plan to work on your own book, if you're spending all your time on someone else's?" He glared at her.

"The opportunity just came up, and I got excited." Cora stood up, turned her back to him, went to the sink, and started rinsing dishes.

"There's always a reason, something you want to do for someone else. You get all caught up in it—our own plans get put off." He paused and took a deep breath. "We're not getting any younger Cora. We're supposed to be retired! It'll take the whole summer, probably longer. I thought we agreed, after the Sag Bridge business, we'd devote more time to ourselves and our family. You seem to have some sort of superwoman complex—just keep heaping things on, good old Cora will get it done."

"My concept of retirement seems to differ from yours. I retired so I'd have time to do things I didn't have time to do before retirement."

"Did you actually listen to yourself when you said that?" He picked up the newspaper from the table, folded it, and then slammed it down again.

Busy at the sink, Cora was torn by the thought that the project might not get done without her. Was she overestimating her importance? But how could she let Nick and Frannie down? It didn't seem the right time to make that argument. On a personal level, her head was so full of ideas, it almost consumed her. She *wanted* to write this book.

"We *did* decide I'd scale back—but can't you see why I'm excited? Native Americans didn't have a written language. This memoir was written by an Indian, and a woman, which is unheard of. It has historical importance, and it just fell in my lap. I didn't go looking for it."

"And *that's* not right either. This man just pops in, and all of a sudden you drop everything and you're ready to commit a year of your life to him. Who is this guy?"

She had spun around. "You have to meet him, Cisco. You'll like him. Let me invite him for dinner so you can get to know him. You'll change your mind once you get involved."

"I know what you're doing—you've explained it in more detail than I wanted to hear, and I *don't* plan to get involved. You want to do this, go ahead, you do it. But leave me out." He had pushed himself up and stomped from the room.

Cora had stood at the sink gazing out the window after Cisco left, tears of disappointment in her eyes. Cisco's words were angry, but true, his arguments were for her own good. How could she convince him when she couldn't even explain her desire to write this book to herself? But... he didn't realize how important this was to her. They both clung to their viewpoints.

It won't be the same if we don't do it together, she had thought at the time, and thought again now. *I want to share it with him, not tell him about it. It's going to be exciting and fun, and he's going to miss it.*

Maybe he'd come around. Dismal as that prospect seemed, it had happened before.

She dried her hands, found Cisco stony-faced playing solitaire on his computer, put her arms around him from the back, and rubbed her cheek on his head. "Please don't be angry, hon. We'll find a way to work this out."

Sitting on the bench now, her thoughts were interrupted by the happy shriek of a young child. Cora looked up to see Nick striding toward her. A lively, one-year-old girl sat on his shoulders, pounding his head with both fists. An attractive young woman bounced along behind, pushing an empty, lightweight stroller.

"Oh, my God," Cora said. "So this is your family. You didn't tell me how beautiful they are!" Nick beamed, Dawn met Cora's eyes with an embarrassed smile, and Rose continued to giggle and pound her father's head.

Nick took the little girl off his shoulders and held her in his arms, bouncing her to make up for removing her from her perch, and handed her to Dawn. Rose immediately started to wail her displeasure, and while Dawn calmed her and settled her in the stroller, distracting her with a toy, Cora appraised Nick's wife.

The tiny, dark-haired woman looked like a teenager, but her dark eyes sparkled with intelligence and good humor that suggested an air of maturity and competence beyond her youthful appearance. The word that came to Cora's mind was "darling." Observing Dawn as she gently but authoritatively calmed the child, she was struck by the impression this young woman was a match for anything Nick, or life, could throw at her. Cora caught Nick's eye. "They're beautiful!" she mouthed at him.

Nick smiled at her, and he and Dawn exchanged a warm look.

A man dressed as a voyageur walked toward them, and Cora recognized Brad, the director of the Isle a la Cache Museum, a portly man in his forties. Despite his jovial demeanor, Cora got the impression he was well aware of everything happening around him. He stooped now and made eyes at Rose. Without fear she focused on him, fascinated, then reached to pull off the red stocking cap he wore. He laughed as they wrestled playfully over it, and Rose squealed, reaching for the fringe on his leggings.

Dawn smiled at Cora and said, "Cora, I presume?"

Nodding, Cora said, "What a delightful baby. Nothing much frightens her, does it? Babies at her age usually cry at anything strange."

"Oh, no," Dawn said. "She's the most fearless little girl you ever saw."

"How does she like her new home?"

"She's all over it," Dawn laughed. "She started walking when she was only nine months, and she's into *everything* now. It's good we decided I'd stay home for a while—I can't leave her for a minute." They began walking back toward the exhibits. Rose was fascinated by the loud sounds of a musket demonstration just off the main path and turned her head, enthralled, until the noise stopped. Cora and Dawn chatted comfortably as they walked, instantly bonding with each other.

Under a canopy next to a grove of trees a small, bright-eyed woman greeted them. "Adorable baby!" she said. She tucked short red curls back under the bonnet she wore.

"Welcome," the woman said, beginning her speech. "We heard there was much need for merchants on the frontier, and much money to be made in the fur trade, so we have come here to trade along the river."

"So this is a trading post? Is there a fort here?" Cora asked.

A man in a black beret joined them. "No, no. Settlements near the forts are regulated, and only one factor is authorized to deal with the fort. Our post is out along the river, close to Indian villages. Indians bring furs to our outpost during the winter, when the animals have full winter coats and the furs are best, and they trade the furs for supplies. We bring furs to the fort in spring and live near the fort until fall. Then we bring supplies to the post along with goods we still owe the Indians from winter trades."

"What kind of supplies?" Dawn asked. The woman was entertaining Rose by making faces and encouraging her to grasp at a wooden spoon.

"Indians want fabric, especially bright-colored fabric, metal implements, and decorations, in that order. They also like cheap blankets made with dye that bleeds. Indians use the dyes for clothing, since they cannot get some colors from nature. Firewater is not as popular as we were led to believe," the man added.

"I'm glad to hear that. We take a beating over that stereotype," Nick said.

"We?" the man asked.

"I'm Potawatomi," Nick said, holding out his hand.

The man shook Nick's hand and dropped his persona. "A reenactor? The day's half gone. Hurry and get into costume, man!"

"I'm not a reenactor," said Nick. "I'm Potawatomi."

The man looked embarrassed. "I'm sorry. No slight intended."

"None taken," Nick said, smiling. "I'm used to that reaction." They chatted for a brief time and then moved on. Nick retrieved a toy Rose had thrown and rummaged in the stroller for a wipe to clean it. When he couldn't find one, he walked off with the toy looking for a restroom to wash it in a sink.

"He's obsessed with keeping her toys clean. I should do that, and I try, but she's always picking something up and it seems hopeless," Dawn laughed.

"It's a guy thing—they think it's easy when they're not there all day. We used to say babies eat a pound of dirt somewhere along the line. They survived somehow," Cora said.

They shared a laugh. "You're easy to talk to Cora."

"Have you made friends here yet?" Cora asked.

"Not yet," Dawn said.

Cora remembered when she had her first son and lived miles away from family and friends. In those days two-car families were rare. She was lonely and starved for adult companionship. She thought she sensed that feeling in Dawn. "It's a great town—I'm sure you're going to love it. Why don't I pick you up some day and show you around while Nick's at work?"

"I'd like that," Dawn said, her face reflecting gratitude.

"We did see a voyageur, but no Indians," Nick interrupted, rejoining them and handing a new toy to Rose. "Strange, don't you think?"

"There's a lot more to see. I don't know how we can cover it all," Cora said, shaking her head.

"Perhaps we should divide up," Nick suggested. "We can compare notes at our next get-together." Cora didn't miss the implication that he expected there would be another get-together.

"Great idea," Cora said.

"Hey, there you are. And who's this?" Frannie asked, coming up behind them.

Rose fastened her eyes on Frannie.

Frannie seemed equally attracted to Rose. Ignoring Dawn for the moment, Frannie's eyes lost their customary saucy look and turned soft. "Babies—I love babies. Do you know how long it's been since I've been around a little girl-baby?"

She moved close to Rose and made a funny face. Rose squealed with delight.

Now they were all together, they forgot for the moment the idea of dividing up and headed instead down a wide dirt path that led away from the crowd and into a stand of thick brush and trees. As Nick and Cora walked ahead, they heard Frannie and Dawn chatting and laughing behind them.

"Frannie will surprise you," Cora told Nick. "Under that brusque exterior you won't find a more loyal friend. It may seem like she's just having a good time, but she'll show up with valuable information we never would have thought of. She's got a knack for finding the obscure but useful."

Soon Cora lost sight of Rendezvous. She and Nick strolled without talking, listening to the pleasant sounds of birdcalls, rustling leaves, footsteps, and the murmur of rushing water that surrounded them. Suddenly Frannie yelled out from behind them.

"Hey! Do I hear water? Didn't I say, no river?" Cora and Nick turned around to see Frannie peering anxiously around. She stopped and pointed to her right. "Is that a river? You brought me to a river? You're not getting me out there!"

Cora tried to placate her friend. "This is called Isle a la Cache, Frannie. Surely you knew from the name we were coming to an island. We're not *on* the water, only near it. You must have been near rivers before."

"Yeah, but that was before I heard about that curse." She looked around at the surprised looks on the faces of her friends, and lastly at Dawn and Rose, and calmed down. "Well, I guess you wouldn't be bringing this little baby here if there was any danger. Just I wasn't expecting this, is all."

They continued a short distance and soon came to the southern tip of the island and full view of the river. The sense of desolation at the spot was mesmerizing, and they were drawn to the riverbank. Frannie held back nervously.

Having forgotten Frannie for the moment, Cora was startled to hear her excited shout. "No! Look! It's out there!"

Cora, and everyone, turned to look at Frannie.

"No!" said Frannie, pointing at the river to the right of where the others stood. "Don't look at me! Look out there, on the water! Do you see it?"

Turning, Cora saw nothing unusual, only the water calmly drifting by, here and there carrying a leaf, branch, or other bit of debris. She caught the eyes of Nick and Dawn, who shook their heads with baffled expressions.

Cora went to Frannie's side and took her arm. "What did you see, Frannie? We must have missed it."

"It was that big water cat thing, like the curse! Just laying below the water, then streaking off real fast. I saw it Cora, I swear I did!"

Nick and Dawn approached. "What did it look like?" Nick asked.

"A big black shadow under the water, real long and thin, like fifty feet, and then it just shot off under the water, but I saw it until those trees got in the way!" She pointed to where trees grew thick along the riverbank.

Cora noted that the direction Frannie indicated was upstream, against the current. Used to looking for explanations of the unusual, Cora spoke up. "Could it have been the shadow of an airplane on the water? That would have looked like what you described."

"I didn't hear an airplane," Dawn said.

"The sun is behind a cloud. Why would there be a shadow?" Frannie asked.

Chapter 6

Frannie loved mail. Every day, she listened for the slam of the mailbox closing, ran down to the front entry, and scooped everything out of the box, hoping for something entertaining. Today's delivery included a padded, nine by twelve manila envelope, lying on the entry floor in front of the mailboxes. *What's this?*

Grinning with anticipation, she dumped the ads on the kitchen table, reached into a drawer for her letter opener, slit the envelope open without examining it further, and reached inside. Immediately she jerked her hand back with a cry, dropped the envelope to the floor, and knocked over her cup of coffee, splashing some of the hot contents on her jeans.

Heart pounding, she mopped at her jeans, reached for the envelope again, and wrinkled her nose with distaste. Handling it by its edges, she dumped the contents on the table and stared at them. Without touching anything, she turned the envelope over to read the address. Then she picked up the phone and dialed.

~~~

"Cora, you got to do something about that crazy Indian dude of yours—thought he was one smart dude, more of a smart *ass*, you ask me. You know what that nutcase did?"

"No Frannie, I have no idea. I'm rushing here. Couldn't this wait until we get together? That's in less than an hour."

"No—it can't wait. I want to tell you what I think before I see him. He sent me one of those padded envelopes, you know the ones to keep things from getting broken in the mail?"

"Yes, I know what padded envelopes are." Resigned, Cora plopped into her office chair with an impatient sigh. "I'm sure it wasn't an *empty* envelope. What was in it? Something you didn't like?"

"Uh, huh. That's right. I reached my hand in there, all unsuspecting, and what do you think was in there?" Frannie sounded indignant.

"I have no idea Frannie. What was in there?"

"A mess of fur and a plastic tube with little tiny beads in it. I just about jumped out of my skin when I touched that furry thing, I want to tell you! And what am I supposed to do with little bitty beads?"

Cora bit her cheeks to keep from laughing aloud. "How do you know Nick sent it?"

"The envelope was addressed to Frannie 'Kemosabe' Berkowitz—who else it's gonna be from? Made me spill coffee on my jeans. Those are *new* jeans. I sure hope the stains' gonna come out."

"*Kemosabe* means something like friend, doesn't it? That doesn't sound mean to me—it sounds like a joke. Did you do or say anything that would make him play that kind of joke?"

"No—well, maybe—I don't know. Before we left the Rendezvous, I was complaining to him. I said I couldn't get that tanner guy to give me any mink samples. Oh, yeah—and I said the guy that was selling the wampum wouldn't give me a sample either. He only wanted to sell long strings of the stuff, way too expensive."

"Well, you see, he's saying you're a friend, and he's giving you the fur and beads you couldn't get, don't you think? It's a gift. Well, sort of a gift. I think it's his way of saying he likes you. Maybe he wants to jolly you out of that scare you had by the river."

"Huh. Strange way of liking someone, that's what I think. How'd he know where I live?"

Cora felt her face redden. "I told him Frannie, while we were at Rendezvous, after we separated. He wanted to know how to contact both of us."

"Huh," Frannie said. "I suppose while you were *talking* about me, you filled him in about how I moved back into Mama's two-flat in the old neighborhood after she died, after living all those years with my white husband and friends, maybe even how I turn my black talk on and off after all of that."

"Guilty," Cora said, her voice barely audible with embarrassment.

"I know you meant well. But now—I got to get back at him, Cora. I can't just let this sit like it is. Think real hard now, what's a good joke I can play back?"

"I'll give it some thought, but it's between you two," Cora said, relieved Frannie didn't seem upset that she and Nick had discussed her personal life. "Are we done now? Can I finish getting ready? I have to get my notes together."

"Yeah, you get organized, you're real good at that. See you in an hour." Frannie hung up without waiting for Cora to say goodbye.

~~~

Cora, Nick, and Frannie sat in comfortable chairs in the library of the visitor's center at the Isle a la Cache Museum, in front of a wall of tall windows, through which could be seen a reconstructed Potawatomi longhouse and the French-style log cabin with vertically placed logs. The frontier landscape was a sharp contrast to the modern library furnishings. The wall opposite the windows was filled with a mural of voyageurs at riverside. All signs of Rendezvous were gone.

Unlike the historical society, the visitor center was air-conditioned. Cora had suggested they meet there to plan the book; they would have ready access to research materials and the setting was conducive to their work. The museum staff had expressed excitement about the publication of a story set during the fur trade era and was pleased to accommodate them.

Frannie hadn't mentioned her "gift" from Nick. Cora supposed this was because she was planning something or because she didn't want to give Nick satisfaction.

"Couldn't talk Cisco into joining us, huh?" Frannie asked.

Cora shook her head and frowned. "Not yet. To give him credit, he has good reasons."

"I don't want to make trouble," said Nick, looking concerned.

"No, no. He might change his mind. I'm here today, at least, to help get things started." Cora checked some notes on her iPhone and then slipped it back in a pocket. "After we split up, I made notes about the longhouse, the cabin, and some things in the museum; snapped more pictures; told the museum staff what we were doing; and arranged for us to meet here."

While Cora spoke, Nick's gaze shifted to the window, his brow furrowed. "Nick?" Cora said. "Is something wrong?"

"Oh, sorry. I was just thinking about something personal," Nick said, turning his attention back to the women. "We talked to some voyageurs. They let Rose play in their canoe. She cried when we lifted her out but stopped when we got to a man who was showing dogs. That was interesting. In those days, Indian people didn't keep dogs as pets, but they *used* them. Small dogs kept the camp clean and barked to give an alarm. Medium-sized dogs flushed game, but didn't chase it. Big dogs pulled sledges. Rose buried her face in the fur of a big, gentle dog that looked like a bear, and she didn't want to let go." He laughed. "I wish *we'd* thought to take pictures."

"They used to *cook* them dogs too, I heard somewheres," Frannie said.

Nick put a hand over his face and peeked between his fingers. "We didn't talk about that."

Frannie said, "Not to be bragging or anything, I got some good stuff. Oh, I got to confess I got lost awhile, learning all about minks and wampum, some stuff we don't need to go into right now." Cora noticed Frannie avoided making eye contact with Nick. "I asked questions about catching and punishing criminals back then. Seems kinda vague, not one way of doing things but different ways, depending on where and who was around."

She picked up a small notebook and thumbed through it. "After explorers, the military, they came to build some sort of road, well…not like a road, more like a path of mud or dust, but better than trails—wider than trails. Then they built forts and a few men stayed to defend them, more like a place for people to come for protection, behind walls. Sometimes they protected whites and sometimes Indians too, from other warring tribes."

She held up a hand as if she thought they were about to interrupt her. "No, listen, let me talk. It gets better—this is good stuff." She read from her notes, poking her finger on the page as she made each point. "The French built the first forts. The French Marines was sent by the king to protect his possessions. But sometimes *Indians* built forts too. The Marines handled crimes by non-military people, not just soldiers. Then the English came, built new forts, and took over some old ones, but for non-military crimes they appointed "sheriffs." Then when the U.S. took over, they wrote a whole constitution, and they didn't only have sheriffs, they had judges that went around a circuit to hold trials. Then there was militia and rangers and vigilantes and posses, too. In Wawetseka's day, *any* of these people could of had a hand in punishing a killer."

She stopped, looked up, and gave them a proud grin, as if awaiting appreciation.

"What did I tell you?" Cora asked, looking at Nick. "That's critical to Wawetseka's story, and she laid it out for us, didn't she?"

"I'm impressed," said Nick, and he touched a hand to his forehead to salute Frannie. "You have details written down there about all that?"

"Of course I do," said Frannie, indignant. "And there'll be more too. I haven't even started researching online—Cora can tell you how good I am doing *that.*"

Pam entered the library and began to search the shelves. She wore a tan uniform today instead of the harlot costume. Pam not only manned the desk and handled scheduling and business matters, but she conducted tours and programs. "I'm an Interpretive Specialist," Pam had laughingly told Cora, "which is a big name for an all-inclusive job."

"Pam," Cora asked now, "were there any Indians at Rendezvous? We didn't see any."

Pam gave Cora a blank look. "Now that you mention it, I didn't either. We just send out invitations and assign spots. Whoever wants to participate shows up. I guess we just didn't get any Indians this time. Usually we do." She withdrew a book from a shelf and left the room.

"I talked to a *black* soldier," said Frannie. "People don't expect black people on the frontier, but there were. They weren't slaves, but not exactly free either, not completely anyways. They had *rules.* Huh."

"Let's move on," Cora suggested. She reached into her oversized purse, pulled out a notepad and pen, and placed them on her lap, poised to make notes. "Did you bring copies of Wawetseka's memoir?" she asked Nick.

Frannie jabbed Nick in the ribs with an elbow. "Cora's organized. She takes charge—keeps us in line. You'll get used to that."

Nick unzipped a carry bag and pulled out three stacks of papers held with clamps, each stack an inch thick. "Yes Cora—here you go."

"About a hundred pages here," Cora mumbled, flipping pages quickly. "They're not numbered…looks like roughly a hundred,"

"They're in handwriting. Lousy handwriting to boot. That's gonna make it a whole lot harder," said Frannie.

"Sorry," Nick said. "It gets worse. This is a translation, remember, from French? The words may not seem in the right order sometimes. The translator didn't do this for a living—he just knew how to speak French. He might have misinterpreted some of it too. You could have some trouble figuring out what Wawetseka meant to say."

"We can't use this like this," complained Frannie. "Do we need to find a new translator? Somebody who speaks French and Potawatomi and knows about Indians way back when, yeah, *that* shouldn't be hard to find. Huh." She made a face. "You still have the original, right? What kind of condition is it in, after all this time?"

"The manuscript's in surprisingly good condition. It's been in a pottery container inside a wooden box." Nick leaned forward and looked at Cora. "*Should* we look for a better translator—maybe we can get a grant—unless you know someone?"

"Not off the top of my head, but why don't we just go with what we have, and if questions come up we'll do what we have to do," Cora answered. "Sometimes too many people slow things down."

Frannie poked Nick again. "See? Organized. What'd I tell you?" She paged through her copy, shaking her head. "So here I'm reading now, and it says 'I Wawetseka she have relative brave prisoner' and I can't make out the next words at all, 'cause of the handwriting. How are we supposed to make this a book? Nobody's gonna read this. And it's a hundred pages. Books are three hundred pages, most times. It's not long enough either."

Nick sounded defensive. "Well, I managed to read it, and I understood the story. I didn't say it was easy."

Frannie looked up and poked her finger on a page. "Here's the part, at the very end, about Mishipeshu—'*Gémojshket* beware of curse of Mishipeshu.' Anybody want to say more about that after what I saw at the river? You're not getting me there again today, by the way. What's the matter with you, Cora?"

Cora took a deep breath. "Just déjà vu all over again," she said, shaking her head. "Let's just move on."

Frannie appeared doubtful. After staring at Cora for a moment, she said, "Okay then, but don't forget what I *saw.*"

Nick and Cora exchanged a glance. "Even if there is such a thing, the curse wouldn't apply to us, remember? The memoir is mine."

Frannie rolled her eyes at him. "Whatever you say, chief. I expect you're gonna save me, there's anything to this curse thing. Right?"

"We won't forget," Nick said, although his expression said otherwise.

"I'm sure there's some other explanation for what you saw, Frannie." Cora reviewed her notes and looked up. "I think we should read Wawetseka's memoir during the week and discuss our impressions and ideas next Saturday. If we have time, we can dig further to get a better feel for what Wawetseka's life was like."

Frannie slapped her leg. "Got your orders straight, Nick, from the lips of the Great Organizer? It's a mystery, right? A murder mystery? Tell me again—we're gonna write a murder mystery, isn't that what we're doing?" Frannie nodded her head, turning inquiring eyes on Nick and Cora.

Chapter 7

Sitting alone at her kitchen table over a cup of coffee before heading to her volunteer stint at LAHS, Cora gave free reign to the jarring memory that had disturbed her since the last time Frannie mentioned Mishipeshu—the memory of an old recurring dream, a dream that began sixty years ago, long before Cora ever heard of the legend. Not for the first time, she wondered how other people dealt with uncanny occurrences in their lives, or indeed how many people even had such experiences.

In the dream, Cora walked on level ground beside a lake, looking across the water at a cliff on the opposite shore. As she walked, a huge creature, like a dragon, a sea serpent, and a black cat all combined, rose from the lake to pursue her. She felt anxious, but not terrified, as if she could escape or control the thing as soon as she figured out how to do it. Sometimes popcorn materialized and she threw it to the monster. It would stop to eat and she'd get farther away. Then she would wake up.

Some twenty years ago, she and Cisco visited Devil's Lake in Wisconsin. As they approached the lake, she felt disoriented, as if living a dream. The lake looked like the one in her dream, but she'd never been there or heard of the place before. While walking on the rocky side, trees with trunks about eight inches thick started shaking; there was no wind, and they couldn't see anything shaking them. Other than the shaking, all was surreally quiet, not even the sounds of birds or insects. Her fear increased when walking on the level side, expecting something to rise from the water at any moment, but it never did. Afterward at the visitor's building, she read for the first time the legend of a monster that lived in the lake. After that experience, she never had the dream again.

Now she couldn't get the idea out of her head that the dream was a premonition related to what they were doing and to the curse of Mishipeshu on Wawetseka's memoir. As she picked up her laptop bag and headed out the door for LAHS, she wished her world didn't seem more complex than that of most people. She could imagine what Frannie would have said, something like, "Here we go again with the crazy shit. Hang around Cora long enough and something like this be sure to happen."

~ ~ ~

"My princesa, let's go visit Mrs. Cora!" Dawn greeted the baby in a cheery voice, hoping the little girl wouldn't sense her gloomy mood.

She raised the window shade, and light streamed into Rose's room, revealing newly painted, soft lavender walls. *Not exactly neutral, but Nick actually picked just the right color,* she thought. Rose babbled and pulled at her socks, happy after waking from her morning nap.

"Let's check that diaper and put on a pretty new outfit, now that you're all bright and sunny and ready for adventure. I bet Mrs. Cora has fun things at that little museum where she works." Dawn wished she felt as happy and carefree as her daughter.

She had to get out of the house. Rose enjoyed long walks in the stroller, and the activity might bring Dawn out of her funk. Alone in the house with Rose all day, she stewed nonstop. Maybe it was hormonal, but she didn't think Nick appreciated her fears over the new development. He wasn't acting right, and she couldn't talk to him. She'd tried, but he didn't seem to take her seriously. In fact, he was part of the problem. She got the feeling something else was going on, but he denied it.

She could call her mother, but that would only make things worse. She didn't really want her mother to know she was upset with Nick. Ma would only preach at her.

The only friend she'd made here was Cora. She needed adult conversation, and the mere thought of talking to Cora gave her a sense of relief. She felt a closeness to the woman from the moment they met. She wouldn't unburden herself—just find something else to do.

Dawn gathered up the freshly changed little girl in her arms and headed purposefully down the stairs.

~~~

"What a nice surprise!" Cora said. "Do you need help?"

"No, we're good," Dawn said, unbuckling Rose from the stroller. "Do you have time for us? Sorry I didn't call ahead."

"Can I show you around?" Cora asked.

"Nick says you have a museum," Dawn said, leaving the stroller against a wall in the church entry.

"We do." Cora glanced nervously at Rose. "We can try that. It's in the basement."

The historical society's museum housed a series of exhibits in the basement, among them a schoolroom, a doctor's office, a general store, and other displays. Only a small rope reminded visitors not to enter or handle the rare and authentic items within.

Almost immediately after entering the museum Rose began to reach for things, wiggling in Dawn's arms to be let down to explore. It wasn't long before she began to scream with frustration. "I guess this wasn't such a good idea," Dawn said. "Is there a park or somewhere more baby-appropriate we can go?"

"I think I have an answer," Cora said, and she led the way to the church sanctuary, closing the doors.

"The doors are much too heavy for her, and everything in the sanctuary is tied down. She can explore to her heart's content."

Built in 1865 from stone quarried in Lemont, the building was originally a Methodist church. The sanctuary seated approximately a hundred in unique curved pews. On the outer walls were stained-glass windows, each named in memory of an original member of the church. The ceiling was tin and a small altar, an organ, and a throne-like, red-velvet chair sat behind a carved wooden railing.

Dawn set Rose down, and she toddled to one of the pews. With both hands slapping the seat, she began to make her way slowly down each row, intrigued by the enormity of the space before her. Cora led Dawn to the front row and they sat.

Dawn's face grew sad. "I wish I had more time alone with her."

Looking up to see tears in Dawn's eyes, Cora was puzzled.

"You're not going back to work, are you? I thought you were going to stay home while Rose was so young."

"It's not that, Cora." Dawn brushed at the tears and then looked off into the distance. "Sorry. I shouldn't burden you with this."

Uh, oh. Something's going on—something not good, Cora thought. "I worked in the medical field before retiring. I'm used to hearing confidences. You can tell me if you like."

"I didn't come here to talk about my problems, Cora. I just thought... I didn't plan...oh, I don't know what I thought...I don't know anyone here—except you." Dawn stared at the floor and after some consideration said, "I'm pregnant again, Cora. I suspected last week, but I'm sure now."

Cora smiled and gave a sigh of relief. "Oh, that's wonderful Dawn," she said warmly. "You must be ecstatic!"

"I wish I could be. I *would* be. But this is the worst time!" Dawn shook her head slowly. "Nick's worked so hard, competing against people as brilliant as he is. He needs my help and support. Rose demands my attention every minute she's awake. How can I handle Rose, manage the house, help Nick, and, now, care for a new baby—I don't know how I can do it all! And on top of things, this *book*...." Embarrassed, she dropped her eyes.

"Well, forget the book for starters—we can take care of that. What about your family? Can't they help? I thought your family wasn't far away."

Dawn shook her head again. "That's another problem, Cora. They'll be so angry. The last thing my mother said to me when we left was to be sure I didn't get pregnant again."

"Why? Doesn't she *want* grandchildren?" Cora's eyebrows narrowed.

"Not *my* mother," Dawn shook her head vehemently. "You have to understand—it's a cultural thing. Generations ago, Indian women didn't have many children—they were well spaced because they nursed them so long and living conditions were harsh. My mother grew up thinking that was the norm. She learned it from her mother, who was the second child in a family of two. I have a much older sister—just Sunny and me— and my mother was over forty when she had me."

Dawn's voice was soft and hesitant, which Cora interpreted as embarrassment. "Then Sunny had seven children, one a year for seven years, and she couldn't handle it. I'm sure Sunny wasn't much fun to live with—her husband left. She was drained physically and emotionally, and in the end, well—Sunny was never stable or responsible to begin with—she ran off somewhere. We've never heard from her. Mom raised Sunny's kids. They aren't much younger than me."

"I see. What does Nick think?"

"He's—I don't know—he doesn't say much, but he acts like it's not a problem. We'd both be happy under other circumstances, but he doesn't seem to understand why the situation overwhelms me. He doesn't see what I do all day. You saw him with Rose's toy at Rendezvous, acting like that was all it took to care for a baby."

She gave a short laugh. "He thinks my worries are in my head. I'm sure you know women do the lion's share of worrying. He's in la-la-land, just assumes everything will be taken care of somehow. He doesn't appreciate how hard it is on me."

Cora saw tears forming again before Dawn glanced away. "Let alone we can't afford it. Tribal scholarships helped, but we needed loans to get Nick through his education and we have to pay those back. We only have one car, so I have to drive Nick and pick him up if I want to go anywhere; otherwise I'm stuck in the apartment. I don't know if I can do it, Cora."

Dawn got up to check Rose and found her crawling under the pews, then pulling herself up and banging on the seats, babbling happily.

Cora remembered how difficult it was when she was home alone all day with her first son, and Cisco's life was centered on his work. He'd come home expecting to play with his baby, walk into a clean house, with dinner ready and a cheerful wife to listen to the details of his day. After all, what did she have to do all day except play with the baby? She was exhausted and resentful, and Cisco couldn't understand why. *Men are more understanding of family obligations now, aren't they, when mothers return to their careers? And help with child-rearing and household tasks?* Some help. Some take responsibility. Two very different viewpoints. Maybe things hadn't changed as much as she thought.

"You don't need to explain the worry part." Cora gave a little snort. "So he's leaving everything up to you then?"

"Pretty much."

"So you're worried, he's not, and you're angry with him."

She nodded vehemently. "Yes! I want him to feel like I do, and he just thinks I'm making a mountain out of a molehill. It's not fair!"

Cora sensed there was more to it. "And you're concerned about your relationship with Nick?"

Tears spilled out of Dawn's eyes and ran down her cheeks. "Yes," she said, her voice choked. "When we came here, I was so excited—just our little family finally making it on our own. It's a crucial time for Nick—he has to do everything right, and I wanted to be part of that. But I underestimated. I'm not really helping him at all. I thought I could take care of a house and baby and still be bright and cheerful, and now that I'm in the midst of it, it's *hard*. I feel like I'm disappointing him, and he doesn't seem to realize how hard I try. I feel alone. I'm not supposed to feel alone. We aren't supposed to be alone if we have each other, but now I don't feel that way. We don't talk like we used to."

Dawn's eyes suddenly blazed with anger. "And what about me? I put my own ambitions on hold for Nick and Rose. It just goes on and on. I'm there for everyone, but no one cares if *my* dreams are shot to hell!"

"What *are* your ambitions, Dawn?"

Dawn sniffed and grew calmer. "Medical school. I want to treat the elderly, to help make their lives better."

Dawn went to Rose, picked her up, and hugged her, as if hugging the baby would give her comfort, but Rose cried out and wiggled in Dawn's arms, so she put her down again.

Cora was touched. She had once wanted to be a doctor too, but she gave up the hope to raise her family. It had been a different time, and few women were accepted into medical schools in the 1960s. Instead, after the boys were older, she chose a career in medical administration and had no regrets. But she understood Dawn's dreams.

"I think there's something going on, Cora—something Nick's hiding. He won't look in my eyes when we talk and gives short answers. I get the feeling he's thinking about something else and doesn't want me to know. We've never done that."

"Do you have any idea what it could be?"

"None. Unless there's trouble at work. But we've never kept secrets from each other."

At least Dawn wasn't suggesting another woman. Cora walked over to Dawn and hugged her. How young she looked, like a child. "Dawn, I don't know if this helps, but I understand. I can't give you a magic potion to make your problems go away, and you don't want that. You just want someone to listen."

She felt Dawn's nod against her shoulder.

"So today we have what we have, and tomorrow—who knows? Maybe a better day. First you go through the motions and your little baby makes you laugh and things don't seem so bad, or else how can you laugh? And then your fears get smaller—maybe slowly, maybe all at once—and you're not so upset with Nick. It may not look that way now, but it will happen. And that new baby will come and be as welcome as Rose was."

"I wish I could believe that."

"You will. Not today maybe, but you will. Would you like me to talk to Nick?"

"No! Please! It has to come from him, not because someone prompted him. Don't tell anyone Cora, please. This isn't like me, to tell such personal...."

"It's not all on your shoulders, Dawn, much as it may seem. People *will* support you, and Nick will too. I can't believe he doesn't share your dreams."

After Dawn and Rose left, Cora reflected on how she had pegged Dawn as someone who could handle anything. She still believed that, but anyone can reach his or her limit. One of her favorite sayings was about how people respect us for our strengths but love us for our weaknesses. Dawn had a firmer place in Cora's heart, as did the whole young family.

She wished there was some way she could help. She'd share her thoughts with Cisco when she got home. Assuming he was in a mood to hear about her new friends, not a sure thing at all. Things weren't all that rosy in her home these days either.

Chapter 8

Cora clicked off her iPhone after checking the time. "Should we start without Frannie or wait for her?"

"We've made amazing progress outlining Wawetseka's memoir, but we still have to agree on how to tell the story and whether we need more research," Nick said.

He stopped talking, leaned back in his chair, and gazed out the window, watching birds at the feeders. Allowing Nick time to pursue his thoughts, Cora's mind wandered too. Nick was a delight to work with; despite cultural and age differences they agreed on many issues. Their laughter brought Cora, embarrassingly, to the pants-wetting stage on more than one occasion. Yet awkward moments sometimes occurred: she was influenced to some extent by Dawn's confidences.

She and Dawn had lunched together at McDonald's earlier in the week. Dawn had revealed a new problem.

"As if things aren't bad enough, I'm getting letters and phone calls from an old friend, Billy. He's had a crush on me since we were kids, and he just doesn't seem to accept my marriage to Nick. I don't know, maybe he thought I married Nick just to give the baby a name and I'd leave him after Rose was born." She frowned. "I don't know how he can think that—I never gave him any such idea. I haven't even seen him for a long time, but all of a sudden he's calling and texting me, stuff like what we're going to do together and how he misses me. Sometimes he just hangs up when I answer the phone, but I know it's him. I'd be more worried if I didn't know he was in Dowagiac."

"What does Nick say?"

"I didn't tell him. They used to be friends. I was afraid Nick would go ape and do something stupid. Ha! Fat chance of that. More likely Mr. Optimistic would probably just say Billy will get tired of bothering me and I should ignore him. Nick just doesn't get it!"

Now Cora wondered what Nick was thinking. Was he still minimizing Dawn's concerns about the new pregnancy? He didn't seem to be the kind of guy who would do that. He probably didn't realize how stressed his young wife was. Or maybe, as Dawn thought, something else was going on. She was uncomfortable knowing things Nick didn't, but she had to stay out of it.

It wasn't comfortable at home for Cora either. Cisco didn't say much, but he had made his disapproval clear and was out of the house more than usual. Cora wondered if that was his way of rebelling or making the best of the situation. When she asked, he just threw her a piercing look and said, "I'm fine," and walked away or changed the subject.

All is definitely not quiet on the home front—for either of us.

Nick's question broke into her thoughts. "Are you ready to tell me about your 'wolf-ly' experiences? I'm interested in predators, remember."

Did Cora want to share that story yet? She decided she did—but where should she begin?

"I didn't want to get into it, because it's not a real wolf. It's a spirit," she began tentatively, watching Nick's face.

"Wow! That's great!" he said, with a grin and twinkling eyes.

Cora laughed at his reaction. "You don't think I'm nuts?"

"Of course not. We have lots of legends and beliefs that relate to both wolves *and* spirits. One of the more important ones is about the water panther, like in the curse. And you know there's a wolf in Wawetseka's story. So how did this wolf spirit come into *your* life?"

"We looked into the Sag Bridge mystery because a woman who was killed there was haunting me. She used a wolf spirit to do some nasty things. After we solved the murder, the woman's spirit left, but the wolf's spirit is still hanging around. It isn't threatening anymore, though—comforting actually."

Nick nodded, clearly enjoying the story. "That's typical of wolf spirits, avenging and protecting—guardians. I bet the wolf is a female."

"It is! How did you know that?"

"Just a good guess. A lot of similarities between women and female wolves!" he laughed and poked an elbow at her. "So what do you mean—she's still around? Does she scare you?"

"No, no—I think she's staying around to protect me. I seem to have some strange status with spirits—they're vicious to other people but friendly to me. I hear her howling sometimes, in the night. She wakes me up. Neighbors think it's a coyote, but I know it's my wolf—the howls aren't the same. I did a fair amount of research about predators even before everything started. I was sure I'd seen wolves, so I started saving news clippings and searching the net."

Frannie strode into the room, dropped into a chair, and made a show of arranging some bags around her. "Finally let Nick in on the great wolf experience, huh? What'd you think of that, Nick?"

"Cool!"

"That old wolf had us running down all sorts of false trails, thinking there was a real wolf out there. We couldn't figure out why it was hanging around Cora. Can't tell you how much time I spent online learning all about wolves. We never did get to visit that wolf ranch like we planned to, though. Things started happening too fast and then it was all over and there was no reason to go."

Brad, the museum director, walked into the room and opened a cabinet. Cora remembered him playing with Rose while dressed as a voyageur at Rendezvous. Brad spent much of his time in his office, but he was anxiously looking forward to the publication of their book and had promised Cora he would use some connections to promote it.

"You *should* go out to that ranch if you want to know about wolves," he said, revealing he had overheard their conversation. "It's a chance to get up close and personal, better than a zoo. The owner will talk your ear off—there's no better place to learn about them. You might even be able to hold a pup." He started moving things around in the cabinet, but kept talking. "He has a few other animals, like a bear and a cougar. And coyotes, so you can see how different they are from wolves. Make an appointment, though. It's not a walk-in kind of place."

"Nick here's a scientist," Frannie announced proudly. "He specializes in predators, and why they're moving back where they haven't been for years. You read about that in the papers? Every now and then a wolf or a bear or a cougar comes around somebody's backyard and gets people riled up. Not to mention those coyotes getting into everything now."

"I heard some graves were dug up in one of those little cemeteries, near where that truck yard is. They found prints and thought it was a cougar that wandered in and couldn't find food. That's what the experts said, but nobody believes it," Brad said, removing a box it seemed he'd been looking for and standing up.

"Why would an animal do that?" Nick furrowed his brow. "There's more than enough deer around. And people are buried in vaults, deep, to protect bodies from animals looking for food."

"Those little cemeteries are real old, some even before permanent settlers arrived. Who knows what they did so long ago."

"Well, wouldn't be much meat left on those old bones to attract no cougar either, if it's so long ago," Frannie said.

"She's right," said Nick.

"Hey, it's not *my* story, I'm just passing it along." Brad chuckled and left the room.

"They've been nice to us here," Cora said.

"They have. They let us meet, answer questions, find references for us, and, since they're all reenactors, they know a lot. We'll have to include them in the acknowledgements, of course, but let's think about another way to thank them," Nick said.

The staff were interested in Wawetseka's story because she lived at the end of the fur-trade period, the theme of the museum. Cora kept them updated on the book's progress. All three staff members did historical research, participated in living history reenactments, and were naturalists. Pam's program management and tour responsibilities kept her in other parts of the building much of the time. Josh, in addition to his time at the museum, was pursuing a doctorate in history. He belonged to a community theatre group and was growing a beard for an upcoming play; his acting experience enhanced his role-playing as a river pirate. He worked limited hours at the museum but was entertaining when he was around.

"Damn!" said Frannie, grinning from ear to ear and banging a fist on her chair. "Cougars, that there water panther curse, wolves, pirates, and Indians! How much fun is this!" She let out a peal of laughter.

"Okay," said Cora, picking up a notepad to hint that they had wasted enough time. She was glad to hear that Frannie seemed to have decided the water panther was fun after all. "We were going to review potential settings for the story today. Let's see what we know and then decide if we need to visit some places."

"Yes, we have a pretty good sense for the people of Wawetseka's time, how they lived and what their life was like," Nick said. "We also identified some historical figures she would have known, like William Clark; Thomas Forsyth; and Chiefs Black Partridge, Keepataw, and Black Hawk," he added, crossing his ankles. "We know what was going on in the world during her lifetime and what was happening locally."

"Don't forget about the justice system, although that's still confusing. If we don't find all the answers we can just let Wawetseka tell it like it was. That's what I think," Frannie said.

"Did you read the entire translation? Do you have any questions?" Nick asked, looking at each woman in turn.

"That translation is a problem—details are lost," said Cora, balancing her notes on her lap and clicking a mechanical pencil.

"Well, I made it through her story," said Frannie. "But one thing threw me. It's talking about those breechcloths, wrapping around the privates and all, and she says one was decorated with porcupine quills. Seems pretty uncomfortable to me. What about that?"

After they finished laughing, Nick explained the quills were woven into, not poked through, the breechcloth.

Cora drummed her fingernails on the arm of her chair. "How do we tell the story convincingly if we can't picture where Wawetseka lived and traveled? Even if we assume this whole area was something like today, there were no roads, for instance."

"Right," Frannie said. "How did she get from place to place?"

"Lots of questions. Did she go about on foot or in a canoe? There were lowlands, swamps, forests, valleys, canyons, and bluffs all around here. Did the river freeze? How did that affect what she did? How deep was the snow?" Cora made notes as she talked.

Frannie blinked rapidly. "How we gonna do all that?"

"Let's visit places that are easy to get to. When we think we have a good lay of the land, we can piece it in with research and Google Maps," Cora proposed.

"So we're finally going to see where Wawetseka lived, like I asked the day we met?" Nick said.

"Let's start with this island," Cora said. "Then the ravines at Black Partridge Woods, the lowlands and swamps along the Des Plaines River, and the bluffs south of Argonne. Dellwood Park in Lockport, to see cliffs. Sagawau Canyon in the Sag Valley. There's another bluff near the old Brown farm." All three wrote rapidly as Cora named places.

Frannie wiggled in her seat. "People are going to love this murder mystery!"

"Wait a minute, Frannie," Nick said. "We haven't decided if the book is going to be fiction or nonfiction."

"It's *got* to be a novel. Otherwise it's just going to be sitting on some shelf. People like stories, not dry academic stuff." Frannie sniffed.

Nick stuck his chin in the air. "Who says a story has to be a novel? It can be nonfiction and tell a story! It doesn't have to be dry."

"People read nonfiction when they want to know how to do something or fix something. If they want a story, they look for *fiction.*"

"What about *The Devil in the White City? In Cold Blood? Seabiscuit?*"

"Didn't sell as much as *To Kill a Mockingbird!*"

"Need I remind you it's my story?"

"Do you want anyone to *read* your story?"

Cora wasn't surprised, having expected an argument would develop sooner or later. Planning the book had been a lark so far, but her friends held strong opinions. Perhaps she could get them to compromise. "Nick, you favor a straightforward, nonfictional representation. Something research or academic-worthy, right?"

"I do," he said. He nodded and bit his lower lip.

"It's your story and your ancestor, and you should make the decision. Would you consider a compromise?"

"We're pretty far apart here," Nick said, shaking his head. "But I'm between a rock and a hard place, since I depend on your help. What kind of compromise?"

"We could write two books instead of one. We write the mystery first, get people interested, and then we follow up with a well-documented and notated nonfiction work. It could come out at the same time, or later. The novel could generate interest in the scholarly work," Cora proposed.

Nick and Frannie considered the suggestion.

"Or, a fictional book could be interspersed with expository chapters every now and then to put it into a historical perspective. This would be followed with an extensive bibliography or chapter notes, or both."

"I don't think I like that," Nick said. "It would slow the reader down and be confusing. People will expect one thing or the other, and we run the risk of turning off both kinds of readers."

"Huh! It would put them to sleep," Frannie said.

"Wawetseka's narrative has gaps, which is why we're doing all this research, to make the story flow better. What we fill in will be our words, not hers. But we could write the story in first person. It would be like she's sitting in the room telling it to us, then we take the story she told us and write it down in our words," Cora proposed.

"Let me think about that," Nick said, bouncing his heel on the floor.

"We could get into her head. We have her words, so that shouldn't be too hard," Cora continued. "She kept on top of what was going on in the world and had strong opinions she wasn't afraid to voice. Of course, it was so long ago the reader won't understand some of it unless we make the history clear. As Ricky would have said to Lucy, 'We have a lot of 'splainin' to do.'"

Nick had a blank look.

"We keep forgetting you're only a baby here," Frannie said. Cora noticed that Frannie didn't look at Nick. In fact, she appeared to be intentionally avoiding meeting his eyes.

"Bottom line, what's more important to you?" Cora asked, giving Nick a serious look. "Lots of readers or a scholarly work?"

"A historical novel?" he asked.

"You could call it that. But you won't be able to call it nonfiction," Cora said. "That's just how it works. Publishers need to know how to promote it."

Nick paused to consider. "All right. Why don't we start writing it as a novel, keep good historical notes, and decide about the final draft after we get some done."

Frannie leaned back in her chair with a grin. "Works for me. 'Long as it's a murder mystery."

"Humor her," Cora said, leaning over and patting Nick's arm.

"So who's gonna do the writing part?" Frannie asked. "I'm no good at that."

"I'd like to—but I just don't have time," Nick said.

They both looked at Cora, who sighed and nodded slowly. "I figured that would happen. Okay—if I can work it out with Cisco. We have to have dinner, Nick, like we talked about, with Cisco. If he hears us talking about our plans, gets to know you—once he understands what we're doing—he won't want to be left out."

"Cisco's *your* problem Cora, but he likes me, maybe he'll do it for me if not for you. Let's get back to business here. So you're gonna write the story, and we'll all get to pick it apart—I mean edit it, right?" Frannie said.

"Hold that thought," Nick said. He stood up and headed toward the restroom.

Cora was still trying to figure out how Frannie thought she could get Cisco to do something Cora herself couldn't. She caught an odd look on Frannie's face. "What?" she asked, raising an eyebrow in Frannie's direction.

"Nothing," Frannie said, biting her cheek.

"Frannie—" Cora began, then she heard a thump from somewhere in the building.

Frannie burst out laughing.

"Frannie—what did you do?" Cora asked, her gaze narrowed on her friend.

"Nothing," Frannie said again, trying to stifle her laughter.

Nick shuffled back into the room, rubbing his head, his face flushed. Straight-faced, he sat down, holding his hand over his shirt as if hiding something inside. Brad, and then Pam, passed by the doorway, grinning widely.

"Okay, Frannie. You got me." Nick started to snicker too.

"Want to let me in on the joke?" Cora asked, looking from one to the other.

"Your friend," Nick said, reaching under his shirt and pulling something out, "planted this on the bathroom mirror."

Cora jerked back in her chair and uttered a yelp as Nick held up a large gray mask covered with fur and set with deep yellow eyes—the most realistic mask of a wolf head Cora had ever seen.

"I went around the corner to wash my hands and saw this ugly thing looking back at me. Banged my head on the wall before I realized it was just a mask. Felt like I swallowed my heart three times before I caught my breath." He turned to Frannie. "So that's why you were late. How'd you arrange this?"

"Brad and Pam were in on it…helped hang it up…kept people out until you went in there," Frannie got out, holding onto her sides and rocking back and forth. Finally she said, "Okay, Kemosabe, back at ya. You got any idea how creepy it is to reach into an envelope and put your hand on something furry?"

"Sure I do, otherwise I wouldn't have sent it," he replied.

Frannie was clearly delighted with the results of her joke. "He's talking about looking for wolves, thought I'd help him find one! I wanted to put him to the test, find out how *brave* he was," she said, with another chuckle at her pun. "Think you passed the rites of manhood? Would your *tribe* be real proud of you?"

"There're no stains on my pants. Does that answer your question?"

They beamed at each other, squabble forgotten, kindred spirits. Cora sat back, listening to them banter and thinking how much she was enjoying herself.

They're probably both planning their next trick. I wish Cisco were here to share the fun.

Chapter 9

"It *would* be vastly different today, like you said. But it's still wild." Nick and Cora leaned against a split-rail fence, studying the Des Plaines River Valley spread out in front of them. After parking in the lot at Keepataw Preserve they had followed a short trail to an overlook.

They stood partway up a bluff on the north side of the mile-wide valley. A long bridge dominated the view southeast, blocking sight of the village of Lemont, which was on the south bluff about two miles east of where they stood. Behind them ran Bluff Road, two lanes that wandered through wooded areas.

Pointing at the bridge, Cora said, "That bridge carries I-355. It's the second-longest bridge in Illinois." In the distance to their right, the tall structures of an oil refinery could be made out, an accumulation of storage tanks and towers discharging columns of steam into the air and looking like a scene from a future-world thriller movie. At this distance, with the quiet rustling of grasses and leaves interspersed with birdcalls, the man-made structures didn't seem intrusive.

"This is a decent place to view the valley, although we're not high enough to see the waterways clearly, only hints of them through the brush," Cora said, pointing at the floor of the valley. She spoke in a hushed voice, as if afraid to disturb the quiet of their surroundings. "You can see the swampy flood pools and wetlands well enough—the largest one we passed on the way here is called Goose Lake. Beyond them are the three waterways. Closest to town is the Illinois and Michigan, or I & M, Canal; in front of that is the Sanitary and Ship Canal; and closest to us you can see bits of the Des Plaines River. I'm sure you've noticed the industry when you cross the Lemont Street Bridge to go to Argonne: the warehouses, truck yards, barge basins on the canal, mounds of stone, sand, mulch...."

"But right *here*, tall grasses and wildflowers, clumps of trees—like a savanna." Nick seemed impressed. "Who knew? It's so peaceful. I can see why my ancestors would build their village here."

"In Wawetseka's day, the river was the only waterway, and it was located where the Sanitary Canal is now. The river was diverted into a new channel; the canal runs where the river once was. It was an awesome engineering feat. The new riverbanks are straight, but the river used to meander, and east of here were three islands, a short distance east of Lemont Road." She pointed southeast.

"The river was only about four feet deep at low level, but it could rise twelve feet or more, overflowing its banks and filling the floodplains—much of the valley floor—after heavy rain."

Nick turned, taking in the surrounding area. "Do we know exactly where the Indian villages were?"

"Indian villages were located along river routes and trails." Cora pointed to the top of the south bluff. "Along that ridge was a major trail that connected the Lockport–Joliet area to the Sag, about five miles east, where it met other trails to Lake Calumet and what became Chicago. Today it's Archer Avenue."

Nick followed her finger. "There was a village at Sag, on a hill known as Mount Forest Island. A church, St. James at Sag Bridge, is there now, on the south side of the river. Legend has it that St. James Church and cemetery are built over an Indian graveyard, and that Father Marquette visited an Indian village at that site when he passed this way.

"Wawetseka's village would have been on this side, the north side—it could have been here, or we will go to another possible location next. One more village was on the opposite side of the river, downstream three or four miles south, near Isle a la Cache where we have our meetings, but on the mainland near where that refinery is now. Upstream from here and across from St. James on the north bluff was Signal Hill, where smoke signs could be seen from both the Des Plaines and Sag Valleys, northeast toward Chicago, directly east toward Lake Calumet, and west toward Joliet. Let's go see where I think Wawetseka's village was."

Cora drove them a short distance east on Bluff Road. A picturesque stone bridge and shelter were on their left, and a few feet farther another car lot, where they parked. A forest preserve sign identified the area as Black Partridge Woods.

"I'm glad Black Partridge was remembered," Nick said as he read the sign. "I didn't expect that."

"Yes, and not just Black Partridge, but Keepataw. Although Keepataw was only a minor chief, he spent most of his time right here. At one time Lemont was named Keepataw, but the powers that be in those days didn't think an Indian name was dignified enough."

They headed into dense woods north of the parking lot, climbing up an unmarked trail. After only a few steps, tall stands of maple, basswood, and oak surrounded them, the ground between the trees covered with dense underbrush. They followed a thin, hard-packed clay trail until a deep ravine opened in front of them. The trail followed the edge of the ravine, snaking up, down, and around. Tree roots like half-buried arms turned their ankles as they walked carefully to avoid missteps or slips on the thick bed of leaves that remained from last fall, fearful they would plunge down the ravine into the rocky stream gliding silently at its bottom. All was silent except the hollow sounds of their footsteps and the light rustle of the brush they pushed past that threatened to overgrow the path. The vegetation emitted odors that were now pungent, then sweet. The sense of isolation was complete.

"This is awesome!" Nick commented. "Go into these woods just a little way, and you lose the whole modern world, don't you?" He stopped at the edge of the gully. "From the road you'd never know this rugged landscape was here, and standing here you could be lost...or fall into the ravine...."

"That's true," Cora nodded. "People *have* been lost here. Even though homes are scattered along this road, people get twisted around in the woods and it's scary. When we first moved here I read in the local paper about a body that was found in these woods. A mentally disturbed man in his twenties had wandered out of his house one winter night, and he wasn't found until the snow melted in spring."

"If I hadn't seen this, it would be hard to picture," Nick said. "And Wawetseka lived here."

"Somewhere here, perhaps where the stream leaves the ravine and the ground is more level. The stream that carved this landscape runs under the stone bridge we saw below and would have had sweet water. The woods and ravines provided shelter, security from strangers, and wild-life for food. And the river was nearby for transportation. We can't know exactly where her village was, but we do know, from artifacts found here, Indian people lived on this bluff. We also know it was across the river from a fur station that was near the south end of the Lemont Street Bridge."

Cora paused. "The only information we had about that fur station was a single mention in the literature that it existed in 1816 near the present intersection of State and Main Streets in Lemont. Wawetseka's memoirs tell us about the people who lived there, what they did, what it looked like. That's what excited me. We don't know exactly where her village was, but she must have roamed through these woods and walked right where we stand now."

Nick stepped close to Cora and pulled her into a hug. "Thank you, Cora. I *do* feel like I'm walking in the footsteps of my ancestors. I can't tell you how much that means to me. I've been wanting to see this as long as I can remember...." His voice shook, and he put his cheek against her hair, holding the hug for a long moment. Cora closed her eyes, feeling the warmth of friendship this young family had brought into her life. Her eyes burned behind their lids with sadness that Cisco had yet to meet these people who were becoming so important to her.

They parted and Nick followed Cora down a different trail back, pass-ing the shelter and crossing the small bridge. They walked in silence, stepping softly on the hard-packed ground. Cora had a desire to reach out, touch Nick's hand or arm, make some physical contact, but she didn't.

After they reentered the car, Cora pulled her hand away from the igni-tion key before starting the engine and turned to Nick. "I know this isn't my business, Nick, but I'm concerned. Is Dawn going to be okay about the new baby? Tell me and I'll shut up if you don't want to talk about it," she added quickly.

"She'll be fine. She just needs time to get used to the idea."

Cora looked off into the woods surrounding them, dropped one corner of her mouth, and put her hand on her key. "Sometimes a woman feels overwhelmed by responsibilities, whether they're real or not. She may know she'll get through it, but that isn't what she wants to hear. She just wants to have her concerns acknowledged."

"No one knows how much Dawn does or appreciates her as much as I do. But if you think it will help, I'll tell her again." He avoided Cora's eyes and raised his chin, a muscle jumping in his taut jaw.

Cora nodded and started the car. She didn't think Nick understood what she had tried to say.

~~~

Later that morning, Pam led them around Isle a la Cache. Cora had walked much of the island on previous visits. It was larger than the others knew.

"Some say the island is about eighty acres, others say more than a hundred," Pam said, circling an arm above her head. Cora struggled to remain serious; outside the museum she still pictured Pam in the flamboyant clothing she wore at Rendezvous instead of the tailored uniform she wore today. "Why the difference, you might ask? Isle a la Cache sits low in the water, and the river floods certain times of the year, covering parts of the island. It's roughly a mile and a half long and about a half-mile wide."

They walked along an inlet. To the west, 135th Street passed over a bridge. Another small island was in front of them, with rapids rushing between the two bodies of land. Frannie glanced nervously at the water but resolutely followed the group.

"I understand the river isn't very deep," Nick said.

"The main channel on both sides of the island can be deep during flood stage, but after floods it goes down quite a bit. Flood stage can raise the depth ten to twelve feet. It's a serious problem for homes upstream when the river runs over its banks."

"Runoff from building in the area, is that what causes the flooding?" Nick asked, ever the environmentalist.

"It doesn't help, of course, but the river has always done that. Farther north of here are places a canoe can't get through at low water. The Indians and voyageurs took advantage of the times the river was high to travel, so they wouldn't have to carry everything on foot between low water areas."

"That's why the Chicago waterways were built, to create passage between Lake Michigan and the Mississippi River by way of the Chicago, Des Plaines, and Illinois rivers," Cora added.

They followed Pam around the island's riverbanks. They passed through woods on the south end of the island, but the east side was too muddy to circle back to the museum. "See those low areas in the center of the island, where it's all muddy? When the island floods, it gets swampy, so little grows there."

At the south end of the island the waters flowed together again. "I can't tell what I'm looking at," Frannie said. Knowing Frannie had seen something in the river right here, Cora noted she stood well back and looked about apprehensively. "The banks cut in and out—what part's the river?"

Pam pointed to the left. "It's over there. There's another good-sized island right in front of you, and a bunch of little islands all along here, but the channel on your right swings in front of you here…," she pointed, "then bends to the right to join the main channel. There are more little channels between the islands. It's rather a jigsaw puzzle."

Cora took some pictures with her iPhone.

They headed back past the museum, turned east, and walked through a picnic area, where they neared the east side of the island. Pam pointed out a pipe and faucet protruding from the ground near the road. "That's a natural spring, a very deep well, and it tastes wonderful. A few people bring jugs to fill, but not many know about it. There were other natural springs on the island and also near Willow Springs, hence the name. Most of the locations have been lost. Indians thought the springs had medicinal value and visited them almost like a vacation destination."

Cora looked across 135th Street at a dense wall of green.

Nick noticed where Cora was looking. "What's on the other side of the road? Is that mainland or island?" he asked.

"It's more island," Pam said.

"What's there?" asked Frannie.

"Nothing," Pam turned and abruptly started back toward the museum. Cora got the distinct impression Pam didn't want to talk about that part of the island.

"If the entire island is more than a mile long and a half mile wide, what we've just seen probably isn't half of it, and we've been walking the better part of a half hour. I hate to doubt your word, but it seems like a pretty big slice of nothing," Nick commented.

"I mean it's not developed. There's no parking there, no shoulder, no place to pull off along the road. The only way to get to it is by boat or to park here, walk across, and try to find your way through brush and bogs. There're no trails, no buildings, no reasons to go there. There could be deer, coyotes, and smaller animals, and I guess a few fishermen go in there, but I don't know anyone who has."

"That's interesting," Nick commented. "I'm sure in Wawetseka's day, and the voyageurs' day, they used the entire island, not just the part south of 135th Street."

As they approached the museum, Cora pointed to a far parking lot near the west side of the island and a man crossing the street on foot. "There's someone going over there now. Does he have a fishing pole? That old truck must be his. It's the only one in the lot."

Nick stopped and stared, his fists clenched.

"What's wrong, Nick?" Cora asked. Something about the truck was familiar—was that the same truck that followed her to the restaurant the day she met Nick? It had been a month ago.

Nick shook his head and resumed walking. "I thought for a minute I recognized that truck."

Cora studied his face. "Must be someone you don't care much for."

"You might say that," Nick said.

Chapter 10

"Wнat the hell was Billy doing out here?" Nick said aloud as he drove home after Pam's tour of Isle a la Cache.

The most obvious thing that came to mind was that Billy was following him for some reason. To aggravate him? He tried to put his anger away. After all, they had lived in the same town until about a year ago. There was no reason to think Billy's appearance here now was anything more than annoying.

Nick saw Billy's truck from time to time, passing local businesses or parked in town. It appeared he was staying in Lemont, but they hadn't run into each other. Wouldn't Billy have made contact by now if he had followed them here? He was probably here for some reason that had nothing to do with them. Wasn't he?

Nick no longer doubted that the words scrawled on his car were put there by Billy. But what did the words mean? Was Billy saying Dawn wasn't Nick's? Or Wawetseka's story wasn't Nick's? Thank God, he hadn't needlessly gotten Dawn upset by letting her know Billy was around.

He turned his thoughts to the conversation he had with Cora. *Was* he being insensitive to Dawn? It seemed that Cora thought so. If he revealed his own fears, wouldn't that make Dawn's concerns even more real to her? How could that help? Wasn't it better to make light of things and not voice his worries?

He had been thrilled to receive the fellowship, proud of the honor that placed him among the top graduates in his field. Once that was completed, he would be in line for the best positions, ensuring his future and fulfilling their dreams—everything they had worked so hard for. But it wasn't turning out to be all smooth sailing. The assistant director, Tony Lombard, continually looked over Nick's shoulder, and whatever Nick did, Tony criticized. The director usually agreed with Nick, and that seemed to put Tony on the defensive. Maybe Tony felt Nick was after his job. Nick had tried to debunk that idea and become friendly with the man, but nothing worked. Every day was filled with tension.

A new baby? He loved children and wanted more, but he refused to admit to Dawn that this wasn't a good time. She was upset enough already, so he told her nothing about *his* stress. He tried to appear confident and upbeat and told her it would turn out fine.

The book—it wasn't a good time to be writing a book either. But he had put it all in motion. How could he call it off now that other people were so involved, so excited? Working on it relaxed him and made him forget his problems. Cora's and Frannie's friendships had proved to be valuable in more ways than one—and fun.

He had always felt confident of solving any problem, but for the first time he doubted himself—a new and disturbing feeling. Should he confide in Cora? Would he feel like a traitor if he told his troubles to Cora but not to Dawn? He couldn't tell Dawn—it would be too hard on her, and above all he had to do what was best for her and Rose.

They would get through it. The rest of the summer, the fall, maybe the winter—then in spring everything would be new and fresh. New baby, new book. And surely he would work out his problems at Argonne by then, and Billy would have moved on. Their problems would be over come spring.

~~~

"What are you doing here, Billy?" Dawn's voice was hushed but exasperated. She stepped onto the front stoop and eased the door closed behind her. "Rose is napping," she added.

She assessed the situation nervously. The weekend had been uneventful, albeit rather noncommunicative. Nick left for Argonne this morning while Dawn was still asleep. It was now early afternoon and Dawn had hoped for some quiet time while Rose napped. Dawn wasn't frightened of Billy, but the encounter was bound to be unpleasant.

Billy was not a large man, but Dawn knew he was stronger than he looked. He had cut his hair to shoulder length and had a dot of a beard between his chin and lower lip, which she thought made him look rather shifty. He stood there staring moodily. He seemed to be at a loss for words now that they were face-to-face.

Billy glanced across the street, where a neighbor wasn't hiding the fact that he was watching the beginnings of what he suspected was a confrontation. "Can't we go inside?" Billy asked.

"Absolutely not! Are you nuts? After your angry calls and hang-ups, and you standing here glaring at me, I'm supposed to let you in my *house?* Whatever you want to say, you can say it right here. Better yet, go away and leave us alone!"

He set his jaw and clenched his fists, hands at his sides. "Your mother said you aren't leaving Nick after all. I had to hear it from you, see your face when you said it."

Dawn backed away a few steps and threw her arms up in the air. "Of course I'm not leaving Nick! Whatever gave you that idea? How many times do I have to tell you? I told you back home and on the phone, and I'm saying it again now!"

He moved a step forward and stuck out his chin. "I thought you were joking! Why do you keep leading me on then?"

"I've *never* done that! Just because I tried to be *nice?*" She closed her eyes tightly, shook a fist in the air, and cried, "Oh!" in frustration. Then she opened her eyes, took a deep breath, and pointed a finger in his face. "There's something wrong with you Billy. Get used to it and move on. Leave us alone!"

He blinked rapidly and looked away. When he looked back his eyes appeared more wounded than angry.

"You've got to get them to stop writing that book about Wawetseka," he said.

Dawn looked confused. "The book? Why do you care about that? It's Nick's project, his ancestor, and he can do whatever he wants with her memoir. What business is it of yours?"

Billy's eyes flared again, and he slammed his fist against the wall. At this the neighbor stood up and moved to his porch railing. It appeared he was trying to decide whether or not to interfere.

Billy glanced at the neighbor, and Dawn watched Billy's face reflect hesitation, then soften, then calculate, and then flare with anger again before he replied.

"It's *not* Nick's! The stories of Wawetseka belong to our band! The decision is not Nick's to make! It's a *tribal* matter!" He backed onto the walkway, as Dawn stood amazed, trying to figure out what this was all about. The neighbor started down his stairs and moved in their direction.

"Make them stop the book. I'm warning you! You'll all regret it if you don't." Billy spun around, stalked down the walk to his truck, and peeled away.

The neighbor crossed the street and approached Dawn. "Are you okay? Do you want me to call the police?"

Dawn gathered her thoughts and gave him a weak smile. "No, don't call anyone, please. It's an old matter. He's angry, but he won't hurt anyone." She put a hand on his arm. "Thanks for being there," she said. "I'm sure it helped.

She went into the house, her legs shaky. *I can handle this*, she thought. She closed the door behind her, leaned against it, put her face in her hands, and dissolved into tears.

Chapter 11

Cora put finishing touches on dinner while Cisco filled bowls and platters and looked for serving spoons. She leaned over and spoke in Cisco's ear. "Well," she asked, "what do you think?"

Cora held her breath. She desperately hoped Cisco would drop his resistance and join them. She felt something was missing, almost as if she was betraying him, when she worked on the book.

Cisco, who had been listening to the merriment in the adjacent family room, let out a roar of laughter and then he too spoke in a low voice, "I like them—nice people—a lot of fun."

"Fun, like when we solved the Sag Bridge murders with Frannie?" Cora reminded him with a smirk.

"That was fun too—part of the time." He looked into her eyes for a moment, shaking his head.

"This time we're only writing a book. What could happen?"

"Look how Rose is hugging that stuffed wolf pup Frannie gave her," he said, instead of reacting to her comment.

"Reminds you of our grandkids when they were that age, doesn't it? Remember how devoted Ryan was to Frannie?" Cora asked.

"You mean before they became walking computer games?"

"Stop. All kids do that these days." Cora scraped food onto platters and set them on the island in the middle of the kitchen. "Soup's on," she called. "I hope you don't mind buffet style. The little chalkboard lists what everything is."

"Damn! A chalkboard menu," said Frannie, shaking her head. "Isn't that just Cora? Even that gal's eating is organized."

~ ~ ~

After dinner, Cora brought out a red velvet cake to celebrate Rose's first birthday.

"Looks like you picked a winner," Dawn said, looking with dismay at her little girl, head and arms smeared red and white with cake and frosting.

"I bet Cora has a plan for cleaning her too," Frannie said.

Cora picked up Rose. Dawn followed them into the laundry room, where Cora sat the little girl on the washing machine, deftly removed her clothes, rinsed them, and threw them in the washer. She filled the laundry tub with warm water and plunked Rose in it. Rose splashed and laughed, playing with an empty plastic squeeze bottle until all remnants of cake were gone.

Dawn delivered the sleepy child, wrapped in a soft towel, to Frannie's waiting arms. Rose promptly fell asleep, cushioned against Frannie's abundant chest. Frannie sank into a corner of the sofa, her head nodding.

"I'll clean up. Go get to know Nick better," Cora said, as she pushed Cisco out of the kitchen. Having discovered a common interest in golf, Cisco dragged Nick to the garage to show him a new club and a GPS device that registered the distance from his ball to the hole.

Dawn, relieved of motherly duties for the moment, helped Cora put away leftovers and stack dishes in the dishwasher.

In a hushed voice, Dawn said, "Cora, I have to tell you—Billy came here. He came to our house!"

Cora's eyes flew open in alarm. "You didn't let him in, did you?"

"No, of course not! Rose was taking her nap so I stepped outside." She proceeded to repeat the conversation to Cora in detail.

"Did you tell Nick this time?"

"Yes, I called him at work. He said maybe Billy will leave us alone now he got things off his chest. I didn't tell him about the phone calls, though."

"Is he right about the book? *Does* it belong to the band?"

"Nick's mother gave it to him. I don't know what the rules are about antiquities or whatever, but his family has always had it. I don't know how the band can claim it, but our views on ownership are a bit complicated."

"We're increasing its value and not harming the document." Cora dried her hands on a kitchen towel and hung it on the stove handle. "Incidentally, has your mom calmed down about the new baby yet? After you finally told her?"

"She's okay, but she's not telling her friends yet, until she figures out what she wants to say."

Cora moved about absently, dried a baking dish, and then pulled out a stack of bakeware and returned the dish to the cabinet. "I think Billy's not ready to give up his anger yet, so the stuff about the book is an excuse to stay mad. His accusations don't have any substance. He got a chance to say what's on his mind—I bet you don't hear from him again."

They were distracted by a sleeping whimper from Rose in the next room. Frannie opened her eyes and gazed at the little girl. She smiled and whispered, "It's been a while since I held a sleeping baby. I forgot all about how sweet it is."

"I hate to break it up, but we should get her into her own bed," Dawn said, smiling at the scene.

"Before everyone leaves, can we settle a couple of things real quick?" Cora asked.

"Cora, you always about business," said Frannie. She heaved an exaggerated sigh and rolled her eyes. "Guess it wouldn't be Cora otherwise."

"What can't wait until Saturday when we get together again?" Nick asked, as he and Cisco reentered the room.

"The reporter from *News Local*, for one," Cora replied.

"Oh yeah, that," Nick said, rubbing his chin. "Isn't it too soon? We don't have much to tell him yet."

"I don't think we should turn down any opportunity for publicity," Cora said.

"Yeah, I agree with that," said Frannie. "We get the guy on our side now he's gonna be there when we need him. Could be helpful in other ways too—maybe someone will call us with stuff we want to know. Can't meet him too soon, that's what I think."

"'Her,' actually—Megan Flynn. How about if we see her on Saturday, right before our regular meeting?" Cora suggested.

"Isn't that the same reporter that screwed things up for your election last year?" asked Cisco.

"It is, but that wasn't her fault, remember?" Cora said.

She stared at Cisco, and all eyes turned to him. "We could use some help," she hinted.

"Okay, okay," said Cisco, wagging his head back and forth and waving his arms. "It's clear you're all going ahead with or without me, so I give. But on my terms." His words said he was agreeing against his will, but his twinkling eyes and tight lips that controlled a smile gave him away.

~~~

"I'm so glad you're going to work with us," Cora said later, glancing at Cisco as he sat, feet extended in his recliner, in front of the television in their family room. "I felt guilty, having all that fun without you."

She wanted to say more, but knew Cisco got the point. She had a tendency to belabor things, which made him crazy. "How many ways are you going to say that? I get it!" he'd say. He would never admit, though, that he did the same thing himself.

He studied her face. "You're the one with the well-developed sixth sense, so why am I the one who gets the feeling something's not right here?"

Cora felt a little surge of apprehension but said nothing.

Cisco drew a long breath. "It might not be as bad as I thought. It's your project, not mine—I don't write books, but I'll lend a hand if you need me. Let me take it at *my* pace, okay?"

"Sure. Don't you like Nick and Dawn?" she asked.

"I said I did, didn't I?" She knew he didn't intend a sharp retort. The response was his way of agreeing with her, but he would want her to think it was reluctantly.

His eyes kept straying to the television. If she didn't distract him right away, the opportunity would be lost. She clicked off and set down the iPhone she'd been using to check emails.

"Can I share some confidences with you?" she asked.

"Should you?" He slowly turned his head toward her.

"I think I should. I didn't want to say anything until you met them."

"Okay—what's up?"

She told him about Dawn's pregnancy and feelings that Nick was oblivious to her worries, that Nick could be hiding something from Dawn, and about Billy. She explained that she thought Nick was hesitant to talk about it, and the moments of distraction she had noticed.

"Trouble in paradise. So you think this guy is stalking her? How serious is it?"

"The fact that he's moved here is scary, but maybe he'll stop fantasizing when he sees them together."

"It bears watching though. It's been a couple of years since they married—don't you think he should have gotten over it by now? You don't think we should get the police involved, do you?"

"I think the most serious thing is how they're not communicating with each other. That's the kind of thing that breaks up marriages. I'm worried about them."

He nodded.

"They remind me of *us* when the boys were young, Cisco. You were busy at work, distracted, and irritable. You thought your hard work was enough and just wanted to crash when you got home, and I was supposed to have everything right. My day was stressful too, and I wanted to unload, but you thought I had it easy." She blinked a few times, recalling her fear of doing the wrong thing, making mistakes, and having the awful sense that she was alone, unable to admit to anyone, especially Cisco, that she was worried about their marriage.

Cisco didn't comment, so Cora continued. "I didn't understand your pressures, and you trivialized mine and didn't realize I needed your support. We couldn't talk to each other. I talked to my friend Lu, and you didn't talk to anyone, but just held it all in."

"I remember. It was pretty awful for a while."

"Your head was in the right place, only you never *told* me. That's what I needed to hear." Her voice shook a little. *Even after all this time!*

"We couldn't talk about it, either of us."

"Until we did."

"Which saved our marriage," he said.

"We were both self-involved and had to figure out how to live like a family. We had to work at it, and it took a while."

"It wasn't easy," Cisco said. "But thank God we did it."

They looked deeply into each other's eyes. Cisco reached over and took her hand, and he continued to hold it as he turned his attention back to the television.

Chapter 12

Megan Flynn, a short, slight woman with a heart-shaped, pixie face; short-cropped, copper-colored hair; and green eyes sparkling with energy, was a true reflection of her Irish heritage. Megan set her mobile phone in the center of a table that had been brought in for them at the Isle a la Cache library. "Is it okay if I record this session? There won't be anything off the record, will there?"

"Nah, go ahead," Frannie replied.

Megan initiated the recording app and glanced out the large window, pausing to study the Indian longhouse and log cabin, and then moved her eyes from Cora to Nick to Frannie. "Isn't it unusual to be writing a book by committee, so to speak?"

The question was unexpected, but Cora answered it. "Probably. But it makes sense. We all come to the project with different skills. Nick owns the manuscript and has the cultural heritage to interpret and enhance the story. Without him there is no story—but he has no time. I have writing skills and historical knowledge, and Frannie has research skills and time on her hands. It works." She smiled. "It doesn't hurt that we're big fans of each other."

"How did you get together?" Megan asked. By turns they filled her in on how they met, who Wawetseka was, how the memoir came into Nick's hands, and the gist of the story. Megan was particularly interested in the curse of Mishipeshu and took it down in detail. Frannie started to open her mouth once or twice, but she thought better of it and said nothing, which was a relief to Cora.

"So you're a Native American? Nick doesn't sound like an Indian name," Megan pointed out.

"It's Nikan. It means 'friend' in Potawatomi," Nick said.

"You never told us that!" Frannie said.

Nick shrugged his shoulders. "It never came up."

"And Dawn?" Frannie asked.

"Wapun, which means 'dawn.' And Rose is Rozene, which means, naturally, 'rose.'"

"Huh," said Frannie, with a little snort. "'Bout time we knew."

"So this book you're writing is a mystery?" Megan asked.

"Right," said Frannie, at the same time Nick said, "Maybe." Megan turned a questioning look at them.

"We're not sure yet. Depends on remaining research and trial chapters. It may wind up a nonfiction, historical biography or a historical mystery novel. Either way, the story involves solving a murder mystery and bringing the killer to justice," Cora explained.

"Why is the story important? Why should people be interested?"

Nick cleared his throat and held up a hand to indicate he wanted to answer that question. "Not only is the story told in the voice of an Indian woman, but there was very little written from the viewpoint of Native Americans at the time, and it corrects misconceptions. Wawetseka was a remarkable woman in any time or culture." He engaged the reporter with one of his charming smiles.

"While those in authority grabbed at easy answers, she had the strength, intelligence, and determination to identify the real killer, and not only identify him but find out where he went, track him down, and bring him back singlehandedly, operating under laws of an alien society. She was a small woman, and this happened during a snowstorm in a brutal environment."

Cora nodded. "It's an important story for Lemont, too, because much of the story happened right here, almost twenty years before the arrival of permanent settlers. It dramatizes not only interesting cultural and historic facts but unique geographic features of the area."

"What do you mean by unique geographic features?" Megan pulled her eyes away from Nick.

"The river, the Des Plaines River, was the primary way people got from place to place in the northern part of Illinois. Throughout its course, especially right here, travelers encountered rocky bluffs, canyons, islands, forests, or swamps. Most of these features are still here today, but we don't notice them amidst all the trappings of suburbia. The story will make people notice," Cora said.

"I'm sold," said Megan with a laugh.

"When do you plan to print your story?" Nick asked.

"Right away—either this coming Friday's edition or next Friday at the latest, early August. I hope to give it a front-page cover and a full page inside. When can people buy the book?"

"We hope to finish in a few months, but then we have to find a publisher. Provided that doesn't take too long—it could be a year," Cora said.

"It *will* be published, even if we have to do it ourselves," Nick said firmly.

Megan turned off the recording and reached into her purse for a camera. "Let's get some pictures with interesting background, especially that big wigwam out there."

"It's a longhouse," said Nick. "It was used for gatherings and ceremonies."

"Can't your phone take pictures? Why d'you need a camera?" asked Frannie.

"Phone cameras are fine for smaller pictures, but they don't have enough resolution for a front-page or half-page photo," Megan explained.

"Okay then," said Frannie. "You gonna need that camera to get all of us and that old long house thing. Be sure you got *me* in that picture. How's my hair, Cora? Does it look crazy enough so all my friends can recognize me?"

After Megan left, Cora said, "I learned a lot about selling books to prepare for writing about Sag Bridge. You have to get people's attention seven times before they're motivated to buy, on the average. Getting publicity this early is a stroke of luck."

"I agree," Nick said. "A few people will be intrigued immediately, and fewer may want to get involved or help promote it. Others need reminders. This reporter can be helpful."

"What's the business for the day?" Frannie asked, clearly expecting Cora to take over.

After summarizing their research, Cora outlined plans for the coming week. "I think we should go to Dellwood Park and the old Brown farm to see limestone bluffs—we might need to describe bluffs in the story—know where they are and how to navigate them. They'll look much the same now as they did in Wawetseka's day."

"You told us about Dellwood Park, but what's at the Brown farm?" asked Nick.

"It's right here in Lemont, one of the first farms, settled in the 1830s. It has a bluff and quarry on the property. It's a private institution now, an inpatient facility for women, so we'll need permission to walk around. I wonder if you could arrange that, Nick? They may respond more favorably to a scientist from Argonne."

"Sure. Hey, I think I'll bring Dawn and Rose to Dellwood Park. That sounds like something they'd like."

"Okay, good." Cora turned to a blank page in her notebook and looked up. "Do we understand enough about how the justice system worked, before statehood, under territorial law? There were a lot of travelers, but few nonnative residents. Wawetseka mentioned a sheriff and a judge, but who accused a killer, who captured murderers, where were they kept, how were they punished? Was her experience typical or unusual?"

"I been digging into that, so I'll stay on it," Frannie volunteered. "Cisco was a soldier—maybe he'd like to check out the military."

"I'll ask him. I'm sure he will." Cora made a note. "And we should learn more about some of the historic figures we identified, like Thomas Forsyth. He's an interesting guy, Indian agent, trader, and spy for William Clark, of Lewis and Clark fame, who was governor at St. Louis at that time. Forsyth was in business with his half brother, John Kinzie of Chicago. Mostly Forsyth was at Peoria, but he traveled to Chicago regularly. Peoria is where Wawetseka's son would have been tried. If nothing else, Forsyth would have at least known what was going on. Let me check." She made a few more notes.

"I guess I'm the one who should check old Indian customs regarding crime and punishment. I'll contact our elders and see how we policed ourselves before the white man—and find out about local Indian leaders of the time. Some of the historic people we named were Indians," said Nick. "Especially Black Partridge. Where was he when Wawetseka's son was arrested?"

Cora started to gather her materials. "I'll organize the information we already have; categorize; and make to-do lists, agendas, and time charts. Frannie, can you look up old trials? This should have been one of the first murder cases in the state."

"Sure—and it goes without saying you'd do all that," said Frannie. "When we gonna start writing this thing?"

Cora noted but did not mind the good-natured gibe at her organizational habits. "Does anybody think we're there yet?" Cora asked. The response was a series of shrugged shoulders.

"I can start organizing the story now, too, I suppose: character lists, settings, key scenes, outlines, list of maps, timelines, stuff like that—locate some maps showing old Indian trails. I'll start a binder." She studied her notes, pulling on her lower lip. "A lot of this has landed on my plate now, but there's no way I can get out of it. Everybody better leave me alone this week."

"I'm sure gonna like seeing us in the paper again," Frannie mused. "Are we sure this Megan person is gonna write good stuff about us?"

"Sure she is," Cora replied. "Why wouldn't she? What reason could she have to make us look bad? She wouldn't print anything at all if she wasn't going to present us positively."

"She didn't stop that bad press you got last year," Frannie pointed out. Nick looked blank. Cora never told him she and Megan had interacted last fall over Cora's library board candidacy.

"It all turned out okay," Cora said. "She apologized for the error and helped correct it."

"That's true, but now I'm getting a bad feeling about this," Frannie said, waving her forefinger in the air. "Things just going too smooth. That's not the way of things. We're all having too much fun. Ought to be some hard spots, something bad due to happen."

Cora noted that Nick's head was down and he was staring at the table.

"Maybe that wolf spirit of yours, Cora, think you need protecting again, getting involved and helping us out some kind of way," Frannie babbled on, oblivious. "Think your wolf buddy be any help if this Mishi-whatever come after us? Or that cougar?"

Brad entered the room as they were talking, and Cora glanced nervously at him.

"Don't let your imagination run away with you, Frannie," said Brad. Cora wondered how much he knew about her "wolf buddy" and "Mishi-whatever." She caught Frannie's eye and jerked her head in Brad's direction.

Frannie looked up. "What?" she said. Then, looking toward Brad, "Oh." She pushed some items around the table aimlessly as she mumbled, "I'm just saying. That's what I think."

Cora thought Frannie's ramblings were extreme, but she also felt uneasily that things *were* going too smoothly. It wasn't just Nick and Dawn's personal troubles, or Billy, but something more. It was silly, an unwarranted premonition. She couldn't shake it, but no one else needed to hear about it.

Chapter 13

"I wish she hadn't focused so much on that curse," Cora said, holding up the local paper and pointing at the headline. "But I guess that's what makes news, and we wanted attention, so there is that."

The story, featured on the front page of the Friday paper as Megan promised, was favorable. The headline read: "Lemont Writers Challenge Ancient Native American Curse." In addition to descriptions of the work in progress and its writers, the story was full of references to shamans and recounted the legend of Mishipeshu, the Water Panther.

Cora read highlights aloud as the writing group picked at a fast-food lunch at Isle a la Cache. Frannie took the newspaper from Cora and examined it, although she had already read it.

Nick had seemed distracted once again when he arrived and made no comment as she and Frannie discussed the news article.

"Is something wrong, Nick?" Cora asked. "Don't you like the story?"

"It's fine," he said, his voice expressionless. He looked undecided, then without further comment he pulled a folded piece of paper from his pants pocket, smoothed it, and handed it to Cora. "Funny this should arrive today, of all days."

Cora stared at the ordinary, copy-machine paper. Neat letters printed in blue marker covered the page. Her heart skipped a beat and her face grew white. She looked up to see Frannie watching her anxiously. "What's wrong?"

Cora read from the page:

You must not continue to offend the spirits!
The curse is real!
Proceed at your peril!

Frannie slammed her hand on the table, knocking over her cup of pop, which, fortunately, was almost empty. "I told you things was going too smooth!"

"Where did this come from?" Cora asked.

"It was in my mailbox this morning, but it couldn't have come through the post office, since the envelope wasn't addressed." Nick produced an envelope, free of any writing.

"Someone local then," Cora said. Frannie was wiping the table with a fistful of paper napkins. Cora caught Nick's eye and mouthed the word "Billy." Nick shrugged and glanced toward Frannie, acknowledging that Dawn must have told Cora about Billy, but Frannie knew nothing about the personal matter.

"I told you I saw that thing in the water, but you all didn't believe me, and now look! This letter have to do with that thing I saw? How could that be? Who would send such a thing? Someone who doesn't like Indians?" Frannie asked.

"I don't know about what you saw, Frannie, but *who* is a good question. It's got to be a *person* behind this. Someone with a grudge against one of us? Someone with something to lose if we publish the memoir?" Nick suggested.

Cora passed the letter back to Nick. "It's not so odd it came today—we were in yesterday's paper."

Nick closed his eyes for a moment and dropped his forehead onto his hand.

"Things always get interesting when you're involved, Cora—too interesting. In fact, things get dangerous," Frannie said.

"That's one of the reasons Cisco didn't want to get involved. But what could happen—you can't believe in a curse!" Cora said.

"We didn't believe in ghosts, either, until last year." Frannie replied. "I'm not so sure anymore. Spirits or not, it's a threat from something or someone."

They stared at each other.

"It's your legend, Nick. I don't know why I was the one saw that thing instead of you. How do you explain this?" Frannie asked.

"I can't explain it," Nick said. "I know the stereotype is that our people believe in good and evil spirits, taboos, fetishes, and the like, but Indian curses have always been debatable. This doesn't make sense to me. I think it's coming from someone who *thinks* he knows more about our culture than he does."

Cora picked up her hamburger. She couldn't understand why Nick was leading the conversation away from Billy, who she thought obviously sent the note, but she played along. Also, even after her experiences, she didn't want to admit a supernatural presence could be involved. But was a human threat any less dangerous?

Finally, Nick wiped his mouth with a napkin. "I don't want to stop. If you guys want to drop out, okay. I'll hire someone to finish."

"No way," said Frannie. "I'm not backing out. Just keep me away from that river. And see what you can do about getting me one of them talismans or something, will you, Nick?"

Cora grinned at Nick. "Looks like we're still in. That doesn't mean we shouldn't take precautions, though. Give me that letter. I'll have Cisco take it to Officer Rogers, a cop we know. No harm having him watching our backs."

Nick opened his mouth and looked as if he was going to object, but then handed her the note.

Thinking further discussion would be nonproductive, Cora suggested they continue with the planned discussion points for the day and try to put the threat out of their minds. She led the meeting, as usual, asking each person to review progress since their previous get-together, and gradually they began to focus on other matters.

During the week they had all strolled along a limestone bluff at Dellwood Park in nearby Lockport and then had a late-afternoon picnic. They laughed at Rose, who hadn't seen a picnic table before and treated it like playground equipment, climbing all over it and jeopardizing the food that had been laid out.

Next they stopped briefly at the Brown property to see a limestone bluff and became interested in a stone barn built in the 1830s. The walls had been constructed with rifle slots for defense against Indian attack, slots that had never been used, since the native population had left the area before the barn was built and did not return.

The group agreed it was time to start actively writing the manuscript. Their objectives for today were to discuss some final details and begin to outline the story.

Cora had located and copied a survey drawn in 1827, only ten years after Wawetseka's story, showing the course of the Des Plaines River, its islands, swamplands, and surrounding prairies; elevation of the bluffs; and numbered land sections for comparison to Lemont's present-day layout. She passed out copies and began the discussion.

"Are we agreed? We'll write the story as a novel, but Nick will write an introduction that gives a serious discussion of the place, time, and issues?"

Nick and Frannie, who had worked out the compromise, nodded reluctantly. Cora had pointed out that some readers would just skip the introduction. Nick insisted that some people wanted to understand what was going on at the time to fully appreciate the story. If they didn't include it, some people would have questions or their thinking would be skewed. Readers could decide to read it or not, which they couldn't do if it wasn't there.

"So, what voice should we use? What will make it compelling for the reader? First person may be easier to write, but I read that more novels today are in third person. Don't know why—maybe just the public's taste."

"I think we should do what comes natural to us and hang the statistics," Frannie said.

"I agree," said Nick, nodding. "Wawetseka wrote it as a memoir, and it should keep that flavor. Writing it in first person will give it intimacy and make it seem more believable."

"It's also tighter, meaning we can tell the story more directly, with better flow, more action, and fewer words. We can explain directly from her perspective and include her opinions. So we agree on first person?" Cora looked around and got the expected go-ahead.

"Next—terminology and vernacular. How will she talk? We have three languages to deal with: French, English, and Potawatomi. How much language authenticity should we use? Before the white man, Indians had different concepts and used descriptions based on experience: moons, suns, seasons, travel—foot, horseback, or canoe. Measurements were based on human anatomy, such as hands, arms, etc."

Nick nodded as Cora spoke. "'A hand of suns ago a man with a scar the size of a man's finger was found when we walked a half day from our village.' Do we want our readers to have to puzzle through that?"

"I do that all the time. I'm a specialist in talking two kinds of ways, but I think I can judge when to use what," Frannie said. "We should make some *rules.*"

"How has it been done by other writers? Are there any first person examples?" Nick asked.

"Yes. Black Hawk wrote an autobiography. He wanted to tell the story of the Black Hawk Wars in his own words." Cora walked to the library shelves and found a thin volume, which she handed to Nick. "As I recall, the book uses a combination of white and Indian descriptions."

Nick thumbed through the pages. "Apparently Black Hawk's inter-preter wrote it down and then a newspaper editor reworked it. And, it was re-edited in 1882. Despite that, it's generally accepted as a rare account from an Indian perspective."

He set the book down and scratched his head. "I know I've taken a stance for authenticity, but I'm not sure it makes sense to be too much of a purist here. The reader might get disgusted and put the book down. Since you're writing the first draft Cora, what's your opinion?"

"I think we should use whatever words were used by semi-educated people of the time, and throw in some vernacular for flavor now and then. In the forward or afterword we can explain that we did this intentionally to make it easier for readers. It'll get a little tricky with dialogue, when she's talking to other Indians, but we'll do our best."

Frannie waved her hand in the air like a schoolchild excited to have the right answer. "How about we pretend *we're* telling the story—tell-ing it as if we're writing it down like Wawetseka told us? *She's* telling the story but we're using *our* words. Isn't that sorta what Black Hawk did?"

Nick blinked. "That frees up the language difficulties and keeps the intimacy. But we have to be sure readers understand that's what we're doing."

Pam walked into the room. "How you guys doing? Need any help?"

"Maybe," Cora said. "We're having some language and point-of-view issues." She described the difficulties and their potential solutions. "What do you think?"

Pam went to the library shelves. "Let me see if there's anything here." She found a few books and set them in front of the group. "See if you find anything helpful. I'll see what the guys think," she said, leaving the room.

Soon she was back with Brad and Josh. Josh, as an actor, advocated strict vernacular. Brad thought excessive vernacular would be confusing. Easy enough to act out, harder to write. After lively discussion about such matters as stiff dialogue, unnatural prose, and breaks in flow, they agreed with Cora's initial opinion.

"We don't want to turn readers off saying stuff all weird," was how Frannie put it. Cora smiled, thinking Frannie's language was nothing to brag about.

Cora scratched her head. "Maybe this isn't a big problem after all. She spoke and wrote French, didn't she? And lived with a French family? She wouldn't have been limited to Indian descriptions."

The others blinked. Cora was right, of course.

"Wawetseka mentioned someone from the fur station helped her perfect her memoir," Nick said. "It seems we had an early writer in the family, who even used an editor. I wonder if she hoped she would be published one day, a gift to her descendants."

Cora withdrew mentally from the friendly chatter to sort out how she was going to proceed. The burden was on her now, and she hoped to develop an outline and first draft of the novel within two months, writing at a rate of two to three chapters a week, estimating the finished work as fifteen to twenty chapters.

She thought it a reasonable plan. Commitments made her anxious, but she worked best under a deadline. A hollow feeling in the pit of her stomach and an acid taste in her mouth reminded her of the curse and the warning letter. She'd let Nick sort out the business with Billy, but she couldn't help but feel there was more to it than that. Like first Cisco and then Frannie had said, something wasn't right, but nothing added up and it didn't seem she could do anything about it. She straightened her back and forced the apprehensive thoughts from her mind.

Chapter 14

THE drive to their son's house, located in a suburb far west of Chicago, took more than an hour. Cora enjoyed the ride, delighting in the display of autumn color in the farm country and western suburbs through which they passed. Cora and Cisco had spent the day with their son, daughter-in-law, and grandsons—a nice day, no special occasion, just the pleasure of being together.

Patrick had announced a promotion and raise—long overdue, in Cora's opinion. Patrick's overfull and stressful life seemed much like her own, and she wondered if in any way she was responsible. Nothing she could do about that now. In any event, she hoped life was about to return to normal for all of them, whatever the implications of that.

Marty had prepared an excellent meal, and everyone, even Sean and Ryan, usually picky eaters, had seconds. Wonder of wonders, the boys stopped gaming and went for a long walk with Grandpa Cisco and Grandma Cora, and they had a lively conversation about things that interested boys, things that had happened, and things they wanted to do. As a result, they stayed much too long.

Now, driving home after dark, she remembered the colorful scenery that began the day and wondered if the long, unusually warm autumn was responsible for the brilliant leaves. This late in October, most trees should have dropped their leaves by now, shouldn't they?

"I never get it straight, Cisco. Are colors more brilliant after a long, hot fall, or after a short, cold one? Is this year unusual?"

Cisco, wrestling with the steering wheel in a gusty wind, shrugged and shook his head.

Well, whatever, this year the color was outstanding and the days hot. The weather *was* highly unusual. Almost November, it was still in the 70s and 80s, one day after another with no end in sight. And tonight's warm wind was from the south, continuing the pattern.

Cora dropped her head back against the car's headrest and closed her eyes. Cisco enjoyed driving and didn't need her to keep him awake. With nothing to do except sit there and wait to arrive home, she let her thoughts wander.

The manuscript was done! Not *exactly* done, but soon to be published, after a few minor tweaks their editor had requested.

Cora shifted her position and drew a deep breath. Cisco glanced her way and asked, "You okay?"

"Fine," she said. "Just sleepy. It's been a long day."

She returned to her thoughts. The writing of the manuscript had gone exceptionally well and far ahead of schedule. Cisco was happy, and Dawn was free to prepare for the new baby. In the immediate aftermath of near completion, Cora felt at a loss for what to do with herself, but knew she would soon get over that. Frannie…well, Frannie was another matter. She was pestering Cora every few hours with trivial questions. Did we remember to tell the publisher our thoughts for the cover? *Yes, Frannie, for the umpteenth time, we told him.* She wanted to say, "Get a life," but she knew being at loose ends was temporary for Frannie too, so she bit her tongue.

The concentrated efforts of "the team" had enabled her to write and edit the manuscript in just over two months. Cisco ensured that she had enough writing time each day: two hours in the morning, followed by a short lunch, and three hours in the afternoon. She locked herself in her office, refusing phone calls or interruptions, and banged out two thousand words on good days, five hundred on poor days.

When she needed information or opinions, she sent off e-mails. Frannie, Nick, or Dawn got back to her with quick answers, doing all the research for her. She did this Monday through Friday, and they all got together Saturday mornings to read the latest chapters and edit the material. She entered the edits on Sunday, reread the edited chapters, and then worked on new material again Monday morning. In the end, they had a 60,000-word manuscript.

Meanwhile, Frannie and Cisco looked for a publisher. Their combined efforts, along with the first three completed chapters of the book, had resulted in a signed publishing contract. The editor their publisher used happened to be free when they completed the manuscript and had returned it quickly with only a few suggestions. It looked as if the book would be released before the end of the year, in time for Christmas sales. Megan Flynn had already published another news story to announce the completion of the book and expected publication date.

Cora's friends at the historical society wished they could have been more involved, and Cora tried to make up for this by keeping them posted and giving them a sample to read now and then. They could not, however, have progressed nearly as quickly were it not for the Isle a la Cache staff, who not only responded promptly to their questions, but also gave useful opinions. The staff wandered into the room during planning sessions and joined in freely. It was clear they felt some ownership in the project.

"Nothing ever came of that threatening letter Nick got or Frannie's fears. It's been more than two months," Cora said. "That whole business was strange. Do you really think it's over? I know you don't like to hear this, but I'm still waiting for something to happen."

"Probably a prank, like Officer Rogers thought. Nick's still acting like he's disturbed about something, though."

"I noticed. Things are probably not any better between him and Dawn. He doesn't talk about it. Remember I told you Dawn is happy about the baby now, but she said they still aren't communicating very well. Billy hasn't made any more trouble, though, so that might be over. Maybe he went back to Michigan. Nick was probably right when he said that problem would go away on its own."

Cora thought there was still something wrong there, but now Dawn wasn't confiding in her either, so she had no way of knowing—except the couple never exchanged glances anymore. She had watched. Sometimes one or the other seemed to clamp their teeth and turn away to stop an angry comment.

Still, she felt unsettled. Why couldn't she shake the feeling things were running out of control? Was it because the entire project had gone so unexpectedly quickly and easily, and she just couldn't square that against past experiences?

She drew a long breath. She and Cisco would try to return to normal now, since the work was done. Done, except for a little editing and decisions about cover and design. The title, they had just decided, would simply be *Wawetseka's Tale–A Retelling, 1817*. Cora liked it.

She opened her eyes when Cisco pulled into the garage and gathered her belongings to get out of the car.

As soon as Cisco turned the handle of the door between their garage and kitchen, Cora knew something was terribly wrong. The door, blown by a powerful gust of wind that blasted through the house, struck Cisco in the head and chest.

"Ouch! Shit!" He winced and jumped backward. His hand flew to his head, and he rubbed it and turned toward Cora. "Maybe I forgot to leave a light...I'm sure I locked the doors and windows."

The garage-door-opener light timed out, leaving them standing in the doorway in semi-darkness, wind whistling around them.

"Something's open *somewhere*," Cora said.

Cisco stepped cautiously into the dim kitchen, lit only by a distant streetlight penetrating the windows. Cora followed closely, clinging to his arm. He flipped the light switch, revealing a scene of destruction— chairs overturned, tablecloth dragging, a bowl of fruit from the countertop smashed and broken, with glass and fruit scattered over the floor. In the family room adjacent to their kitchen, a lamp lay on its side. The leather sofa was slashed, its cushioning poking through multiple gashes. A shattered kitchen window accounted for the wind, shards of broken glass glittering on the floor in front of it. The blinds were bent and hanging lopsided, and the curtains were in tatters. Cora watched the curtains blow violently and heard the blinds bang as they struck the walls. She grimaced at an overwhelming foul odor and noticed what appeared to be animal feces on the floor, wet with stinking yellow puddles. She gagged.

"What the...!" Cisco reached out an arm, which prevented Cora from going any farther into the room. "Get out! Call 911! Someone could still be in here!"

But they stood frozen, staring with open mouths near the door that was banging now against a wall. Cora was horror-stricken, and a hollow space opened in her gut.

Then, a sudden cessation of wind and soft padding sounds, muffled on carpet, drew their attention. They turned their heads toward the dining room at the other end of the kitchen, to the archway that separated the rooms. At first Cora saw only two pale-gold eyes, unblinking, that appeared to shine of their own light.

"What...." Cisco stopped, and they stared as a large gray animal slid into view and stepped into the room.

"Christ! A wolf! Not again!" Cisco cried, as he moved in front of Cora and began to push her backward.

Head held low, mouth a horrible grimace of sharp pointed teeth, the animal advanced menacingly toward them.

Cora was unable to move. Cisco pushed her through the kitchen doorway, crouching and throwing his arms in front of his face and neck in a protective stance.

A loud thud, scraping sounds on the floor, and another snarl came from near the broken kitchen window. Cora peered out from behind Cisco and saw that another, much larger, wolf had landed in the room.

"Oh, my God!" Cisco yelled.

The attacking wolf, distracted by the second beast, halted its rush and turned its head toward the new arrival. In that moment of hesitation, Cisco pushed Cora into the garage and grabbed the door to force it closed between them and the attacking animals.

The last thing Cora saw as Cisco pulled the door shut made her realize that the second wolf was not rushing them, but instead launched its massive gray body at the attacking wolf, snapping powerful-looking jaws at the animal's throat, forcing it to the ground.

Snarls, yelps, and thuds were heard through the door, sounds of a furious battle. Cisco grabbed Cora's arm and pulled her away from the door and farther into the garage.

Hands clasping her head in terror and confusion, Cora demanded, "What's happening?"

"Just get in the car!" Cisco cried. Flinging open the car door and shoving Cora into the seat, he slammed her door and ran around and got in the driver's side. Safely inside the car, he pushed the button to activate the garage door opener and backed the car out before the door was fully open, scraping the top of the car.

The tires squealed as he raced down the driveway and onto the street. He skidded to a stop and pushed the remote to close the garage door. "Call 911! We'll stay here on the street until help gets here!"

"What's happening?" Cora repeated.

"Damned if I know!" Cisco said.

WAWETSEKA'S TALE

A RETELLING
1817

Nikan Pokagon   Cora Tozzi   Frannie Berkowitz

AUTHOR'S NOTE

WAWETSEKA, A POTAWATOMI woman, is my ancestor. She was born in the latter half of the 1700s in a village along the Des Plaines River where Lemont, Illinois, is now located, and she lived into the mid-1800s. When she was a young woman, she was educated in a Jesuit mission. While there, she was baptized in the Catholic religion and learned to read and write French. Later she returned to live with our people and married a Potawatomi man.

Indigenous people take great pride in their clan identity and ancestors. I grew up on stories about Wawetseka, and I often begged my mother to repeat my favorites. These stories, passed down through many generations, grounded me to what I found most valuable in my Native American heritage. I believe that the memoir Wawetseka wrote in her own hand, which is now in my possession, was written by her as a gift for her children, my children, and my children's children.

Wawetseka was proud of both her white education and her native culture. She knew others were coming to her land, but like most American Indians of her time, she was hopeful she could maintain her traditional way of life. Her memoir relates a personal experience that included the sometimes-baffling changes she observed and her feelings about those changes, before the great disaster happened to her people. Later, when others of her tribe left the area, she made a decision to live among white people rather than migrate. Her story and her observations revealed the ultimate sense of loss she must have felt. The poignancy and loss resonates across almost two centuries.

Most of our people lost their homes to treaties and left Northern Illinois for reservations in the West, especially after the Treaty of Chicago in 1833. Not everyone left. Some remained in the Midwest, and they still live in small communities in places such as Dowagiac, Michigan. Among those who stayed were people who were educated by missionaries, Catholics, and people who had established friendly or favorable relationships with white people. Wawetseka and some others from her village stayed. She lived in a small cabin near friends. There she improved her language skills to make possible the writing of a document that recorded an important event in her life.

As her memoir begins, Wawetseka describes the arrival of men from Canada and eastern parts of the newly formed United States. As the Illinois Territory awaited imminent statehood, each man, whatever his origin, was convinced the land was rightfully his. Their reasons were as varied as were their origins.

The Indian's belief in his right to Illinois land was rooted in semi-migratory culture and seasonal moves. We farmed in the summer and hunted in the winter. We established lodging patterns traditional to our tribes and sacred areas to bury our dead. We did not live in a single place but habitually returned to the same places.

Indian farms in the Illinois Territory were extensive and well laid out, capable of producing crops for sale or trade. When we left our summer villages unoccupied to travel to winter hunting grounds, we expected to return to our fields, much as "snowbirds" do today when they move from northern states to warm climates in the winter. We defended these home grounds from tribes that attempted to steal them and eventually from white men who thought our land was unoccupied.

First to arrive, in the mid-1600s, explorers and priests came and established missions. Fur traders set up trade posts at approximately the same time. Missionaries taught religion to the native population, but they also taught white culture, including language and reading. Women and children attended mission schools, but our men were more interested in trade. They brought furs to the posts and bargained for items available only from white people. Native people initially welcomed them, anticipating trade for things we desired but did not have, items such as cloth, kettles, metal tools, and weapons.

By the time of Wawetseka's story, white newcomers desired not only our furs but our land, spreading across the territory from crowded colonies in the East. We faced a dilemma. The fur supply was becoming depleted, leaving us with little to trade. The reduction in game forced us toward starvation and dependence on land to grow crops. We could fight for the land the white men wanted and become farmers, or we could trade land for annuities on which to survive.

Illinois tribes knew when white men would arrive. News traveled west, spread by Eastern tribes and by honeybees that announced their coming, penetrating the forests fifty miles ahead of the frontier. Surveyors had already arrived and other men would follow to occupy the northern part of the new state. Wawetseka knew that Illinois was about to be granted statehood and what that meant.

Many of these men viewed us as intellectually inferior and called us "savages." We had no written language, but we were shrewd negotiators. We generally got the better part of trades. Why, then, did we lose our land?

"Americans" of the newly formed United States did not understand the migratory nature of the Indian and thought unoccupied land was just that, available.

Nor did Americans understand our communities and personal customs; they thought one Indian tribe represented all Indians and negotiated land purchase with any tribe willing to deal. A tribe may have known the land in question was occupied by others, but thought they were being presented with gifts. As a result, Americans thought they had bought our land, another tribe thought they were recipients of good fortune, and we who had resided on the land for generations returned to find our traditional homeland forbidden to us.

By 1817, the area of Northern Illinois that presently includes the cities of Chicago, Peoria, and Rock Island was sparsely populated but widely traveled by a startling variety of people. This is contrary to the prevalent idea that prior to the Indian removal period, which began after the Treaty of Chicago in 1833, only Indians lived in Northern Illinois. The following are some people Wawetseka would have encountered, and why they claimed a right to these lands.

French priests followed a mission to educate and convert natives to what they believed was a better way of life. They thought of everyone as God's people, and they lived in God's land.

French traders and voyageurs had lived in the country since the sixteenth century and saw no reason to cease fur trade operations. Brides were sent over from France, and families gathered into hamlets. Some men lived with the Indians and intermarried. Both parties benefited from this "kinship" arrangement.

English trading companies established trade routes and had won the right to do so in the French and Indian War. The Northwest Territories were part of the United States by 1817, but the English didn't all agree to abandon their successful private trade interests and relationships with the Indians.

American traders disagreed with English and French traders and attempted to license those who could trade legally. The territory belonged to America. And they believed only Americans had rights there, and others should leave. They had fought and won a war to make it so.

Frontiersmen had already developed paths and small settlements as they pushed westward. These men had unique appetites: they craved adventure and were wanderers and explorers. They wanted to be the first to experience a new land and perhaps stay.

Soon to follow frontiersmen were the earliest settlers, mainly from Eastern states and emigrants from Europe. Why did these people leave the comfortable Eastern Seaboard for the hardships they would encounter in Illinois? In the early 1800s Eastern cities were already centers of industry, commerce, and finance, with factories, universities, and cultural activities—desirable places to live. But opportunity favored the wealthy. In cities, no jobs were to be had for common people who lived in crowded conditions. In rural areas the rich lived in mansions, while small farmers made small profits. Property went to the oldest son, leaving nothing for other family members. The young country was outgrowing itself. But land—and opportunity—awaited those willing to work for it in the West. Invaders fanned out like rivers and disappeared into the wilderness of the West.

Men who fought in the War of 1812 discovered the open lands of Illinois and found them attractive. After the war, they returned with their families for a chance at a better life than they had in the East.

Still others sought to lose themselves in the sparsely populated land. Some had miserable lives, were misfits, or unlucky at love. Some were lazy and deluded into thinking life would be easier. The poor and the well-to-do alike came, bringing all their possessions with them. Land would soon be available for purchase. Surveyors were already mapping out a new canal. The area was about to become prosperous. They wanted to be the first to stake claim to the best piece of the pie. Craftsmen and tradesmen followed the settlers, knowing their goods would be needed and their fortunes would soon be made.

Criminals, speculators, con artists, and opportunists, knowing the newcomers were carrying all they owned and were vulnerable, looked for easy pickings in a land with little if any law enforcement. Military and rangers were sent to build blockhouses and forts to protect and attempt to keep peace between the varied groups. Volunteer militias were raised among the frontiersmen, and agents were appointed to represent and trade with Indians. Judges rode circuits and sheriffs covered vast areas, alone but for men in positions of authority at trade posts or settlers they could recruit. Vigilantes enforced their own interpretation of justice.

And we Indians—invaded, bewildered—struggled to survive.

In this time, and in this place, Wawetseka lived. This is her story, and the authors of this book would like to tell it to you as we think, were she here today, she would tell it.

Nikan Pokagon

AUTUMN AT BLACK PARTRIDGE'S VILLAGE

THE DEAD MAN arrived in autumn, swept by rising floodwaters, caught in the flood plain at the base of the bluff, below Black Partridge's Village.

Our children had found the body and spread the word through our village. I was not there to hear it, as I was on top of the bluff, searching the woods for the last few nuts and acorns hidden beneath the crisp fallen leaves. We had gathered rice and dried and smoked fish and harvested our crops, but much still needed to be done to prepare for winter. The harvests were plentiful this year, but now the dried peas, beans, and squash had to be packed into pots and baskets; the corn pounded into flour; and the acorns boiled, so they would not make bitter flour. The tobacco was not yet stored, nor were the mats woven for our winter houses. With all that to be done, it was a relief to wander peacefully in the quiet woods, enjoying the last warm days and the sweet-smelling leaves.

My peace was disturbed by rustling noises from somewhere in the trees. Startled, I turned toward the sound, but I saw nothing moving. I wondered if I should stop gathering and return to our village. It was well to be cautious these days—not only of large animals, but also of men who came now, men with unfamiliar ways, who could be a threat to a woman alone, away from her village.

The sounds came again, closer, and then I heard a high-pitched whine, and M'ewé, "wolf" in the white man's tongue, emerged from behind a large tree that had fallen to the ground. She crept toward me, her head held low, and then she bounded to me and put her paws on my shoulders. With a cry of relief, I laughed and allowed her to put her jaws affectionately about my chin.

I will tell how I came to be friends with a wolf.

The day I found M'ewé she was crying and rooting around beside her dead mother's body. The she-wolf had starved; perhaps her mate had been killed, leaving no food to nourish mother and pups. M'ewé was the only pup alive, sightless and weak, barely alive at all, and too young for solid food. I held her gently in my hands, then warm against my body for comfort, although the day was hot, and I carried her home.

Our people viewed animals differently from the way the white man did. When I lived with Alain and his family, they allowed a dog into their cabin, and they touched it fondly and called it a pet. We thought animals must be useful in some way. We did not play with them, although our children sometimes did. We did not want to interfere with what dogs were meant to do.

Our women said I should have left M'ewé to fend for herself like other wolves, but she would have died. Perhaps I did not do so because my own little daughter was weak, and I could not bear to see any creature die, no matter how wild, if I could make it live. Perhaps I had enough of death, having lost my husband that year, when he died in great pain of some white man sickness. Perhaps I thought his spirit was in the desperate pup, since wolf was my dead husband's totem.

When I found M'ewé, I was still nursing my little daughter, so I was able to squeeze some milk from my own breasts into my palm to feed the tiny pup. I hid her from our men, but the women soon discovered what I was doing and called me *kyesh'at*, "fool." They said M'ewé would never live on woman's milk. When she did live, they thought some magic was involved, or that M'ewé was not a wolf but a spirit come to dwell among us. When I lived among white men I had come to disbelieve magic, but the women's suspicions amused me. I was not sure about spirits.

M'ewé was of great comfort to me that winter, when my daughter lost her struggle to live. It could be I was not meant to have a child at my age, as I had no need to return to the women's hut after her birth, and it was known that children born to women at that age may not survive.

My husband was an only son, with no brother to take us in after his death, so my son, Nagmo, and I lived with my kin. Nagmo soon took a wife and left our home to live with her. Living with kin meant being agreeable and humble, which was not my nature. I was inclined to go my own way, my opinions different from others, and I had to stop myself lest I speak too freely. But such was our custom, so I made it work. Our people protested when I appeared with M'ewé, but I think the women allowed me to raise her because they were sorry for me.

M'ewé grew strong over the winter, and when we returned to our summer home she followed me, attached as closely as a child. Her silly ways helped me with my grief. She tumbled playfully with our village's children, pretending to nip at them, and they became fond of her.

Amazed visitors spread word of her, and we became known as the "Village of the Wolf." Some held M'ewé in awe, and others feared her. Some believed she was inhabited by a spirit. This opinion spread when she grew to her full strength, and wolf ways stole into her nature. She never hurt our children, but she began to attack our small dogs. The women complained, and I knew she could no longer live among us.

I had to drive her away then. Before I took her back to the woods, I taught her to live in the wild; otherwise she would not survive because I had always fed her. We played games to give her the skills she would need: pull and tug to strengthen her jaws, chase, knock down, and attack and kill small prey.

When she was ready, I took her deep into the forest. We walked that day and the next, and then I chased her away, acting angry. She thought at first it was another game, but I hit her with a stick, and she yelped and backed away. I held up the stick again, waving it around my head, yelling at her as if she did something bad, "Go away!" "Bad girl!" And so she slinked away, glancing back after every few steps. And then I cried.

Now and then, like today, M'ewé visited me when I went to the woods. She had grown very big, bigger than most male wolves, the size of a full-grown doe. Perhaps she grew so large because I fed her well as a pup so she did not have to depend on hunting.

Or, as some said, maybe she was not an ordinary wolf.

In the woods that day, the day the dead man arrived, she was the same gentle companion I remembered. I rubbed her shoulders and pushed my face into her thick fur. After a time she dropped to the ground and, whining, rubbed against my legs, losing a bit of urine onto my moccasin in excitement. I dropped beside her and held her head in my hands.

"*Kyesh'at M'ewé*," I said to her. "Foolish wolf. Will you never let my feet stay dry?"

Later, as I approached the village with my birch-bark basket of acorns and nuts, my friend Shawnash waved to me. She waited for me outside our village gates, which told me she had news. Shawnash, "Warm Wind" in the white man's tongue, walked uphill to meet me. Something must have happened while I was away from the village. Seeing her, M'ewé disappeared into the trees.

The men of our village—and women, too, sadly—considered Shawnash to be simple, pleasant, but of little use. A large woman, tall with a thick waist, she moved slowly, a blank look on her round, flat face, which made others think she was dull-witted and lazy. They did not see that her slow movements were skilled and efficient, or that she often did more than her share of work. As her only close friend, I knew her unrevealing face hid a woman of intelligence, deep thoughts, and a keen sense of humor.

"Wawetseka," she called. "A very bad thing has happened! A man has been found in the river!"

I smiled. "A man, Shawnash? Surely you should be happy to meet a new man, as the ones in our village are all taken, or of such poor quality no woman wants them." Shawnash was over thirty years of age, no longer a maiden. She had not been able to interest a man even from neighboring tribes.

"No, Wawetseka. He is a dead man, a dead *white* man! He is caught in a deadfall in the river, and Poji has gone to the station to tell the white men so they can come to get him—and find out who he is. We do not know him."

"He must have been traveling on the river then." I had many questions. "How is he dressed? What sort of man is he? How did he die?"

"It must be Mishipeshu, 'Water Panther,' as the man is in the water. What else could be the reason?"

Our people were terrorized by Mishipeshu, a huge beast that resembled a big cat but was covered with spikes and scales. He lived under our lakes and rivers and guarded valuable metals that were found there, and he brought death and misfortune to people who trespassed in his waters.

This was why we sprinkled tobacco on the water as an offering when we traveled—to protect us from Mishipeshu.

"Mishipeshu? Why do you think it was not just a mishap?"

"Do not let your time at the mission and living with the French family blind you to our beliefs, Wawetseka. I did not go to see the man myself, but...our women say the body is horrible. His face and his manhood have been torn away, and there is a great wound in the back of his head. Some very powerful force must have killed him, they say. Some terrible thing—like Mishipeshu."

I was not sure about Mishipeshu, but my alarm grew for other reasons. This could mean trouble for us: a white man found dead near our village, and mutilated. I hoped he was not scalped, or one of our men would be blamed. White men always look for ways to blame us.

"Where is Nagmo?" I asked.

My son, Nagmo, "Sings All The Time," lived with his wife's tribe, as was our way. He came to visit a few days ago but did not give the reason, and he soon left on a hunt with our braves, his old friends. I suspected trouble between him and his wife, or with her family. They were married only since early summer, and although he did not speak to me of this, I saw much confusion on his face when he did not know I was watching. Wabmimi, "Gray Dove," was very young and appeared lazy and spoiled. Their first year could be hard, but she was a delightful child and will make a good wife—if their marriage can survive until she grows out of her young girl ways.

I wanted to advise Nagmo. Mothers want to do that...but I would not unless he asked.

"A man who returned early from the hunt said Nagmo went his own way and has not been seen since." Shawnash, who cared for Nagmo as if he were her own son, seemed worried. She shuffled her feet and looked away. I knew she was curious about why Nagmo was not home with his wife and hurt that I did not talk to her about it. She would not understand why he would leave the hunting party either.

It was not unusual for Nagmo to go off alone, but I was worried too. He was a skilled hunter and a clever tracker, trapper, and woodsman. He was not a large or powerful man, but he was cunning and the best of marksmen, and I should not fear for him. But a dead white man was found and we cannot know what trouble might be coming. I did not like to hear that Nagmo was missing.

Our camp was built into a bluff that overlooks the She-shick-ma-wish-sip-pe River, or "Soft Maple Tree River," which white men named Des Plaines. Most villages were built close to rivers, but when heavy rains fell far upstream and rushed down, the floodwaters overflowed our river's banks and filled our valley. The arrival of floodwaters sometimes warned us of approaching storms. So we made our home on the slope, above the floodwaters. On top of the bluff lush forests and grasslands grew, and it was there I had gathered nuts that day.

Shawnash took my basket and we started down the slope. We approached the palisade that surrounds our village. We did not fear attack these days, so we did not need a palisade or guards, but the enclosure was there from the past. Beyond was the longhouse and our round-topped family lodges, looking like a herd of huge, sleeping brown beasts. Our village was twenty-four houses, an exact number; the priests taught me numbers when I was a child at the mission school.

I wondered if recent turmoil among the whites would cause us to need the palisade after all. I hoped we would not have to go to war again. The United States paid us annuities for using our land, but they did not always pay the right tribe. And, some British still wanted to trade with us, but we were told we could not do that. The white men would figure things out at some time, but until that happened there was much confusion, suspicion, and conflict. White men came and went on the river almost every day. We did not always understand what they were about and merely watched from our heights.

I was not like most of the women in our village, who did their own work and left worldly things to men. I was curious about things I heard and things I saw. Our men did not like to hear my opinions, which did not always agree with theirs, and I discovered it was best to not give voice to my thoughts. That did not stop me from listening and forming my own views.

We entered my home, and I took the basket from Shawnash. She waited while I found the right woven bag and poured what I had gathered into it, fastened it tightly to keep out mice and insects, and stored it on a platform near the back wall. We went down toward the river. Like everyone else, I wanted to see what was going on.

Two nights before there had been a violent storm, but this day was sunny and clear. Still, the rain had filled the valley. Even though the river was back in its bed now, it was tricky to move from tussock to tussock, to make our way through the swampy lowlands to the mainstream of the river, which divided itself into many narrow passages around islands. The storm must have uprooted and washed down the tree in which Shawnash said the man's body was caught. Uprooted trees caught against the banks were not unusual, but dead bodies were.

Most of our people were gathered in small groups near the river's edge, talking excitedly. Children jumped from pool to pool, splashing and laughing, pushing and daring each other, darting at the deadfall, and attempting to poke at the dead man with sticks.

I caught sight of Poji, "Wrong Way," who it seemed had returned after telling the white men at the fur station across the river.

Poji was Nagmo's best friend since they were young boys, a huge man of important bearing and great strength, and the opposite of Nagmo, who was short like me and slender and cheerful. Together Poji and Nagmo were a formidable pair, Nagmo for his cunning and marksmanship, and Poji for his skill, intuition, and brute strength. In our village Poji and Nagmo were known for their jokes and laughter and were always up to some prank.

Poji's name did not describe him as his namer intended—Poji was a guide and tracker, whose skills in the backwoods and feats of strength were legendary. He was sought out by many, even the military, for his services. Those men did not know the meaning of his name, and our people thought this was a fine joke. It was said that his name had to do with how he was born.

Sometimes this naming business worked, but other times we were stuck with a lifelong joke. I am another example of poor naming, as I am anything but a "pretty woman." I am a little plump, and everything about me droops: the skin below my eyes and cheeks, my upper arms, and especially my breasts, which were never firm and uplifted as breasts should be. Even my hair is thin and limp.

Our men could pick a new name from their manhood vision, but women had to keep whatever was shown to the namer in a dream. Nagmo's name suited him, as he was a cheerful and kind man. Secretly, I had a hand in this; having had enough of serious and angry men, I had no wish to raise one. The evening before Nagmo's naming ceremony I put some herbs into the namer's evening meal to be sure he had the most pleasant dreams—pleasant dreams to make him think of a happy name. Nagmo's vision quest later made good the namer's choice.

Shawnash and I arrived at Poji's side, where he stood watchfully a short distance above the deadfall. "Poji, what is happening?" I asked.

"I told Davey Leckey at the station about the dead man. He will come here as soon as he finds others to help. He cannot untangle and move the man alone, and he does not wish to involve us. I promised to watch that no one disturbs the body."

I was relieved that Poji was there to speak the white man's language, as otherwise our village would have sent me, and although I speak French well, my English is poor. Poji speaks many tongues, but at the mission, and later when I lived with Alain LeClaire, his wife, and baby, we spoke French. Alain taught me to read and write French, as it was my duty to keep records when he was away. Poji did not have these skills, only speaking. Sometimes we went together to interpret when both speaking and reading in white tongues was needed. It could get complicated.

"How many men are at the station today? When do you think they will come?"

"The blacksmith, Jim Penney, and his helper are there. Lemuel has been away hunting all day, and Philippe—he is not much help for this sort of thing. There is a visiting missionary. That is enough."

I was pleased to hear a missionary was visiting. I had liked the mission, and priests were kindly men. I missed them after the mission closed. "A visitor? When did he come?"

"He has been there some days. Leckey said he wants to build a school on the river. He knows about medicine. He might know how this man died."

"Have you been near the body?"

Poji looked away and dug the toe of one moccasin into the grass. "It is unpleasant," he said simply.

"Yes, I heard that. Can we walk down together to see?" I looked at

Shawnash, who gazed at the ground and shook her head. I thought she was reluctant to view the dead man up close, which could have been for superstitious reasons. I was undecided about superstitions. I grew up with our native beliefs, but after learning about the white man's God, I did not place as much importance on legends as most in our village.

Poji helped me get near, guiding me to the highest ground to avoid the muck through the floodplain. I must have been concentrating on my way too closely. From above the river I had seen mostly a mass of tangled branches at the riverbank. When I glanced up again at the deadfall, I was disturbed by the most ghastly of sights.

A DEAD MAN

MY GAZE LOCKED on the sight before me. I missed my step and stumbled, plunging up to my knees in cold murky water, slimy from mixing with rotted plants on the valley floor. I threw out my arms, struggling to keep from falling fully into the cold water. Poji caught me and pulled me back to higher ground.

The man was about ten feet away. A large uprooted tree was wedged against the bank, catching more trees and branches as they washed down, blocking the river, the water swirling around the jam. Massive roots reached upward into the air, and caught between them, held fast, was the body of a white man. I had thought I would see blood, red or black where he was battered, and blood spilled onto the tree or his clothes, but the man was naked. Where his face had been was only ragged flesh and bone, shades of gray and white, bloated, with no color at all. He was tangled in the tree roots, as if only lying on his side. Where his man parts had been was much like the face, gone, only a hole in the flesh that was mottled blue and pink. One arm was pinned in the roots and had no fingers on it, only a stump of a hand. The other arm dangled in the water, and, as the water flowed, the arm, white and bloated, moved up and down like a gruesome joke, as if beckoning us to come closer. I could not take my eyes away from that arm, and I knew it would haunt me from that day on, not only in my dreams, but I would look for an arm every time I approached the river, to be sure there was no arm there.

"There is no way to recognize that man," I said. "I wonder if he is from here. I wonder if we know him."

"He is taller than any man from the station but for Jim Penney, and thinner than Penney. He is probably a traveler, on some white man's business, not from here," Poji guessed.

"Poji," I noted and pointed at the man's shoulder, "do you see that he is tied to the roots? Does it not look like cords are holding him to the tree? Why would that be? And where are his clothes? This man did not drown and get caught up in the roots. Someone *put* him there."

"Your eyes are sharp, Wawetseka," he said, staring at the body. "What you say is true. He is bound at his shoulder and at his thigh." A look of concern came over his face. "No matter how this happened, it will be trouble for us."

I knew what he meant. White men always blamed our people. Once we handed over one of our men in good faith, expecting the man would be found innocent and released. Instead, he was executed under the white man's law, only to find when it was too late that it was a white man that committed the offense.

"What can we do?" I asked. I felt my face tighten with worry.

Poji was quiet and I knew he was thinking hard. He was a shrewd man. I tried to feel confident as I watched his face, hoping to read there that he knew the right thing to do.

"We must let the white men take the body and examine it. It is too late to do anything else," he said, pointing at two canoes, one bigger than the other, halfway across the river and heading toward us. "But we must listen well and remember what they say. We must try to know what they think. *We* must look carefully at the body too, to protect ourselves in case they try to accuse one of us. If a white man did this and they do not look for a white man, we may have to tell them how this man died."

"Let us hope this man is not a surveyor," I said.

Surveyors came to our valley last year to mark out a route for a new way to Lake Michigan by water. The new government would have them describe our land so it could be bought by settlers or given to soldiers as payment for their services. The arrival of surveyors was a sign we would have to leave. It was a dangerous job.

"Maybe one of us *did* do it. What will we do then?" I asked.

"If one of us did it, we must find out why. If it was a just reason we must prove that. This does not seem the way one of our men would act, but the canoes are here now—watch what the white men do. The dead man will be gone and we will not have another chance. We will talk after they leave."

He was right. When I was living at the mission a man was found, killed by a person, not by an accident. A runner was sent to the nearest fort, and men of authority came to investigate. I watched them then as they wrapped the body to protect it from insects and took it away. White men would take charge this time too, and, if they decided who committed the crime, that man would be hunted down and we would have little to say.

We watched from the closest firm land nearest the deadfall. The rest of our people were a short distance away and had fallen silent, waiting to see the white men retrieve the body.

"Poji," a man in one of the canoes called, and I recognized Jim Penney, the blacksmith. Penney's assistant, Emmett, was in the canoe with him. Everyone knew Penney was a capable man who often took charge, even when it was another man's responsibility. But it was Leckey, not Penney, who was in authority at the station. "Can you see how we can get our canoes close to the body?"

Penney was a large man, at least a head taller than any man from our village, and heavily built, his forearms bulging with muscle. One would expect such a man to have a fearsome appearance, but Penney's eyes sparkled with good humor and he laughed often and heartily. He had a thick red mustache on his well-tanned face. He spoke English and French— and some native languages well enough to communicate. He was well-liked by us, and Leckey's young sons frequently hung around him at his work, as Penney was more entertaining than their own busy family. He was observed to treat his assistant kindly. Emmett was a young man, quiet and serious, who seldom engaged in conversation, as he spoke with a stutter and twitches of his face.

Poji pointed out the best spot, and Penney maneuvered the canoe there. He set his paddle inside the canoe and reached out to grab a branch, using it to pull the canoe as close as possible to the body to examine the man.

The other canoe steered closer to the bank to view the man from a different angle. This larger canoe carried Leckey, the station commander, and a second man I did not know, who was wearing the clothes of a priest.

Penney called out, "From the looks of him, I see a savage hand at work here—can't imagine a white man would be this brutal. Well, there is nothing for it but that someone will need to get out and work their way above him on the tree roots to untangle him, so we can get him into the canoe. We will likely get wet."

As Penney leaned forward to get a better look, a slight breeze blew toward him, and he jerked back and turned his head away. "Christ! What a stench!"

The breeze carried the odor to where I stood, and I covered my nose with my hand.

"Perhaps Emmett should untangle him," Leckey suggested with a frown. He did not look at Penney. I did not know if he was concentrating on what was to be done or if he was angry that Penney was giving orders Leckey himself should have been giving. "His lesser weight is more easily supported by the roots and less likely to break them. And we can support the weight more easily to catch the man when he comes loose. What a mess!"

I thought Leckey was a good man, although not given to much talk. He was serious and hard at work whenever I saw him, but he treated me politely and answered questions carefully. He was tall and thin with long, light-brown hair tied at his neck and neatly trimmed hair on his face, below his nose and around his chin. He dressed in the white man's imitation of our traditional clothing—a deerskin shirt with sleeves, britches, and white man's boots instead of moccasins.

I wondered why Leckey came to live here. Station commanders were expected to be important men, whether or not they had the right experience or intelligence. Leckey did not seem the sort for this position. Penney had a more commanding manner so travelers often turned to him instead. It appeared that Leckey intended to stay, since he brought his family, his wife and three sons, and also a young, simple woman, a companion for the younger children. He had a big, but gentle, black dog, which he said helped him get from place to place and pulled a sled when snow was on the ground.

"Have you a knife?" Poji called to Leckey. "You can use mine."

"A knife?" Penney turned to Poji with an attitude of surprise. He looked again at the body, and it seemed it was only then he noticed the cord that attached it to the roots. "God Almighty!" he exclaimed.

Emmett looked apprehensively at Penney. "N-n-n-now?" he asked, with a little jerk of his head. Penney gave an impatient wave, and Emmett grabbed a large root, pulled himself out of the canoe, and looked at the bound man. His face paled. His eyes closed involuntarily, and he put his free hand over his mouth, but it was ineffective in stopping the vomit that rushed between his fingers. As he turned away and his stomach emptied into the river, Penney said, "Oh, for Christ's sake, get a hold of yourself, man."

Leckey, who was closer to Emmett, reached out and passed him his knife. "Take it easy—just get above him and cut the cords. There is no need to touch the man, as we will do that part." The priest sat silent, offering no assistance, and I wondered for what purpose he had come along, and why he was at the station at all.

Emmett cut the ties that held the body in place, and Penney and Leckey placed the man in Leckey's canoe to be taken back to the station. Watching them move away, I hoped that the spirits would be good to us and that would be the end of the matter.

A KILLER IS ACCUSED

NAGMO, MY SON, was accused of killing the white man found in the river, even though it was still not known who the man was or how and why he was killed.

I did not know what to do. Not for the first time I wondered how we could live among white people in our land. I *had* lived with white people, learned how they did things and about their God, not only at the mission but living with a mixed family when I was a young unmarried woman. I learned to write, figure, and keep records as they did, and I thought I understood a great deal about the white man's ways and could help our people come together. It appeared I did not know how they thought after all. Although many treated us kindly, they had no respect for our knowledge, experience, or traditions, but only tried to persuade us to adopt theirs. Most did not care about *us* at all. They were afraid of us or wanted us to go away and leave our land to them.

I had long ago accepted that these men would dominate, but I had hoped we would live peacefully together. The more contact we had, the less I held that hope. When the men took Nagmo away, I knew I must look for solutions under their laws, as they would ignore ours.

Our hunting party returned the day after the dead man was taken from the river to the station, and Nagmo came back alone another day after that. He arrived at our village near sundown and gave little reason for his absence, only to say he separated from the party after an argument about where to find game. He was sure he knew a better place, but in the end he was not successful, although he stayed another day in an effort to prove himself right. He was clearly disheartened by his failure. The hunting party was not successful either, bringing in only a few birds and small game, no large game for our women to prepare for winter.

This autumn had been much warmer than usual, but the movement of game led us to expect a hard winter. It could get worse: travelers warned us of more and more settlers coming. Soon our once-plentiful hunting grounds would not feed us.

After Nagmo returned, I tried to talk him back to his usual good humor, but he would not say what was bothering him. It was not unusual for our men to hide problems, especially from women, but Nagmo and I had always shared our thoughts. I was worried about what could be so bad he would not tell me, but a mother would not ask.

I thought he was upset about his marriage. Among our people a woman could always leave a man if she thought she made a mistake and go live again with her family. Perhaps Nagmo was afraid of losing Wabmimi as his wife. Fearing to make matters worse, he took a short break to hunt with our men, to restore his confidence, only to be disappointed again by his failure to find game during the hunt. He could have been feeling a loss of personal and tribal esteem. That was what I thought.

Near midday two days after Nagmo's return, a delegation came from the station to our village. All the white men were in the party, and I thought that was a bad sign. Penney, Leckey, and the missionary—who was called Father Pascal, we were told—came in one canoe. In another canoe was Philippe Villeaux, a Frenchman who had been in the fur trade but now lived in a cabin outside the station with his métis daughter, since he was no longer strong enough to carry fur bundles. In his canoe was Lemuel Reddick, a young man who came here this summer with his wife, who was to have a child. They planned to settle here, as more will be coming this way and they wanted to pick the best place. Another man, unknown to us, was introduced as Hardy Findel. He seemed to be a jolly man, and he said he was exploring the river for business reasons and did not want to miss what he called "all the fun." Emmett, the young assistant who became sick at the sight of the dead man, did not come.

We watched the men pull their canoes onto our side of the riverbank. The river had receded by then, and washed-out areas on both sides of the river had dried but provided poor footing on the hard, dry mud. The men's ankles twisted and they held their arms out to keep balance as they crossed the uneven ground and then straggled up the slope and walked into our village without asking permission to enter. In an effort to show that we were friendly and accommodating, our palisade gates were taken down two winters ago, when the last war between the Americans and the British ended.

The men seemed serious and stern. They asked for Poji, and he came, although it sounded to me more like an order than a request.

Leckey greeted Poji pleasantly enough and asked if he would gather the men who had been on the recent hunt and who had been away when the body was found.

Many of our people came and I joined them; we murmured among ourselves. What trouble was this? The visitors' grim faces indicated the visit had a purpose that was not a friendly one. Was there some new thing, or did it have to do with the dead man? I looked nervously about for Nagmo, but he was nowhere to be seen.

Our people still thought the man had been killed by the Water Panther, but I disagreed. Mishipeshu could have caused the mutilations, but how would that explain the naked body and the ties to the tree roots?

Poji talked quietly with our hunters. Who would represent our men, and where and how should they converse? To stand here in the entrance to the village did not show respect and would appear threatening. Everyone could go to the longhouse, but that would take preparation and ceremony and imply serious decisions our men were not prepared to make, as they had no idea why the white men were here. After much discussion while the white men grew impatient, it was decided to gather around an unlit fire pit, and the men were led there. The visitors were seated on the ground, along with three braves who had been on the hunt. We had picked these men to represent us. Poji would translate, and I was also sent for.

Penney stood up and held a tomahawk above his head. He did not smile and his brows were low and close together. "Which of your braves does this belong to?" he demanded, waving the tomahawk and then holding it where the men could see it clearly.

I held my breath. Every man in the village would recognize this tomahawk. A brave's tomahawk was a very important and personal possession, used not only as a weapon of warfare but for hunting, cutting, chopping, and striking blows. A metal or stone head was shaped and fastened securely to a short handle of very hard wood. One side of the head was sharp for chopping and cutting, the other blunt for pounding and striking. The making of a tomahawk was a difficult project that required patience and skill, and tomahawks were much prized by their owners. Although many braves now used metal tomahawk heads they got from white men, Nagmo's was made in the old way, of carefully selected and crafted stone, tied with sinew to a handle of the hardest maple, both sinew and handle treated for strength. This handle was carved with red-painted songbirds, symbols to represent his name, "Sings All The Time."

Our men looked from one to another. Poji's face was still, and my heart beat so hard in my chest I thought all could hear it. The tomahawk had what appeared to be dark blood on the sharp, or cutting, side. Poji looked at me. We could not deny the weapon belonged to Nagmo—it was too well known. But, as it was used to skin or prepare game, it was not unusual to find blood on it.

Why did the white men have it? Nagmo carried his tomahawk at all times. Only something very important would separate him from it.

I calmed myself and nodded to Poji, who said, "That is the tomahawk of Nagmo, Wawetseka's son. How is it you come to have it?"

The men looked at each other but did not reply. Finally, Leckey spoke, in a manner less aggressive than Penney. "We would like to talk to Nagmo."

"He is here," I said. "I will get him."

I went in search of Nagmo, but could not find him in the village. One of the boys said he saw Nagmo walking toward the river, and then I saw him returning from there, still some distance away, and I sent a boy to fetch him. I went back to tell the men we would be there in a short while, and I walked down to meet Nagmo, to question him before we talked to the men.

"Why were you down by the river?" I asked as soon as he was close enough to hear. My voice sounded sharper than I meant, but I did not correct it.

He was plodding up the bluff, concentrating on the ground. But at my question he lifted his head and gave me a look like he does when he thinks I should stay out of men's business, and he said, "I was looking for something I lost."

"Might that be your tomahawk?" I replied. I sounded like I was accusing him of something wrong—but I hoped that was not true.

With surprise he said, *"Ne'ni, how would you know that?"*

"The men from the station are here and they have it. They want to talk to you." I rested my hands on my hips as I waited for him to come closer.

He stopped walking. I saw a muscle in his jaw twitch. Then he turned away and gazed silently at the river.

Sudden fear sent a cold wave down my back. "Nagmo, what is going on?" I asked. "How could you lose your tomahawk? It is like a part of you, like your arm. It is always to hand."

He looked at me, let out a long slow breath, and then dropped down onto a fallen log. He motioned to me to sit beside him, and I did.

When he spoke it was not of his tomahawk. "I fear for my marriage," he said.

I said nothing but waited for him to go on. I could see that he was struggling, but I would have let him tell his story when he was ready even if that were not so, as that is our way.

"I love Wabmimi, but she does not want to be with me." He paused again. *"Ne'ni,* we are not yet husband and wife—we have not done what a husband and wife do." His face was dark but the muscles stiff, and I sensed he was fighting to keep it so. "She pulls away if I touch her. I do not know what to do. Am I to force her? Will that not make her *more* distant from me?"

I remembered my first days with my husband, which were very different. His touch thrilled me and I could not get enough of it. I imagined I could feel his touches whenever he was away, longed for every moment we could be together, was filled with heat and desire at the most embarrassing times. I tried to understand how Nagmo felt...Wabmimi is so young....

It must have been very difficult for Nagmo to talk to his mother about this. His desperation, hurt, and unhappiness tore through me like physical pain, but should a mother talk of such matters? Was my son hurting now because of something I should have done or something I did wrong? It was not my place to try to better the relationship between my son and Wabmimi, but I could not stop wanting to.

"These things take time," I said. "You must be patient, as she is like a child still."

"What kind of man am I, despised by my own wife?" His eyes flashed with strong emotion in that stony face. I thought he was angry and that he did not want to think he was to blame. "I came back here, where I am respected, and here I would figure out what to do, then go home to her. But I only get worse." He stopped, pulled a weed from the ground, tore leaves from it, and threw them into the breeze, then reached for another. He stood up and began to pace in front of me as his words poured out, speaking from his heart.

"On the hunt, I was useless! I could not think of anything but Wabmimi and my failure, and the others looked at me with slanted eyes and surprise on their face, as I did not seem myself."

He stopped pacing and stared at his feet. His anger faded and his voice became soft, his words breaking. "I decided to go away alone, like on my manhood vision quest, and see if a quest of a different sort would help. I fasted and I grew weak and I ate the wild herbs that make visions come. And I slept, but no dreams came. When I woke, I was insane with hunger, and I killed a squirrel and ate it without cooking. Crazy with thirst, I ran to the river and drank, and only then realized I did not have my tomahawk—left where I killed the squirrel. When I went back, I could not find the place. I looked for two days and could not find it. Just now I thought I might know where it was, but it was not there, and then the boy found me as I was coming back."

I thought it strange that Nagmo, with his tracking skills, could not find the spot he had just been. This was a sign my son was in a bad way and that saddened me. But I believed his story about losing the tomahawk and was relieved. I hoped the white men would believe it, too, and not conclude it had anything to do with the dead man. Much as I longed to hug my son, it was not our custom. So instead I stood up and looked into his sad eyes and put my hand over my breast to show my love, and I said, "Let us go explain to the white men."

When we returned, the men, who had been wandering in the open area, seated themselves again around the fire pit to question Nagmo. He told the men that he separated from the hunters, became hungry, killed the squirrel, and lost his tomahawk. The men looked back and forth at each other, and I could tell they did not believe the story, but thought we had made up a lie before coming to them. They had more questions.

"Why did you not stay with the other men on the hunt?" Leckey asked.

Nagmo said he was upset with his wife and wanted to be alone to think about what to do, but he was ashamed to let the braves know this. The hunters exchanged glances and nodded, as Nagmo's words had the ring of truth.

Penney, who had been seated while Leckey asked questions, stood up and began to pace. He stopped in front of Nagmo and studied him. Nagmo avoided his eyes, looking at the unlit fire pit. Penney pointed and accused, "We have the bloody tomahawk, and he was in the right place at the right time, with no alibi. I don't think he told us the whole story about his wife. Maybe the dead feller violated her and Nagmo killed him for vengeance. That would go along with stripping the body, the mutilations, the privates, face, and hands. I bet he stole something from the man, as he had opportunity to do that." He reached out and grasped the bottom of a decorated bag Nagmo wore around his waist. "Look, he's wearing both a bag and a pouch. He must show the contents."

The white men murmured and nodded. The hunters also nodded, and one said, "Show him Nagmo, that this is only suspicion. There is nothing in your bag or pouch to fear discovery." Nagmo nodded, opened his bag, and spilled the contents on the ground in front of the men. Inside were a pipe, a scraping tool, some dried meat, hard bread, a length of cord made from local vines, and flints for making fire. With reluctance, as a medicine pouch is where braves keep their most valued items, things that related to their vision quest and personal spirit, Nagmo unfastened his pouch.

Nagmo's eyes widened, he stuck out his jaw, and the muscles in his face tightened. Everyone in the circle stared at the contents of Nagmo's pouch: tobacco; the beak of a small songbird; and a man's gold ring with a large red, brown, and yellow stone that looked very valuable.

AT THE STATION

DAVID LECKEY TURNED me away again. He still would not let me, or Poji, talk to Nagmo. He was polite, even kindly, but he was firm.

Three days had passed since the men imprisoned Nagmo at the station. After seeing the contents of his bag and pouch, they were convinced Nagmo killed the white man. Penney looked fearsome, but he allowed Leckey to pick up Nagmo's own cord from the ground and tie Nagmo's hands with it before he led him to a canoe. Nagmo walked with Leckey meekly, looking around as if he was confused by what was happening.

Poji and I, and the men of our village, although alarmed, did not interfere. We thought this was a mistake that would soon be explained.

Leckey told us that when a crime was committed against a white man, the white man's laws would be followed. We were not allowed to follow our own customs, which served us well before they came. If we interfered, more would be punished. Leckey said he would personally see that Nagmo was well fed and cared for while they held him. Nagmo was locked in a storeroom, and no one was allowed to visit him. He would stay until a judge decided if Nagmo was guilty.

Leckey said Nagmo could have no visitors, but still every day I paddled across the river and asked to see him, and every day I was turned away. I went through my tasks with the other women, but I did not speak and constantly had to look away so they would not see the tears in my eyes. I thought of nothing else. But, no matter how hard I thought, it made no sense to me. And I did not know what I should do, other than I had to see my son, and I had to find a way to free him. This morning I headed alone once again to the station to try to visit Nagmo.

Paddling Poji's canoe awkwardly across the river, I forced myself to think of something else, to relieve my mind for a brief time. I thought about what the men said when Fort Dearborn was rebuilt more than a year ago, that when the Illinois Territory became a state many changes would happen. The changes would not be good for us.

Already there was more travel between Lake Michigan and the Mississippi River. Visitors passed this way almost every day now, planning to make fortunes. Some were on horseback, following our ancient trails, but most were on the rivers, not only in canoes but also a few in boats large enough to carry more belongings. After picking up supplies at Fort Dearborn and managing the portage, travelers were ready to rest, trade, or talk by the time they got here. This was why the station was built in this place—to accommodate traders and travelers. It happened quickly, only a year or two; white men moved in to take control, driven by ambition, heedless of *our* presence.

I reached an area of packed earth near the fur station and lifted the light canoe onto land. I walked from the river to the station, only a short distance.

Before reaching the station, I passed Penney's cabin and forge, which were outside the palisade walls near the river. The forge was a large building shaped much like our wigwams, but pointed at the top like a giant anthill. Smoke and heat came out a hole, and over a great fire Penney made metal tools and other things after much pounding and clanging. He said the abundant wood and limestone, along with iron that arrived at Fort Dearborn by ship, made this an ideal place for his business.

Penney had many plans. If he mixed our native sand with a metal called galena, or lead, he said, it made a sort of pottery that could be seen through, called glass. He could get galena from mines near the Mississippi River, and he wanted to be the first man in the area to sell glass. Glass was valuable to white men. Under their law, a settler had to build a cabin that had one or more pieces of glass, called windows, before he could say the land was his.

Penney's cabin looked sturdy enough, but he had no glass, only wooden boards that covered a hole in one wall and opened to let in light and air. The boards and a door hung on metal hinges, which Penney made in his forge. Both Penney and Emmett lived in the cabin, and Emmett took care of their garden, in which were many weeds and food half-eaten by animals or left without being harvested. I shook my head, as I knew that such poor habits would bring skunks.

I approached the station's palisade, made of logs and about eight feet high. The buildings inside were surrounded by a large yard. Leckey said most palisades were taller, but it was made for gathering, not protection, now that we no longer fight each other. Like our village, the gates were open, so I was able to walk in to find Leckey.

Leckey said he was American. He was adamant he was *not* British, as he had just fought the British. The British were no longer allowed to trade with us, only Americans. We thought the two were not much different, as they did much the same business and looked much alike, and they spoke the same language—the tongue that Poji spoke but I only poorly. The British who traded here until the end of the war two years ago treated us more fairly than Americans did. Americans just wanted our land.

Leckey made an exception for Villeaux, who was a voyageur for a French company until he got too old for that work. Leckey liked the pleasant man and allowed him to do a little trapping and make small trades. Villeaux spoke French and some Algonquin. He was short and muscular, with much hair about his head and face. Villeaux told me voyageurs grew their hair to control insects, and they laugh and sing a lot.

Villeaux's cabin was in the woods a short distance away, hidden by trees, but I had been there many times. His cabin was made with thin logs that stood upright, not like Penney's cabin and the station building that were made with thick logs stacked on their sides. Villeaux's home was neat, and his garden well tended, as his daughter did these tasks. He stayed mostly to himself, but our children liked to visit him to listen to his songs and tales, as he spoke our language. His daughter was called Amelina. She was a very large woman with a kind face but not pretty at all.

These were the only people who lived here until this summer, when Lemuel Reddick and his young wife, called Amethyst, came. They did not come on the river, but by land. They chose land near the station, close to the river on the bluff. They did not have time to build a cabin before winter, so they dug into the bluff, using its stone for the back wall, and made front walls from blocks of clay mixed with grass. They would build a proper house next summer, they said, after they cleared land for their farm, using the trees they cut down. I doubted their dug home would be comfortable all winter, but perhaps someone else would take them in during bad days. We would have let them live with us, but we went to our winter camp when the game moved away. They refused our offer, not wanting to leave their belongings behind as we did. I thought they made a poor decision, because the young wife would bear her child alone this winter.

The fur station building had six rooms in a long row. Leckey and his family—his wife Lilly, their three children, and the simple woman who lived with them—occupied two rooms on one end. Two more rooms in the center had rough bedding for travelers who arrived on the Des Plaines River, on foot or on horseback. At the other end were Leckey's office and trading counter and a storehouse where goods were stacked— supplies for trade and furs for transport to Fort Dearborn. Each room had only a small slit near the top of each door for light. Penney said he would put glass windows in the doors someday. In the end room, the storeroom, Nagmo was imprisoned.

Leckey was friendly, but it was clear he must listen to people on his side of the river when it came to this killing. He was sad about Nagmo's situation, but he did not seem convinced Nagmo was without blame.

Poji has been talking daily with Leckey, who told him what the white men did before they came to get Nagmo. After they brought the dead man to the station, they prepared him for burial and placed him in a box in a shallow grave outside the palisade, so jackals—what white men call coyotes—and red fox would not molest the body. The body would stay there until it was identified and claimed.

They knew the body had washed down from somewhere upstream. So they searched, and a short way upstream they found Nagmo's toma-hawk. They did not find anything that told them where the killing happened, who the man was, or how or why he was killed. They stopped looking, as they thought Nagmo was the killer.

Poji said they would keep Nagmo locked in the storeroom until the men decided if Nagmo killed the man and then how he would be punished. It could be many months before that happened. Leckey promised

to make him comfortable and feed him well, and I believed Leckey—
but I wanted to see Nagmo myself.

Two days ago, seated at the same spot where I sat with Nagmo before
he was taken away, on the tree trunk overlooking the river, I talked with
Poji. "Why do they say it is Nagmo?" I asked. "Is it just because of the
tomahawk? We explained that to them."

"The tomahawk is an important reason, but there are others," Poji
answered. And just as Nagmo had done, he also pulled up a weed and
began to tear the leaves off of it. "They say he was in the area where the
killing happened at the same time it happened. No one can say he was
somewhere else when the killing happened, as no one saw him in another place. They think it is strange that he left the hunting party and went
off alone. So he could have done it, and no one knows something that
will prove he did *not* kill the man."

"Is that not true of everyone else? How do they know *when* the killing
happened? How do they know *where* the killing happened? How do they
know Nagmo was there at that time? They do not know *who* this man
was, so how can they know this other?" I waved my arm in the air after
I said this and gritted my teeth very hard until my jaw hurt.

"The dead man was attached to the tree, so they know the tree came
from upriver. And he must have been tied to the tree before the rains, or
he would not wash down with the tree."

"Well, that is true," I snorted, "but it does not say much. How far up
the river was the tree? How long before the rain was the body tied there?
How do they know it was during the time Nagmo was missing or that it
happened where they found the tomahawk?"

I lifted my face and Poji met my eyes. "They do not talk about such
things," Poji admitted.

"No, because they have decided it is Nagmo, so they do not ask questions that might have different answers," I said, and I pounded my closed
fist against the tree trunk.

"Wawetseka, there was blood on Nagmo's tomahawk."

"It was a squirrel he killed—and why wasn't it washed by the rain?"

"*They* do not believe that. And the cord in his bag was the same as the
vine the man was tied with." Poji threw down the weed, brushed off his
hands, and wiped them against his leggings.

"That vine grows everywhere. Many use that vine to tie things." I shook my head. "Why would Nagmo do such a thing? None of us even know this man."

"They say the man is not from here, as no one has heard of a missing man. They say he is a traveler who took Nagmo's wife against her will. Nagmo admitted to a problem with his wife. That is why they say the body was naked and mutilated, because of what the dead man did to Wabmimi." Poji would not look at me then, but gazed instead off into the distance. I wondered if he suspected his friend.

"There is no reason to say that, only because they invent a reason, because they want to blame an Indian. Indians do not behave this way, or for these reasons! This is not an Indian killing!" I made a rude gesture with my arm. "They would make a better argument if they blamed Mishipeshu for the mutilations to the man's body, like Shawnash. At least that sort of thing is in *his* nature."

"They think Indian men do things for the same reasons and the same ways white men would. They do not understand otherwise. They do not know Indian ways."

"They are wrong, Poji! We must tell them."

"I have tried, Wawetseka," he said, and his voice sounded tired. "They ask me to explain why Nagmo had that ring."

"There must be a reason. Nagmo can tell us."

"We must talk to Nagmo."

That was why I went to the station that day, and why I would keep going. I wanted Nagmo to tell me why he had the ring, so I could convince Leckey that Nagmo did not do this thing.

But again today Leckey would not let me to talk to Nagmo. Leckey spoke but a few words in our language and in French, and I had only a few words of his tongue, and so it was hard for us to make our meaning clear to each other. But in the few words we had, and with gestures and reading our faces and hands, he let me know that the other men were convinced of Nagmo's guilt and that he could not prove them wrong, and it appeared Nagmo did this crime. He did not look in my eyes, but he touched my shoulder kindly and wiped under his eye. And he made a similar gesture toward Nagmo in the storeroom, to show me he was sad and fond of both of us. But he could not help us. And so I walked away, as there was no more I could do.

Somehow I had to prove he was wrong.

I stopped at a large tree inside the wall of the palisade. I squatted there under its shelter, to be alone and think of what else I could do. Since I could not talk to Nagmo, I wondered if there was anyone else who might know something to help explain things.

The only other person there today was Leckey's wife, Lilly, with her youngest son, whose name I did not know. He was too young to walk and was sleeping on a blanket in the shade at the end of the post building. Next to the boy was the simple woman who helps Lilly, since Leckey had no daughters to assist with women's work. The woman was called Nell.

As in our own village, some persons stayed like children in their minds forever. Their bodies grew, but they moved awkwardly and they could only do things children can do. They were helpful in small ways that made our lives easier and were most pleasant. Little things made them happy, even the smallest attention. They especially liked to be praised.

Nell, I was told, had nowhere to go when her family died of a disease that ran through their small settlement. Leckey and his wife took her to live with them, and they seemed very fond of her. She was very large and wide, of a similar age as Lilly. Her movements were slow and clumsy, her face flat and without expression much of the time, but when pleased her face lit with a lovely smile. She liked to visit our village and was popular with our people, who liked to hear her pretty singing voice. She appeared happy at most times and often sang to herself, repeating words she heard over and over, not seeming to understand their meaning. Because of this, so like the meaning of Nagmo's name, I called her Nagmo-Nell.

Today it appeared she had been asked to watch the baby. She sat next to him and sang, and now and then she leaned forward to brush an insect away. If the boy waved his arms or startled in his sleep, she stopped singing and watched him closely. After he was still, she sang again. I tried to catch her words, and I heard them but did not know their meaning. They sounded like nonsense: "Aye, aye, keet aye, keet aye aye, preet aye aye, keet."

Sleeping next to the baby was a big black dog with thick fur and a huge head like a bear. He was almost the size of the small bear he resembled. We were sometimes attacked by white men's dogs because we were strange to them, but this dog was friendly and gentle even to us. In the winter Leckey tied him to a sled that carried supplies, and he traveled with Leckey from place to place, following along the shore as Leckey paddled his canoe. We had dogs in our village too, but none as large as this, and our dogs were not gentle, but snarled and bit.

As I watched Nagmo-Nell, Lilly came out of her building carrying and stroking a heavy animal she had told me was called a cat. Our people know bobcats and large and dangerous panthers, but the cat she held was neither. It resembled a bobcat in some ways, with its pointed ears with tufts of fur on the tips. But bobcats were a little bigger and had only a stump of a tail. In other ways this cat was like a raccoon, with its thick fur, similar size, and long bushy tail. It was mottled brown with silver streaks all over, no dark stripes like a raccoon or spots like a bobcat. It was a friendly creature, and once Lilly showed me how it talked back to her, making a lot of loud and silly noises that made me laugh. Lilly also had me count the toes, and the cat had seven toes on each foot, which was very odd. She called it simply, "Cat." It was clear that she was quite fond of the animal, and the whole family liked to play with it. It was the same with the huge black dog, which they called "Dog." It seemed to me that names were less important to them than they were to us.

Until I nursed M'ewé, I did not understand the white man's closeness with their animals, their big black dogs and this thing called a cat. We did not hold or pet or cuddle animals, as Lilly did. Our dogs roamed freely in our camp, and we threw them scraps to eat. They belonged to all of us, not one person.

Lilly wore a bonnet and carried a hoe, and she smiled when she saw me. "Hello, Wawetseka," she called. I knew these words, and I smiled back at her and waved but stayed where I was. She walked away to her garden.

I saw no other people, other than two of Leckey's sons sweeping and dusting around the post. The missionary and the other traveler were not about. All was quiet.

What else could I do? I had to prove what these people believed about Nagmo was wrong. Perhaps *I* could find where the man was killed, when and how it happened, and who he was. Maybe there was another way to find out how Nagmo came to have the ring. I could go upriver, before the cold and snow started. Perhaps I could find something the white men missed, since they stopped looking. I could look again at the tree where the dead man was found. It was on the bank now, and I could look more closely.

I had to find out more about the white men, too, because, if Nagmo did not do this thing, then one of them could have. If I found out where and when the killing happened, I could see if any of them was away at the time and might have done it, and I could look for a reason. I would need Poji's help.

First I would explore the riverbank and upriver, so I would have good questions to ask.

FACTS ARE FOUND

"Look at this, Poji!"

I pulled a heavy branch from the debris caught in the tree and shook it with difficulty. The tree was firmly locked in dry mud on the floodplain. Poji and I were poking through its roots and branches, looking for anything that might tell us what happened. The river was back in its proper bed and likely to stay there until spring rains.

What I held was a branch about eight feet long, with huge oval leaves and large, soggy green fruit bigger than my hand. The branch had been wedged between the roots of the tree near where the dead man had been tied, its fruit rotten, smelly, and squishy. I broke one of the stinking things open, which revealed dark brown seeds that resembled large beans. The juice ran sticky down my arms. "Do you know what this is?" I asked.

"That is a pawpaw, is it not? Those huge leaves and big fruit are unlike any other. They are no good to us because they rot so fast, almost the same day, and we cannot store them. They do not grow here." Poji's words were clearly meant to let me know he thought what I found was useless.

"Yes, but it *is* important to us!" I insisted. "Pawpaw grows no closer than the land near the portage. This branch, with the fruit already overripe, is twisted in this tree. The tree must have come from farther upstream than the white men said, not where Nagmo was and where they found his tomahawk."

I tore another leafy branch away, dipped it in the water, and used the wet leaves to rub the sticky mess from my arms.

"Could the branch have washed down days later and been caught after the tree was already lying here in the water?"

"No Poji, it could not have happened that way—and the man was killed sooner than everyone thinks. Here is why. This fruit ripens and falls to the ground weeks before this dead man was found. Because the fruit is still on the branch, the branch must have been tangled in the tree weeks ago, before the fruit ripened and fell. That was long before Nagmo came to our village and went on the hunt. And look, parts of the same vine the man was tied with are tangled with this pawpaw branch. The branch was tangled in the tree before the man was tied to it, earlier than the men think."

I was very excited, but Poji was doubtful. "Will the white men think this as important as the bloody tomahawk and the ring? I do not think so. They do not know about the pawpaw—where it grows and when it ripens. They will think we are telling another story to get them to release Nagmo."

"They *may* think that, Poji." I began to walk toward Poji's canoe, dragging the branch. "But now *we* know—this proves the man was killed when Nagmo was not near and we can find *more* proof. We know when the man was killed and where it was done, and we can find out who was away at that time. We know the man was killed no closer than the portage, and we can look for other evidence between there and Fort Dearborn. They have only looked a short way upstream. We must talk to the white men."

Poji looked skeptical. "I will go with you, Wawetseka, and talk to the white men. But they are growing tired of us, and it may do no good, only make them angry. They will not want us to interfere in what they consider their business."

Would they tell us anything if they suspected we were trying to prove one of *them* was the killer? We had to be careful who we talked to, what we asked, and what we said. That was not an easy thing when so many languages were involved. We decided Poji would talk to the new arrivals, the priest and Hardy Findel, and I would talk to Philippe and Amelina Villeaux. Then he and I would discuss what we learned.

We went immediately, and I found Amelina and Philippe at their cabin, but Philippe was sleeping, which he often did around midday. Amelina was turning over the garden and gathering root crops into baskets, but she stopped her work and asked me to come inside. I preferred to sit outside on their wooden porch. She went in to wake her father. She brought a sweet drink for me in a metal bowl, and it was very cool and pleasing. Her father joined us, and I relaxed, knowing we would talk well together. Not only did I speak their French language, but, since they had kin in a nearby village, they spoke our tongue. They expressed sadness that Nagmo was to be brought to Fort Clark for trial, but they did not seem to doubt he had killed the white man.

"I do not believe Nagmo killed the man," I told them. "This is not like something an Indian would do. An Indian would not hide a man in this way or tie him to the roots of a tree. Why would Nagmo kill this man? We do not even know who the man is. If it was because the man was trying to kill him and he killed in defense, Nagmo would not mutilate the body or tie it to a root. This killing does not make sense for an Indian man."

"What you say may be true," said Philippe. "But there is much evidence against him. There is a story about Nagmo and his new wife...."

"The story about Nagmo's wife has no truth to it. It is simply the girl is very young." I said this convincingly, I thought, but I saw their eyes meet with a look of doubt.

Amelina got up to get a drink for her father and then sat down in a chair next to his, a chair that moved back and forth on curved pieces of wood. She stayed silent, but I knew her to be a smart woman who would speak up if she had anything important to say.

"Philippe, I wonder if this killing may have been done farther away, perhaps on the way to Fort Dearborn. A traveler might have seen something that would help Nagmo." I looked through the trees as I said this, not at Philippe, hoping my words were true.

"I went that way myself, about a month before the flood. I was gone for ten days," Philippe said. I counted out the days. That would have been during the time I figured the killing happened.

"Did you go all the way to Fort Dearborn? Is that not a long trip for you to make?"

"Oh no," he said. "I went only to see kin at the Sag village."

"The village where the two valleys come together, at the cliff that looks over the Des Plaines River?" There were many villages in the area Philippe visited. The great trail divided there, one branch going through the Sag Valley to the east all the way to Lake Michigan, along which was the village where Nagmo lived. The other trail followed the Des Plaines River through its valley, past the portage to Fort Dearborn farther north. Where the routes met there was a bluff from which a man could see anyone traveling by canoe or boat, or anyone walking through the Sag Valley.

"Yes," Philippe said. "That is the place. I went to make arrangements, to find out who would be bringing furs in the spring, and what was expected in trade goods, to tell Leckey what goods to have on hand. But it was a wasted trip, as while I was there the nephew of my dead wife saw Leckey traveling on the river toward Fort Dearborn. Leckey must have decided not to wait for my information. I later found out he left early so he and Reddick could travel together. Reddick did not want to be away from his pregnant wife too late in the season."

"So you, Leckey, and Reddick were all away from the station at the same time?" I was pleased with this information, as it opened many possibilities.

"Yes, and not only the three of us, but Penney went that way a few days later. I understand he is paying a man at Fort Dearborn to send settlers his way to buy windows, as he plans to bring in the galena this season, before the snow starts. I thought perhaps he went to complete those arrangements." Philippe rested his head and closed his eyes.

"So no men at all were in the station?"

"Only the women, children, and Emmett."

"Pa, did you not see our visitors too?" Amelina asked.

Philippe opened his eyes and lifted his head at Amelina's reminder. "Oh yes, that is also true. The priest and the other man, Findel, who is looking to set up a business. His wife will be joining him later, he said, to help him. I did not know that then, of course, since I saw him only from a distance, but later when we talked at the station."

"Were the priest and Findel traveling together? I thought they did not know each other."

"Oh, no, they were in separate canoes. Findel arrived first, in the morning, and stopped on the bank. In the afternoon, the priest came. They talked for a while and made a fire, so they probably ate some food. Then the priest went on, but Findel stayed the night on the bank and left the next morning."

"That is puzzling. I thought Findel did not come to the station until after the dead man was found."

"No, you are right. After the two men met, Findel went back upriver, toward the portage. He did not show up at the station until right before they came for Nagmo."

"It is strange he would go back and forth like that. So they were not strangers when they arrived at the station, as they said?"

"At that distance there was no way to tell how well they knew each other. I knew them only by their clothes."

"That is interesting," I said, and stood up to leave.

I went to the station to talk with Lilly while I waited for Poji to finish questioning Findel and the priest. I liked Lilly. I guessed she was glad that Amethyst Reddick lived there now, and she had another woman for company. Amelina was pleasant enough, but she was quiet, stayed with her father, and did not seek out the company of other women. She could have felt unwelcome since she was mixed blood and did not speak the English language that was usually spoken at the station.

Lilly left her gardening for a time and stood with me in the shade of the great tree, took off her bonnet, and wiped sweat from her forehead. Lilly speaks only a few words of French. "Nagmo is well," she told me haltingly. "My husband says he asks for you, but it is not possible. He is patient. He says you and his friends will bring him home." She looked at me with a smile that looked warm but doubtful, which made me think she did not believe what Nagmo said would happen.

"We will try to find a way," I told her. "A way that the men will agree with, not a violent way."

She relaxed a bit but would not look straight in my face. "I hope so."

"Is it true your guests do not know each other?" I asked. "Villeaux says he has seen them talking together."

"Oh no, we had to introduce them when they came, some days apart. They nod and speak a little now to be friendly, but they do not converse."

So I thought they were pretending something that was untrue. I had to talk to Poji about that.

Lilly went into the building and came out with Nagmo-Nell. Nell carried a large basket filled with dry beans and Lilly a large earthen bowl. I watched as Lilly showed Nell how to break apart bean pods and collect dried beans in the bowl. Then Lilly returned to her garden, and after a time Nell began to sing again as she worked. Her words were a little different today, and I repeated and remembered the sounds, "Aye mah nay, aye aye mah nay, preet mah nay, aye aye, preet aye." I still had no idea of their meaning, or even if there was a meaning.

Seeing Poji coming through the open gates, I went to meet him, and we left the station. I had enough of the station. These people locked up my son, and I could not feel good about that, no matter how nice they acted toward me. I could not get the idea out of my mind that it was false politeness, and I was tired of pretending nothing was wrong. I wanted to be away from here, to *stop* pretending, until they set Nagmo free.

Poji and I went to the river and sat in the canoe but did not yet start across the water. I could tell Poji was trying to hide his feelings and not let me see them on his face. He sat on his hands waiting for me to ask him what he found out from the visitors. I thought he was playing with me to put me in a better mood.

"What is it, Poji?" I asked. I fear my voice did not sound very much like I wanted to play a game.

"The priest was helpful," he said with a grin. "He is a man of medicine, and he knows much about wounds and such."

"Yes?" It was not respectful to act impatient, but I circled my arm for him to hurry his words.

"He said that the wound on the man's head would kill him, but that it was a wound such as is made by a rounded thing, not a sharp thing. If it was the tomahawk that killed the man, he was hit with the pounding end, not the cutting end."

"But our men would strike with the cutting end!" I exclaimed. "And it was the cutting end that had blood on it. The blood of the *squirrel*," I insisted.

"Yes, but there is more. The mutilations might not have been made by the killer. The man's body was in and out of the water, we do not know for how long, but at least days. And the water was warm, so the body would decay. He said fish and other creatures of the river, crawfish and insects, would be attracted by this and eat away soft parts, like the face, the manly parts, around the wounds, and the hands and feet. We did not see any blood, and the wounds were smooth, not ragged. He may not have been cut but decayed and eaten." He gave me a sideways glance. "He smelled bad enough for this to be true."

"So he was struck in the head and tied under the water to rot? Why were the fingers gone? Did he think the creatures in the river also ate his bones?"

"He did not say. But if the soft parts were gone, there would be little to hold the bones in place, and washing down the river was a rough thing, so perhaps they would break away."

This news was in Nagmo's favor. I caught some of Poji's good humor and tried a little joke. "Maybe Shawnash was right, and Water Panther was responsible."

"Do you not wish it was that easy? I hear Water Panther especially likes white men's clothes and boots," Poji said, amused eyes sparkling.

"Did the priest say why he came here?" I asked. I told him how Villeaux saw the priest and Findel talking and wondered if they knew each other. "If so, why do they pretend they do *not* know each other?"

"He said he was sent to look for a place to build a mission, like the one you lived at. He is to explore and give an opinion about the best place and then bring back more people to build it and live and teach in it."

"What about Findel? Did he say anything useful? Why is he here?" I ran my hand absently along the side of the canoe.

"He is friendly enough. And he speaks many words, but the words do not say much. He says there are people behind him with a great deal of money and that money is more valuable than trade goods. He has been sent to figure out where people will settle and what they will need, so they can put the right business in the right place and have even more money. Why this need for money I do not know, as before they came we had no money and we had all we needed. It is perhaps this money that makes it hard for us but good for them."

"Villeaux tells a different story, about Findel's wife joining him. That is strange, do you not think? Well, maybe Findel and the priest do *not* know each other then...."

"I do not know, Wawetseka. Maybe this all means nothing."

"Poji, Nagmo was the only man who was *not* where the man was killed, but he is the one accused. Except for Emmett, every man from the station—Leckey, Penney, Villeaux, Reddick, Pascal, and Findel—every one of these men was *away* from the station, upstream, and could have done the crime. The killer could be one of them, but which one, and why did he do it?"

"What you say is true, but I do not know more."

I gave a great sigh, thought quietly, and then said, "At least we know none of the women did this thing, as none of them left the station." I had a pleasant thought of Nagmo-Nell singing to the baby and on the porch as she worked, and I smiled and told Poji about it, to take my mind off our troubles for a short time.

"Probably she is repeating words she heard, or her own sounds for something she saw. That is what she usually does. She makes me smile. She is such a happy and pleasant person to be around, or even think of."

"I wonder if the words have meaning to her," Poji said.

"She keeps saying 'aye' and other sounds like 'keet,' 'preet,' 'mah,' and 'nay.' These sounds are a bit alike and that is what she does, says like sounds over and over. I wonder what she saw or heard that put those sounds in her head."

"The word 'aye' means 'yes' in the English tongue, and 'nay' means 'no.' Could be she was singing about things she likes and does not like. The other words have no meaning to me."

"We cannot know her head, Poji. Not only does it work more simply than ours, but it is a white person's mind as well. That is too confusing. Nagmo-Nell is like a child playing."

My mind turned away from amusing thoughts to Nagmo in jail, and I came to a conclusion. "Poji, will you go upriver with me, as far as the portage? We may not find anything, but I think we should go, to try to find something the men will believe—free of excuses they may make to say we are wrong."

THE VOYAGE BEGINS

"I wish you would not do this thing," Shawnash protested. She looked worried. "The white men do not listen to us. They have not and they will not. What good will it do for you to go upriver? It could be dangerous. Water Panther may have only increased his appetite with bites of the dead man and is waiting for more to come his way."

"No one else is doing anything, Shawnash," I told her. "The white men think they have the killer, so they do not look. If I do not find the real killer, no one will, and Nagmo will be found guilty. I do not have a choice."

"Send the men then," she said.

"Our men are busy and have given up too. I cannot trust them to notice things I, Nagmo's mother, would notice."

"But Mishipeshu—"

I interrupted, holding up a leather pouch and waving it. "I *have* tobacco, Shawnash. I promise, I will sprinkle it on the water to appease Mishipeshu when we begin and every day we travel on the river."

I was impatient to begin the trip, but the men at the station had sent for Poji. With Shawnash as companion, I waited on the riverbank for him to return. I paced up and down, staring into the water but seeing nothing, rearranging over again the few supplies to be loaded in the canoe, questioning yet again if we were bringing too much or too little, trying to quiet Shawnash's complaints despite my own fears.

With only Poji and me to carry the canoe through the portage, we took as little as possible, our only food a pouch of dried fruits, dried fish, and corn cakes. We would hunt, fish, and gather if food ran short. I carried a knife and had brought blankets in case of cold nights or wet days.

Poji had his knife, his tomahawk, his bow and arrows, and the pouch he always carried with important items such as pieces of chert to start fires.

When he returned, I did not ask Poji what went on at the station, as the day was already half wasted. Shawnash and I put the supplies in the canoe. I said goodbye, and she held her head high but did not speak, only put a hand to her cheek, her eyes shining with moisture. Whether she was sad at our parting or concerned over the dangers of our trip, I could not tell.

More for Shawnash's benefit than our own, I opened my pouch and made a show of chanting and sprinkling tobacco on the water as an offering to Mishipeshu.

Poji was strong and skilled, and we did our best to battle the current as we went upriver, but due to the delay we would not be likely to reach the portage until nightfall the next day. With little moon and hazards on the river such as floating tree branches, it would not be wise to travel upstream in darkness. We would have to sleep a night on the bank before going through the portage. We did not have days to waste if we were to find something to save Nagmo, as cold weather would soon make travel difficult.

If we found no answers near the portage, we would go on to Fort Dearborn and talk to the men there. All the men from the station except Villeaux, and even he was questionable, had stopped at the fort. Someone there could have seen something helpful.

I turned to wave to Shawnash a number of times as we went up the river, but before long we lost sight of her, of our village, and of the station. The current was swift and our progress slow but uneventful. With no recent storms, little was floating on the river to impede us, so we traveled as fast as could be hoped for. The day was clear and the sun bright. Trees on the banks glided before our eyes, a few branches hanging low, some bright red, orange, or yellow, trailing in the water and making ripples in the river's flat brown surface. The quiet and peaceful scene and the steady rhythm of the paddles gradually took the edge off my fears, and I asked Poji what had happened at the station.

Poji did not reply or look my way at first, but only continued to apply his paddle with long deep strokes, first on one side of the canoe and then on the other, as I steered from the rear. After a while he turned a num-

ber of times and opened his mouth as if to speak but said nothing. I suspected there was something he did not want to tell me. Finally he said,
"The station is filling up with white men. Since we left there yesterday
afternoon, two more visitors have come. One man came in a canoe, and
the other came on a horse and led another horse, and he had one of those
great black dogs like Leckey has."

"Were they from Fort Dearborn, traveling downriver?"

"No, and that is unusual for this time of year. They were traveling upriver as we are."

"Yes, that *is* strange. Men do not bring furs from the outposts this time
of year, when pelts are poor. This is the time they travel downriver, out
to the posts and villages with supplies for the winter. Did they carry supplies? Or was there some other business? Why did they ask for you?"

I did not look at Poji as I asked my questions, but watched the river.
Again he did not answer right away, but I was patient. We would be on
the river a long time to talk. And what could these new visitors matter to
me? But why did Poji hesitate to speak? When he turned around I saw
hardness in his eyes and his jaw was set hard too, before he looked away
again. He pretended to examine the trees on the shore, and I thought
he wanted to hide his face from me. My mouth became dry.

I called to him and held out my hand to show I would wait for his reply.

Soon he spoke. "The man on the horse was a sheriff—a lawman—and
he came to take Nagmo to Fort Clark."

It was my turn to be silent, thinking on his words. My heart fluttered
in my chest, where there was a sudden pain, and my eyes became hot and
wet. Then I asked, my voice shaking, "What will happen at Fort Clark?
Will they decide Nagmo is guilty and punish him?"

"There is a great white man's village at Fort Clark now, Wawetseka,
and many white men live near *our* villages there. Many speak French,
but some come from New Orleans and St. Louis where they have long
lived, traveling on the Mississippi River. It could be that Chief Tecumseh's prophecy and the great earthquake drove them north to live on the
Illinois and Des Plaines Rivers. Travel between these places takes only
a week, and even less to Fort Dearborn. Even Black Partridge now lives
near Fort Clark."

I knew all of this as well as Poji did and had known Black Partridge well before he took some of our people with him to start his new village. I waved a hand impatiently. "We have heard that before Poji. There is much mingling between our people and the white man. Even our great Chief Gomo was raised by a French trader before he returned to guide our people. But why is this sheriff taking Nagmo to Fort Clark?"

"This far north it is only at Fort Clark that men are punished by white man's law. A man, circuit judge, goes there, and people gather to tell what they know about men who are accused of wrongdoing. If it is decided a man is guilty, this judge says what the punishment will be. So they will bring Nagmo there and wait for circuit judge to come."

"When will he come?"

"They did not know. Perhaps soon, or he may be there when the sheriff arrives with Nagmo. But if not soon then he will not come in winter —not until spring."

"Where will Nagmo be until this is decided?"

"They have a building there for accused men, and he will be locked in that building."

I rested my paddle in the canoe and put both hands over my ears, and then I covered my eyes with my hands. When I could speak again I asked, "What is the building like? Will Nagmo be warm in the winter? Will he be well fed, and will he get to move around so his muscles and bones do not grow weak?"

Poji said quietly, "I do not know, Wawetseka. But this I do know: there is only one such place. White men commit crimes too, and they are put in this place. Surely they will treat Nagmo the same as they treat white men. I was told the white man's law says that Indians and white men who are criminals are treated the same."

I made a quick sound through my nose, like the snort of a buffalo. "They say that to get us to do what they want. Have you seen them treat Indians the same as white men?"

"I have not seen *anything* like this before, Wawetseka. I do not know. But I do know this: Thomas Forsyth, our agent, is now in charge at Fort Clark. He has been fair with us and speaks for us. He and Black Partridge know each other well, and Black Partridge says Forsyth is our friend. We must believe that Forsyth will see that Nagmo is treated fairly."

Black Partridge was an important chief who had lived at our village and was respected by white men because he helped some escape during the killings at Fort Dearborn. With both Black Partridge and Forsyth in Fort Clark, my mind was a bit easier.

"But what if they decide Nagmo is guilty?"

Poji looked away again. "For killing a white man, the only punishment I have ever heard of is death."

I had expected he would say this. I picked up my paddle again and dipped it into the water. My jaw was hard and my thoughts clear. "We cannot let that happen, Poji. We must prove Nagmo did not do it. But that is not enough. If they are to believe it is not Nagmo, we must find out who *did* kill the man and bring him to Fort Clark for the judge. We have to do it before the judge gets there."

We paddled a long while in silence. Then I asked, "Why did they send for you?"

"They wanted me to explain to Nagmo, so he would go with the sheriff peacefully."

"And did he?"

"They were not to leave right away, but Nagmo said he would."

"What is this sheriff's name? What did he look like?"

"He is called Peniston Wayne. He is tall and strong with a serious look on his face. He puts grease in his hair to keep what is left of it close to his scalp, and he has a great long mustache that hangs below his jaw."

"And he travels with one of those big black dogs? Why?"

"Leckey says the dog will help him if they need to transport anything and can chase Nagmo if he tries to run away."

I gave my buffalo snort again. "I know those dogs. They are big but so gentle the only thing Nagmo would have to fear from such an animal is being licked raw."

We paddled a long time. I was trying to figure out how the new information affected what we had to do. Then I remembered there was a second man.

"You did not tell me about the other man, the one in the canoe. Did they know each other?" I asked.

"I think they know each other only a little. He is called Noah Taylor, and he is looking for his brother, who came this way some months ago and has not returned."

I immediately thought of the dead man. "Looking for a missing man? Who is his brother, and why did he come up the river?"

"His brother is Simon Taylor, and he was taking a message to Fort Dearborn from Thomas Forsyth. Both brothers speak many languages. Noah Taylor asked if I saw his brother. He said they look much alike, only Simon does not walk with a limp but Noah does. Noah wears buckskins with fringes and a cap made from a raccoon skin—tail and all. He is tall and thin and carries a pack on his back and a long rifle, like trappers and guides. He has much hair everywhere hair can grow on a man's face. His eyes are small and sharp, and he reminds me of a weasel. I do not trust the man."

"What did he say to you?"

"He and his brother came to the Illinois Territory from the east because their older brother inherited the family's farm, and they heard there were opportunities here for hard-working men. He said powerful men in the Territory do not agree about things, and they send messages back and forth because one man wants to have more power than another. He spoke of William Clark. Do you remember Clark? He is the man who went with Lewis all the way to the great sea in the West some ten years ago. This Clark is governor at St. Louis now, and Forsyth is his great ally. Taylor, Simon Taylor that is, was doing something for them but did not return. Noah Taylor has come to find out what happened to his brother and if the message was delivered."

"Do you think, as I am thinking, that this Simon Taylor could be the man who was found in the river?"

"I did think that too, although many men were traveling to Fort Dearborn and through the portage in both directions at that time. It could be any man."

"But this man is *missing*. We have not heard of any other missing man. Did Leckey say they would disturb the dead, dig up the body, and let Noah Taylor see if it *is* his brother?"

"Not in my hearing. The dead man was greatly disfigured, remember?"

"Yes, but a brother might know." A chill went up my back thinking about the dead and our ancient gods. Despite my belief now in the Christian God, I have not forgotten our own beliefs. "And there is the matter of the ring to be settled. He should know if his brother had such a ring. Was there no talk about that? The men at the station must have thought about all of this."

"I agree with you, but they did not say such things to me."

"This man, this Noah Taylor, if it is his brother who was killed, he would want to carry out orders from Forsyth and Clark, but he would have personal reasons, too, and want to know how his brother died. Might he try to harm Nagmo before he gets to Fort Clark, if he believes the white men, if he thinks Nagmo killed his brother?"

"That could be true, Wawetseka."

THOUGHTS IN THE NIGHT

I woke long before sunrise and could not return to sleep, despite the comfortable bed we had made along the riverbank. Poji, from the loud snoring noises I heard, had no such difficulty. Indeed, the sounds he made would keep away any forest creatures that approached; even human enemies would be likely to stay away, unable to identify his strange and frightening sounds. I smiled at the thought that this added protection could reduce the need for guards during the night and might well be one of the reasons his services as guide and interpreter were so popular. But it was not Poji's noises—but my own disturbed thoughts—that kept me awake, staring unseeing into the darkness on that moonless night.

Although I spent much time thinking about what Poji told me during the long afternoon as we paddled up the river, things often seemed clearer at night—clearer but also more troubling. I may have made the distractions of river travel an excuse because I did not *want* to think too deeply.

Now, I tried to stop it, but a picture kept forming in my mind of Nagmo hanging from a tree with a cord about his neck, as we were told the guilty were punished this way. My eyes flew open but saw nothing in the darkness. My heart pounded, and my chest felt tight. Nagmo, my only son—more important than my own life.

I pushed the painful image away and sniffed. Panic and pity would not be of any use. I turned on my side and forced myself to review our plan. Perhaps it was ill-formed. Would this trip accomplish anything? What did I expect to find near the portage? I already knew the vine that

146

tied the man to the roots grew there, and the tree was uprooted there. Would finding the place the tree fell into the river mean anything? I was not sure, but I thought it was the right place to start.

A weapon? Something heavy and round, a bludgeon, like the pounding side of a tomahawk, a club, or even a rock. How would we recognize such a thing? Would blood not be washed away by now? We would search, but I doubted we would find anything helpful.

Would we find anything to tie the dead man to that place and show what happened there? Perhaps the victim and killer struggled over some valuable item. But we would not find such an item—the killer would have taken it.

Was this then a useless trip?

I wondered *why* the man was killed. If we knew the reason or the killer, it might tell us what to look for. Not knowing, we might pass over the proof we sought, not recognizing its meaning.

We had already learned that any man from the station could be the killer, but we could not be certain it was not some *unknown* man.

My head went in circles.

I assumed it was Simon Taylor who was killed, while taking a message to Fort Dearborn from Forsyth, perhaps on the orders of Clark. Did someone want to prevent that message from getting to Fort Dearborn? Was Forsyth a spy, as some said? What might the message have been?

Forsyth, our Indian agent at Fort Clark, controlled trade with us and distributed our annuities. Was there some conflict about trade profits or annuities? The time of year was right for settling matters about annuities, which were paid before the cold months.

Poji said powerful men were arguing about business, and those men placed great value on money and position. Did Simon threaten some important man's business?

It had been some time since Simon Taylor left for Fort Dearborn. Had he already delivered his message and was headed back downriver when he was attacked? People at Fort Dearborn would know if Simon ever arrived or not.

Perhaps it was not the message, but something about Simon's return or something that happened on the trip that was the reason for the murder. That could be anyone or anything, but I did not know *other* persons, so I started with those I *did* know, the people at the station. Why might they want Simon dead? I did not consider Peniston Wayne or Noah Taylor. They were in Fort Clark when Simon Taylor was killed.

I turned onto my back and opened my eyes, seeing only movements of branches, darker against the darkness of the night.

I knew of six men who could have killed Simon: Villeaux, Leckey, Penney, Reddick, Hardy Findel, and the priest, Father Pascal.

I liked Philippe Villeaux, but if I considered *everyone*, I had to include him. Villeaux said he went only as far as the overlook and headed east, not north up the river. Did he go to visit kin as he said? Maybe he traveled by canoe to the base of the bluff and returned to his canoe later and went upriver. Why would he do that? If Simon stopped at the station on his way upriver, they may have met and something happened that made Villeaux follow the man. Did Simon stop at the station?

Maybe Amelina knew Simon Taylor, or Simon did something to Amelina. Poji said Noah Taylor reminded him of a weasel, and Noah said he was like his brother. If Simon hurt Amelina, Villeaux would be very angry. Villeaux was old—could he kill a man? He once had great strength, and if he struck with a rock from behind or while Simon slept, yes. I could not discount Villeaux.

Poji called Leckey a friend, and Poji was usually right about such things. Leckey was kind to us and seemed a fair and hard-working man. He had a great deal of responsibility, so it was odd that he left suddenly for Fort Dearborn, taking Reddick with him. Did Leckey go to Fort Dearborn for supplies, as was said? Or was he meeting someone or expecting a message? Messages came to Fort Dearborn every month by trail from Indiana. Would he not have known that and arranged his trip, not left unexpectedly? His story was suspect.

Leckey was very fond of Nell. I had seen him interrupt his work to go to her with an explanation, a kind word, a gentle touch, or a pat on the head. Nell liked these little attentions, but I wondered if Leckey was too fond of her or touched her too familiarly. As with Amelina and Villeaux, if anyone hurt Nell, Leckey would have wanted to punish that person. Did Simon stop at the station and harm Nell? I liked Leckey but could not say he did not kill the man.

The Americans who managed the new fur company expected Leckey to be sure only Americans with licenses traded there, since unlicensed traders made prices go up and down. I did not think Leckey had the experience or temperament to command the station. Poji said Leckey was avoiding Penney and speaking to him shortly, as if they had some quarrel. Yet Penney was his happy, friendly self.

Penney was always cheerful and laughing, willing and able to do any task. Our children liked him, and children had a way of knowing good people. Penney let them watch him work and pounded out little gifts and toys from metal scraps. Leckey did not have the natural outgoing manner and air of authority as Penney, and people often turned to Penney instead, who seemed more capable than Leckey. But it was not Penney's job, and he had his own ambitions. Something was not right between these men, but what could it have to do with Simon?

Penney's trip to Fort Dearborn was also sudden and the reason unclear, something about plans to be sure people at Fort Dearborn sent travelers his way. He did not return with supplies, but perhaps he did not need supplies or planned to get them when he went to Galena for lead. Penney could have killed Simon, but what could be the reason?

I knew little about Lemuel Reddick. I never talked to him, but his wife, Amethyst, seemed a pleasant young woman. She had light-colored hair, blue eyes, and a pretty smile, but she was quiet and looked at the ground a lot, with both hands held over her growing belly as if to protect her unborn child. It was said Reddick spent all his time cutting trees and digging land. They brought two oxen with them from the east and traded with our tribe for a horse. I did not understand why he was making a shelter for his animals before he built a cabin, since his wife was to have a child and animals could live outside as they were born to do.

Why did he go with Leckey? He could have asked Leckey to do his errand and stayed home to work, but that was not what he did. I had questions, but I saw no reason Reddick would kill Simon.

If Leckey and Reddick traveled together, one man would have known what the other did. Did this mean neither man did it? Or could it mean they acted together? Or did they separate during the trip? I should find out.

Poji let out a loud gasp in his sleep, as if he had been holding his breath, and then he breathed more regularly with softer snoring sounds.

Returning to my thoughts, I also knew little about Findel. If what Poji said was true, that was the way Findel wanted it. I had no reason to suspect Findel, but I distrusted anyone who seemed to be lying and acting overly important, as was my opinion when I saw him the day he came with the men who arrested Nagmo. He was tall and slender, but his clothing draped over thick arms and thighs, revealing that he was muscular and strong. He wore a thick leather belt over his shirt with a pouch that held a large knife. His forehead was lighter than the rest of his face, which told me he usually wore something to cover his head. His dark, almost-black eyes moved quickly and constantly, seeming to miss nothing. He made me think of a fox.

Findel came down the river after the dead man was found, after the arrival of Father Pascal, who he said he did not know. But the killing happened *upriver*, and we knew Findel was somewhere upriver, so he could have killed Simon. Many things about him were suspicious, but nothing connected him to Simon. I hoped we would find some such thing.

Father Pascal seemed to have the quiet, serious manner one would expect of a priest. He was helpful to Poji about the condition of the body, even though his opinions cast doubt on the white men's charges against Nagmo. He had good reasons for coming here, reasons that would benefit both Indian and white people. I had been taught by priests and respected them. I did not know why a priest would kill Simon.

Yet I had questions. Why would he pretend he did not know Findel? Or, was Villeaux lying about seeing the men together? The priest was at the station before the body was found, but where was he when the killing took place? Poji said he had taken many short trips both up and down the river, but always returned to the station.

I could not exclude a single one of these men. Each one could have been where the man was killed and have a reason to kill. There could be other people I did not know, too. Much as I did not want to think it, an Indian could have committed this crime—but not Nagmo.

This was not going to be easy to do, to get Nagmo set free. But freeing Nagmo was my life. I had no purpose now but to save my son.

When daybreak came, we would finish our trip to the portage and search there for signs that one of these men, or any *other* man, killed the man who was found at our village. We would look for something to show the dead man was Simon and the killer had left something behind to tell us who he was and explain what happened.

Having thought this all through, I was sleepy at last and closed my eyes. As I drifted toward sleep, I thought I heard the rustling of something large moving around nearby. I listened alertly for a time, and, just when I was once again on the edge of sleep, I dimly heard a sound like metal striking a stone. My eyes flew open, unseeing again in the dark. No animal, only a man, would have a metal thing and make a metal sound. A traveler would approach us, not hide. Nervous in the night, I listened for the sound to be repeated. The idea came into my mind that someone at the station did not like the questions we asked. Did the real killer, alarmed, follow us?

As time passed and I heard no further sound, I thought that, half awake and half asleep, I only imagined the sound, and, exhausted, my eyes closed once again.

THE PORTAGE

AT DAYBREAK THE river was peaceful. And there were no signs of a visitor during the night—no footprints, scrapes along the bank, or any other indications.

"Someone passed on the river during the night," Poji said, when I told him of the sound I heard. "Or you were dreaming. You were very tired and in a strange place."

That did not explain the rustling sounds nearby, but I did not argue. What he said about dreaming made sense now that it was daylight, and I trusted Poji to find signs, if there had been any.

The whole day we saw no travelers on the river, and I wondered why, as people had been passing our village just about every day. I watched for, but did not see, anyone following us. The trip was uneventful, but we did not get near the portage until the sun was descending.

Poji insisted we should not risk leaving the river to enter the portage area late in the day, as it would be dangerous. Although I expected it to be a difficult process to carry our belongings and canoe, inspecting the area as we went, I wondered why he was insistent. I thought we could just stop along the way when it got dark and urged him to continue while the light remained.

"Rather than argue with you, Wawetseka, I will show you why we are not leaving the river until there is enough daylight to finish the trip," said Poji.

The river went straight north here, and Poji paddled toward its eastern bank, a thin strip of mud. Trees here were so close their branches trailed in the current, some with trunks in the water. He pointed out many inlets hidden by the dense growth. I had traveled along this river many times but had not noticed the inlets before. Poji headed the canoe into one of them.

Almost immediately we were surrounded by trees, thick growth of shrubs, and many kinds of water plants. The water was motionless with floating green scum, stumps of dead and dying trees, and other once-living things. I wrinkled my nose at the rotting mess and swung an arm wildly to ward off clouds of gnats and mosquitoes. Black mud was on both sides of us, and before long we could not proceed without the need to constantly free our canoe from areas too shallow to keep it floating as it caught in the soft, marshy bottom. This went on as far as I could see ahead.

Poji freed the canoe and paddled back to the river, and after a few powerful strokes we came to another such inlet. Entering it, the experience was the same as the first.

Back on the river, we passed, close to each other, inlet after inlet, more than I could count. "How can anyone find a way through this? Where does it end?" I said. I had pictured a well-worn path through a forest, a wide dry area traveled by many men, with ample room to carry canoes and walk side by side, connecting the Des Plaines River to Chicagou's River. I did not expect this maze of bogs and wetland.

"The white men call this Mud Lake," Poji said. "It is well named. When it rains farther north, especially in the spring, water flows down the river to fill the swamp. Sometimes canoes can pass, but usually some part must be portaged. That is why travel is best in the spring. At other times it is like this and the portage harder to do. There is a wider channel, which we will come to soon, and it is not so discouraging as this, but now you understand the danger of being lost here."

After some time we came to a creek wide enough for large canoes. Along the bank people had carelessly left waste to be carried away the next time the river rose.

"The portage?" I said.

Poji nodded. "We will make our way down this channel and then carry our things to Chicagou's River."

"Will we stop here then, and wait for morning?" I asked.

"Not here. It is best to be cautious while we sleep. We will go a little farther, hide our canoe, rest until daybreak, and then return." Although we saw no other canoes during our trip, the portage was known as a busy place, and we expected to meet travelers. Not all travelers could be trusted.

The next morning, we returned to the creek and made our way through Mud Lake and many low, swampy areas, heading east. A breeze was sharp and cool, and despite the bright sun I wished I could wrap one of our blankets around my shoulders, but it was impossible to paddle that way. The activity gradually warmed me. As on the previous day, we came upon shallow areas barely able to float our canoe, and in the end we had to get out and pull it. When we could go no farther, we unloaded the canoe and lifted it onto dry land. There were trees and undergrowth ahead, but through the trees we saw the edge of a prairie.

We heard voices at a distance. We carried our canoe into the woods, placed it behind the undergrowth, and hid it with branches that still had dry leaves attached. We would watch—observe the men and where they stepped, what they carried, and how they portaged and repacked canoes. We could have hidden ourselves, but we wanted to talk to these men. It was wise not to act in a suspicious manner, so we stayed in the open to let them know we were no threat. Many men came into sight, loaded with bundles on their back. We recognized voyageurs, who came in canoes large enough to carry eight men and their goods.

Such travelers were not unusual. The routes travelers used through our land were few and used by many: voyageurs, frontiersmen, military, merchants, explorers, and Indians.

The distance from Fort Dearborn to the portage was not far, and these voyageurs, accustomed to strong paddling and heavy work, could easily load supplies and travel to the portage in a few hours, even upstream. Travelers usually exchanged news when they met, so Poji and I assumed these men would want to talk with us. We also expected them to be friend-ly, as men who traveled in the large canoes traded with our people. If they were not friendly, then they were either pirates or up to no good. In either case this was no business of Indians, and they would not bother with us. So we did not foresee trouble no matter who the travelers were.

But travel at this season was unusual, as supplies usually came in warm months. When the men arrived they acted surprised to see us sitting there. One man, loaded with large bundles, called out to the others, pointed with his chin, and nodded in our direction. He and another man set down their burdens and talked together, waving an arm at us. Before long one picked his packets up again, struggling to balance one on top of the other, and the second man walked in our direction, leaving his packets on the ground.

These men were not as tall as our braves and had short but powerful-looking legs and large shoulders and arms. Villeaux told me men must be built this way to work for the fur company, as long legs did not fit in the canoes and much strength was required to carry heavy bundles. They were dressed in baggy clothes and had bright-colored cloth wrapped about their foreheads, and much hair on their head and face, like Villeaux. Each man carried two heavy-looking bundles stacked on his back. The man who came toward us seemed to be in charge.

"English?" he asked. *"Francais?"*

Poji stood up and looked into the man's face, pointed at himself and said, "English." Then he pointed to me and said, *"Francais."*

The man smiled with his mouth, but I did not see warmth in his eyes. Speaking French, he asked, "Where is your canoe? How did you get to this place?"

I saw no reason I should not tell him, so I said, "We have hidden our canoe until we talked with you, in case you were thieves."

The man's eyes grew friendly, and he laughed heartily. "So even the natives have fear of these river pirates. One must be careful these days. We carry rifles now not just for game but to protect ourselves from these evil men. The river is not as peaceful as it once was. Maybe we should just leave it to the Americans, like they demand."

"We have no love for Americans either. They give us promises in exchange for our land. Your men treated us fairly and lived among our people. Then Sauganash men, Englishmen, came. They were not so fair, but they gave us goods for furs and left our land to us."

I stopped, wondering if I said too much. But the man's expression seemed to indicate he approved of my words, so I went on. "Now Americans say the land belongs to them. We have no more wish to fight, so we must learn to live their way."

He let out a long slow breath and shook his head slowly. "Your words are true. These Americans are many, and now they say we can no longer trade, only American men. This could be our last trip to this country."

"Is that why you have come in fall? We are used to seeing you *after* the cold months," I said.

The man looked at Poji, pointed at me and then to his forehead, as if to say I was smart for an Indian woman. Then he asked, "Why are *you* here, instead of preparing for winter camp?"

"We look for a white man who came this way some time ago with a message to Fort Dearborn. This man was traveling alone, with no supplies, and probably in a bark canoe. Do you know of such a man?"

"Not many men are at Fort Dearborn, just the commander and a few soldiers with little to do but get ready for winter. Few live at the fort, but it is still busy, with many people coming and going. A ship came some time ago with supplies for the fort. Some people come to trade, some get news or mail, or some meet other men. Both white men and Indians come, but more and more are Americans, less and less are French or English—as they must have a license to trade and licenses will only be given to Americans."

"But the man we look for? Any news of him?"

The man opened his mouth as if to say no, then stopped, and gazed past the woods to the water in the distance. He may have been thinking that now the supplies were moved they still had to carry the large canoes, load them, pull them through the swamps, and reach the river. He turned back to me.

"We were not long at the fort and did not see such a man. But there was *talk* of a man who came from the west far downriver. He waited for a canoe to come across Lake Michigan from Indiana and met with the man who arrived in it. It is said the man was an important person with a letter from William Henry Harrison. These men talked a great deal and then left. The commander of Fort Dearborn seemed impressed by the visitor from Indiana but did not know what the men talked about. That is all I know."

"It is said Harrison still has much to do with Indian matters but no longer has authority in Indiana, only Washington. Many of us have no fondness for Harrison," I added.

"It may have been some such thing," the man said, but he shrugged his shoulders as if he did not know or did not care.

"Do you know how the man looked, the one from the west?"

"It was said that he was tall and slender, dressed in rough clothing, and he glanced about a good deal as if he was afraid to be discovered at some crooked thing. That is one of the reasons there was talk at the fort, because he was an unimportant-looking man engaged with such an important-looking visitor."

The man kept looking toward his men. The last man was already headed back in the direction of the canoes. The first of the large canoes appeared, carried easily by two voyageurs. Three women came from the woods with baskets. I guessed that they had been sent on ahead to forage in the woods while the men unloaded, as the women would be responsible, among other tasks, for preparing meals. The voyageur began to shuffle his feet, a sign he had enough of our questions. We bid him farewell and watched as he hefted his bundles to his back and turned away, his powerful legs seeming to carry the burden effortlessly.

"What do you think?" I asked Poji.

"I think we should not search here today but go right away to Fort Dearborn and talk to the commander. If Simon is the dead man and the man we just heard about, we should find out what we can as soon as possible. Anything that a quick search would find here was probably already discovered, and anything not found yet would take more than a fast search and be here when we return. We may have a better idea what to look for after we visit the fort."

I agreed with Poji.

FORT DEARBORN

WHILE THE VOYAGEURS loaded their canoes, Poji took ours from its hiding place. I wrapped our possessions in a single blanket that I threw over my shoulder. Poji carried the canoe easily. Indian canoes were made so that a single man can carry one, even great distances. They were strong but light, and the crosspieces that supported the frame were placed so the canoe was well balanced when carried overhead. Poji moved out in front as I plodded along behind.

The portage did not turn out to be as hard as I feared. It did not take long to cross the prairie, an empty, treeless area. We soon arrived at the bank of the river we called Chicagou's River, where Chief Chicagou drowned some years after he returned from France. Half a day of light remained, and we used it to get nearer our destination. Unlike the trip to the portage, Chicagou's River on this side of the land bridge flowed downstream into Lake Michigan, and with the favorable current we drew near Fort Dearborn well before nightfall.

After passing through areas of forest and marshland, the riverbanks grew higher, and we saw a flag and then the fort on a high bank in the distance. On the shore just short of the fort, at an area only wide enough to lift our canoe out of the water, we made a shelter under the canoe, not wanting to risk being turned away at the fort too hastily.

"Once I came here shortly before the sun set. The men at the fort had finished their work and did not want to be bothered with Indian matters at the end of their day," Poji said. "We will be more welcome after sunrise."

The night was bitter and frost was on the ground in the morning, but I was too worried about our quest to feel the cold. We set out early, shading our eyes to avoid looking into the sun as we headed toward the fort. I was restless and feared I would drop my paddle. I had never been to Fort Dearborn, although Poji had been many times.

The banks at this part of the river were about eight feet tall, but the ground above them was flat. Before we reached the fort we came upon a clearing, and under one of the few trees at that spot was a log building surrounded by some small wooden structures and a garden. The building had porches from end to end at both front and back, to welcome many people, Poji told me. This was where Jouette, the Indian agent, lived. Before entering the fort we would talk to him for his advice about the best way to get the information we sought.

Then there stood the fort, surrounded by a palisade of wooden pickets, atop a promontory at a bend in the river. Poji said that a second wall was a short way inside the outer one. Two tall wooden structures called blockhouses allowed men to see great distances and defend the fort, but the large gates in the south wall were open. A few buildings were outside the fort and a large area of cleared, flat ground was on the side away from the river, where Poji said soldiers marched with their rifles. There was a large garden nearby.

A battle during the last white man's war destroyed this fort, but it was built again in the same place and in much the same way.

The fort was very like the station near our village, only larger and stronger. I could not take my eyes from it, and I knew it must have taken much work to build such a remarkable thing as this. Poji explained that men lived inside the fort, in buildings that surrounded a large open area and were almost as tall as the blockhouses.

Flying from a tall pole was a flag that could be seen from a great distance. I thought this flag would be seen even from Lake Michigan, and its purpose could be to tell boats this was where they were to come. Large boats—ships, with great white sheets like wings that filled with wind—traveled on the great lakes and arrived at the fort loaded with supplies. These ships stayed in the deep water nearby, but large canoes pulled up to a landing where smaller boats were kept to go out to the ships to unload them.

Men who visited our station told us this, and they said more ships and large canoes were coming. There would be many changes now that the Illinois territory would be a state, and settlers would be allowed to buy the lands we had traded to the government. When surveyors came last year, although we resisted at first, they offered gifts, and, knowing we had no choice, we took the gifts rather than lose the land and gain nothing at all. It made me sad, but we could do no more.

We paddled around a corner of the fort and lifted our canoe onto the sand of the landing area. A small building stood next to it, and a few canoes, one small boat with a flat bottom, and a large wooden raft were at the landing. They were empty, so I thought they were kept there for use by those who lived at the fort.

Across the river from the fort was a large house. Poji told me it was owned by an important man named Kinzie, who was the half brother of Thomas Forsyth, the agent at Fort Clark. Sometimes white men seemed many, like grains of sand—too many to count, which made me fearful. Then it turned out they knew each other, and it seemed they were few after all.

Kinzie's house was tall with two rows of glass windows, tall trees, and a large garden. Poji said Kinzie bought the house and land from a black man who built it many years before. Kinzie hoped to get much money here. I did not understand why a man needs such things for just himself.

We left our weapons in the canoe and covered our possessions with blankets. Standing back, I knew that anyone passing could easily steal from us. But what else could we do? We could not prowl about to look for a hiding place, since anyone watching would think that suspicious. And to appear peaceful, we could not enter the fort with our weapons. We left them behind nervously and walked around the fort to Jouette's cabin.

Jouette, a giant of a man, was stacking cut logs against his cabin. He wiped his hands against his cloth britches and came forward to greet us, pleasantly enough, but his lowered eyebrows said plainly that he wondered why we had come. He addressed Poji in our language.

"What brings you here? There are no payments due, and I see you haven't brought anything to trade," he said.

"No," Poji said. "We came for information about a man, nothing more."

"Why would that be?" Jouette said, frowning.

Poji explained at some length about the dead man and Nagmo's capture. Jouette rubbed the back of his neck and then motioned toward the porch. He took a seat on the steps, and we sat stiffly on the edge of the porch, our feet in the dust of the yard.

Jouette shook his head and tightened one side of his mouth, indicating the response we should expect at the fort. "You're here to prove a white man committed this crime, and you expect that someone here will help you do that?" he said.

"A white man, if that is the case—or an Indian man. Someone who is not Nagmo, who did not do it," I said firmly. He finally looked at me.

"This is Wawetseka, Nagmo's *ne'ni*—mother," Poji said.

"Ah!" Jouette said and swung at an insect. "Damned bees, get pesky this late in the year." He thought for a while, and we waited patiently and did not prompt him. At last he said, "A man did come, could be a month or more ago. Sent here by Forsyth—you know Forsyth? The agent at Fort Clark?"

Poji nodded and pointed toward the fort, "The man whose brother owns that large house across the river?"

Jouette nodded. "I didn't know anything about the man's business, and he was gone before I knew he was here. I thought it odd that he didn't visit me. I thought if Forsyth sent him it would have been on Indian business, and I should be kept informed. But no one at the fort seemed to know what it was about, or they weren't willing to tell. There was some talk about Forsyth being a spy."

"Perhaps they will tell us, but who should we ask?" Poji said.

"Damned if I know," Jouette said, shaking his head. "The commander, Major Baker, should know everything that happens at the fort, but he's so involved with digging out that sandbar. Damn foolish thing if you ask me. God put it there for a reason, I say. Anyway, the man you look for and the man he met, both are long gone, but if anyone knows it would be Baker."

Jouette had nothing more to tell us, so we walked back to the landing to see if our canoe and possessions were still there, and they were. We headed to the large open gates in the south wall of the fort.

We saw no one inside the fort when we entered, but it appeared we had been seen. A man in a soldier's uniform, probably a guard, climbed down from the east blockhouse and approached us, asking in English why we had come. He looked toward the gate, probably thinking there should be more of us. We realized that, like Jouette, he expected us to be carrying furs or other trade items. When Poji explained that we had not come to trade, he lost the friendly manner with which he greeted us—a poor enough pretense to begin with—and looked upon us with suspicion. Even if we meant no trouble, he seemed to feel our visit would be an annoyance.

Poji asked to speak to Major Baker, and the soldier motioned at the opposite side of the fort, pointing to a long building with metal tools, kettles, cooking items, clothing, and bolts of cloth stacked near its door. Poji said this was the trade post. We squatted in the shade at the far end of the building, away from the trade goods so as not to be accused of stealing. The soldier went to a large building with many doors like our station and entered a door at one end. While we waited, a woman came out of another door. She was my age, dressed in fine clothes, and wearing a hat with a large brim, tied under her chin with a thick yellow ribbon. She went into the same doorway as the soldier.

After some time the soldier returned with word that the commander was too busy to talk to us. I was angry and wondered what he could be so busy about with so little going on—but what could we do? The woman had not come out, so perhaps it was she who made the commander busy. The soldier clearly thought he had finished with us and expected us to leave, and he walked off without another word.

We would not be dismissed so easily. While we stood near the gates and discussed what to do, we saw a small canoe coming down the river. A lone white man got out and lifted his canoe next to ours. He wore a deerskin shirt and a battered dark hat with a wide brim, and he carried a long rifle.

Poji's eyes opened wide in surprise. "That is Noah Taylor who I talked to at our station, the brother of Simon, the man we are seeking. I thought he would go with Wayne and Nagmo to Fort Clark. Why is he here?"

We intended to watch and find out.

Noah strode with purpose into the fort. He limped badly, but this did not slow him at all. The same soldier who had left us standing approached him. They talked for some time, both men waving their arms toward the river and motioning toward the commander's quarters. Finally the soldier turned away and Noah followed him toward the major's quarters. They were gone a long time. I was starting to get hungry, and the sun was high in the sky when Noah came back alone. He walked to the trade post, not noticing us where we sat at the end, and spent some time inside. Then he came out, walking slowly and looking about with great interest. We followed at a distance as he left through the gate and found a log to sit on near the landing. He placed his hat on his knees, set his rifle on the ground in front of him, and sat staring at the water, or perhaps at nothing at all, with his chin resting in one hand.

Poji and I looked questioningly at each other, and at Poji's nod we went to where Noah sat. Noah startled when he noticed us, as he had been deep in thought. Just as Poji had described, he resembled a weasel or some other small, sneaky animal, with a narrow face and tiny dark eyes that held no warmth or welcome in them but darted around in all directions as if he were expecting danger. He made small restless movements with his head, his hands, and his legs.

"Haven't I seen you before?" he asked, squinting at Poji.

"Yes, at the station where you stopped before coming here," Poji replied. "You were looking for your brother, and I interpreted for an Indian man who might have seen him."

"Ah, yes. You're the friend of Nagmo, the man who killed my brother."

"I do not believe Nagmo killed your brother. I wonder why you have come to Fort Dearborn. It seems you did not follow us, since you did not recognize me," Poji said.

His eyes turned in my direction, and it seemed he just then noticed two of us were standing there. Despite Poji's words, I wondered if this man *had* followed us and was responsible for the sounds I heard that first night. He waved a questioning hand at me.

"This is Nagmo's *ne'ni*, his mother, Wawetseka," Poji said. "We have come to try to find out who killed your brother, as we have evidence Nagmo did not."

He jerked his head and narrowed his eyes again. "What evidence?" he demanded.

Poji explained what we had found: the pawpaw, the opinions of the priest, and the blood on the wrong side of the tomahawk. The man nodded his head as Poji talked. He remained silent for a long while. Poji and

I squatted nearby and remained silent too. It was our custom to allow men to think and choose the best words, not to say many words that have little purpose other than to fill silence.

Noah looked out at the water. When he spoke it had nothing to do with Nagmo or his brother.

"Do you know what Baker has his men doing? Why there are so few men here today?" he asked. When Poji shook his head, Noah continued, "He has his men digging away a sandbar that makes it impossible for ships to come close to the fort. Have you ever heard of such a thing?"

I agreed this was a strange thing to do. Would it not be easier to bring the boats as far as they could come and unload the supplies there, than to change the course of the river, which was wide and deep at this point except for the sandbar? But that was apparently what white men did, the hard thing instead of taking the land as it came. Neither Poji nor I said anything, but waited for Noah to go on.

He took in a deep breath at last and said, "I don't think Nagmo did it either. What they said at the station doesn't make sense to me. I also don't think the way this happened is what an Indian man would do. That's why I came here, to follow my brother's steps and see if I could discover the true story. What you told me confirms my instincts. And you said that's why you're here too."

"Yes," I said simply.

He got up, went to his canoe, and fumbled in a large pouch. "Let's eat while we talk," he said, and he asked Poji to build a fire, indicating a spot a short distance from the landing near a tree. "Let's make ourselves comfortable. After we tell each other what we know, we may all be nearer to the truth."

NOAH

WE ATE HEARTILY of Noah's food—pemmican, corn biscuit, and something he called "portable soup," which was a mixture of dried meat, vegetables, fruit, and nuts. He added water to this and then heated it in a pot. After eating his fill, he walked away behind a tree and I heard him relieving himself. Poji took the opportunity to lean close to my ear and whisper, "Do not trust him too much, Wawetseka. I do not like the look of the man. He is hiding something, or up to something, and it will not benefit us, you can be sure!"

Noah returned, adjusted his clothing, reached under his canoe for a blanket, and made a seat of it. We had answered all his questions and were anxious to be told what *he* knew.

Before he left the station, Noah told us, Peniston Wayne seemed jumpy and anxious, pacing and mumbling that he had to get back to Fort Clark with his prisoner. Perhaps he wanted to avoid the cold or other expected danger while traveling overland, or perhaps he had urgent business at Fort Clark, but he gave no reason. Noah said he did not trust Wayne. "What sort of man takes a job as a sheriff, chasing down bad men, locking them up, and executing them? Not the sort of man I want to associate with. And if the man he brings in is innocent, so much the worse. What sort of man brings an *innocent* man to be tried and convicted?" I nodded my head. Those were my thoughts too. I also thought there was little trust of anyone, of us for the white men, and these men for each other. This was not good.

"I talked to Wayne," he went on, "and he refused to consider a different killer. That was not his job, he insisted. His job was only to bring in the accused man, alive if possible, but if not alive, bring him back anyway."

Hearing these words, a sharp pain gripped my chest and my heart missed a beat. I sat cross-legged on the ground, stared at my moccasins, and shivered as a chill went down my back. I had thought we had time to bring in the real killer, but it never occurred to me that a man like Wayne posed a threat, too, as he might find it easier to bring Nagmo in dead. I could not stop another picture from forming in my mind, this time of Nagmo's body draped across the back of a horse being led by a law man. I looked up to the skies with a prayer to the Catholic God that Nagmo would go peacefully and not incite Wayne's anger along the way.

"Did they start for Fort Clark before you left?" I asked Noah.

"Wayne had some business with the blacksmith, a message from Galena, he said. The blacksmith was away for a day or two on an errand. His boy didn't know much, just that he was expected back soon. Wayne had to wait for the man, but I left to follow where Simon had been sent, to see if I could find out what happened. The story made no sense to me."

So Penney had left the station too. If it was not Noah who followed us, it could be Penney—if I had not dreamed the noises.

"Why did you not believe the story?" Poji asked, sounding suspicious. It seemed Poji still thought the man was up to something. Whether or not the man had followed us, I hoped Noah's words were truthful.

"Simon carried nothing valuable and had a reputation as a friend of Indians," Noah said, looking into Poji's eyes. "An Indian man would lose more than he gained by killing him, as he would be caught and punished, which turned out to be what happened. Why would a man like Nagmo want to kill my brother? Neither man had anything the other would want or anything to quarrel about—they didn't even know each other. And I didn't think an Indian would hide a dead body or tie it to the roots of a tree. You have respect for the dead and fear spirits of the dead, more so if you think you dishonored the man in some way."

He turned his eyes from Poji and looked at me. "They let me talk to Nagmo. He was frightened, but sincere, and I believed his story."

Noah's eyes appeared truthful, but now I was angered and looked away. Poji and I could not talk to Nagmo, but they let this stranger do so.

Noah began picking up handfuls of sand that he let run through his fingers onto the ground. He glanced at Poji and then back at me. "I must admit my purpose was not so much to prove Nagmo innocent, but to find the man who killed my brother."

Poji looked thoughtful. He directed a hard stare at Noah nonetheless, and I thought he was reluctant to give up his opinion of Noah's character. "But he had your brother's ring. What did he say about that?"

Noah frowned. "My brother had no such ring. At least he didn't when he left on his journey. There was much talk about the ring and that angered me. Leckey, Findel, Wayne—all made a big deal of the ring sealing Nagmo's guilt, and even the priest agreed. When I told them the ring didn't belong to my brother, they insisted it *must* have been his, where else would it come from? If Simon didn't have it before the trip, then he got it at Fort Dearborn, they said, but it was surely his. My brother saved what money he earned to put into land—he would not buy such a useless thing. No, I can't believe that ring belonged to my brother."

"Perhaps he did some favor, and it was given to him in payment or gratitude?" I suggested. "Perhaps he planned to use it to trade."

Noah snorted. "Who out here would trade for such a thing? That's for wealthy people in big towns, not out here on the frontier. Food, land, things we need to work the land—those are of value here, not fancy rings."

"Then how did the ring get in Nagmo's pouch?" Poji asked. "I was there and saw it fall to the ground out of the pouch. There was no mistake."

"I can't explain the ring, but it has nothing to do with my brother," Noah insisted. "Wayne told me Nagmo said he was going to give the ring to his wife, as such a present would help their marriage. But when I asked Nagmo he only looked confused and said he had no idea how the ring got in his medicine pouch."

"So Nagmo denied having the ring?" asked Poji.

"Poji, it cannot be," I said. "Wabmimi would value such a gift, but I cannot believe Nagmo stole it. Did anyone else hear Nagmo say such a thing, or only Wayne? Wayne could be lying. Or maybe some other person told him this, not Nagmo—someone who wanted Wayne to believe Nagmo was guilty, or someone who slipped the ring into Nagmo's pouch."

I was confused by this too. I could not see how anyone could put the ring in Nagmo's pouch. Nagmo was away the morning they came to accuse him and carried his pouch with him, as always. I was with him the entire time after he returned until the ring spilled from it.

"Did you have reason to suspect anyone at the station?" I asked.

"Not before I arrived here, but after I talked to the men at Fort Dearborn there are many suspicious things."

We had been sitting long and Poji got up to move about as we talked. I only straightened my back and raised my face to the warm sun, stretched my arms to feel a cool breeze, and tried to calm myself. Soon it would be bitter cold, but this day would have felt pleasant were it not for the things we talked about.

"You are saying that Major Baker had much to tell?" I said.

"Not just Baker, but his aide, and then Baker's wife joined us, and all had interesting observations about what went on while Simon was at the fort."

Noah brushed off his hands, wiped them on his pants, swung one leg over the log, and sat on it as if he were riding a horse. "Forsyth sent Simon to Fort Dearborn to meet a man carrying important information from William Henry Harrison, representing the U.S. Government about Indian affairs. The messenger came from Fort Wayne. So Fort Dearborn, midway between Fort Wayne and Fort Clark, was a logical place to meet, as he could travel down the St. Joseph River and across the bottom of Lake Michigan. Forsyth is an intermediary for William Clark, the former explorer, Indian agent, and now governor of the Missouri Territory."

We did not interrupt Taylor's words to tell him we knew these things about Forsyth, Clark, and Harrison, but allowed him to tell what he knew in his own way. He might tell more than he intended.

"According to Baker, who knew nothing about either man or about the nature of the information, both men arrived and talked privately, and the man from the east left shortly afterward. Baker's wife said she had the impression Simon felt something was wrong as soon as he arrived at the fort, even before meeting Harrison's man. Simon seemed angry and distracted. He wandered about restlessly the entire time there, looking about him and over his shoulder."

"The message must have been disturbing," said Poji. He stopped pacing and sat down on the ground next to me.

"Was Simon upset when he left Fort Clark?" I asked.

Noah shook his head. "He was smiling and looking forward to the trip."

"Then perhaps the message he carried was not what upset him, since he was not upset when he left. But he was upset *before* he talked to Harrison's man." I said.

"You are implying something happened after he left Fort Clark and before he arrived at Fort Dearborn, and perhaps that's the reason he was killed?" said Noah.

I nodded. "Do you agree?"

"Maybe it happened as soon as he got to the fort, before the messenger arrived," Noah suggested.

"Do you know who was at the fort?" I asked.

"Yes. The aide had a log of visitors, and he let me examine it. During the time Simon was at the fort, in addition to the men assigned there, Simon, and the messenger, who signed only the name of Harrison, there were four other men: Davey Leckey, Lemuel Reddick, Hardy Findel, and Father Andri Pascal."

"Did you see the names of Jim Penney or Philippe Villeaux?" I asked.

"I did not," Noah said. "Penney? The blacksmith? Who is Villeaux? Were those men supposed to be there?"

I looked at Poji, who shrugged his shoulders. Poji has many good qualities, but sometimes he does not keep pace with my thoughts.

"Villeaux is an old man who lives near the station. Both men went in the direction of Fort Dearborn while your brother was there. Since they were not at Fort Dearborn, it seems unlikely either would be suspect, unless their names did not get entered in the log. Can you see any reason the men there or Baker, his wife, or the aide, would want to harm Simon?" I asked.

"No reason comes to mind. They seemed honest and friendly. They didn't exchange glances as if they were hiding anything, and they answered all my questions fully."

"Did they notice anything unusual about the other visitors?" Poji asked, as I was opening my mouth with the same question.

Noah smiled widely, the first smile I had seen on his narrow face. "Oh yes, plenty. As soon as Reddick caught sight of Simon, he ran up to him, threw a punch, and knocked him down. They had a furious argument and had to be pulled apart."

"What did they argue about?" asked Poji.

"Aside from a lot of name-calling and nasty words, the man who saw the incident only heard Simon say, 'It never happened.'"

"They knew each other then," I said, thinking. "What did Leckey do?"

"His behavior was odd too. Aside from angry glances at Reddick, who he kept at his side after the fight, he went about his business, picked up mail and supplies, and left quickly. I talked to the trader at the post, who wouldn't look me in the eye. All he would say was that Leckey complained about his trades and that he opened a letter and started swearing. I had the feeling Leckey and the trader had an unhappy exchange."

"Did either of them have contact with Simon?"

"Not that anyone mentioned, but they said it was a busy day with a great deal of going here and there. Everyone I talked to said the same."

"What about Findel?" Poji asked.

"Ah!" said Noah, and laughed loudly. "That man is not what he seems! A businessman all right, but criminal business. The aide recognized him immediately. He's the head of a bunch of bandits from the east, although he wore fancy clothes to mislead everyone. Here they call them river pirates. They travel up and down the rivers, disguised as merchants, businessmen, or some other thing, but what they're really doing is looking for people traveling alone or in small groups. They rob them, kill them, and blame it on the Indians—oh, sorry."

I took no offense and waited for him to finish.

"The aide seemed to enjoy talking about this. Many of these men are criminals who left the east because they committed some crime there. They're swindlers and pickpockets and skilled at tricks that deceive the eye. Findel is a known counterfeiter and the idea man for the band. Undoubtedly he passed through your station to see what sort of profit could be made on that part of the river. And the priest? He was recognized too, and he isn't a priest at all, but a member of Findel's band in disguise."

THE SWAMP

"Why do we need him?" Poji hissed near my ear. We had stepped a short distance away while Noah put his canoe in the water and loaded his possessions. Despite Poji's suspicions, although Noah probably did not fully trust *us* either, we had agreed we would learn more and faster if we worked together.

"He knows about his brother, he knows about how white men act, and he is on our side," I whispered.

Even though it was pleasant that day, Poji said snow would start soon. He was skilled with signs that predicted weather and spoke of mares' tails, low gray clouds, a ring around the sun, what birds and insects were doing, and more. I believed him about such things. With nothing further to be learned at Fort Dearborn and bad weather coming, we left immediately for the portage, Poji leading the way with Noah in his own canoe close behind.

The upriver trip on Chicagou's River was short and the portage also short. And with fair conditions on Mud Lake and a downhill current on the Des Plaines River, we could have made the trip to our village in a single day, if we had left at daybreak. This was why the station was built near our village, because it was a journey of one day from Fort Dearborn, and men would be ready to rest there, after going as far as possible in daylight.

But it was late when we left and past sunset by the time we crossed the portage. We decided not to search the portage trail. With so many passing that way, a crime would be too easily seen there, and a man could not carry a body, a canoe, and belongings through the vast swamp by himself, if the killer acted alone. The tree to which Simon was tied must have been along the Des Plaines River or the storm would not have carried it to our village. We reasoned the killing must have happened near the river.

We camped under the trees, since we could not cross the swamp in darkness. We created what shelter we could under our canoes and built a fire. The night was cruelly cold with a strong wind off Lake Michigan.

At daybreak, the swamp was covered with a thin sheet of ice. Even in the short time since we had been there, the swamp had drained a good amount, lowering the level of the water such that it was no longer possible to paddle easily through Mud Lake. We made forked poles from saplings to pull our canoes, sticking the poles into frost-covered tussocks of grass and roots. At times we got out of the canoes, broke the thin crust of ice, and waded in mud, sinking even to our waist into unseen depressions. Despite the thin ice at the surface, the cold had come so quickly that the water below, although stinging our bodies, still held the awful black suckers that found their way through openings in our clothing and attached themselves to our skin.

The sky was gray with no sun. To keep our direction, we searched the sky continuously for spots that now and then brightened slightly, where the sun was hidden. Our only consolation was that the cold kept away the awful mosquitoes that would have plagued us in warmer weather.

It took an entire day to travel the cursed swamp. We were fortunate Poji was a skilled tracker and we did not lose our way. We arrived on the bank of the Des Plaines River, exhausted and shaking in our cold, wet clothing, just as the sun was setting. Now that we no longer needed it for direction, there the sun was. Poji took some tobacco from his pouch and mixed it with water to form a paste to put on the suckers, and this was successful in ridding them from our skin, as they only broke in pieces if we tried to pull them off. Mishipeshu would need to make do with smaller tobacco offerings.

We made camp a short distance inland and huddled, shivering, around a fire, our skin blue, trying as best we could to dry our wet clothes—our overturned canoes a poor barrier to the wind. Noah, expecting his trip would continue well into winter, had in his canoe a thick buffalo robe, which he laid over the three of us. With this and the cheap blankets we had brought, we made it through the night.

The sun was absent again when we woke, the sky gray, the wind fierce. From here our village was downstream, and the remaining trip would be quick with little danger, provided we did not delay until the approaching storm arrived. We would not get another chance to search here, as all signs would be gone once the land was covered with snow. So, despite the cold, we looked for anything to tell us where the killing occurred, how it had happened, or who may have done it.

"You see the short trees with the long, yellow leaves still attached to them, the leaves bigger than your foot?" I pointed out. "Those are pawpaw trees—the branch that was caught in the roots of the tree with the body. See the soggy, green, mushy patches on the ground below the trees? These patches are rotted pawpaw fruit. Based on the time the fruit ripens, the man must have been killed more than a month ago."

Noah walked over to examine the trees and ground. "The man...Simon...yes. You say these trees grow nowhere except here?" he asked.

"Not between here and our village. Not farther upriver. Perhaps far off, or farther downstream, but not nearby, no other place the river would carry it to our village. Since this portage is the route white men take, it must have happened here." Noah nodded his head as I explained, a serious expression on his face.

Having made that point, I went on. "You see how, even after the river has dropped, there are trees with trunks in the river? Simon would have been tied to a tree such as that one," I said, pointing to a tree that, although some feet from the river bank, had many tangled roots above the water, like the loose, sloppy nests sparrows make.

"I see what you mean," Noah said. "It would have been easy to bring a canoe right up to a tree like that and tie a man to those roots, wedged under the surface of the water." He looked back at the dense growth of trees on the riverbank, many of which were vine-covered. "Those vines," he pointed, "are they soft and pliable enough, and strong enough, for that purpose?"

"Yes," I said. I watched his face as he thought this over.

"Why would the killer do that? Why didn't he just leave Simon where he was, drag him into the trees, dispose of him in some other way? Why tie him to a tree?"

"People go by here. Perhaps he did not want to chance Simon being found by anyone who had seen them together. If he left the body on land it could be found. Birds, flesh-eating scavengers, insects, foul odors—any of these things could call attention to a body left on land."

Noah turned his head away. His voice was coarse and a little shaky. "Why not just leave him somewhere else in the swamp?"

"Maybe he feared someone passing by and seeing him with the body or was afraid of getting lost back there—we do not know what level the swamp was at when he was here. And since the level goes up and down so quickly, the body could float right up or onto a dry area. He would not want it to wash downriver where it could be found. To bury it would take too long." I shrugged my shoulders. "He would not expect the tree itself to wash downriver. Maybe he was not a very smart man and that was the only thing that occurred to him."

This brought a laugh from Poji, but he stopped laughing when he looked at Noah, who was blinking his eyes rapidly and holding his jaw tight. I did not say more but allowed him to grieve.

"So we will look here to discover where he was killed and perhaps find some useful information?" Poji said.

"For what purpose?" I asked.

"What do you mean? Is that not why we came?"

I glanced at Noah to see if he was following my argument. "Three things happened. First, Simon did something that made someone want to kill him. Where did that happen? It did not happen at the fort, it appears, but before he got to the fort. So on the trip to Fort Dearborn they ran into each other." I waved my arm to indicate it could have happened anywhere from here in the direction of the fort.

"After Simon delivered his message and left the fort, he would have passed here again on his return. The killer either followed him or waited for him here. Next, he killed Simon, after they went through the portage, and probably after the swamp, as he could not carry canoe, supplies, and body. Possibly before he got to the river, or perhaps along the river, near here.

"The weapon was a rock or some such thing, unless the false priest was lying about the head wound. What should we look for and where could it be? If it is a rock it would be washed clean by now. If it is a man-made weapon, the killer would have been careful not to leave it behind. He took it with him or hid it, or someone found it and picked it up by now. How could we find such a thing? And if we did find it, how would we know who it belonged to?"

It got clear in my head as I spoke. I could not stop the words from tumbling out—out of control like a stream running with snowmelt on the first warm sunny day.

"And then, the killer hid Simon's body. I do not think that was here. I think he would want to get away and hide the body somewhere fewer people came, perhaps upstream since not many people go that way. I think the killer planned this, to wait for him here, and then brought the body upstream and tied it to a tree root." I stopped to see if the men agreed with me.

"We should be sure there's nothing to be found here," Noah said. "And we should see if what Wawetseka says can be proved, if there's a landing upstream and anything left there. Maybe downstream too."

"Where is Simon's canoe?" I asked.

Noah and Poji looked at each other in surprise. "His canoe?" Noah asked.

"Did he not travel here in a canoe? Where is it?" I asked.

Both men shook their heads thoughtfully.

"Here is how you can help," I said, looking at Noah. "Why might someone want to kill your brother? We already decided it was not for the message he carried, but some other reason. And you said your brother was not carrying anything of value, so it was not to rob him."

"Was it not the ring?" asked Poji.

"I told you he had no such ring," Noah said through gritted teeth, and I wondered why he was so adamant. Poji and Noah glared at each other.

"Unless he got the ring on the way here," I suggested.

"Fine. I can't prove it, but I don't think so," Noah said. "Again, what did it look like?"

"It was a thick gold band, carved very fine. It had a large, dark-reddish-brown stone, oval like a dried bean, but bigger, and a bright-yellow line glowed down the center of it. I have never seen such a thing."

"I recognize your description," he said. "It's called a cat's-eye stone. Many wealthy men in the east have them. The stone looks valuable, but it's not costly unless it's unusually large, colorful, or bright. The gold band would be more valuable than the stone, most likely. But again, it would be of little value here, where we have more important needs than fancy rings."

"Why else might someone want to kill your brother?" Poji asked.

"What about the man who attacked Simon at the fort? Reddick? Or the pirates?" Noah said.

I thought about this. "It seemed they did not meet before they got to the fort. Did you not say Simon was upset when he arrived at the fort, before that argument? If they ran into each other sooner, why did he not kill him then instead of letting him travel on to the fort? Also, Leckey was with Lemuel Reddick the whole trip. So Leckey would have to be involved, or at least know about it. Yet neither man admitted to knowing Simon when his body turned up."

"It was badly disfigured," Poji said.

I snorted. "If they tied a body to a tree, they did not expect it to come downstream. How many bodies tied to trees would wash to our village? They would have to know it was Simon and be hiding the fact."

Poji turned to Noah. "Reddick recognized Simon when he saw him and was angry. Reddick only recently came here from the east. Perhaps your brother did something back east that made Reddick angry. Stole from him or hurt someone in his family or some such thing."

"I know of nothing like that. Surely I would know, as we came west together," Noah said.

"Perhaps it is someone who is hiding here now, who does not want anyone to know who he is, someone that Simon recognized," I said, looking off across the water. I shook my head. "That is the sort of man who becomes a pirate, to hide his past. But if it was Findel or the priest, why would they hide the body at all? And why did they stay so long at the station instead of moving on as soon as the body turned up there?" I put my head in my hands, rubbed my eyes and face, and took a deep breath.

"I cannot think so long. Let us look around here before we go upstream, and I will think again later."

We looked carefully for some time around the riverbanks and into the edges of the forest. We found things that could have been left by anyone, but nothing to connect these things to a murder or to any person we knew. We got into our canoes to search upriver for a nearby landing place where a tree could have uprooted and fallen into the river.

MISHAP

THE DRIED MUD of the bank was still covered with a sheen of frost. The river had fallen, making the bank wider than when Poji and I had stopped there days ago, a short distance upstream of Mud Lake. Today the three of us went separate ways to examine the bank and look for worn trails where the woods began.

Near the trees we found remains of fires, but otherwise only animal trails, nothing to suggest men had left the river's edge. Poji stood near the water and looked up and down the banks on both sides of the river.

"Do we need to cross to the other bank?" I asked, shivering in the damp and cold wind. Discouraged and miserable, my body was begging me to return to my warm home, but I was desperate to prove what we believed about the killing.

Poji's sharp eyes fixed a short distance downriver where the bank narrowed and met the water. He pointed. "There. Look. The branches on that tree, the one hanging over the water across the river, are they torn? It is more than the wind. It is as if something large broke many branches that have not yet fallen from the tree."

The whole side of the tree that faced the water was covered with brown leaves clinging to torn branches, the exposed wood shining white. This would not have been caused by lightning, but by something large that fell on or struck the tree. It was hard to notice, since brown leaves filled the woods.

We crossed the river and approached the tree for a closer look. "See there," Poji said again, pointing at the surface of the water a few feet out into the river. The water swirled oddly, ripples where there was no clear cause.

Noah took off the warmer raccoon cap he wore that day instead of his wide-brimmed one, and he rubbed his forehead. "You're suggesting a tree used to be there and fell against this other one?" he asked.

Poji nodded, still searching, until his eyes stopped again. "Something was dragged there," he said, pointing a bit farther downstream.

I could not see anything until we went to the spot. Just below the tree line was a scrape in the dried mud, a partial print of a moccasin, and some almost unnoticeable crushed vegetation leading into the trees, as of a trail made by small woodland animals. We pushed some branches aside, and a short distance away a large dead tree lay on the forest floor. Behind it, covered carefully with branches and leaves, was a canoe.

"Is it Simon's?" I asked Noah.

Noah approached the canoe reluctantly. We pulled the branches away and uncovered the canoe, which was turned upside down, its birch bark resembling another tree trunk. It would not be noticed unless someone were searching for a canoe or remembered that no birch trees grew in this place. Most travelers, especially white men, stayed on the portage side of the river, the east bank, and would not go to the west side.

Noah turned the canoe over. It was empty, but in the ground below it, hidden by a thin layer of dirt and leaves and weighted with a rock, were a white linen shirt, a pair of britches, a pair of moccasins, and a coonskin cap.

Noah put a hand over his eyes and then dragged it down his face, which was white with anger. "These are Simon's clothes." We waited for him to say more, but he did not.

Poji broke a forked branch from a nearby sapling and poked and swept it around the forest floor, but nothing else turned up. "The clothes were purposely hidden, but the killer must have taken his personal possessions, any pouches, and valuables, as they are nowhere. Perhaps only a robbery after all. Look here...."

He walked to the trunk of a nearby tree, covered with vines like those used to tie Simon. Vines had been pulled from the tree, either torn or cut through.

While Poji and Noah examined the vines, I looked inside the canoe.

At first it appeared empty, but then I found a small, round, black object about the size of a dried bean, wedged under a rib of the frame. I thought at first it was a pebble, polished by the river and caught there, but, when I pried it loose, it was a piece of dark metal with two small holes in its center.

I had seen such things before. Visitors from the east sewed them to cloth with sinew, and they held clothing together, instead of tying with strips of cloth. Some were very fancy, but this one was rough and plain.

I showed it to Poji and Noah. "Have you ever seen this?"

Both men nodded. "Something like it, but not this one," said Poji.

Noah turned it over in his hand. "It's a button, but Simon's were not like this—I have never seen one like this. It would do the job, but people would use better ones, not this rough ugly thing."

"It could have been ripped from the clothing of the killer," I said. "He might not have noticed such a small, worthless thing. We will keep it. Perhaps someone at the station will recognize it."

Having found what we went to find, there was no reason to stay longer—there was nothing more the areas around the portage or on the river had to tell us. It was not yet midday. We started back to our village with little help from the current, which was light and sluggish after receding waters and the light freeze. It would take a bit longer, but we would easily arrive in less than half a day.

As we passed the inlet that led to Mud Lake, we saw a group of three large canoes, the kind that carry many men and supplies. Men were gathered on the bank, some beside the canoes rearranging bundles and others taking a break. From the manner of their dress, I thought they were an American company. These men seemed less skilled than French voyageurs, but they were young and strong. They probably came to build or supply a post before winter. They might stop at our station, and it was likely, with so many strong paddlers, they would pass us on the way. We went around a bend and lost sight of them before they got into their canoes.

Sometime later we heard singing behind us and then a warning shout from one of the men. Startled, I turned to see why he was shouting and in the process dropped my paddle into the river. I leaned to grab it, and our canoe tilted to one side. Poji, who was also grabbing for the paddle, lost his balance. We hit something large. Distracted by the shouting and lost paddle, I had not seen it. Our canoe lurched violently, and Poji fell into the river.

I was a poor canoer and a worse swimmer. I left the fallen paddle and crawled to the front of our canoe to get Poji's, the canoe rocking from side to side and threatening to dump me into the water too. The danger was not great. The river was not more than four feet deep in most places, and the current was slow. Poji would be cold and miserable and that was all. I grabbed the paddle, but while I was doing that the canoe drifted away from Poji. I called out to Noah, but he did not come to help. The other canoes were moving in our direction but were still a way off.

Floating nearby was a large, dead deer—the obstruction we had hit. Perhaps it was wounded by a hunter and fell into the river trying to escape.

I saw Poji floundering, and his head bobbed above and then below the water. "Mud!" he yelled, and I realized then he was stuck in the muddy river bottom, which was pulling him down like quicksand.

"Noah!" I called. "Help us!" But Noah appeared stunned and was unmoving, and his canoe went past Poji as Noah watched, a look of terror on his face.

The deer carcass drifted away, and Poji continued to flail at the water, unable to free himself from the mud. Unskilled as I am, my progress toward him was unbearably slow. "Stay calm!" I called. "I am coming!"

One of the Americans' canoes reached Poji before me, and the men pulled him from the mud. Gasping, Poji clung to the side of the canoe, which was so loaded with supplies it had no room for him. Despite his near exhaustion, Poji decided to swim the short way to the riverbank, so as not to overturn our canoe while trying to get in it. The bank had no clear landing place, only a swamp-like area filled with mud, grass, and twigs. Poji dragged himself onto the mud, which, it appeared, was firm enough to hold him while he regained strength. We headed toward him.

Before I drew next to Poji, followed by the large canoe, Poji cried out in terror and jumped, scrambling violently to move away on the uncertain surface. I was too late to help. I watched in horror as the creature coiled beside Poji lifted its head and rose for a moment with fangs bared. I saw the terrible white inside its ugly mouth as it buried its fangs into

Poji's ankle—fangs that in my panic appeared as large as bear claws. Getting near Poji's side, I raised my paddle and beat at the awful thing until the dark snake, about four feet long with a body as thick as my arm, slithered into the river and away across the surface of the water.

Through all this, Noah hung back and did nothing. The Americans joined me, and, with great effort, we managed to get Poji into our canoe.

Poji became weak almost immediately. His eyes were dazed, and he moved his mouth open and shut but did not speak. He would never be able to take us home.

One of the men in the canoes offered to help. At last Noah joined us, and he and the American made Poji as comfortable as possible and wrapped him in Noah's buffalo robe. Before he was covered, I saw that Poji's leg was red and swollen.

The American got into our canoe. The young man was strong and took us swiftly toward home. I steered the canoe, if for no other reason than to distract my fear by staying busy. The entire way I watched Poji. His breathing was troubled and he trembled fiercely and continuously. He was too still, not lifting his head or moving his arms or legs. I feared he would die before we got to our village.

Mixed with my fear was fury at Noah. Why did he not help? Why did he not pull Poji out of the mud and into his canoe? Was he the friend I had convinced myself he was? Or had Poji's suspicions about him been right all along?

HOME

Noah's face turned red as I scolded. It amazed me that a white man's face could get so bright, the whiter the man the deeper the color, and yet they called *us* red men.

"Why did you not help us?" I demanded. "You were right there. All you had to do was steer a little to one side, but no. You just put your paddle down and drifted by and watched Poji almost drown and get bitten by that snake. And now he could die!"

When we arrived at our village yesterday, Shawnash was waiting. One of the children saw our canoes on the river and set up a cry. Shawnash's welcoming smile quickly faded when I called out that Poji was hurt.

Shawnash could move fast when she had to. She told one of the children to get help, and before I knew it we were lifting Poji, buffalo robe and all, out of the canoe. Men carried Poji to Shawnash's wigwam. Uncertain about when our village would move for winter, Shawnash had set up a wigwam close to her summer house. It would be easier to care for Poji there than in the crowded space with my kin.

Shawnash did not waste time with words. She assessed Poji's grave condition and shouted for the medicine man to be found.

Many medicine men were old and wrinkled with thin hair. They appeared frail, but when making medicine they were surprisingly strong. This was explained by their vast experience with the spirits who possessed them. Our medicine man was no exception. He was with us for many years, and we knew he took much care to sing the necessary songs while gathering and preparing medicines, even growing herbs from seeds of plants that did not grow here. I had seen him put his medicines right into a person's body through a hollow goose bone.

When he arrived he shook his head. After careful examination of every part of Poji's body, he mixed many herbs together in cold mud and packed the mixture around Poji's foot and leg. He made us wrap Poji in many warm blankets and move him near the fire. He sat by Poji's side, put his hand on Poji's chest, and murmured ceremonial chants for a long time. Then he talked to me.

"We will wait," he said. "He will get better slowly, or he will get worse slowly. Either way, he will fight the poison. I will perform the indicated ceremonies, move my sleeping pallet here, and stay with him while I await the healing dream. If he is not better in four days, I will mix other medicines. He is a strong man. Perhaps he will live, if the spirits will it. It would not hurt to ask for their favor." The fees had already been arranged, so he went to his mat and fell asleep.

Shawnash had made arrangements for the shaman's fee when he first arrived. I had heard white men say medicine men are greedy. But we believed the mind plays a large part in any illness, that larger fees are more likely to produce better results, and that treatment will fail without a fee. Shawnash was very skilled with quillwork and had recently finished a lovely bag. Our medicine man was in need of such a bag to store cures, and so the fee was paid.

After all was done, I told Shawnash what had occurred and about my disgust with Noah. "I cannot understand why a snake was where it should not be, why it would be trying to sun itself on a cold and cloudy day," I said.

"It could be that is why it was there," she said. "The cold came fast, and the snake was sluggish and confused and looked for sun to help, even if the sun was not there."

I moved my sleeping pallet into Shawnash's wigwam then, and we settled in to keep watch. Exhausted by the trip and events, my thoughts jumped from one thing to another, and I could not relax or focus my mind. Our people did not touch each other a great deal. We rarely hugged or embraced. We preferred to keep emotions private. But that night Shawnash moved her pallet close to mine and, sensing my anguish, put a hand on my arm. With the comfort of her touch I fell into a rest-less sleep.

The next morning when I confronted Noah, I was tired and irritable. He looked at the ground, but, little woman that I am, I got right under his face and glared up at him.

He turned his face away and mumbled his excuse. "I can't swim."

I threw my hands up in the air, almost dropping my robe, and spoke louder. "You could have stayed in the canoe and pulled him out of the mud! That you cannot swim is a poor excuse!"

He let out a slow breath and said, "And then I started to help, but Poji was already swimming, and..." He stopped and then went on in a weak voice. "I'm terrified of snakes. I panic—my head spins and my legs grow weak. That was a *big* snake! I wanted to help, but I froze."

I threw my hands back into the air; stamped my foot until it hurt, say-ing "uh" with every stamp; and spat out with disgust, "*Kyesh'at!*" The man *was* a fool. Then I turned my back, leaving him standing there with his head hanging as I stomped away.

I walked for a long time through gently falling snow. The wind had howled all night but the morning was calm. Each day was colder and again a film of ice was on the river, and, as Poji had predicted, the snow had started to fall—a few light flakes that melted on my face and hands. Only a light brushing of white appeared in patches where it blew against trees and tall grasses. It was early for such weather, which was not expect-ed for another month or more. Maybe Shawnash was right about the snake.

I walked up the hill to the top of the bluff where I had gathered nuts the day the dead man was found. I thought about everything that had happened, trying to make sense of all we now knew and feeling alone and frightened now that my anger had died down.

Shawnash heard the women's gossip and told me Nagmo went peace-fully to Fort Clark with Peniston Wayne soon after we left for Fort Dear-born. Things were quiet at the station, but the women thought some-thing was wrong. Everyone seemed uneasy and did not speak in their usual friendly manner. Findel and Pascal were still there. Men on both sides of the river wondered why they had not left. They did not know these men were pirates.

The American men in the big canoes stayed one night, sleeping on empty ground inside the palisade walls. They were off again at daybreak. I thought they were anxious to stay ahead of the snow and ice that threatened their trip. We would not be likely to see them, or other groups of visitors, until spring, although a few men came on horseback or on foot after the river froze.

The early frost and coming storm surprised our men too, and they postponed our move to winter grounds. Deer had returned to our woods once more, but if they left again we would follow our food supply. Meanwhile, our men would hunt nearby and do some trapping. Our women were adapting our houses for winter or setting up winter wigwams—temporary arrangements until a decision was made.

I thought about the trip we had just made, and I wondered if we had accomplished anything at all. We knew more, but how would we use what we knew to free Nagmo? We still had all the same suspects and had found no new ones. We still did not know why Simon was killed. The only real change was that Poji could no longer help me. He might even die. That was a very bad outcome.

Soon I would be an old woman. And I was not skilled in the ways of men, even Indian men. I did not hunt and I did not travel alone. Yet I *was* alone, the only person trying to rescue my son, the person I loved most. I had to do something—but what?

I sat on a fallen log, pulled my robe close around my arms and chest, tormented by my fears, feeling I did not have the cunning or strength to save my son. Once again M'ewé came from the forest to cheer me. Silently she padded one slow step at a time on the frozen ground and then rested her muzzle on my knee, looking up at me with her yellow, sorrowful eyes in the gray light, seeming to sense my distress.

I put my hand on her neck and stroked it, and then I buried my face in her thick fur and let a few tears escape. When at last I lifted my head, I knew what I must do.

I could not do this alone. Perhaps the answers I sought were in the things we found. But I did not understand white men's ways enough —so the answers eluded me. I needed a white man to think with me, to put together what we knew, to figure out who did this thing. I needed

someone strong to capture the killer once we found him. I needed someone I could trust, who was not himself the killer.

If no one fit *all* that, well, no one else being available, trustworthy or
not, then I needed Noah Taylor.

UNCERTAIN ALLIES

SHAWNASH WENT TO find Noah. He had not yet gone to the station.

"What did you say to that man?" Shawnash asked. "He looks like a dog that has been in a fight and is tending his wounds."

I shrugged. "He should look that way, Shawnash. If he had helped perhaps the snake would not have bitten Poji."

Noah approached me apprehensively, and I thought his limp was more noticeable. He swung his body as if one hip did not move. One leg appeared to be shorter than the other. I wondered if this affected his ability to swim and if I had misjudged his actions on the river.

I was not ready to think kindly, and I greeted him with "humph," and a sneer. But I made a sign that he should walk with me.

He limped along by my side. I saw him clenching his jaw. He said nothing, probably fearing that anything he said would start another outburst, but wondering why I sent for him. He moved quickly, and I thought his deformity did not seem to slow him at all.

I asked, "How do you come to walk this way?"

He turned to me and blinked, then turned his head away. "Not all canoes are light like the ones we use. Some are made from trunks of large trees and are very heavy. As a child, I was playing where I shouldn't have been, and one of these fell on me. I almost died. When I recovered one leg never grew right."

We were well away from the village, approaching the top of the hill where I had left M'ewé. I had a sudden picture in my mind of her bounding out to greet me and how Noah might react, and I giggled. He looked at me oddly. Giggling was the last thing he expected me to do.

I took in a deep breath and let it out slowly. "I am going to pretend I am not angry, because if we are going to solve this killing of your brother we must work together. Neither of us can do it alone."

He walked along, not saying yes or no or anything at all. I decided that meant yes.

"Nagmo has been taken away. We already talked to everyone at the station and everyone at Fort Dearborn, and we went everywhere Simon went. So there does not seem to be anyone else to talk to or anywhere else to go."

He continued to walk in silence. I did not look at his face, but I felt that some tension went out of his body. We had been walking fast, but we relaxed our pace then, our moccasin-covered feet making only light crunching sounds in unison on the lightly frozen ground as Noah adjusted his awkward stride to my short one.

He finally broke his silence. "Unless the murderer is someone we don't know."

"The answers may not be in what we have learned, but we *do not know* what we do not know, so we can only start with what we *do* know. We must look at what we know in every possible way. We must throw out every fact that does not bear on the killing and consider every suspect. If we prove any person did not do it, then we gain knowledge because there are less people who could be at fault. We have a chance to find answers. What other way is there?"

He turned to me and looked into my face. "I think you are better at this than I am, Wawetseka," he said. "Let's get started and you lead the way."

Shawnash's wigwam was more comfortable and less crowded than my lodging, which was packed with kin. We sat on mats, warm by her fire, talking quietly so as not to disturb Poji who slept opposite us. Shawnash joined us and that was comforting to me, not just for her friendship but so I did not have to be alone with Noah.

I began. "We must say if every fact is certain or is only our reasoning and tell what it has to do with the murder. We may discover answers if we do this together."

I wished that I could write down what we said, as I used to do when I lived with Alain, but we did not have writing tools.

"The man who was killed was my brother, Simon," Noah began.

"This is true, because we found his clothes and his canoe. The man tied in the tree wore no clothes and his canoe was missing."

"Yes," Noah went on, "and he was tied with vines from the same place we found Simon's canoe, the same place a tree was uprooted from the river."

"So we know that someone killed your brother near that place, probably by hitting him in the back of his head, and then hid his canoe and tied him to the tree roots to hide his body. The tree was uprooted by floodwaters and swept downstream and washed up here."

Noah nodded, "Didn't we guess that?" He seemed unimpressed.

"It is no longer a guess. It has become a fact. And—" I said, and I jabbed a finger in his direction to emphasize that even if he did not think that was important I did, "we know *when* it was done, because we know when he left Fort Dearborn and how long it took to get to the river. Knowing when and where he was killed we can put him and the killer in the same place at the same time. Fewer people could have killed him."

"It doesn't eliminate any of the people we suspect," he said, and crossed his arms over his chest.

Shawnash was taking it all in, and she asked, "You suspect people? Who are they?"

I was still thinking over Noah's comment. "Villeaux never came to the fort. He said he went to the Sag village, not to the fort. We have no reason to say he was not telling the truth, but we can send a runner to the Sag village to see if he was there when the killing happened."

"Providing we can get through before the storm starts… Villeaux is unlikely, don't you think?"

"I like Villeaux," Shawnash cut in. "I always liked him, and his daughter too."

I smiled. "That does it," I said. "Villeaux is not the killer. Shawnash has a good sense for such things." I thought I would get her alone later and ask her feelings about Noah.

"So we are down to five suspects," said Noah.

"Penney did not come to the fort either," I said. "He did not explain where he went or why, which is suspicious, but he did not know Simon —unless they crossed paths." I held up a finger to count each person I named. "Leckey and Reddick, who saw Simon at the fort, both acting angry, Pascal and Findel, who we know are up to no good."

I explained to Shawnash that we found out Findel and Pascal were thieves.

"We have a rusty button and a cat's-eye ring," Noah said. "If we knew the button belonged to one of these men, and how the ring got in Nag-mo's pouch, it could lead to my brother's killer."

"We must to go back to the station and ask more questions," I said, standing up.

NELL

WE WASTED NO time, as there was none to waste. The morning was bitter cold, with ice forming at the riverbanks and snow in the air but not yet on the ground. We did not want to risk the river freezing over, so we got quickly into Noah's canoe.

We went to the trade post first, where we found Leckey moving goods from the open porch into the storeroom to prevent damage from the approaching storm. His manner was friendly, but his eyes kept straying. It was clear he was impatient to answer our questions and get back to work.

When we asked again about the ring, he said, "The ring came out of Nagmo's pouch. We were both there when it happened. Wawetseka—you saw it too." His irritated tone gave the impression he had no doubt and we were disturbing his work only to ask questions he had already answered.

I showed him the button and asked if he had ever seen it. "It's a button, of course, but I have not seen this one," he said. "It looks like someone made it from a piece of iron, maybe Penney. But I have not seen buttons like this on his clothes. If he made it, perhaps he gave it to someone or maybe he had nothing to do with it at all. You should ask him. He may know where it came from or whose it is. But it's of little value, so I wouldn't be too concerned about returning it," he went on, mistaking the reason for my question.

I looked at Noah, who nodded. The connection to Penney made sense.

"Why are Findel and Pascal still here? Shouldn't they have finished their business by now and been on their way, especially with bad weather setting in? I wouldn't have thought they would stay so long." Noah took up the questioning.

"I don't know either, but I think they're readying themselves to set out now. Although it *is* odd they would stay when the weather is good and travel when it's bad. But it's not my business."

"They are traveling together? I thought they didn't know each other." Noah then told him what we found out about the two men at the fort. Leckey was stunned.

He went into his office in a rush and came running out a moment later, carrying a rifle. He entered one of the visitor's rooms, and I heard him say angrily, "You two aren't going anywhere until you show me what you're taking!"

"Hold on, Leckey!" It was Findel's voice I heard. "Put that thing down! What's got into you?"

"I know who you are! I'm not letting you out of this room until you return what you stole!"

"Whatever it is you think you know..."

Pascal rushed out of his room and entered Findel's. "Oh for Christ's sake! Calm down you two. Let him look, Findel. We have little enough of value, and we're soon away from here."

I didn't want to be around when Findel and Pascal found out Leckey got his information from us. I grabbed Noah's arm and pulled him around the building, and we went through the garden behind it. Our attention was caught by a yowling sound, and a large, brownish-silver animal walked in our direction. I recognized Cat. Noah gave a little laugh and said, "Here, kitty, kitty." Noah approached the cat and ran his hand over it. It arched its back in obvious pleasure and then curled around his legs, rubbing against them.

"What is that word you said, 'kitty'?" I asked.

"Ah, that's right, you do not have cats here. They are quite popular back east, where they keep homes and barns free of mice. Young cats are called 'kittens,' and the way you call any cat is how I just did—'kitty,' an affectionate term for cat."

I ran that over in my mind. I could not figure out why what he said seemed familiar—and then suddenly I knew.

"Keet aye, preet aye—kitty," I said.

"What?" Noah said.

"That is what Nagmo-Nell was saying. She was talking about her cat. Let us talk to Lilly before we talk to Penney." I hurried around the building toward Lilly's rooms.

"What for?" Noah asked, trailing after me. "Who's Nagmo-Nell? What if she *was* singing about her cat? How does that help us? We don't have time for this now!"

I remembered that Noah knew nothing of Nell and her songs, but I did not want to stop to explain. "Please," I said. "I have a feeling." It was suddenly urgent that I talk to Lilly Leckey.

Noah swayed his head from side to side and rolled his eyes. I suspected he was thinking that Indian women get notions just like white women do. But I was glad he was there to speak English and make it easier to talk to Lilly.

Lilly looked at me blankly when I had Noah tell her about Nell's words and my interpretation. "Singing about Cat? Why would Nell sing about Cat? She has lived with Cat for years, and she never sang about her before. Fond as we are of Cat, those eyes of hers—no, I would never call them pretty—sly or sneaky maybe. It is more likely Nell saw something or heard something that has nothing to do with Cat. Did she say anything else?"

What Lilly said explained *preet aye*, "pretty," too, and she spoke of Cat's *eyes*. Poji had not told me the English tongue had more meanings than just "yes" for the sound "aye." We had only been entertained by Nell's singing, never thinking there was anything important about the words she sang.

"Another day, Nell sang, '*Aye mah nay, aye aye mah nay, preet mah nay, aye aye, preet aye,*'" I said. I clearly remembered the words from the pleasant rhythm and Nell's sweet voice that I could still hear in my head.

The wind increased in strength. As we talked it blew swirls of snow over the packed earth that surrounded that end of the building, across the porch, and under a roof near the door to Lilly's rooms. Lilly wiped her hands on her apron and hugged a thick shawl more closely around her shoulders.

"I can tell you that one," she laughed. "*Mah nay* would be 'money,' what she calls Penney. You know, money—coins—one called a penny?

She gets it confused, calls it all money. And since Penney is named like a coin, she calls him money too. I do not know why she would think he has pretty eyes. She likes Penney a good deal, perhaps too much—whenever I go looking for her she is following him around. But the Cat business, no, I do not think you have that right." She shook her head.

We left Lilly and headed back into the wind and blowing snow. I asked, "That stone in the ring? Did you not call it a cat's-eye?"

Noah stopped, drawing his eyebrows together. "What if I did? She was singing "kitty," and a "pretty eye." What does the stone have to do with that?"

I put a finger to my eye. "She calls Cat "kitty," but if someone told her the ring was called a cat's-eye, she would say "kitty," and the stone was pretty, so "kitty," and "pretty" and "eye," that is what she was singing. She meant the ring!"

I could see the idea forming in his mind, and I went on. "And *mah nay* means she associates the cat's-eye, the pretty stone, with Penney! She liked him—Lilly said she followed him around. Maybe she saw the ring and knew it was his."

"Let's go see Penney!"

"Not yet. Let us see Findel and Pascal, before we leave the station—before they leave."

As we approached, we heard Findel's loud indignant voice through his partially open door. He was speaking in French. "Bastard! What other crap is going to happen before we get out of this cussed place. We should have left yesterday instead of waiting on that whoremonger. Fat lot of good that did us, only gave him the opportunity."

Pascal appeared in the doorway and then turned back to Findel. He made a sign of the cross in a mocking way and put his hands together as if in prayer. "Thank the good Lord we had nothing of Leckey's."

Findel looked up and saw us. "And you two, revealing our identities to Leckey. Thanks to you, now we cannot operate anywhere from Fort Dearborn to Fort Clark. Haven't you done enough? What do you want here?" He glared at Noah and moved a hand toward his knife sheath.

Noah said in a firm but quiet voice, "Calm down, Findel. Your identities were known at Fort Dearborn, and word had spread already. We did nothing—unless your plan was to rob Leckey."

Pascal said, "Too late for that. That other prick, Penney, beat us to it."

Noah's eyebrows came together. "Penney? Penney stole from Leckey? Is that where Leckey is—gone after Penney?"

My eyes turned in the direction of Penney's cabin, although it could not be seen from inside the station. I worried that we would not be able to talk to Penney if Leckey was confronting him about stealing.

"Huh!" Findel exclaimed with disgust. "Tarnation! Luck be with him on that. Seems Penney found where Leckey kept his cash and disappeared in the night—not only with Leckey's valuables but with ours, too. We think he had that simple woman who's so stuck on him sneak in here—no one would suspect her. But we'll catch him if we have to call up our whole band!"

I paid little attention to his words after he said Penney disappeared.

"Please," I said. "We must talk to Penney. If the man is gone, then you must tell us what *you* know. Please." It is not our custom to beg, but I would go to any lengths to find out what happened.

Findel looked about to push past, but he stopped and looked at me. As he considered my plea, it was clear he was calculating whether it would be to his benefit to tell us what he knew. A kind heart I never expected. It would not be pity but anger and revenge that motivated the man. If he could not punish Penney himself, he would take satisfaction in turning the Indian nation and American authorities against him.

Findel snorted, shook his head, and then turned to Pascal and made an arm gesture toward the door. "Pascal," he said, "finish bundling up our possessions—or I should say whatever of value that lick-spittle arse left us. We'll leave as soon as I finish with these two meddlers."

Findel went to a platform heaped with bedding and sat, leaving Noah and me to stand awkwardly. "What are your questions?" he said, his arms crossed over his chest.

I took out the button and asked if he had seen it. "Perhaps...perhaps not." He frowned impatiently. "It's a rough thing, such as a blacksmith might make, not fine goods from the east. Why are you bothering me about this thing?"

I told him I found it in an abandoned canoe along the river and thought it might belong to someone here.

"So what? It's not worth anything."

Noah explained who we were and that we were trying to save Nagmo. We thought the button might lead to the real killer.

Findel laughed heartily, stood up, and paced the room, stopping now and then to emit a fresh roar at the ceiling. Finally he said, "Well, you have, at last, come to the right place to find your story. And you have come at the right time, too. I was sworn to keep a secret, and until this morning would have done so. But now with Penney's treachery I don't give a fart. In fact, maybe you two can be useful. Tell me what you know." He sat back down on the bedding.

Noah told Findel of our trip to Fort Dearborn, what we found on the river, how we thought Simon encountered someone on his way to Fort Dearborn and that that person killed Simon on his return trip—although we had no idea why.

I told him I thought the ring found in Nagmo's pouch belonged to Penney.

He looked as us with a crooked grin. "You are right in your thinking and right also that I can tell you the rest of the story. But why should I do that? What is in it for me?"

I had been watching the man and I thought I had his measure. I had met men like him before, men who love to brag and tell stories, who only need a little poke to get them started. I thought I knew what would work and took a chance.

I challenged him with my eyes. "This man tricked you and made you very angry. You will want to expose him, especially to someone who can bring him harm. If Penney caused Nagmo's arrest, you have our promise we will find Penney and bring him harm. So you will have made sure of revenge even if you do not do it yourself."

Findel and Noah both looked at me with surprise. Findel caught Noah's eye and pointed a finger at me. "Well, now," he said, "the Indian woman has me figured!" He made a lavish gesture of respect in my direction, then threw his head back and laughed.

"Make yourselves comfortable. This will take a while." He leaned back and crossed his legs.

I lowered myself and sat cross-legged on the floor. Noah looked around, unsure of what to do. I indicated the only chair in the room, and with relief he sat in it.

"Let's begin with the ring," Findel said. "The ring *does* belong to Penney. He paid me to put it in Nagmo's pouch."

"But…I was near Nagmo the whole time he was with the white men and saw nothing. It was not possible," I argued.

He laughed once again, quite amused by us, it seemed. "You know who I am," he said. "I'm quite good at my profession. Sleight of hand is nothing to me. I would be ashamed if you had detected how I did it."

I looked at Noah, who returned my look and shrugged his shoulders. If Penney arranged for Nagmo to appear guilty, no one would look further for the killer.

"You did this for money?" I said, anger in my voice.

He leaned forward and made a gesture, his hands out, palms up, and eyebrows raised. "I am what I am."

I was too angry to speak. If it were not for this man, Nagmo would be free! Noah continued questioning Findel.

"Then Penney hired you to help him hide the fact that he killed Simon and put the blame on Nagmo?" said Noah.

"Yes."

"Did he tell you why he killed him?" Noah asked.

"Simon recognized him, and Penney thought Simon was going to expose him."

"Expose him for what?" I asked, regaining my voice.

"Recognized him as who?" asked Noah at the same time.

"For killing a man in Harrisburg, Pennsylvania," Findel said.

Noah jumped up and began moving randomly about. "Simon and I lived near there before coming west!" He stopped as if having a sudden thought. "I never met this man called Penney, not in Harrisburg, and not here. He was away the first time I was here and gone again now. I never had a chance to recognize him."

"Likely he had a different name back east. Before Penney came to the territory, he was engaged to be married. But his business fell off, and he started drinking and turned mean. He even knocked down his future bride. She asked the pastor of her church for advice, and Penney thought she committed adultery with the man. He flew into a rage and struck down the minister with a rock, in front of witnesses. Penney had to flee, as he would have been hung for the murder of a man of the cloth."

"How do you know this?" Noah asked.

"When Simon arrived at Fort Dearborn, he told me of Penney's former identity. He feared Penney, but he felt a responsibility to expose him. As far as Simon knew, I was the respected businessman from back east I claimed to be, and he thought I would help him figure out what to do. He was reluctant to involve the military for some reason."

Perhaps Simon, working with important people in Illinois, did not want to involve them in a murder and so avoided the military. Or perhaps, having spent most of his life in the east, he was unsure about how things were done on the frontier and turned for advice to the only man from the east who was available.

"And how did you advise him?" I asked.

"I told him to leave the man be. He led a decent life and was no longer a danger to anyone. I had no idea if this was true, of course, but it's my nature to side with the criminal, as I would be two-faced otherwise." He winked.

Noah continued pacing, his arms behind his back. "So Simon left to return to Fort Clark, his message delivered. But Penney thought he was going to be exposed, so he waited for Simon and ambushed and killed him. He hid the body and the canoe and came back as if nothing had happened."

"Yes. Until the body washed up here. I would have liked to see Penney's face when he got that little surprise!" Findel grinned.

"And then he had to be sure there was no search for the killer, so he hired you to help him make it look like an Indian did it," Noah said.

"Yes."

"You did it for money." I said again, still amazed at that reason.

"That, and when I got here he recognized me from past travels and threatened to expose me unless I went along."

The rest seemed clear now. When we brought Poji back yesterday, I had spoken about our trip freely to the American man who brought us home. He must have told our story at the station, and Penney thought he would be found out. Having run once, he had to run again, lose himself, and take on yet another identity. During the night, using his influence over Nell, he stole whatever valuables he could from Findel, Pascal, and Leckey and was gone this morning.

I stood, folded my arms across my chest, and asked Findel, "Will you try to get your valuables back?"

"Damn right, and dang it all to hell if he gets away this time!" said Findel. "We know the direction he went. When we found our money pouches missing, we went to his cabin and found his helper sitting with his head in his hands, so upset he could hardly get a word out, jerking his head like a fish on a line. Finally he managed to tell us he saw Penney load his canoe and paddle upstream—must be heading to Fort Dearborn or north to Wisconsin. We'll catch him." A thoughtful look appeared on his face, and he rubbed his chin. "You made a promise in exchange for what I know. You will join us."

Noah started to agree, but I said quickly, "You must start without us, as you are ready to leave. We have some business to attend to, but we will catch up."

Noah opened his mouth to object, but I gave him a hard look and he closed it, with a puzzled look on his face.

GOING OUR OWN WAY

"Why did you say that?" Noah demanded as we crossed back over the river. "We want to catch Penney! Wouldn't we be better off in a group than alone? They're sure to be better at this than we are!"

"I do not think that is so," I said. My voice was firm, and I could feel that stubborn look on my face. Nagmo said he always let me have my way when he saw that look on my face.

"Why the hell not?" Noah stroked angrily through the water against the cold wind. From the tenseness in his body and face I thought he would have stamped his foot if he were on land and only stopped himself from doing so now for fear of destroying the canoe.

"Penney is cunning. Why would he head upriver, against the current in stormy weather—to go where? Back to Fort Dearborn and risk being identified again? Farther upriver to Wisconsin, a man battling the current and foul weather alone? What is there for him in Wisconsin? Only more places like here and Fort Dearborn, where he might be discovered or where he is already known. He will want to avoid such places."

"But Wawetseka, Emmett saw him! He was going upriver! We *know* that's the way he went," Noah insisted.

We hit a thin layer of ice when we reached the bank. Noah made as if to stomp away, but I grabbed his arm. "It is a false trail," I said, glaring at him.

I watched his eyes look up and down the river. He removed his hat, ran a hand through his hair, and then set the hat back on his head again. In a calmer manner, he reached for my arm and pulled me with him as he walked slowly toward our village. "Explain."

I took a deep breath before I spoke. "Penney went north only to throw off anyone following him. He wants us to *think* he went upriver. That is where the pirates will chase him, and they will look for signs he landed on the south bank. But Penney knows people will look for him on the river. And the storm will soon put an end to river travel, so he will travel on land instead. He went upriver to mislead, and he will leave his canoe on the north bank, as he did when he hid Simon's body. Then he will travel by land in the opposite direction."

"Where would he be going if that's his plan? What's for him in that direction?" Noah was clearly not convinced.

"He would want to avoid places where people from the east come. To escape and hide, he would go downriver. He will come to the Fox River and could take it to Wisconsin, but I do not think he will do that either, as there are settlements of people from the east in Wisconsin, too." Noah seemed to be considering what I said.

"I think he will head for the lead mines at Galena, where people are from the south and the west, not from the east. He has been there already, his skills will be needed there, and he can make a living." Noah looked at the ground as he walked and said nothing.

"He will start his trip heading south and will stay ahead of freezing water. He will buy or steal a canoe when he passes one of our villages, and I think he will follow the rivers to the Mississippi and up the Mississippi to Galena. If the weather does not permit canoe travel, he will stay on land. Along the way he will meet native people and Frenchmen, who do not care who he was in the east. That is the way he will go."

We struggled uphill into cold wind and blowing snow—the snow still fine with only traces clinging to the crotches of tree branches. After a long silence Noah asked, "What do you think we should do then?"

"Penney would not go far upstream. He would double back on foot and pass behind our village, then follow the river toward Fort Clark. We should go a short distance upriver and search for signs of landing on the north bank to pick up his trail."

After a while Noah said, "Despite what he said, maybe Findel is not to be believed. I heard him and Pascal arguing, something about whether Penney would rob that too. They were swinging their arms, Pascal pointing downstream and Findel pointing upstream."

"You see," I said. "They are not sure which way Penney was heading either, but they decided to go upstream."

Noah made no further objections. "What if we do not find signs of landing on the north bank?"

"It will *not* be easy, as Penney will try to hide such signs. He has a half-day start, so we have time to follow only one trail. Let the pirates look for him upstream on the river and south bank while we look closer on land, on the north bank. If we do not see signs to show where Penney stopped, we must leave our canoe and retrace the river on foot."

Noah rubbed his chin. "And if we catch Penney, then what do we do?"

"I do not know," I said, dropping my eyes. "But we will figure something out. We must bind him, take him to Fort Clark, and tell our story, so they will put Penney in their jail instead of Nagmo."

"He is a big man and strong, Wawetseka," Noah said. "Perhaps we need help."

No man from our village could be spared to accompany us. The early storm had found our village unprepared either to move to winter grounds or to spend the winter here. Every man was needed, and we could not say how long we would be gone. It was just as well, as it was my feeling that white men would be more sympathetic to the brother of the murdered man and an Indian mother than they would be to a group of braves.

The men helped us gather what was needed for travel in bad weather. We loaded Noah's canoe with blankets and warm robes of buffalo hide. I put on my warmest dress, the long one that covered my arms, and I tied on leggings and pulled on winter moccasins. We took knives, flints, a tomahawk, strong binding materials, and Noah's rifle. We tied dried meat, fruit, beans, and nuts in large pouches, enough for a week. We would hunt if our food ran out.

I asked Noah about his rifle, which was different from those our men used. He explained that he got it from a soldier during the last war. The soldier thought the accuracy of the new rifle would be an advantage, but he did not realize how difficult it would be to reload nor did he think about the need for a bayonet, which the weapon did not have. It was a poor war weapon but a better hunting weapon than we had.

We stopped at the station to see if anyone there would go with us.

Only Leckey, Reddick, and Villeaux remained, and they could not leave responsibilities or family at such a time. Emmett, who might have joined us, left with the pirates in hope of transport to Fort Dearborn. I thought that too was just as well. Emmett was a slow and weak sort, more likely to hold us back than be of much help.

Leckey wished he could go to recover his belongings. In his place, he insisted we take Dog with us, as Dog would be useful, he said, if we needed transport or something retrieved from the river or if we needed to run down Penney. Noah wondered how we would get the huge animal in our canoe and how we would feed it. Leckey laughed and assured us that Dog would follow our canoe on land, would gladly jump into the water to cross the river, and required little food, which he would scavenge himself.

So the three of us set out near midday. As promised, Dog jumped in the icy river and swam beside us, shaking himself when he reached the north bank, then loping along on land, great pink tongue hanging from his massive mouth, as we labored upstream. We hoped it was not already too late to catch Penney.

Our river changed constantly, as did the land on both sides of it. This was our biggest challenge but also the reason for our success. First we passed shallow marshland that forced us to stay in the mainstream, and we lost sight of Dog. We would find no signs if Penney landed there, but Penney would not have struggled with his heavily laden canoe through swamps in the bitter cold, especially at night. So we passed the swamps and looked for a better place to land, although we still watched for any sign he had taken this harder route.

I asked Noah to pull into the first area of dry land on the far side of the swamp, reasoning that Penney would be anxious to land at the first suitable place. I thought he would carefully hide his landing here rather than waste time looking for a better spot farther upriver. Even if Penney was a skilled river traveler, he had likely been more concerned with business matters and not so familiar with the lesser-traveled side of the river and swamps.

Before long, Dog came from the trees to join us, as Leckey had said he would. He shook his big head, flinging gobs of drool in all directions, and appeared happy, standing nearby and watching every move we made.

Farther up the river, the bank was densely covered with trees growing into the water, impassable to a man carrying a canoe. Yet another large swamp could be seen beyond. The landing we were on was a thin strip of only fifty yards of bank, but even this small area was hard to explore closely. A sense of urgency drove us, as we had to find evidence of Penney's trail before snow hid any traces he might have left. Noah tied Dog to a tree to prevent the animal's footprints from damaging any signs while we searched.

Noah saw it first, and at his excited call I hurried to the spot—a poorly defined depression the size of a man's foot in the earth and, adjacent to it, faint regular white streaks in the partly frozen mud. Gazing at the mark, I felt a thrill. I realized we were looking at brush marks where Penney had used a branch to rub out his prints. Working in poor, if any, light, it might not have occurred to him that when the ground hardened the marks would be highlighted by a dusting of fine snow. I grinned at Noah, who shrugged his shoulders, but I could see he was biting the insides of his cheeks so I would not see his smile. I had proved to be right!

To make sure it was Penney's trail we followed we had to find the canoe and discover the way he went. Where a thin deer track penetrated a densely forested area, we found occasional brushings of snow and followed them into the trees. At last we found a canoe, just as Penney had hidden Simon's—lying behind the trunk of a fallen tree, covered with leaves, at the edge of a small clearing that was hardly bigger than our longhouse.

The grasses in the clearing were well matted, as if much activity had taken place there. At the edge were the cut stumps of two small trees, and nearby trimmed branches littered the ground. I did not need to explain this to Noah.

"He cut two poles and made a travois," he said. "With many belongings, that would be the best way to transport them on foot—he had more than he could carry. He would have kept his best tools, and tools are heavy. He's probably wearing his clothing in layers for warmth, but buffalo robes would be burdensome. And we don't know what valuables he stole and how heavy they are. A man alone—that would be the thing to do."

I grinned. "This is good for us. He probably got here at first light—this would be hard in the dark. That puts him less than a half day ahead of us. This took some time to do, so we are closer to him. He will hide his trail at first, but once he thinks the trail well hidden he will stop covering it to travel faster. The marks of the poles bearing such weight will be easy to follow. And he will need to rest, as he would have had little if any rest during the night."

"Yes, but what direction did he go from here?" Noah asked, turning around the clearing and shaking his head, indicating he saw no answer to his question.

Leaving Noah to examine the ground, I studied the trees circling the clearing, which were less dense here, meaning Penney could drag his travois in any direction through them and then cover the beginning of his trail. I came to a decision and pointed straight north. "There," I said.

Although faint, slight differences could be seen in one place compared to the rest of the trees around the clearing. The layer of snow was thinner on the lower branches with less snow in the crotches. A few branches were broken, the bright color of their insides a contrast to the bark of those that were undisturbed. Noah at first could not see what I pointed out, but he walked to the place and found signs of snow knocked from branches as someone pushed through that way.

"He is going directly *away* from the river, not following it," he observed.

"He will double back before long," I said. There was sureness and pride in my voice. Being proven right in predicting Penney's moves this far made me feel more confident. Noah probably thought it would now be even harder to argue with me.

"We should get moving," Noah said. "The snow may get heavier. Before that happens, we want to pick up the trail he leaves when he stops trying to hide his way."

"Yes. But would it not be better for us to quickly make a travois here too—where everything we need is at hand? Dog can pull it, and we can travel faster than Penney with his burdens if we are unburdened ourselves."

Noah nodded. "Let's get started."

PURSUIT

BUILDING OUR TRAVOIS turned out to be short work. Leckey had given us the harness and saddle and all the cushions, straps, and bindings we would need.

Noah cut two strong saplings and removed the branches, making two drag poles eight feet long. He notched the leading ends so they would fit together and hold firm when tied, and he trimmed the far ends so they would drag smoothly. He carved smaller notches along the length of the poles and laid thin branches into them, tying them in place with wet sinew that would shrink and tighten as it dried. When finished, we had a ladderlike frame of crossed sticks between the poles, forming a platform on which to tie our load. We placed the poles close to allow passage on narrow trails. This method was used by us for many years because materials were easy to find and a travois easy to build.

While Noah did this, I sorted ties, straps, sinew, and rawhide, and I attached the saddle and harness to Dog. He stood patiently, his long ears pitched forward, tongue hanging, exhibiting as much excitement as the gentle beast could muster. Leckey told us Dog could easily pull a load of a hundred pounds. Our supplies were less than that. "This will not be a burden for you, will it?" I said to him, holding his massive head and looking into his gentle eyes as he drooled onto my foot. "You enjoy testing your strength? Well, this time your load will be light, but better you have the burden than us." Over the saddle I tied a cushion of buffalo hide to protect Dog's shoulders where the poles crossed.

We carried our supplies from the landing, and Noah hid our canoe in a different place than Penney had left his. "If a man wants to steal a canoe, we shouldn't make it easy for him to take two instead of one," Noah said. I did not say that it was unlikely anyone would steal either canoe in such a remote place. I do not understand men's concern about such things.

Pleased with our efforts and the short time they had taken, we wrapped robes and blankets around our belongings, tied our bundle to the platform, and bound the travois to Dog's harness over the cushion. Dog turned his head to look at us, panting, as if smiling and anxious to be on the way.

Noah tucked his knife and tomahawk into his belt, from which also hung a small pouch with flints, powder, and bullets. He slipped his rifle strap over his shoulder and hung a pouch of water from his belt. I wore my knife and carried a pouch of dried fruit, nuts, and meat on my back. We would eat while we walked to make better time. I led the way, followed by Dog, and Noah at the rear to untangle the travois if it got caught in the brush.

As we walked, I imagined myself in Penney's place. How might his escape have differed from our pursuit? Penney must have been tired when he reached this forest. We knew he left the station in the middle of the night, and I figured he left the river near daybreak, the first chance he had enough light to find a landing place. Then he built a travois, loaded his belongings, hid his canoe, and obscured his trail.

Alone, it would have been hard and tiring work. He might have grown careless due to fatigue and needed to rest; but, fearing pursuit, he would have wanted to go some distance in the new direction, west, before he stopped. Traveling through wooded areas, pulling a heavy travois, he would have broken branches and left footprints, and he would have needed to conceal these. He would have hidden his trail where he started and when he changed direction, but then he would have relaxed his efforts to travel faster.

With that in mind, and because our lighter burden gave us an advantage, I thought it would not be hard to follow him once we were sure of his direction. The trail would be lost shortly before he turned, where he took efforts to throw off pursuers again. I also expected him to turn left, to follow the river toward Fort Clark, but inland from the river to avoid our villages and the heavier woods and swamps that filled the valley. I thought he would stay on higher ground, on top of the north bluff of the valley, where he would see the river but it was easier to travel through the thinner woods and occasional prairies that grew there. But first he had to climb uphill. Pulling a heavy load.

As I expected, after a short time Penney's trail became easy to follow. The cold ground was too stiff to show more than an infrequent moccasin print, but the ruts dug by his travois poles were clear and wide, proving the heavy weight he was dragging. Occasional branches were freshly broken, and streaks of bright white, yellow, or green stood out against gray or brown bark.

It occurred to me that Penney must have unusual strength to drag such a burden uphill and stay ahead of us. Perhaps fear of being hunted and captured increased his strength.

After about an hour's walk, during which the only sounds we heard were those of our footfalls crunching through crisp, dry leaves, his track disappeared, and we guessed he would have continued only a short time in the same direction from this place before turning left and heading west.

Instead, shortly after reaching level land at the top of the bluff, to the right—the east side of the trail—we noticed the leaves that covered the ground were not just dry, crisp leaves but were mixed with damp, musty ones and some earth, indicating they had been hurriedly placed there.

"He is not too tired to remain clearheaded," I observed. "He is laying another false trail and will soon double back to the west. If you follow where this leads, I will go on ahead and look for a place where he crossed back."

The false trail either took many twists and turns or Penney did not spend much time hiding it. Only a short distance farther I again found damp leaves mixed with dry ones and then a rut dusted with fine snow, a bright pointer revealing his direction. The marks went east and west. I called to Noah, and he quickly joined me. Once more, Penney soon stopped covering his trail. Then, after another half hour's walk, it disappeared again.

"He must have stopped nearby to rest," I said. "We should not look for a trail, but for a resting place."

Noah and I searched in opposite directions, and then we zigzagged back and forth on both sides of the trail, looking for a trampled area or some other sign of camp, but we found nothing. It seemed Penney had been careful.

It was then that Dog proved his usefulness. At first he seemed confused about which of us to follow, but when I looked back his large head was lifted with his muzzle pointing in the air. Then he lowered his head and marched in a straight line through the brush, pushing it aside as he forced his way through. The travois tangled on a branch; I freed him and he tugged in the same direction, so I followed, certain he knew something.

Dog led me to an area of disturbed leaves in a depression behind a large tree trunk. Although nearly invisible in the dim woods, once found, the disturbance was clear. I pictured Penney in my mind, dragging his travois behind the tree trunk, covering it with branches, laying down buried between the travois and trunk, and taking his rest.

I wondered how long he had rested and how far ahead he was now. I added together again the time it would take him to travel to the landing, make his travois, hide his trail, travel as far north as he wanted to go pulling the heavy travois uphill, lay a false trail, and get to this point. I figured he would have reached this place a couple of hours after daybreak before his energy gave out. There was no sign of a fire, so he would not have slept long in the cold—wrapped in a robe under the leaves—perhaps two or three hours. So he would have left here mid- to late morning, and it was now afternoon. We were gaining on him, and we were still fresh. We would stay on his trail until we lost the light or were prevented by weather.

I knew the woods here extended for many miles to the north on top of the bluff. At the bottom, in the valley, this side of the river was marshy most of the way to our village, where we had begun our chase. There was only one way Penney could go now—along the edge or top of the bluff. And it would not be easy for him to drag his possessions through miles of forest until he passed about a mile north of our village, where he would think he had escaped and fooled those who followed him.

He had no way to know we were gaining on him or that we moved faster than he did with our lighter load and Dog to pull it.

"If he is going as you think, Wawetseka, we waste too much time looking for his trail. We should just go quickly through the woods and look for where he came out," Noah said.

That did not seem a very good idea to me, and I wondered if Noah really wanted to catch Penney after all or instead wanted to assist his escape. "The trail is clear enough and following it slows us hardly at all. If Penney turns off of it for any reason, we would never know and would waste time looking at the far edges of the woods and lose him," I said.

Noah frowned but made no further argument, and we continued to follow Penney's trail.

After a time, Noah asked, "What does the man look like?"

"Look like? What do you mean...oh, that is right. You never met him, did you?"

"I have been thinking, if Simon recognized Penney I should too. Mostly we knew the same people. But Findel's story doesn't mean anything to me."

I described Penney, but Noah only shrugged his shoulders and shook his head.

We walked at a steady pace, as quickly as we could without tiring. My mood had changed many times since morning, excited when we made discoveries and our guesses proved to be right, anxious and fearful when I realized we had no plan for what we would do when we caught up to Penney. Now, as the sun descended, the light became dimmer and the shadows long and dark, and it was difficult to tell if the shadows were of trees or something else. We had only to follow along, my mind no longer busy with figuring our way. Unoccupied with immediate thoughts, I grew more anxious.

Nothing moved, and the silence was disturbing. I had a feeling of being in some other world, a dream place. I put one foot in front of the other as if I was being led instead of doing the leading. I wondered if Noah felt the same. Dog suddenly stopped, turned his head behind him, and stared at something I could not see, the hair of his neck and back raised, a low sound coming from his throat.

"He hears something behind us," Noah said.

We squinted in that direction but saw nothing and heard no sound. So Noah prodded Dog, who moved forward again, occasionally turning his head.

We heard it then, faint rustling sounds such as would be made by more than a single large animal. And at the disturbance Dog stopped and stared as before, and then we moved on again.

"Whatever is back there, it's big," Noah said. "Maybe a deer. I hope it's not a bear."

The man clearly did not know much about woodland animals. "Deer and bear do not stalk men. If we see them, it is only that we came on them suddenly."

"What, then?" he asked. I could not tell if he was scornful or embarrassed by his lack of knowledge.

"There are four animals who stalk people," I said. "Bobcats, wolves, and panthers."

"That's three animals."

"And men."

We went on and did not hear the sounds again, and Dog happily plodded along. "Let's hope it's bobcats," Noah said.

"Not likely," I replied.

"Because?"

"It sounded like more than one, did it not?"

"I think so."

"Bobcats hunt alone, not in groups."

"So do panthers," he said.

"Yes. So wolves, or men," I concluded. I rubbed Dog's thick neck without slowing down.

"What do you think we should do?"

"I do not think we should confront them, nor should we lie in wait for them. We do not know how many they are, and the woods do not give us any advantage."

"So?"

"So walk next to Dog, not behind him. Watch him—he will tell us if anything approaches. And have your rifle ready. There does not seem any other way to prepare."

Noah did as I suggested, but his eyes were wide, his face was drained of color, and his teeth were clamped tightly together. If I wanted a brave man to accompany me, I had made a poor choice. But then I already knew that when Poji fell in the river.

We heard no further sounds and all seemed peaceful, although the cold became bitter and a fierce wind blew into our faces. We thought whatever was behind us had gone another way.

In late afternoon we came to a large prairie. Away from the woods that had offered some protection, the wind across the prairie was even more chilling. We could see many miles to the west, and to the southwest there were glimpses of the river in the distance, most of which was still hidden by trees. I knew the river turned from southwest to almost directly south there. If Penney was following the river he would turn again. We figured that Penney was now only a few hours ahead of us.

We were miserable, exposed on the plain, despite the layers of clothing we wore. Only Dog did not seem to notice the weather and trotted along unbothered, with no trees or underbrush to catch the travois. The snowfall increased and began to cover the ground. The gray sky foretold that snow would be heavy during the night, so we were anxious to stay on Penney's trail and close the distance between us. We needed to start thinking about shelter.

Penney no longer made any attempt to hide his trail, probably thinking it would soon be snow-covered. We thought we were not far behind him since his trail, no longer thin ridges into which dustings of snow settled, was a depressed area a few feet wide where the grasses were crushed as Penney moved through them. It was more important than ever to stay on Penney's heels. If we lost the trail in piling and drifting snow, we could only guess where he was heading. We hurried on as dark closed in.

The river was seen dimly in the distance, directly south. A narrow, dark ribbon between expanses of white revealed the mainstream, still unfrozen, with black-looking clumps of trees blocking the view of the river here and there. I knew the area well. The banks of the river were firm here, but only a short way ahead was another swampy area, worse than the floodplains near our village.

Our women foraged here for many years, gathering rice that grew wild in the swamps; nuts that fell in the forests; berries and plums that grew in the shrublands beside the prairies; wheat, sage, herbs and sunflower seeds that were found in the grasslands. Even our houses were made from rushes cut at the edges of the swamps and woven into mats for the walls of our wigwams and our beds.

The river widened here, which the voyageurs called Goose Lake after the flocks of migratory geese we hunted in spring and fall. Beyond the thick woods on the north bank were marshes and impenetrable floodplains studded with islands, too shallow there to support a canoe. To traverse the floodplains the women had to get out of their canoes and pull them. Penney would avoid this area, as there was no passage on foot, even without a travois.

Beyond the floodplains, the river itself was filled with islands that were so close a man could leap from one to another, which made it difficult to find the main channels into which the river divided—channels that came together a few miles downstream to form dangerous rapids.

Penney's trail turned south, toward the river. If he did not know the area as I did, we might catch him near the riverbank, as he would soon find he could not follow the river due to the swamps, and he would turn back to cut through or circle the woods. If I was right, we could be close enough to catch him when he turned back.

Unless we were wrong.

Unless the storm prevented us.

Unless he hid on the large island.

A large island separated the main channels here, surrounded by a maze of smaller islands. The French called it Isle aux Cerfs or Petite Tasseau, the Americans Little Holding Place. Unlike the surrounding swamps, the island stayed dry in all seasons and was a refuge for men and wildlife. We sometimes buried things there instead of carrying them with us when we went to winter grounds. Voyageurs, too, hid valuables, baggage, or pelts—burying them or hanging them in the large trees that covered the place. It had springs of sweet water, which were desired as these were thought to bring cures. For these reasons, our people and the voyageurs had stopped there for many generations.

Penney must need to rest; he would not want to travel a second night in the dark. If he knew this place, he might leave the land trails to spend the night in the safety of the Petite Tasseau. If he could get to it. From what I could see, the river appeared to be low, but the swamps would still make access by land almost impossible.

SHELTER FROM THE STORM

DOG STOPPED, TURNED, and growled a number of times as Noah and I crossed the prairie. There no longer appeared to be any doubt something, or someone, was behind us again. Still we could see nothing. What, or who, could it be? I became anxious to find a place of safety, hoping in the process we would escape whatever pursued us, but I did not tell Noah of my fears. He was fearful enough.

With no alternatives, we plodded through accumulating snow, heading into the wind, pushing ourselves to reach a place we could shelter before full dark. The day had been impossibly long, our emotions jumping from triumph to determination, from urgency to uncertainty, from enthusiasm to exhaustion. We thought now less about our quarry and more about escape and rest. But the prairie offered no place to stop, and so we went on, encouraged by the untiring energy of Dog.

The day was almost over, and we could see only a short way in the failing light. A strong wind blew snow in swirls on the prairie, the tops of tall grasses flowing like waves with each gust, first in one direction and then another. A few times we thought we saw shadows or motion that could not be explained by wind. We suspected we, the trackers, were in turn being tracked.

"I wish I knew what is following us! I could circle back and look for prints in the snow," Noah offered. He did not look at me but squinted about nervously in the dim light. I thought his suggestion a weak offer—what he really meant was that he wanted *me* to look. I still had some doubts about Noah, and it occurred to me that he could be looking for a chance to leave me or to meet up with someone following us.

He could even be working with Penney and wanted me out of the way.

"I do not like that idea," I said. "It would separate us and make us more vulnerable to attack. We are too open here. We must get to the woods, make a camp, and rest. It will be easier to guard."

Noah did not reply, but he looked relieved.

Once again the sounds and Dog's alerts ceased, and I hoped whatever caused them had gone another way.

Penney's track turned before we reached another forest. In front of us was a break in the trees and a cluster of small ponds before the woods began again and ran along the river. Penney's track went straight south toward the river, past the ponds. We thought he was trying to shelter near the river, but before long we found tracks that doubled back and headed west between the ponds and the woods.

"You see what he did?" I asked, after I figured out Penney's movements. "He tried to reach the river and found it too swampy, so he turned back to circle the woods instead. He will soon try to reach the river again. This is why the track is now so clear. It must have taken him an hour to realize he could get no farther the way he was going. We must be close."

It was almost dark now, and if the snow continued there would be no moonlight. If we stopped, we would lose Penney's trail and be forced to depend on reason or luck when we started again. But even if we managed to catch him in the dark, we were too tired to struggle with the man—we had to rest. We entered the woods.

"We have flint, steel, and tinder, but where will we find dry wood and kindling in the snow?" Noah asked. "Will we have to suffer the cold without a fire?"

Potawatomi were not called "Keepers of the Fire" without reason. We would make a fire. Penney would never see smoke through such snow.

Shortly after entering the woods we came across a stand of pine trees—a fortunate find in a snowstorm. The large pine branches drooped almost to the ground, making a natural shelter behind them, which we could build up with piles of snow. The inner dead branches with their dry needles would start a fire, and the sap in every part of the tree contained pitch that would feed the flames. On the surrounding ground were pinecones, which, even damp, would smolder and keep the fire going.

As Noah tore off branches and laid out the fire, I unpacked our belongings and freed Dog from the travois. He immediately bounded off into the woods to explore and, probably, to relieve himself and hunt some small creatures to satisfy his appetite. He seemed attached to us now, and I felt confident he would return. I took out the small iron pot we had brought, filled it with snow, and added a few handfuls of dried meat and beans. After this simmered on the fire we would eat right from the pot. Our robes and blankets were placed on the ground near the fire.

Our camp made and the fire started, Noah grinned proudly. I let him think he had accomplished the tasks on his own. What good would it do to point out that without my direction he knew only how to strike the spark? But I admitted he had caught on quickly and performed the tasks efficiently.

While we waited for our food to warm, he spoke of a concern. "I used all our tinder, Wawetseka."

I took an impatient breath and turned away so he would not see my face as I rolled my eyes. "The trunk of the tree," I said. "The ground will not be frozen. Take your knife, or your tomahawk if the knife is not enough, and dig down through the dirt until you find it dry. Drag out the moss you will find there. Take some of your dry branches and shave a little wood from them. Then rub the moss and shavings together quickly between your hands until they are dry. Replace the tinder from your pouch with this."

Dog came romping back, drawn, perhaps, by the smells of our meal, and he shook snow from his thick fur. He must have eaten during his absence, because, although he followed our food with his eyes, he lay with his head on his paws and made no move toward it. When we were finished, I let him lick the pot and then scrubbed it clean with handfuls of snow. Eventually Dog curled himself against me and fell asleep, twitching now and then as dogs do.

We were not sure we had been followed into the forest and the sounds of pursuit seemed to have been left behind on the prairie, but our situation called for caution. There was little chance that Penney knew we were following him or where we were, but it was not *impossible* Penney could try to kill us while we slept. Our spot was secluded, but we could not see outside of it either, so an intruder would be upon us before we knew. It was best to be armed and alert. We decided to sleep in shifts of a few hours, taking turns staying awake and holding Noah's rifle.

Noah took the first shift, wrapped with a blanket and buffalo robe. I took the other blanket and robe and curled around Dog for warmth. His thick fur was bad smelling, as if he had been rubbing against some dead thing, but the warmth was welcome. I soon fell asleep.

I was startled awake by a rifle shot and a shout, violent thrashing, yelps and snarls, and the realization that Dog was no longer at my side. The glowing embers of the dying fire revealed a wolf lying motionless and bleeding on the ground. Noah was striking a second wolf with his rifle butt, trying to dislodge the fangs that were dug into his leg. Dog was facing a third wolf, both animals circling each other and preparing to engage. Noah's wolf let loose for a moment, and Noah turned as if to flee. "No!" I called. "Do not run! Face the wolf! Wolves *chase* prey!"

I drew my knife, not knowing what else to do. But before I could move still another wolf, bigger than the others, rushed into our camp. Instead of setting upon Noah, Dog, or me it leaped at the wolf Noah had beaten off and, snarling, bit at its neck, flanks, and rear. M'ewé!

The attacking wolf backed away when M'ewé confronted it, and through a gap in the branches I saw it run off a distance, turn back, and stand its ground. The remaining wolf also retreated, and Dog turned on M'ewé, who leaped to avoid his charge. I shouted for Dog to stop, but I had to wrap my arms around his neck to keep him from following as M'ewé ran off with the two fleeing wolves.

With Dog restrained, I looked around our shelter. One dead wolf and Noah, moaning on the ground near the fire, where he had dragged himself. Blood was seeping through one of his leggings, a lot of blood, and below the knee that leg hung at an unnatural angle.

I was on my own now, with the additional burden of Noah to care for.

A WOMAN ALONE

WHAT WAS I to do? I was on my own. I had always had the support of my tribe—I had never faced an emergency alone and did not know if I could. Somehow I must figure this out, as there was no one else to do so.

I could not sit here feeling bad for myself. I could not give up, and I could not give in to panic. Noah was thrashing about in pain. It was up to me to help him.

I forced my mind to review my situation, and in the process I became calmer. I had been making decisions since Nagmo was arrested, so what was different now? Everything, I admitted. I had not realized how much I depended on Noah, not only for strength but also for company. And when I knew something Noah did not, I felt surer of myself.

So it was a family of wolves that followed us, not Penney or any other man. The dead wolf was likely M'ewé's mate, the two other wolves her almost-grown pups, which was why she was able to drive them away. She protected me and would lead them to some other prey—I no longer feared an outside threat. What I feared was deciding what I could do for Noah. What I hated was being forced to give up my pursuit of Penney and what that meant to Nagmo.

Noah struggled to sit up, grimacing in pain with every move.

"Noah, let me see what damage has been done," I said, squatting down beside him to examine his leg. I did not touch it—any pressure or movement would cause him agony. One legging was ripped and covered in blood, exposing torn flesh and bite wounds. His lower leg bent away from his body—it was badly broken.

His eyes were wide and he breathed rapidly. "It's bad, isn't it?" he said.

"We will figure out what to do," I said, expressing a confidence I did not feel.

"It's not just the bite, is it? The leg broke when I fell?"

I could not lie to him. He must have fallen across a rock after the wolf let loose of his leg. "It is broken," I said.

He closed his eyes and gritted his teeth. "It's my good leg, Wawetseka. Even if it heals I will have no good leg now."

I felt very bad for him. "Then we will make it heal," I said.

"How?"

"I will do what I can and then go for help."

I moved away, pretending I was busy and knew what to do, allowing him to compose himself while I worked things out. There was a foot of snow on the ground, and the storm was getting stronger. Things would get worse, but there was not much I could do in the dark.

We had to get through the night, so I set about to stop Noah's bleeding, lessen his pain, and keep him warm. I melted some snow with which to clean his bites, and, using my knife, I cut strips from a blanket, wrapped the wounds tightly, and supported his injured limb. In daylight I would check his wounds again and deal with his broken leg—there was little else I could do by firelight in a fierce snowstorm. Noah, Dog, and I huddled together, covered with buffalo robes.

Not only in pain but exhausted and shocked, Noah slept only fitfully, and I, despite my own exhaustion, could not sleep. My eyes closed, but my mind conjured up a view of a night sky—a clear night glittering with the light of many stars, not the descending snow that now fell. I felt fear, the deep fear one feels when considering eternity. Fear that was made greater by the knowledge that Noah's life depended on me. In the light of dawn, would he still be alive? And what would I do then to save him? After a long time, I slept, disturbed now and then by Noah's restlessness.

In the morning the storm had ended. Two feet of snow lay on the ground, some less and some more where the wind had blown it into drifts. Despite the protective branches, half that amount had blown into our shelter and weighed down the robe that covered us. Noah was awake, his wide eyes looking frantically about, his face pale. I would tend his injuries quickly and then try to relax him and keep him warm. It would be unpleasant work.

I pushed the heavy robe away, and Dog shook himself and ran off to do whatever it was that dogs did, peeing and searching for food I supposed.

I unwrapped the strips I had tied around Noah's wounds last night. He watched nervously but quietly. The wounds looked clean, although it was early for the bright-red skin edges that would be a bad sign. Noah winced when I bathed the wounds again and rewrapped them. Despite the pain, clearly much worse when the leg was moved, he gritted his teeth bravely. The broken leg was the biggest problem.

The leg had to be straightened before it became fixed in a position that would forever keep Noah from walking. He would not have much of a life if both legs were crooked. I was uncertain where I could find help and if I could return quickly enough. In any case the leg must be fixed before he could be moved, even with help. Best to do it now. I had a plan, but it would be hard. And it would cause Noah considerable pain.

I told Noah the plan. A look of terror came into his eyes. Then he nodded, realizing there was no other choice.

I removed the saddle from Dog's harness; prepared two thick, strong branches; and cut strips from one of our blankets. Lying on his back, Noah used his uninjured leg to push while I dragged him to the trunk of the pine tree. He put his hands above his head, and I used a harness strap to tie them securely behind the trunk.

I managed to get the saddle under Noah's leg and set the blanket strips and sturdy branches next to him. All was ready to move quickly— in order to cause less pain.

I called Dog and attached him to his harness, tied a strap to Noah's ankle, and attached the strap with a short line to the other end of the harness.

I looked at Noah. "All is ready," I said.

Noah closed his eyes, then took a deep breath and nodded without opening his eyes again. I touched a thick piece of wood to his lips, and he opened his mouth to take the wood between his teeth.

With a hand on Dog's harness, I urged him forward. The line pulled tight and then tighter. I waited for the sound—a scream, a groan, or some other outcry that would tell me the bones had been pulled into position and that the leg was straight. When the scream came, Dog tried to turn back, but I commanded him to stay and he did, keeping the line tight while I hurried back to Noah's side. He was breathing rapidly but visibly struggling to be brave—I had to respect the man. I had to cause him pain once again to see if we had done any good.

I had seen such injuries before and knew there were two bones below the knee, and the ends of both must line up to heal straight. I pressed where the break was, but I felt the bones still overlapped, so I went to Dog's head and pulled him a bit farther. When at last I thought the bones were in the best position we could hope for, I strapped the saddle tightly around the lower leg to hold it and then tied a branch securely on each side of the leg, fixing all in place with blanket strips. Then I undid Noah's arms to let him rest before I settled him and went for help.

"There is a village not far from here, but it will not be easy to get to," I told Noah when I thought he was clearheaded enough to follow what I was saying. "Where this forest ends there are bogs along the river, but there is a large island in the river there, Petite Tasseau. With good fortune the ground will be frozen enough for me to get through the swamp and somehow get to the island and use it to cross the river. On the other side of the island and river is a Potawatomi village."

Noah nodded his head, and I saw a glimmer of hope in his eyes. He wanted to believe I would succeed. I turned my eyes away from him, not wanting him to see the doubt in mine.

"If this tribe was as surprised as we were by this early storm, they have not left for winter lodging—or at least a man or two has stayed behind with the elderly. If I can cross the river, I will signal them. If someone can come back with me he can help me bring you there. This village is less than two miles away, much closer than my own, which would take days to reach in this snow. If I have good fortune I will return before nightfall. If I am not successful, I will be back this afternoon and we will decide on some other plan."

Noah tried to smile. "That's a lot of ifs," he said.

Noah had to be kept warm while I went for help, an important thing for men who had experienced as much shock as he had. He would need a fire that would last until I returned, and he would need to be covered, but smoke would suffocate him. Nagmo had told me what the braves do to avoid smoke when they need to cover a fire at night. That would work for us.

I looked for a white oak tree, the bark of which burns almost without smoke but gives a great amount of heat. In this dense forest such a tree should be easy to find. But when I left the shelter of our pine, with each step I plunged deep into the snow. My progress was slow and tiring. When I found a suitable tree, I removed a quantity of bark. If needed, even a little amount was enough to keep feeding the small fire for a couple of days. I returned to Noah, who was still at the base of the pine, and helped him sit up, his back against the trunk.

I dug a hole near his hip, a small hole, not much bigger than Dog's head, and I crisscrossed layers of bark to fill the hole. Using Noah's flint and steel and a small amount of the tinder he had prepared the night before, I lit the bark. Once the embers were glowing, I covered the hole with the dirt I had removed, leaving only two small air holes. I placed Noah's rifle beside him and left his fire-making supplies and dried food within reach. Snow would satisfy his thirst, and the remaining white oak bark and buffalo robes were close at hand. Dog nestled beside him. I threw a blanket over man, dog, and fire. Soon it would be a warm, smokeless room under the blanket, and the warmth would last for many hours.

I stepped away, hoping Noah would sleep at last, and paused in front of the pine that had been our home since last night. I wished I could lie down with them. My situation and loneliness suddenly seemed unbearable, and I let out a sob. Then I wiped my wet eyes with the back of my hand, raised my head, closed my eyes, and pointed my chin toward the sky. My work was not yet done.

I did not have the time or materials needed to make snowshoes in the traditional way, but I had to have some sort of device if I was to make any progress in the deep snow—my efforts to locate the white oak tree had convinced me of that. From nearby shrubbery, I found two of the thickest branches that were still bendable, tucked them under my clothing to warm them, and curved them into rough circles with two ends crossing. Where the ends crossed I tied them firmly together with sinew from the travois, leaving a few inches of the ends jutting out at back. I thought they looked a bit like teardrops, which described how I felt.

I crossed a few branches over the circle, covered it all with a web of sinew and blanket strips, and worked another strip through this webbing under which I could slide my foot. They were poor-looking things and would not last, but they would serve the purpose. The last blanket, other than the one that covered Noah, I tore into wide strips to wrap around my clothing for extra warmth and to cover exposed areas of skin.

I picked up an edge of the blanket that covered Noah and Dog and found them asleep in the cozy warmth. I tied the blanket strips over my head, ears, neck, and hands, and wrapped a buffalo robe about me. I would leave the safety of the forest and set off once again onto the barren prairie, but this time alone, with only my knife and Noah's tomahawk tucked into the beaded belt around my waist.

The familiar presence of my belt was reassuring. It was one of the few possessions I valued. It was never meant for carrying a tomahawk, but, like the impromptu snowshoes, it would do the job that was required. I remembered for a moment how proud I had been the day I finished beading the belt, when Nagmo was just learning to toddle around the village. I had carefully dyed quills and worked them in a complicated design with patience and skill. I had hoped to get some silver from the Shawnee, as they once had silver in large quantity. But they had lost it all, and so I finished it without silver.

I stepped tentatively onto the snow beyond our camp and breathed a sigh of relief when the make-do snowshoes kept me from plunging down through it. I took a few cautious steps, then turned back to part the branches of the pine tree for a final look at the mound that represented my last tie to companionship, human or animal. Then I took a deep breath, raised my chin, and walked the short distance to the edge of the woods and the beginning of the grassland.

PETITE TASSEAU

As I LEFT the woods, bright sunlight almost blinded me. I rearranged the strip of blanket that covered my head, wrapping it so that only slits remained over my eyes, to shade as best I could the reflection off the broad expanse of snow. It was bitterly cold, but the skies were clear, and there was no wind in the crisp, early morning air.

Although it took great effort to walk on top of the snow, as I struggled to keep the bulky devices on my feet and was burdened by the heavy buffalo robe, I could not help being impressed by the beauty of what lay before me. I was surrounded by glimmering silver dots sparkling like stars in a sky of pure white, twinkling in the ground on which I walked, as if heaven and earth were reversed, an other-worldly sight.

I had only to go from one place to another, nothing to figure out, no more plans to be made, and that relaxed my mind into a momentary sense of freedom. The necessary delay in the pursuit of Penney, even if only for the moment, lessened my anxiety. Perhaps my mind could stand no more and had forced a brief rest. I would have almost enjoyed my walk had it not been for the urgency of the situation, the uncertainty about whether or not I would be able to complete my mission, and the disappointment over quitting Penney's chase.

The water route in this area was more familiar to me than the land route, but I knew enough to get where I was heading. Circling the forest around the far side of the woods, I would arrive downstream of Petite Tasseau Island. But the river there was wide and filled with rapids. I would try to follow the mainstream of the river on land, going back north to the southernmost tip of the island, hoping the ground was solid enough in the freezing weather to support me through the swampy land, assisted by the combination of thin ice, frosted grasses, and snowshoes. I would have to find a way to get across shallow but raging rapids, jumping the few feet from tiny island to tiny island, until I got to Petite Tasseau. If all of this went according to my plan, then I would cross that island and arrive in sight of the village. I would not be able to cross the branch of the river between Petite Tasseau and the village, but I hoped to attract the attention of someone there by making a fire or waving. Or, having gotten that far, I would find another way.

As Noah had said the previous night, a lot of my plan was uncertain, and even doubtful.

As I plodded along peacefully, some optimism returned, perhaps brought on by the brightness of the day, perhaps by pride in having gotten this far. I had treated Noah's injuries, made him warm and safe, and used what was on hand to ready myself to complete his rescue. I allowed myself a little smile. Before long I would be an old woman, but I would be a capable old woman.

I had given up all hope of tracking Penney. Even if he was not far ahead of us, I could not capture him and bring him back alone. His track was lost now, covered in snow. I would have to assume he made for Fort Clark, and I would head that way when the weather cleared—once I got Noah to safety and if I could find a companion, now that both Noah and Poji were injured. I would think about that once the immediate emergency was over.

I busied myself by studying the surface of the snow for signs of life— there was nothing else to do but follow the edge of the woods and let my mind wander. I welcomed distraction from unpleasant thoughts.

Along the way were tracks of small animals that inhabited the woods and plains. First I came across the Y-shaped prints of a rabbit, zigzagging playfully and disappearing into the plain. I wondered what food he would find in the vast expanse of snow-covered ground. But then rabbits were merely busy beings, not wise ones, unlike the fox, whose tracks I noticed next. These tracks started in the woods and went straight onto the prairie. I knew from the inverted V-shaped pad below the four toe marks that it was a red fox, not a gray one. The pattern and distance between the prints told me the animal was running, probably after the rabbit. The scene would have been beautiful—the fox's red fur shining in the sun, his luxurious tail brushing the top of the sparkling snow as he streaked after his prey. He would normally hunt at night, but he would have been hungry this morning after waiting out the storm, and the rabbit presented a lucky opportunity. Whose side was I on? Did the playful rabbit escape? Did the fox feed his family?

I saw evidence of smaller animals too, mice and squirrels, and these prey brought larger animals out of the forest. One track seemed to be of a much larger animal, but it was that of an opossum, a mess of a thing. The large, protruding thumb made its back feet twice the size of its front feet, and the prints overlapped, with the mark of its ugly tail dragging over the top. The animal itself was ugly too, and so were its habits, like drooling and giving off a foul odor. I was glad I saw only the track that morning and not the animal itself.

I noticed a spot where many tracks came together and entered the woods. I wondered if small animals used this trail to get to the river. If I continued the way I was going, the forest would go on for at least another mile. A mile out, a mile through, a mile back—it would take hours to circle it on snowshoes. But if a path went directly to the river where the bank was not surrounded by swamp, such as woodland creatures would know, then the river was not far and would be reached quickly. I decided it was worth a try to follow the trail, since I would discover soon if it did not to go to the river. I turned into the forest, pushing aside branches of undergrowth as I went, but making reasonable progress.

When I thought I was about halfway, another track, each print an inch wide and looking like little stars stamped in the snow, joined the one I was following—a mink. It would have been hunting at dawn and returning to its burrow in the bank of the river. I smiled, not only because of the pretty little stars in the fresh snow, but because this told me my instincts were right—there was a riverbank nearby, not a swamp. Soon the trees thinned and I saw the river in front of me.

I gave a cry of dismay. Although indeed there was a small, dry bank and the island lay in front of me, getting to it appeared impossible.

The river surged through a torrent with rock ledges on both sides. Petite Tasseau was on the other side of this torrent. Although I could see the river bottom, which was not more than three feet deep there, the current raged over and around rocks with such force it would carry away anything in its path. From one side to the other was only fifteen to twenty feet, but it was as impassable as if it were miles.

How could I get to Petite Tasseau without being swept away, without freezing, without losing the snowshoes and buffalo robe I depended on? I pictured it in my mind: I was wrapped in waterlogged fur, tumbling uncontrollably in a torrent, flailing my arms, trying to grab for my snowshoes, and being pulled down into deeper parts of the river—Mishipeshu lurking in a cave nearby, then stealthily following....

I looked downriver, the route I had planned before I turned onto the trail, to see if I should go back and circle the forest. That was not possible either. If I could cross the bogs, I would only arrive at this same place and have the same problem.

I dropped onto a fallen log. What could I do? Staring at the river, looking up and down as if that would bring answers, I did not at first notice the soft crunching sounds, but gradually I became aware of them and felt a tingling at the back of my scalp. Filled with dread, I turned to look over my shoulder.

M'ewé!

I stood as she padded slowly toward me, her head carried low, and then I dropped to my knees in the snow and threw my arms around her neck, burying my face in her soft, clean fur. Tears came to my eyes, but I did not know if they were from joy or disappointment. I *did* know I was no longer alone and that was a big thing.

"M'ewé," I said in a choked voice. "It seems I see you only when I am crying and you are comforting or rescuing me."

I withdrew my arms and lowered myself to sit on the ground. M'ewé lay beside me, her head on my leg, her eyes soft with affection, and I considered my dilemma with determination instead of despair.

The water was not deep, and the water was not wide. I could stand an icy wetting if I could be sure of dry clothing afterward and if I could survive the current. I looked around for ideas.

Plenty of old branches stuck through the snow, left there after floods. I could gather some and build a platform; remove my clothing, snowshoes, and robe; and tie them to the platform. Without clothing I could brave the short distance across the rapids, free of burdens to fight the current, dragging my dry possessions on the platform.

What could I use to hold the platform together? I looked at my snow-shoes, and I remembered the strips of blanket I had wrapped myself in. I could use the sinew and strips and put everything back together when I reached the island.

I gathered wood and heaped it at the edge of the water, unwrapped the net of sinew from the snowshoes, and tied the bundle together. It was not so much a raft as a pile of small logs and sticks, but it would float, it would not tip, and it was high enough to keep my clothing from getting wet.

While I did this, M'ewé jumped about, grabbing some of the sticks playfully, and I had to scold her, mildly, to keep her from pulling apart what I had made.

But could I make it against the current?

I had another idea. I ripped some blanket strips into thinner pieces and connected them into a long rope. I attached one end of the rope to the raft and the other around a branch as thick as my arm. I took off my clothing and wrapped it and my other possessions in the robe, tying it all on top of the platform. Then I stood there, unclothed, shivering in the bitter cold, hoping that M'ewé would remember the game we played when she lived with me.

I talked to myself aloud. "If there was ever a time to have a strong arm, to throw like a man and not a woman, it is now." I picked up the branch, drew my arm back, and heaved it across the torrent. It landed on the island. "Get!" I called to M'ewé.

M'ewé bounded happily into the water, heedless of the cold, thinking only of the game. She splashed onto the island and grabbed the piece of wood between her strong jaws.

"Tug!" I commanded, remembering how when she was a young wolf I pulled on a stick M'ewé held in her mouth to help strengthen her teeth and jaws.

M'ewé tugged, the branch in her mouth, and I could imagine her play-ful growl, although I could not hear it over the roar of the rapids. The line lost its slack and tightened, and the raft started to move. Before it entered the water I grabbed the line, praying it would hold, that M'ewé would not drop that piece of wood, and that our combined strength would be enough for both me and the raft to get across without being carried away by the river.

"Tug!" I called again, so M'ewé would not be distracted by what I was doing. She pulled, her head low, teeth clamped firmly on the branch, her body straining backward, all four feet fixed against slipping, trying to tug harder by throwing her head from side to side, enjoying the old game.

My feet lost all feeling in the cold water that struck against my legs and then against my abdomen. I had to face into the current rather than walk directly toward the island in order to keep from being swept off my feet, and I did that. I sidestepped one small step at a time, not looking down, testing for sure footing before shifting my weight, afraid of losing my balance or turning my ankle on some slippery stone under the water and falling into the river, which would mean sure death.

"Tug!" M'ewé tugged. I could no longer feel my feet, but I felt the raft behind me, caught by the current, twisting and turning, wrenching with each step—but the crude thing held together and did not overturn. I grabbed a bush growing near the bank, and I climbed out of the water. I hauled the platform—M'ewé still pulling—onto shore.

M'ewé dropped the piece of wood and bounded to me, and I collapsed against her, laughing and catching my breath.

I felt her stiffen and break away. Her lips split into a grimace, a snarl emerged from her throat, and she stared at the woods that edged the bank.

I followed her stare to see Penney standing in front of the trees, a rifle pointed at us. "What do you know? A naked Indian! What marvels this island holds!"

CAPTURE

My HEART SEEMED to stop inside my chest. Yet somehow I knew my only salvation was to stay calm and pretend I had not been trailing Penney. He might suspect I had followed him, but he could not be sure.

Penney aimed his rifle at M'ewé. I called out a single word in our language, "*Kwaskso'on!*" M'ewé jumped straight into the air at the same moment Penney's rifle discharged. She dashed into the trees and disappeared. It was another game we played, intended to train the baby wolf raised in a safe environment—a tactic to escape threats in the wild.

"Damn animal!" Penney grumbled, lowering his rifle as his eyes roamed over my naked body. "Well, if my shot had to miss, at least I drove it off. Wawetseka, isn't it? Look different without clothes. Aren't you going to thank me for saving you from that beast?" I took his comment as mocking—M'ewé was talked about at the station and Penney must have known this when he saw me hugging her.

"Stop staring at me and let me clothe myself," I replied in a sharp tone, faking a confidence I did not feel. I went to my bundle; untied it; and reached for my dress, leggings, and moccasins, glancing at him a number of times as I dressed. Seeing that he watched every move I made, I turned away from him. I did not need to *pretend* embarrassment, but I made a clear show of it so he would not see me hide my knife and tomahawk. I had once had a different opinion of this man, who now seemed a stranger. Exposed and defenseless, I feared his next move would be to molest me, yet he let me clothe myself.

I shivered and clasped my robe close in an attempt to bring some warmth back to my frozen body. I picked up the rope I had made, untied it from the raft, and fixed it around my robe, to make Penney think it was to secure my clothing. I wanted it because it could be useful. I assumed he would not let me leave. I wanted as many tools as I could keep at hand in case I managed to escape.

Penney was thoughtful, as if trying to make a decision. Finally he asked, with narrowed eyes, "Why are you here? Why did you go to so much trouble to reach this island? Why aren't you at your village?"

I acted as if this were a casual meeting to give the impression he had nothing to do with my being there. I lowered myself to the ground and sat cross-legged, shivering despite my robe, which I hoped he took for cold and not fear.

"I was on my way to Fort Clark. Nagmo, my son, has been taken there. Noah Taylor, who is the dead man's brother, was traveling with me, but he was set upon last night by wolves and injured. I am trying to get to the village on the other side of the river for help, to bring Taylor there." He must have known some of this, but I did not want him to think I knew much of what went on at the station.

He narrowed his eyes and watched my face, likely to decide if I was telling the truth. I forced myself to meet his gaze without wavering. "What makes you think there's anyone in this village? Wouldn't they have left for winter grounds?"

"The storm is early and the deer have not left, so our people have not gone to winter grounds yet—we were not prepared. Perhaps we should have left sooner. I hoped this village made the same mistake we did, and someone would be there to help. It was too far to go back. I thought this was the thing to do."

He looked doubtful and studied the raft I had built.

"You must be strong, Wawetseka, to pull that contraption across that raging current."

I raised my chin in the air. "It was hard," was all I said.

He shuffled his feet and leaned his back against a tree. It seemed he did not know what to do with me. He set his rifle against the tree too, but it was still close to his hand. My eyes kept going to it. "Before you left, was there talk of me at the station?"

"I was not at the station." It was my turn to challenge Penney. I stared at him with suspicion. "Taylor and I left from our village, and he did not speak about you. I am surprised to find *you* here. Why would there be talk? Why are you not at the station? Why are you on this island? You must have traveled during the storm. That is strange."

"Pretty inquisitive for a squaw, aren't you?" Penney said. "I thought you squaws were quiet and respectful."

I only returned his gaze and said nothing, acting the way he expected.

"I had enough of that place," he said after a moment. His gaze turned away and he went on as if talking to himself. "The plans I made did not turn out. It's my habit to act quickly once my mind is made up, storm or no storm."

I pretended to believe him, although I knew his words were false. I knew of no reason for him to stop at Petite Tasseau unless he wanted to hide. He was covering his trail in still another way, figuring pursuers would not expect him to stop. He would likely continue his trip after allowing enough time for anyone chasing him to pass him and stop searching. He could make a camp here on the island and wait, perhaps for much of the winter. There was plenty of game on the island and ample wood to build a rough shelter, and he had his tools. He could make a home here indefinitely if he wanted to, with little fear of discovery. He must have thought the tribes would have left the area and expected travel on the river would stop in winter, and if anyone did come to the island that person would only shelter and move on, not search for occupants.

Or did he come here intentionally? Did he need to get something he had cached here, away from the station? Or had he come to steal someone else's cache? Or to meet someone?

He narrowed his eyes again and watched for my reaction as he suggested, "Perhaps I should return with you to rescue Taylor?"

I hoped my eyes did not show the anxiety I felt at his words. I thought frantically. "That would be kind of you, but I hope the village will have more men and means to transport us, not only across the river, but to bring Taylor to their camp. He is in a lot of pain. They could move him more safely and comfortably than you and I could."

He took a step away from the tree, picked up his rifle, and motioned with his thumb through the woods. "Well, come with me or not, as you wish. I'll help you see if there is a way to get off this island and over to the village. I killed an opossum this morning, and it's cooking while we stand here jabbering. You might as well have a full belly before we try to do anything. Follow me." He turned his back and walked into the trees.

I stood for a moment staring at his back. I suspected he was stalling until he decided how to get rid of me. I made this trip to capture him, not eat with him and risk becoming *his* prisoner. And, I hated those ugly opossum!

Penney had made a crude shelter in the woods, finding a place where a large boulder sat near the trunk of a big pine tree. He had placed his travois a few feet from this natural shelter, dug a bit into the ground which had not yet frozen under the tree, and covered the whole thing with branches and leaves.

He made a sign that I should enter and crawled in behind me, setting his rifle at the entrance. Inside was a nice, warm hole with an overhead opening the size of a fist to draw off smoke. He had stored some possessions inside the shelter, close to hand. When my eyes became accustomed to the dim light, I saw ammunition, some dried food, a kettle and spoon, knife, axe, blankets, and robes. Very simple. With little work he could have done this easily in the morning, and it was comfortable enough to stay even through the winter.

What should I do? I did not believe Penney would help me get Noah to the Indian village. If I found a way to surprise and subdue Penney, it would not do me much good here—how would I get him off the island and to Fort Clark? And what about Noah? It seemed I had to accept Penney's offer of assistance to rescue Noah after all and hope to find some way to escape.

The cooked opossum did not smell as bad as I expected. Penney pulled off a leg and handed it to me. I was hungrier than I realized and managed to swallow a few bites before the picture of that ugly thing faking death and drooling got to be too much for me, and the meat in my mouth made my stomach churn. "Perhaps I am too excited to eat," I said, dropping my hands. Penney shrugged his shoulders and took the remaining meat from my hands, finishing it in a couple of bites.

"Will you come with me to get Taylor?" I asked.

He looked at me with suspicion. "I thought you didn't want my help," he said.

"I think it would be best after all. You are here and we are ready, and it is less than an hour away. If we can get him here we can keep him comfortable and feed him until I get help or until we find a way to get him to the village. He will be that much closer."

Penney considered, rubbing his hands on his coat. "All right," he said, nodding his head, but not looking at me. I thought he planned to deal with me when we got off the island. I wondered why he did not do that now. Perhaps he thought Taylor was a threat or wanted to see if Taylor knew anything about those chasing him, and he needed me to show him where Taylor was. Or it could be Penney and Taylor were working together. Whatever the reason was, it would be easier to get to Taylor with me as a *willing* companion rather than as a guarded prisoner.

I must get off the island but keep Penney from Noah.

"How will we get back across the rapids? And get Taylor to this island?"

"It's easy, if one has the right equipment," he said. "I have rope, ties, and hooks to assist our crossing and oiled cloth to keep things dry." This explained how he got to the island despite his load.

"You won't mind taking your clothes off again?" he asked with a wink.

Disgusted, I turned my head away but nodded. Penney had done nothing but joke about molestation, but I could not dismiss that thought.

"I used the materials from my snowshoes to get across the rapids. I need to remake them," I said.

"I have two pair," Penney said, arrogance in his tone. "In case one broke, it would not be safe to travel a great way without a spare."

So his plan was to travel a great way. To Galena, I suspected.

"Getting Taylor on the island will take some doing, but we will manage," he said. I thought he said this to convince me. I doubted he intended to bring Taylor to the island.

"Dog is with Taylor," I said. "Perhaps Dog can help bear the burden."

"Dog? Leckey's Dog? Why?" I could tell from his face that he was suspicious again.

"Leckey thought Dog would be helpful, as we were traveling in winter."

He said no more but picked up his rifle. He loaded it, added some ammunition to a pouch hanging from his belt, brushed off his hands, and stood up.

"Let's go," he said. He left the enclosure, and I heard him uncover his travois and move items around.

When we got back to the river and the rapids, Penney made a big deal of M'ewé's paw prints at the river edge, entering the water. "So much for your wolf friend," he said. "I thought she was some kind of spirit that was supposed to protect you, that's the rumor. But then, spirits don't leave tracks do they?" He laughed loudly at what he apparently thought was a great joke.

This hateful man had deceived all of us into thinking he was friendly and helpful. At that moment I wished Shawnash's belief in Mishipeshu was true and that the beast would rise from the river to grab this man and pull him into the depths, never to be seen again.

Using Penney's ropes and hooks to provide a line to cling to as we crossed the rapids, we made short work of what had seemed impossible a short time ago. We tied our dry clothes and snowshoes to a loop that slid along the line. Once across we dressed quickly. I untied some of the strips I had used to make my rope, wrapped exposed skin, and covered my face as before, and the rest held my robe closed.

"Can't you dress faster?" Penney said.

"It is how we travel in cold weather," I told him.

We followed the animal trail back through the woods. I wondered if Noah would be able to identify Penney when he saw him. After all, both brothers lived near Harrisburg, and Penney had killed Simon to keep his identity secret. If he thought Noah and I were following him, he would want to take advantage of an opportunity to kill both of us. He was likely using me to get to Noah.

Penney made me walk ahead. He said that was because I knew the way, but it was probably to watch me. He kept his rifle ready, although not pointed at me. He was not a woodsman, though, but a tradesman, and he knew little of the sounds and signs of the forest. We heard noises from behind us. Penney stopped, turned to look, tightened his grip on his rifle, and began walking again.

I had recognized the stealthy light crunches made by M'ewé as she tracked us from a distance, hidden between trees, her gray coat blending into dark bark, white snow, and gray shadows. I could not see her, but I knew she was near. Her presence was comforting, but I was also afraid she would show herself and Penney would shoot her.

"It's only the snow melting," Penney said. "Keep going." I stayed on the trail, watching the ground in front of me.

When we came out of the trees, our eyes were immediately struck by bright sunlight, intensified by reflection off the snow on the prairie. I knew this would happen and had wrapped strips of blanket to protect my eyes from the glare, but Penney had not known and was momentarily blinded. This was my opportunity.

He winced, shut his eyes, and turned his head away. I took a few steps in another direction and screamed, *"Nsat!*, 'kill someone!'" as loud as I could. *"Nsat!"* I yelled again. And M'ewé came streaking from the edge of the woods—huge leaps, bounding, crashing, and leaping again. A gray streak in the bright sunlight, resembling a lance of pure silver, M'ewé skimmed over the top of the snow, which had developed a crust when the early morning sun compressed and hardened it. M'ewé rapidly closed the distance between herself and Penney.

Penney, squinting against the glare, turned and hastily discharged his rifle, but his aim was poor. The shot missed, and he dropped the useless weapon and fled in panic, a reaction that ruined any possibility of his escape.

Hampered by his snowshoes, his frantic bounds made little progress, and the race was soon lost. M'ewé instinctively pursued him and fastened her jaws around his lower leg, snarling and tossing her head to dig her fangs deeper. Penney screamed, fell to the ground, threw one arm across his face, and flailed at the wolf with the other.

As soon as Penney was down, I made my way clumsily to his rifle, picked it up, and stumbled over to him. M'ewé was still fixed to his leg, dragging him over the crust of snow. I raised the rifle butt and brought it down on his head, once, twice, until he stopped moving, and his eyes glazed and closed. Then I put my hand on M'ewé's back and commanded her, *"Ngashek*, 'stop!'" And I fell back into the snow, exhausted, but not taking my eyes off the unmoving Penney.

Later, when Penney woke, I sat on the snow next to him, pointing his rifle at his face. He blinked to clear his head, and with a sneer he tried to grab the rifle from me, but I had used one of his own ropes to tie his hands firmly behind his back. If I had not wanted my face to show I was in command, I would have laughed as I saw his expression change from one of arrogance to surprise, to frustration, and, finally, to fear, as he struggled against the ties.

After I had struck him senseless I pulled M'ewé away. I checked to see if he was dead. He was breathing, although with short breaths. Before he could wake again, I tied him securely, went through his possessions, and sat to watch and wait.

I realized I had been wise to stop hitting him when I did—to render him asleep instead of causing his death. Had he died, I would be no further ahead, only an Indian who had killed another white man, and I would be chased and imprisoned too. There would be no one to explain the story and no guilty man to bring to Fort Clark to prove Nagmo's innocence.

A look of hatred came to Penney's face now, and his sneer returned. He said through clenched teeth, "That rifle's no good to you. I discharged it missing that fucking wolf."

I said nothing but reached to my waist and pointed to his ammunition pouch, which I now wore on my own belt. "There are no stupid 'squaws' out here," I said.

"I bet you don't know how to shoot that thing," he argued. He began to blink rapidly.

"I do. But no matter, as I can do without the rifle—I have other ways to force you to do what I say." I pointed at his feet, and he looked at them. "I have wrapped the wounds M'ewé made, but you see I have also lashed your snowshoes to your feet, which you cannot remove with your arms behind your back. I am light and can walk free on the snow which is firm now, so you cannot outrun me. I should say, you cannot outrun *us*, as there is another reason you will not flee."

I made a sign, and Penney turned his head and saw M'ewé not far away. Her face was a horrible grimace, her yellow eyes glared, and she snarled, jaws dripping.

"Get up," I said. "We will return to Noah, and then you will make a travois for him. I will have this rifle, in case I need to use it. M'ewé will watch you, just in case I miss. But there is also plenty of ammunition in this pouch."

I grinned, swinging his ammunition pouch back and forth in front of his furious eyes.

NGWESÉS

THE SNOWSTORM IN October of 1817 did not announce the permanent arrival of winter. After I captured Penney, the bright sun stayed out, and throughout that morning it got steadily warmer. The crust of remaining snow was slippery, but it did not cave under our feet. And with some practice it became easy to walk on the hard crust that remained. By late morning we reached Noah and found him alert and rested. He had pain still, but endured it.

With no need to fight the weather, we would make it the four miles home well before dark, even pulling a travois. Our village was on the near side of the vast forest we had gone through when we left our canoes, so part of this trip was across the plain and pulling the travois was easy.

I thought how the storm had changed our situation. Only four miles from our village, I would easily have been able to reach help for Noah there in other weather and never would have tried to reach the closer village and found Penney on the island. Nor would a shot from Noah's rifle have brought anyone to aid us—even if it could be heard so far through the storm. It would have been thought to be from a hunter.

My plan had almost been undone when I arrived with Penney at the sheltering tree and Dog and M'ewé tangled with each other. The outcome was decided quickly but with a great deal of confusion. Dog jumped at M'ewé, I ran to them, and Penney took advantage to move away. M'ewé broke away from Dog and ran after Penney while I held Dog back. Noah dragged himself out of the shelter and into the open, his rifle hanging on his shoulder. Struggling to a sitting position, he kept his rifle on Penney. I had dropped Penney's rifle to break up the quarreling animals, but I managed to get to it before Penney did. We then had three against Penney—M'ewé, Noah, and I. I tied Dog to a tree, and we had no further trouble from Penney as he completed the tasks we set him to.

I was pleased to see Noah had regained some strength during our absence. We had Penney make a sling from ropes and attach it to the poles from our travois. I fashioned a new harness and replaced Dog's saddle, as his saddle still supported Noah's leg. Noah was much heavier than the burden Dog had pulled the previous day, but there were two to pull now, as Penney was also put to use.

Once Dog was attached to the travois and we started off, the animals settled into the same pattern they had followed the previous day, with M'ewé trailing and Dog making the occasional growl.

When our little party returned to the fur station, it did not take anything on our part to convince Leckey to lock up Penney, as he knew of Penney's guilt before we left. With Leckey, Reddick, and Villeaux the only men at the station now, secure locks were placed on one of the storerooms and a slot was devised to provide food. Thus Penney could stay imprisoned there until either the winter was over or until Peniston Wayne or some other authority transported him to a cell at Fort Clark to await trial. Men from our village helped to guard him, and Amelina took on the task of providing meals.

Leckey and Reddick took advantage of a warm break in the weather to make a trip to Petite Tasseau. One of our braves traveled with them. On the island they easily found Penney's possessions and the stolen goods and valuables and brought them back to the station.

Because of suspicion that Penney went to the island to retrieve something hidden there either by himself, by Findel and Pascal, or by someone else, Leckey and Reddick stayed at Petite Tasseau for two days and searched it thoroughly. Some of the places travelers were known to hide possessions were in the upper branches of trees, in the ground or near tree trunks, in caves, or behind earth or rocks. After searching, Leckey and Reddick were convinced nothing was cached on the island. "Believe me," Reddick said when they returned, "I could well use whatever money such valuables would bring. If there were anything to be found, we would have found it."

Lilly discovered that Penney had planned an escape which involved

Nell. He used Nell's fondness for him to persuade her to hang around the room in which he was locked, instructing her to fetch some tool that would help him escape. Lilly discovered what he was doing, scolded Nell, and confronted Penney. I never found out what Lilly said to them, but apparently it kept Penney and Nell from talking anymore.

We never heard from Emmett, Findel, or Pascal again.

A runner from our tribe was sent to Thomas Forsyth, the Indian Agent in Fort Clark, bearing a letter that explained what happened. The letter, written in Leckey's hand, begged Forsyth to arrange the release of Nagmo, as Penney would be brought to the fort. It also asked for Peniston Wayne or another authority to be sent to bring Penney there.

By return letter, Forsyth advised that there would be some delay while matters went through the proper "channels," but that Nagmo's release was "guaranteed," based on the written "testimony" of Leckey, who was a respected and honest post commander.

With help from our medicine man and some supplies and advice from Leckey and Villeaux, Noah and Poji both survived their injuries. Poji's recovery was complete, but Noah's limp would always limit his activities, especially travel. He became a better man, as our experience gave him confidence and courage he had lacked. He faced life thereafter with humor and determination. He visits from time to time, and we have become friends. He has taken a young Potawatomi woman as his wife, from Black Partridge's tribe near Fort Clark, and Noah is now kin.

I had been surprised to find Wabmimi waiting in my house when I first returned from Petite Tasseau with Penney. It seemed she had been anguished when Nagmo left their home, and the despair of his absence and possible loss quickly matured her. We had long talks during which I told her my experiences of Nagmo's arrest and the identification of the killer and his subsequent capture.

"I could never be so brave as you, Wawetseka," she said. I looked at her fondly and thought that she was wrong in that opinion. I saw strength in her that had not been there before.

We stayed in our village that winter, as did Wabmimi. She said she was determined to follow her husband to Fort Clark and would insist on seeing him.

Peniston Wayne himself came for Penney at the beginning of the month of March. They were in no hurry, as the judge was not expected until early summer. Wayne said they reasoned that Leckey could have the expense and responsibility for holding Penney instead of the authorities at Fort Clark. He asked for an escort of braves from our village to ensure that Penney, who was a powerful and devious man, did not escape again. We thought he should have brought his own people, especially since Wayne and Penney would be on horseback and our men on foot, and the whole business had nothing to do with Indian matters. However, we agreed, since the more important thing was the exchange of prisoners.

When Peniston Wayne arrived, Wabmimi had one of the braves take her across the river to the station. She demanded to speak to Wayne and talked him into taking her with his little party to Fort Clark. The fact that I had not been allowed to talk to Nagmo did not convince her. Perhaps they would be more lenient at Fort Clark, or a wife may succeed where a mother would not. And so she went.

The cold weather was slow to leave, and I waited through two more bad months. Nagmo did not come, nor was there word of Wabmimi. Much of this time the river was impassable and there was little land travel. Runners or smoke signs could have gotten word to me, but none came, and now that all knew Nagmo would be set free, what was there to send word about? There was only a worried and lonely mother waiting for word of her son, not important enough for runners or smoke signals.

The weather finally warmed a little, and Wabmimi arrived, traveling with some traders from Fort Clark. While they stopped at the station, she asked Villeaux to bring her to visit me. We sat near still-glowing embers in my wigwam, as even in late spring the weather remained cool.

"They are still holding Nagmo, until the final word comes from the circuit judge, who is due to arrive soon. In only a short time now he will be released, but they have to settle every small detail. That is what the lawman says—that the white man's law is very 'particular.'"

"They were kind to you? They let you talk to him?" I was full of questions, desperate to know not only the outcome but also how Nagmo was bearing his imprisonment. "Is he healthy? Has all this time locked in the jail changed him? Is he the same happy man, or other?"

Wabmimi smiled at me and reached out and patted my arm. "They were very kind. They not only let me talk with him, they let me come and go from his room, and they fed me. I could be with him whenever I wanted." Her smile widened. "Mostly I wanted. I am to have a child, Wawetseka! This is why I am traveling now, before Nagmo is released, so I can prepare for the child."

I did not know what to say. Tears filled my eyes, and I put a hand over my mouth. A child! My grandchild! I took my hand away from my face, and my fingers fluttered and then dashed away the tears from my eyes before they fell. I tried to rest my hands in my lap, but they shook. I feared my face did not show the happiness I felt, but something else, I don't know what, as I tried to control my emotion.

Wabmimi touched my arm again, and her hand stayed there. *"Koyake',"* she said. "Grandma."

When Wabmimi returned to her village, my mind still would not rest, even with such happy news. Nagmo was not yet home, and until I saw him with my own eyes I could not help but feel something could still go wrong. That was the way with mothers, and if that was not the way with *all* mothers, at least it was the way with me.

I had done all I set out to do, and the outcome was successful. I should be proud and content, but I missed Nagmo and did not know when I would see him again.

"You are sorrowful, Wawetseka," Shawnash said when we finally had a warm day. The ground no longer frozen, we worked it with our garden sticks to loosen it so it would be ready by planting time. The winter, although long, had not been severe, and we would be able to plant early crops as soon as we prepared the soil.

I did not reply.

"You should be happy. Nagmo will soon return to his village and to his pregnant wife—if he is not there already. And our lives have returned to normal."

I blinked rapidly, but I did not reply, wondering if my life would ever be normal again. What was normal for a woman who was educated beyond her family and friends, who has experienced such adventures, who must now live away from those she loves and forget her past? How does a woman do that?

"You will soon have a grandchild. And Nagmo will visit, as he did before, and they will come then as a family. You can visit them, too." She worked at a particularly large and hard clump, using her stick like a spear to break it into smaller pieces. She did not talk while she concentrated on this.

My efforts were less energetic. I poked the stick into areas that were already loose and stirred the stick around with no purpose.

"I suppose Nagmo went straight to Wabmimi and his family and did not stop here, but he will come when he can. He will want to thank you for setting him free, once he visits his wife and his home." Taking a break, Shawnash leaned on her stick and looked into my face.

"He will do what he will do, Shawnash. He has his own family now. I am happy all has turned out so well—I just wish I could see it with my own eyes."

When Shawnash glanced at me I think I did not look happy, despite my words. Her eyes appeared worried, but without saying more she went back to work.

More days went by, and the first seeds went into the ground. Still I had no word from Nagmo, and I thought perhaps I should send a runner to his village to see if he had arrived there safely. The runner would think I was a *kyesh'at*, a foolish woman. He would talk in the village, and the women would think I was a *kyesh'at* too, the sort of mother who was afraid to let her son lead his own life. His wife's family was now his home, and mothers did not come before wives. Which was as it should be.

The sun was nearly down, and a cold breeze swept down the side of the bluff toward the river, but I felt a need to walk alone. I headed up the bluff toward the woods at the top, where I had been the day this story began. I looked at the ground as I walked. I could not shake my sadness. Perhaps M'ewé would be up there to comfort me, though I had not seen M'ewé since she ran off when we got in sight of our village, the day we brought Penney back. I worried if she had met with some accident too, as she was gone so long.

I caught a distant motion—something big and dark on this side of the woods—and I looked that way, but it was directly into the setting sun and it blinded me. I put my hand to my brow to shade my eyes, hoping to see M'ewé, but no. It was a man approaching, not a wolf, a man coming from the direction of the trail on top of the bluff, the trail we took heading toward Petite Tasseau, the one that continued on to Fort Clark.

I heard the man give a cry, almost a moan, and he began to run toward me.

It was Nagmo!

I stood still and let him come to me, tears coursing down my cheeks, my hand over my mouth. My knees grew weak and I started to fall, but he caught me, his strong arms reached out, his hands grasped my shoulders, and he steadied me until I could stand tall and look deep into his eyes—eyes I had feared to never see again—the beautiful, smiling eyes of my "Sings All The Time," my Nagmo.

Without taking his shining eyes from mine, he gently touched my cheek, and said, "*Ne'ni.*" Mother.

I breathed a soft reply, pressing my cheek against his fingers. "*Ngwe-sés.*" My little son.

He lived under our lakes and rivers and guarded valuable metals that were found there, and he brought death and misfortune to people who trespassed in his waters.

—Wawetseka

Cora

2013

Chapter 15

"**W**Hat is it with you people and wolves?" the Lemont Police officer asked, scratching his head and staring at the dead animal lying on Cora and Cisco's kitchen floor.

"And I wonder why every time we place a 911 call, you wind up answering it," Cora said. "Are you the only officer who takes wolf calls?"

Cora winced. Using witty sarcasm as a coping mechanism during stressful situations was a habit she had picked up from her father. The result was sometimes inappropriate. She hoped Officer Jeff Rogers would realize she was joking.

She thought she and Rogers had gotten off on the wrong foot last fall, when a priest had been attacked by an animal at their home and Rogers investigated the matter. He hadn't given much credibility to her story that a wolf had attacked the priest—which was understandable. Neither the department nor animal control had been able to locate the animal afterward.

Today he threw his head back and laughed. "Luck of the draw, I guess. Or the guys at the station are pranking me." The man had changed since Cora last saw him, letting his brown crew cut grow out to a more fashionable style. And he must have gotten contacts or laser surgery, since he no longer wore wire-rimmed glasses.

Tonight two police cars had responded to their call, and a number of officers were searching outside while Rogers talked to Cora and Cisco. Cisco had left a golf club leaning against a family room wall, and Rogers poked the animal with it. "Hey!" Cisco said.

There was no sign of life when they first checked, and there was none now. "Sorry—here," Rogers said, handing the club to Cisco, who frowned at it, walked into the adjacent laundry room and placed the club in the washbasin.

"Well, it's dead, all right, and I'll be damned if it doesn't *look* like a wolf this time...," Rogers said, walking around the animal to view it from every angle.

Cora wasn't normally squeamish, but she had avoided looking directly at the mess on her kitchen floor, afraid the scene would haunt her. She made quick peeks at it now. The animal lay on its side. It appeared to be about a hundred pounds. Its gray coat looked clean and healthy, she noted. Its eyes and jaws were open, its tongue hanging onto their oriental rug, almost as if it were trying to lap up its own blood from the large stain under the gaping wound in its neck.

Stifling a wave of nausea at the thought, she turned away, noting as she did so the sickly odor and the blood, urine, smears of feces, and hair on the rug and uncovered areas of the floor. She thought they might as well wrap the wolf in the rug to carry it away. Even if they could get the stains out, she'd never want that rug in her house again.

Rogers interrupted her thoughts. "We'll send it to the lab. Is this what attacked the priest last year?"

"No," replied Cora, at the same time Cisco said, "yes."

Rogers rolled his eyes. "Here we go again."

Rogers radioed dispatch, then glanced around the room, his face expressing disgust. "Can we talk somewhere we don't have to look at—or smell—this thing?"

"So let's go over the story again," Rogers said, taking a notepad and pen from his pocket as they seated themselves in the living room. "You came home, not suspecting a thing, entered through the garage, found the kitchen torn apart, and that wolf jumped at you...." He waved an arm in the direction of the kitchen. "Before it was dead, of course."

Even though she was seated on the sofa, Cora's knees trembled. She tried to concentrate on Rogers's questions. "Yes."

Cisco started to wave an arm and opened his mouth, but Rogers held up a hand. "Wait."

Cisco shut his mouth and crossed his arms over his chest.

"You said you were able to escape and shut the door, but before that you saw *another* wolf jump into the room through the broken window. Do I have that right?"

They nodded. Cora started to open her mouth, and again Rogers raised a finger.

"You heard a lot of snarling and gnashing of teeth, got into your car, called 911, and waited for us to get here. We walked around back—noted that the back of your house was secluded from casual observers by landscaping between homes—and found a broken kitchen window. Flashed our lights through the windows—saw the dead animal on the floor. We made noise to see if we could flush an animal, nothing. Our men searched the house and found this mess, nothing else, no second animal—wolf. Is that all?" He looked at them questioningly.

Beyond the chair where Rogers sat, Cora saw flashlight beams through the window, bouncing around the front of the house and down the street. She glanced through the dining room window, where their backyard was lit with a searchlight. Neighbors were probably gathering in the street or watching from inside their homes, she thought. Two hundred yards away where their street ended, she supposed another searchlight lit up the farmer's field or soon would. The empty field would be a logical place to look for a missing wolf—but the officers wouldn't find it.

She and Cisco nodded to Officer Rogers's last question. Cisco asked, "What now? Do we have to leave that thing there or what?"

"We have to find the other animal—it could hurt someone, could have rabies. We've notified County Animal Control, but it's Sunday night...," Rogers said. He seemed ready to pass that responsibility to someone else. He flipped through his notes and then pointed the end of his pen at them. "Okay, now the fun begins—what do you think happened here? How did a wolf get in your house, and what killed it?"

Cisco cleared his throat, fist over his mouth, and glanced at Cora. At her nod, he said, "We have no idea why this wolf was here. It looks like the second wolf killed it. This must be related to that threatening note I brought in a couple of months ago."

Rogers eyed them with interest. "I was wondering when you'd get to that. Remind me how you received the threat."

"A note, on paper—oh, you mean how did it *come?* In Nick's mailbox, but no postage. It must have been slipped in the box after the mailman came," Cisco said.

"Right—you're writing a book, and Nick's one of the writers. You thought the note might have come from an old boyfriend. No problems since then?"

"No—until tonight."

"And you kept working on the book the whole time?"

They nodded.

"What did the note say again?"

Cora had memorized the exact words. "You must not continue to offend the spirits. The curse is real. Proceed at your peril." Cora started to explain, but partway through Rogers held up his hand to stop her. "Enough—for now—I remember. This is all getting weird again, as if the whole thing isn't weird enough to begin with. Let's not go any further down this road." He shook his head yet again. "Any idea who wrote the note?"

They shook their heads. Cora was relieved she didn't need to try to explain Mishipeshu.

"Any idea what's in those memoirs someone doesn't like?"

They shrugged their shoulders and glanced at each other. "We brainstormed this. We didn't see anything we were doing that anyone would object to—that's why we went ahead," Cora said. "We thought it was the old friend or a crank."

"And now? You think someone is trying to kill you?" Rogers asked.

Cora blinked. "I hate to think that, but I guess we'd better take the warning more seriously."

"Or take it at face value, a couple of wolves trashed your house looking for food." He dropped his chin and leveled his gaze on them, a habit Cora figured was from looking over the top of the glasses he no longer wore. "Please tell me you don't believe that curse."

This brought a wry grin from Cisco and Cora. "We don't believe the curse," Cisco said, as she nodded.

"Any last thoughts about that second wolf?"

Cora and Cisco exchanged a glance, then shook their heads.

"Are you going to go ahead with this book?" Rogers asked.

Cora took in a deep breath and let it out slowly. "We'll talk about it. It's not our decision alone."

"I'd advise against it." He took down names and contact information for Nick, Dawn, and Frannie. He stood up and handed a card to Cisco.

"Take this and call the station if you want the name of a company that does blood and biohazard clean-up—I know I wouldn't want to do that. Someone will come by to pick up the carcass. Stay somewhere else until that's done if you like, but let us know how to reach you. I'll talk to these people, check out the old friend, a search will be made for the missing animal—again—and we'll let you know if we find something or if we need anything else. Call me if you think of anything useful."

As Rogers left the room, he added, "I must say things never get boring with you two in town." Cora thought he was trying to suppress a grin.

Chapter 16

"**N**o sign of another wolf," Rogers said on the phone early the next morning. "I'm not surprised, and I guess you aren't either?"

"No, you're right," Cora said, standing next to her nightstand, still in her pajamas.

"But listen to this—a neighboring station got a call from some guy —owns a wolf ranch about seven or eight miles from here. Seems they had a break-in last night and one of his wolves is missing. I repeat, *one* of his wolves."

"Did you talk to Billy yet?"

"Still looking."

The call from Rogers cleared up one matter that had been puzzling Cora: the condition of the dead wolf's coat. The coat had shown signs of care, not the dirty, matted coat that would be expected of a predator living in the wild.

She didn't think Rogers would be receptive to her opinions about the second wolf, though. And she couldn't be certain her friendly spirit had saved her from the attacking wolf. But as she told Nick months ago, she suspected her life was overseen by a protective presence since her experience with a spirit at Sag Bridge last year, perhaps now taking the form of a wolf. Not only had she heard it howling in the night, but after a deep snowfall last winter she had found signs of trampled snow, prints of a large predator, and the remains of hawk feathers in her yard. Why a spiritual being would leave prints and eat a hawk made no sense to her, but she didn't try to figure it out. She didn't want to think too much about matters she couldn't control, afraid if she gave in to such thoughts they could easily monopolize her life. Provided, of course, they no longer seemed to present a threat....

~~~

"Let's get this show on the road," Nick said when they assembled at Isle a la Cache at noon to discuss the situation. "I'm taking a long lunch, but it's a busy day."

"I'm sure you realize Cora or I could have been badly hurt or even killed," Cisco reminded him.

Cora was relieved Nick objected to the endless rehash of events. She handed a sheet of paper to each of them. "You all know everything that happened, but we have to figure out if there's anything we can *do*. I made a list of things we should talk about...."

Frannie waved her page in the air. "We should be used to this by now. Cora can't stand it when we're not getting things done. Look at her, trying to smile and act patient, but her foot's been jiggling for the last ten minutes."

Cora knew her friend's comment was intended to lighten things up, but she didn't think that was called for under the circumstances. "I hate to waste time in general and now in particular. If there's anything we should be doing, the sooner the better, before something else happens."

Cisco glanced at Rose, standing by a child-sized table, picking up wooden blocks and banging them on the tabletop. Dawn hovered nearby. "I'm glad you could come Dawn," Cisco said, but his tone sounded doubtful.

"You think I'll be distracted?" Dawn replied, catching Cisco's meaning. "I'm used to it—I'll take her out if she gets fussy."

"This affects Dawn, too," Nick said. "She'll have input."

"Of course," Cora said.

"Just when we're all set—book all written, working out the cover, thought we'd be done before Christmas—and then *boom*, this happens. Shitty timing," Frannie said.

"I think that was the idea," Nick said.

"Whoever did this knew the book was coming out soon, you mean... and tried to force us to stop?" Cisco rephrased.

"I called the owner of the ranch," Nick said. "His wolf was quite friendly, a pet. He thinks whoever took the wolf drugged it. That's why it was aggressive when it woke up—in strange surroundings."

"Glad Rogers found out right away. There aren't many places to get a wolf around here—zoos probably have better security," Cisco said.

"Seems there'd be a lot easier ways to go about things. At least there's no unnatural crap going on this time," Frannie said.

"Yeah, well, where did that second wolf come from? Or go?" Cisco asked.

Cora stared at her agenda, not volunteering her opinion.

"Cora?" Nick persisted. "Thoughts about that?"

"That's right, I forgot that part," Frannie said, before Cora could reply. "That second wolf—out of nowhere, it killed the first one and disappeared—no sign of it anywhere. Like it was protecting you guys. Like before…this some kind of annual wolf caper? And what about that pishy-mishy-whatever thing?"

Cora saw Nick and Dawn exchange glances and concluded they had discussed Cora's previous experiences with wolves and spirits. She glanced around, but no one from the museum staff was nearby. The others caught her meaning.

Cora didn't think the second wolf was part of the original plot. It made more sense that it foiled the plot rather than completed it. If it wasn't her "spirit wolf," what other explanation could there be?

"It's hard to believe a spirit wolf intervened, but hard to ignore too. The important thing is how the attacking wolf got in our kitchen, who put it there, and why. That's what we need to know to *stop* this," Cora said.

"It has to be someone who knows about the book and about the curse. Knows that we're interested in wolves and that there's a wolf ranch in the area," Nick said, holding up a finger as he made each point.

"Could we be overreacting?" Cora asked.

"Overreacting? Cora, someone put a wolf in our kitchen! We're lucky we weren't killed!" Cisco said.

"Maybe he just meant to warn us again, like the letter. Nick said it was a tame wolf. Maybe he wanted to scare us—like Frannie scared Nick with the mask—and take the wolf back after we ran out. He didn't know the wolf would get violent and attack us when the drug wore off."

"You're too generous, Cora. Guy's a nut case, you ask me. Stealing a wolf, drugging it so it goes ape in your house—how'd he get an idea like that in his head?" Frannie said.

"Do you think he was trying to make it look like you did it, Nick?" Dawn asked quietly.

Nick turned to her with surprise. "What makes you say that?"

Dawn looked at the others. "If he was upset with Nick or wanted to be sure the book wasn't published—if it *looked like* Nick did it, like he wanted to get the rest of you out of the way, it would discredit Nick. The publisher could drop the book, and Nick could even lose his fellowship over something like that."

Dawn glanced at Rose, who seemed engrossed with the blocks. She took a few steps toward the others. "Nick studies predators, including wolves, and it got around about Frannie's prank."

"Why would someone go to that extent to hurt Nick or stop the book? And who would know all that?" Cisco seemed puzzled. "Nick doesn't know many people here yet—would it have to be someone from Argonne?"

Cora glanced at Dawn and Nick, expecting one of them to bring up Billy, but they didn't. "*Anyone* could know that," she said. "The media's been loving this stuff. The newspaper made a big deal about the curse and the wolf in Wawetseka's story, and people have been talking about it, which we've been encouraging so the book will sell better."

"That's true," Nick said. "We joke about it at Argonne. And back home...Mom talks about it."

"And the people at the historical society know everything, including the contents of the book. They're expecting to sell it," Cora said.

"All of Lemont knows—anyone that reads local news," Cisco said, nodding his head.

"My neighborhood knows too," said Frannie. They looked at her. "What?" she said. "I'm in this for fun, didn't I say? They all like to hear about the scary parts."

Rose toddled toward the bookshelves, so Dawn picked her up. Carrying the wiggling girl, she said, "And then there's Billy, who threatened us when we were just getting started."

At last, thought Cora.

"But he backed off," Nick said, seeming surprised she brought this up.

She shook her head. "I didn't want to worry you. I thought I could handle it. Nothing really, just…I see him around now and then."

"And you didn't tell me?" Nick frowned and crossed his arms.

"When I told you about his visit, you acted like it wasn't important. I thought you didn't want to hear anymore. So I didn't tell you about the phone calls."

"The phone calls?"

"Billy started calling and texting me back in July."

"And you didn't think I'd want to *know* that? Especially after I saw him in town, and he left the message on my car, and I spotted him later here on the island?"

"What are you talking about? *You* didn't tell me any of that!" Tears sprang into Dawn's eyes, and Rose started to cry. "We don't talk anymore! I can't go on like this, Nick! We have to *talk* to each other!" Dawn walked out of the room, hushing Rose as she went.

Nick ignored his friends and followed Dawn.

"Uh, oh," Frannie said after they left.

"I was expecting something like this," Cora said, meeting Cisco's eyes.

"What? You two know what's going on here?" Frannie asked.

Cora told Frannie about Dawn's encounters with Billy. "But I don't know what Nick was talking about—the message on his car and on this island. Unless… He did act strange when Pam showed us around, when he saw that guy in the parking lot. Remember?"

"No. Should I?" Frannie said.

"Probably not. He just thought he recognized someone he didn't like. Maybe it was this Billy."

~~~

Dawn left the museum and carried Rose to a grass and stone outdoor auditorium, built into a short hill nearby. She set Rose down on the grass to explore and then seated herself and wiped her eyes. Looking up, she saw Nick striding toward her with an angry expression. He stopped, standing in front of her and leaning forward.

"What's the matter with you?" he demanded. "I didn't know we had any dirty laundry to air, but now all our friends do!"

"How could you not know? Don't you realize we never talk to each other anymore?"

"Of course we talk! We're talking now!"

"We're *screaming* now—but that will be an improvement if it makes us finally talk things out. I've been telling you, but you just look away or say some placating words and change the subject. And I know there's something going on with you, but you refuse to admit it!"

"I was only trying to make things easier on you! So what the hell's wrong with placating words? Let me try to understand this—you're angry at me because I try to make you feel better?"

"You just don't get it!"

"You're right, I don't!"

"Problems don't go away because you say, 'Gee, things are going to get better.' They go away because we discuss them, find solutions, and make them work—*together*, not you by yourself."

"Seems like there's a double standard here. Or didn't I just find out that Billy was harassing you and you never said anything?"

"How could I when you're acting so dense? I didn't want to upset you, and I thought I could handle it."

"And you decided that, by *yourself!*"

"Yes! I did!" Dawn got up and walked to where Rose was pulling blades of grass and saw that she was safely occupied. More composed, she went back to where Nick had seated himself on the first riser level and sat a distance away from him. She cleared her throat, stopped, and then opened her mouth and closed it. Nick stared in another direction.

Looking at her feet, she finally said in a quieter, but still angry, voice, "It's been going on since we moved here, Nick. I can't talk to you anymore, and you don't talk to me. I love you, but our closeness is gone. And I'm losing trust. We're not doing anything to fix it and it scares me. I know there's something you're hiding, Nick. I can sense it. Is it about us?" Her eyes shone with tears.

He still didn't look at her. "It's not us. Work is harder than I thought. Some personality issues. A lot of pressure. I can handle it."

She rubbed her forehead and then put her chin in her hands, relieved that he finally revealed what was bothering him.

Nick said, "Our friends are waiting inside. We should go back."

"Cora knows about Billy, and maybe Cisco, but Frannie doesn't. What should we say?"

"I saw him some time ago, the first day I met Cora and Frannie." Nick told her about the encounter. "I thought he was just passing through and that was the end of it, until I saw him here at the museum and then he came to see you at the house. That was alarming, but I didn't really think it would go any further. If I knew he was also calling you, I would have been more worried. He was always such a nice guy—you know that."

"Do you think he put that wolf in Cora's house?"

He shook his head. "I just don't know. I don't think so. But I don't know what else to think either. What do you think?"

She shook her head too. "I can't believe he'd do anything like this, but everyone else will. The police are looking for him."

"Look, I'm sorry to have upset you, but we've got to go back in and figure out how to deal with Cora's break-in. This discussion isn't over —we'll talk things out tonight, okay?"

Chapter 17

Nick and Dawn rejoined their friends but avoided looking at each other.

"Pam said she'll keep Rose occupied while we finish talking," Dawn said.

"Sorry," Nick said, his eyes fixed on the agenda Cora had given him.

Cora cleared her throat and glanced from Frannie to Cisco. "Do we need to know more about this Billy, Nick?"

Nick sniffed and rubbed his forehead. "Billy used to be a friend, but we had a falling out long before we left home. I guess he's still angry and followed us here. I'm pretty sure he left a nasty message on my car, and he went to the house and told Dawn we didn't have the right to publish Wawetseka's story."

"This is the same guy we saw here in the parking lot?" Cora asked.

"Yes."

"So that's why you were upset. What was the message?"

"It just said 'not yours' and a lot of exclamation points written in the dust on my car door."

"And you thought he was referring to the book?" Frannie said.

Nick blinked a few times. "I thought he meant Dawn. Now I'm not sure."

Frannie's eyes widened with comprehension. She opened her mouth, then closed it again.

"Could this Billy be responsible? Do you think he did all this?" Cisco asked.

Dawn had been sitting quietly with her hands in her lap. She lifted her head. "Billy's not…he's all mouth. He doesn't have a lot of confidence, and he's hurt. It's like him to be angry and say things he doesn't mean, but I don't think he'd actually hurt anyone—intentionally."

Nick shook his head. "The note in my mailbox maybe—I just don't know. I wouldn't have thought so, but he hasn't been acting normally. I'm uncomfortable about implicating him. Can we discuss other possibilities?"

"I think we should," Frannie said. "Pinning this on Billy is too neat—the answer can't be that simple."

"Why not?" Cisco asked. "This is real life, not some crime show. The police want to talk to him, so he's in it already."

"A lot of people know about the book, but why would someone want to stop us? They know what the book is about already, so what's the harm if it's published?" Cora asked.

Nick shook his head slowly. "We went over and over this while we were writing it. We never came up with anything. Everything happened so long ago, and it was all resolved."

"Except the people that disappeared—Emmett and the pirates," Cora pointed out.

"You're hinting that something valuable was left undiscovered? Something the pirates were doing, maybe? Somebody wants to find it before we do, or found it and doesn't want anyone to know?" Cisco asked.

"Wawetseka didn't know either, or left it out when she wrote her story. Maybe *she* was hiding something…or maybe she left a clue…." Frannie's gaze wandered to the window.

"Something valuable revealed in our book—something we didn't notice. Someone figured it out and wants to keep it secret," Cora repeated.

Frannie rubbed her hands together excitedly. "I bet it has something to do with them pirates in some kind of way—buried treasure! Or maybe that Penney guy hid something on the island and went back for it. Leckey and Reddick went back to look, remember, and didn't find anything?"

"What about business or politics? Forsyth was a spy for William Clark and sent Simon Taylor to Fort Dearborn with a message. Maybe someone's upset by the idea the iconic William Clark was up to no good," Nick said.

"Why did Reddick hit Simon when he recognized him at Fort Dearborn? Wawetseka never explained that," Dawn said.

"We know Findel and Pascal were pirates, but what did they do *after* the story? In fact, what did they do *before*? They could even have been working for Forsyth too," Cisco said.

"Mishi-pissy-thingy?" Frannie asked. They all laughed. "No, seriously," she went on. "Maybe it's not some supernatural thing, but the guy who did this wants us to *think* it's a supernatural thing—that's why he used a wolf, because it was too crazy for a real person to do. And that stuff by the river, to throw us off, so we'd think it's supernatural after all—he wanted us to remember the curse."

"Or coincidence. The mind, it boggles," Cisco said.

Cora wasn't sure if Cisco was commenting on the number of possibilities or Frannie's rambling suggestion. "A wolf just happened into our kitchen, like Rogers said? Isn't coincidence even more of a stretch?" she said.

"Maybe it doesn't have to do with a secret in Wawetseka's book. Maybe it's something else—something current," Dawn suggested.

"Yeah," said Nick. "There's a guy at Argonne who's been giving me trouble. He's just the unstable kind of guy to pull something like this, and he's jealous of me."

Dawn shot an angry look at Nick, frowned, and bit her lip. "Or Billy, who actually issued a threat."

Nick returned her look. "We were considering *other* options here. Someone else back home? Maybe to keep the memoir private. Or because it reveals something about an ancestor. Or a blood quantum issue."

"Blood quantum?" Cisco asked with raised eyebrows.

"A calculation of how much Potawatomi blood, by tribe, or band, a person has. It determines such matters as tribal citizenship, per capita payments, casino profits," Nick said.

"Like if a person is one thirty-second percent Pokagon or has ancestors in multiple tribes—which tribe does he register with and how much money does he get?" Cisco asked.

"Sort of. Blood quantum determines tribal membership and benefits," Nick said.

"So if someone lied, or it turns out he had an ancestor who lied, and he doesn't want to be found out because he'd be kicked out or lose benefits, and that was revealed in Wawetseka's story—that could be a motive?" Cisco asked.

"People think the benefits are much more than they actually are though," Nick said.

"Whoa," said Cisco. After a moment he turned to Cora. "Anyone at the historical society that could be a suspect?"

She shrugged. "I can't think of anyone, but I can't rule it out either. Could be anyone in town with a grudge or a vendetta or with something to hide or something to gain."

"Or someone here at the island. The staff has been in on everything we do. They wander in and out and could have heard anything."

"Who knew you wouldn't be home yesterday?" Dawn asked.

"That's a good question," Nick said. "Whoever did this had to know you wouldn't be home so they could plant the wolf—or two wolves if you don't believe in spirits."

They looked at each other. "As I said, the mind boggles," Cisco said. "We can sit here all day and make guesses and we're no further ahead."

"Okay then," said Nick. "Let's sleep on it and talk again—when? Tomorrow night? Can we all make that?"

"Two days would be better—I can make two days work," Frannie said.

"Okay, two days—if the police haven't solved this by then. This place isn't open at night. Can we meet at your place, Cora?" Nick said.

"Providing the clean-up guys are done."

Frannie wiggled the fingers of both hands and said, "I'll start digging into *whatever*—but wait! What about the book? Are we going to release it?"

"Is it too late? We have a contract. Would whoever's doing this leave us alone if we cancelled it? After all, the book already exists. Maybe it's not about the publication—it could be something *we* know," Cora said.

"I doubt cancelling the publication will stop this person, but we can stall it until we know more," said Nick.

"You're probably right," Cisco said.

"What about the police?" Dawn asked.

Nick turned to Cisco. "Yeah, what about the police?"

"Why you all looking at me?" Cisco asked.

"Because you hit it off with Rogers. He likes you," Cora said.

Cisco drew in a deep breath and blew air forcefully through his nose. "Okay, I'll keep Rogers informed."

"What you going to tell him now?" Frannie asked.

"I'll tell him we're working on it."

Chapter 18

Treasure! Frannie wiggled a little in her seat, delighted that her logic and research had taken her to the very place she wanted— searching for treasure. Her friends didn't want to seriously entertain the idea of curses and monsters, and they were probably right. But it was in her nature to investigate ideas and places others wouldn't. She sought unusual and creative solutions—fun—that didn't come to mind at first. Like treasure.

Frannie woke that morning at five and was too excited to return to sleep. After yesterday's meeting, she had cancelled an appointment for today and brainstormed the ideas she wanted to investigate. She could hardly wait to get started. She made coffee, dressed in comfortable clothes, and was now happily reading website after website, trying to find treasures that could still be around since Wawetseka's time.

Her first search, for motives, was easy. She Googled "common reasons for crime" and read the top search results, making a list of thirty-one motives. She drew a line through those she felt irrelevant, like serial killings, political or religious, gang violence, hit man. The top three motives were profit, passion, and mental illness. She put a question mark next to "passion" and stars in front of "profit" and "mental illness." She also added survival, robbery, jealousy, greed, hiding a secret, fame, and power.

After comparing the list to their situation, she formed the opinion that whoever was threatening them stood to gain or lose something valuable, either of actual value or of personal importance. She made a mental leap and wrote "something valuable—treasure" in large letters and drew a circle around the words.

She picked up a pencil and hovered it over a notepad, gazing out her dining-room window as she decided what to do next. Built in the 1930s, the two-flat building Frannie inherited from her mother was located in a pleasant, working-class community on Chicago's South Side, an island of safety near areas known for high crime rates. She was gradually rebuilding relationships among neighbors and old friends, having moved back into the building after her white husband, and then her mother, had died. Most of her close friends were white and too uncomfortable visiting her neighborhood.

The dining room that was in style when the place was built was useless as such for Frannie's purpose, so she furnished the large space as an office. A row of windows faced the brick wall of a building merely eight feet away. Frannie had placed her computer in front of the unclad windows so she could look out while she worked. She often wondered what the builder had been thinking to put a bank of windows overlooking a blank wall, but she was glad the windows were there. They created a false sense of expansiveness. She often stared out when problem solving and found it effective.

She did that now. If there was a "treasure," it must be related to their book. If someone was protecting something valuable, something revealed in the book, what could it be? How did it get there? Who might have put it there? Who knew it was there now? Where? Who? What? She wrote the words on her notepad. She idly filled in the loops of the words.

Not everything they had researched ended up in the book, but any of it could be helpful now.

Where? If it's still here today, *where* could it be?

Wawetseka's story took her from Black Partridge Woods, where her village was located, through the Chicago Portage and to Fort Dearborn —now downtown Chicago. Frannie jotted down the locations and put question marks after the Portage and Chicago. These locations were too far away in Wawetseka's day, and Chicago was too public now. She added a star in front of Black Partridge Woods. The site of the former village was secluded now, easy to get to then—a better choice.

She wrote down the fur station, where the south end of Lemont's high bridge was now, and put a "no" after it. Too well traveled now for anything to be found there today.

Keepataw Preserve was where Indian men had hunted, where women farmed and gathered, and where trails led from the village to the river and flood plains. She added the location and put a star in front of it.

The island where Wawetseka had found Penney was now called Isle a la Cache, where she and her friends met to work on their book. Aside from the museum, the island had infrequent visitors, and the north side of it few to none. It was a known hiding place even during the Indian period, and much of it was remote now. Frannie put another star.

The woods and prairies through which Wawetseka and Noah Taylor had tracked Penney was now the site of Argonne Lab where Nick worked, and Waterfall Glen was a forest preserve that surrounded the lab. The area had never been heavily populated and now contained recreational trails, but off the trails it was secluded. Signal Hill was located there; it had once been frequented by Indians, but today was "somewhere" in the woods. There was a rarely visited cemetery, Saint Patrick's, on the slope of the bluff. Perhaps more than bodies were under that hallowed ground…. She put another star.

She would begin with the four locations she had starred: Black Partridge, Keepataw, Isle a la Cache, and Waterfall Glen.

Having narrowed down *where*, she turned her attention to *who*. She tore the first sheet off her pad and started a new one. She wrote: "Who hid something?" and "Who found something?" After giving that some thought, she decided to leave "Who found something?" to the others and concentrate on "Who hid something?" She wrote down two more words: "Who?" and "What?" She'd start there. *What* might have been hidden in one of those locations that would be valuable today?

As she considered the people Wawetseka encountered, a few stood out.

What were the pirates up to? The memoir didn't mention them after they took off in pursuit of Penney. Maybe they came back. Frannie would research pirates in Illinois—Hardy Findel in particular.

Penney might have known of or hidden something. Cora had asked her to check his trial—it would have been one of the first murder trials in the new state of Illinois. Perhaps there was a clue there.

Was a mission really being planned for the area? Was Pascal a rogue priest? Or just a pirate in disguise? She would look up church records, starting with the Jesuits.

What was the message Forsyth sent via Simon Taylor? Important people were involved, like William Clark and William Henry Harrison. Did it have something to do with politics? Or with business, aka greed? They had read some of Forsyth's documents in the Draper Manuscripts at the Wisconsin Historical Society while doing research for the book. She would look there for more.

Questions about Reddick and his past remained unanswered. What was his history before he moved west? She'd search genealogy resources for Lemuel Reddick.

She hoped finding answers to her questions about *where* and *who* would lead her to *what*.

The coffee she drank earlier had left an unpleasant taste in her mouth. Frannie stepped into the kitchen, put a cup of water and a tea bag in the microwave, took a sip, and returned to her desk. She grabbed a stack of paper and loaded it into her printer. She opened OneNote and labeled a tab, typed "lost treasure Illinois" in her browser's search field, scanned a long list of articles, and began to click through them.

Chapter 19

No sooner had Nick entered his office Tuesday morning than Tony stormed in.

"When are you going to let me have that report? I asked for it a week ago—the statistics from the Worth filtration area," Tony demanded. Typically, Tony stomped in already fuming, unwilling to consider any reply Nick made.

"I gave you that report a week ago, right after you asked for it," Nick said. He got pleasure from staying calm and polite, which he knew annoyed Tony.

"You certainly didn't. I'm still waiting, and I'm sick of it. I've had to hold things up. It's making me look bad." Tony marched out of Nick's office, slamming the door. Nick *had* given him the report, but that was life with Tony.

Nick went to the break room, poured a cup of coffee, and then descended a concrete stairway, leaving the building through a fire-exit door. As he stepped outside, a warm wind whipped strands of hair around his face. He wondered if the unseasonably warm weather was about to change. He hoped the break and fresh air would help him calm down.

Nick's fellowship was more difficult than he had expected, and he wondered why Tony appeared to consider Nick an opponent. Nick was proud of his fellowship at Argonne. He bragged about the national lab's part in the Manhattan project and its commission after World War II to develop reactors for peaceful uses of nuclear energy. Now he was one of the scientists researching advancements in clean energy and the environment. It made him feel important. It *was* important.

But any job was bound to have some frustrations. Progress was slow: getting cooperation through channels, dragging out information from busy people, completing forms. Wait some more, one step forward, two steps back. Others putting pressure on him to prepare reports from information he couldn't get.

Nick sensed elements of competition, possessiveness, and jealousy from a few scientists; Tony was not the only one who appeared remote. It hadn't taken long to get frustrated with layers of administrative complexity, research stumbling blocks, and a few brilliant but egocentric personalities. Nick's good nature only made matters worse. What sort of satisfaction was there in mistreating someone who smiled back at you?

But do any of these people, even Tony, dislike me enough to sabotage what I'm doing?

Cora told him things came easy to her, almost as if some spiritual entity prepared her way. Nick's success had also seemed easy, almost too easy. That could be one reason he and Cora became friends so quickly. Now for the first time life presented him with challenges he wasn't sure he could meet.

Why had he thought this was a good time to present Wawetseka's memoir to the world? It never occurred to him it might be better to postpone the book until life wasn't so complicated. That decision almost cost the lives of his new friends.

He tossed his empty cup into a trash can and walked toward a nearby line of trees into the woods that surrounded the complex. He tried to think of Potawatomi people who could be behind the attack. His father was dead. It couldn't be his mother, of course, or Dawn's mother, and he was an only child. Most of his friends were like him, ambitious, intelligent, dispersed throughout the country to launch careers and reputations. He no longer had contact with them—until Billy showed up.

The three of them never wanted things to turn out like they did. Inseparable childhood friends, sometime during their teens both boys realized their friendship with Dawn had become infatuation. At first it was a friendly competition, but when Dawn began to return Nick's feelings, Billy was hurt, then devastated, feeling betrayed by both friends. In an effort to mitigate his pain, Billy simply refused to acknowledge the reality of Nick and Dawn's relationship. But their closeness, of course, was gone, and had been for years.

Nick couldn't believe Billy had a mean streak, and his first instinct was to protect his former friend. But had Billy's inability to face reality gotten so out of hand that he followed them to try to get Dawn back, despite the fact she had never been his to begin with? Had his disappointment developed into obsession, anger, and hate? Was he using the book to punish them because it was important to Nick? Would he go so far as to use a wolf against Cora and Cisco, since he wouldn't want to chance hurting Dawn? Was his family at risk? Nick had to act as if they were. Or was Billy's presence in Lemont only a coincidence?

Nick started to lean against a tree, noticed ants on the trunk, and changed his mind. He kept walking aimlessly.

The manner of attack suggested an Indian, he thought. Animal legends and especially those of wolves abound in Indian folklore. Non-native Americans would be unfamiliar with Mishipeshu and wouldn't think to use the curse to threaten the writers.

If Billy wasn't behind the attack, what other motive could there be? Personal greed? Blood quantum decisions? Something valuable inherited by a citizen? Something that threatened the ownership of tribal land? Something that would embarrass a descendant? A group that felt the memoir belonged to the band and Nick had no right to profit from it?

He stopped and closed his eyes as fear suddenly ate at him, burning in his throat, hot tears forming under his eyelids. He could not endanger his family by what he thought of at that moment as "that damned book." At all costs he had to protect Dawn and Rose.

If some lunatic had a grudge against Nick, the book was a vehicle, not the cause, and cancelling publication would just redirect the vendetta and solve nothing.

Would it be dangerous to hope it was over and wait for something else to happen? Cora said she was a big fan of letting things work themselves out unless forced into action, but that wasn't his style.

Yesterday Dawn was in tears because they weren't being honest with each other, and it tore at him to see that. But if he shared his worries with her, wouldn't that only magnify her fears, rather than alleviate them? Wouldn't it be better to give her the impression he could take care of her and Rose?

He hoped she felt better after his apology. They still had to talk things out—it wouldn't be a good idea to put it off again tonight. But there was so much going on right now....

An unrelated thought came to mind, a note he saw on the department's bulletin board, a coworker advertising a fixer-upper car available for next to nothing. Dawn needed a car. It would be safer than being on foot or locked in the apartment and vulnerable twenty-four seven. Cora talked about this sort of thing—what she called incubation—her mind gave her answers when she was *not* looking for them. He'd check out the car today.

One thing he could put out of his mind—the Water Panther. He emitted a little snort of humor, thinking about Frannie's overreaction to that shadow in the water and her preoccupation with their legends. Nothing supernatural about that all-too-real wolf. But the second wolf... *that* was freaky.

~~~

"How can you just sit there and calmly read the paper like nothing's going on?" Cora glared at Cisco across the table. She took a sip of coffee, picked up a slice of toast, and set it back down on her plate without eating any of it.

Cisco closed the paper, folded it, and looked up.

"Okay. You want to talk, I take it?" His voice was calm.

"Of course I want to talk. What's been happening here? Did someone try to kill us? What attacked the wolf? Don't you think we should be trying to figure it out?" Her voice was *not* calm.

"You decided it was your friendly wolf spirit that attacked the wolf, didn't you?"

"Until a better idea comes along, yes. What about the rest of it?"

"The police are taking care of it, aren't they? What do you want *us* to do?"

Cora assembled her thoughts. "Frannie, Nick, and Dawn aren't sure Billy did this. Could it be someone else?"

"Do *you* have any ideas?"

"How about if we try to shorten the list by eliminating some suspects?"

"Like...?"

"I'd hate to think it was anyone at the historical society, but they know everything about our book. Maybe someone found something we missed."

"And they want to keep it to themselves, you mean, because they can profit from it?"

"Yeah."

"Is that what you think?"

Cora drew in a deep breath, sniffed, and dropped her chin into her hands. "No. Not really."

"You think someone there wants to steal our story?"

"Someone might *like* to do that, but I don't think anyone would." She picked up her toast and set it back down yet again. "The people at Isle a la Cache know the whole story too. They've been helpful, but maybe that's an act. We finished faster than anyone expected—I wonder if they want to stall publication while they beat us to it and get out their own version. One of them, I mean, not all of them. This sort of thing isn't unknown in the world of publishing, you know."

Cisco looked at Cora over the top of his glasses. "Which one?"

"Well, Brad is in charge—maybe he feels *he* should have written a book—he knows more about the history of the period than anyone there, and he's been looking kind of funny the last few times we've been at the museum."

"Maybe he's just tired of you guys talking and laughing in his library all the time. Maybe you're getting annoying."

"Or Josh—what about him? We don't know him as well—he's part-time. He's an actor, so if he's up to something he could hide it easily. He's a hard guy to figure out—always 'on stage' when you talk to him. I never know how to take him. Seems pretty serious about his career though. He's been working on a doctorate in something or other, Pam says. Maybe it has to do with that?"

"Something that would prompt him to threaten us by stealing a wolf, drugging it, and putting it in our kitchen? Would a doctoral candidate, a smart guy, do that?" Cisco refilled his coffee and sat down.

"Well, he's a naturalist. He knows a lot about wildlife, more than we do. All three of them do, as a matter of fact." Cora knew she wasn't making a very good argument.

"So what about Pam then?"

"She was there every single time we were and in the room a lot. She also lied to us about the north side of the island, told us nothing was there, but I think I read there used to be homes and businesses on the island. They're all gone now, but there's got to be something left, even if only foundations. I can't believe she didn't know that. But I have no idea what any of that has to do with our book."

"Everyone knows about it. Megan's given us press—what—four times? People ask me for updates, people I don't even know."

Cora thought about that. "Why would it be that important to someone in town? If it had to do with an ancestor, inheritances, property rights, anything embarrassing, that would all be settled long ago and who'd care? If they found something valuable, why not take it, get rid of it, hide it, or whatever. Who'd ever know?"

Cisco shrugged his shoulders. "What about Megan?"

"Megan? Why? She's helped us."

"I don't know. Maybe she wants to write a book too."

"Let her write her own book. No, I don't think so, Cisco. Not Megan. But what if someone got an idea from what we were doing and went out and started digging around. There's been archeological finds in the bluff before—Indian artifacts, fossils. What if someone found important remains, a village, a burial ground, a mastodon, or a mammoth?" Cora held up a hand when she saw Cisco was about to object. "That's not far-fetched. It wouldn't be the first time mastodon or mammoth bones were found in Illinois. Or Indian bones. Some of the ones at the Field Museum came from Sag Bridge."

"Are you done now?" he asked.

"I guess so. I can't think of anything else." Cora finally bit into her toast.

"I wasn't counting, but I don't think we eliminated anyone," Cisco said.

"Not really."

"So am I supposed to tell all this to Officer Rogers?" Cisco asked.

"Whatever. He should at least know we're cooperating...some of our thoughts. Things you think might help him, not crazy ideas."

"Aha—crazy ideas. He didn't want to hear about the curse. At least you're not blaming your wolf this time, so I can leave that out when I talk to him?"

"Just you shut up now," Cora said, laughing, her mouth full.

Chapter 20

The sleeping girl's lips were slightly parted, making a little "o." As Dawn watched, a bubble formed between them, and then another and another as air passed in and out of Rose's tiny mouth. The cluster of bubbles grew until it looked as if a foam marble balanced there. Dawn smiled—an endearing sight, a reward of motherhood.

Her daughter fast asleep with one arm over her head, Dawn moved to the rocker near Rose's crib. Some light and a warm breeze came through the closed blinds and partially open second-floor window.

She should be doing tasks but the balmy day made her lazy. What incredible weather for late October! Weathermen were calling this Indian summer, but that was supposed to come after frost, and this fall had been unseasonably warm without a break. Sometimes weather patterns like this led to violent storms, but Dawn put that thought aside. She had more important things to worry about.

She sat down carefully, holding both chair arms, and leaned her head back, remembering how she visited store after store until she found just the right rocker to create her personal spot in the nursery. Dawn took advantage of Rose's afternoon nap to rest. If there was any truth in the notion that high activity levels indicated intelligence, Rose was destined to be another Einstein.

She stretched her legs and placed her hands on her softly swelling belly, caressing the small mound and rocking the chair gently. Cora had been right—her initial feelings of panic had subsided over time and now Dawn was devoted to the new baby. If it drained her, no matter, she would care for it lovingly, without complaint. There would be years later on, when her babies were grown, to regain her energy. Assuming they got through their current difficulties.

She looked through the open window at gold and orange leaves waving in the breeze. She was deeply disturbed by the attack on Cora and Cisco, but the more personal situation with Nick monopolized her thoughts. They hadn't talked things out last night after all. When Nick got home from Argonne it was after eleven o'clock, and he was in no mood for conversation. He took her in his arms and said, "I'm sorry if I've been an idiot, Dawn. I was doing what I thought was best for you. We'll find a way, but I'm just too tired tonight."

Her reaction had been stiff and resistant. She had waited anxiously all afternoon and evening, going over and over what she would say to him, preparing to talk it out at last. Was that weak apology the best he could do? But to force discussion then would only have made matters worse.

She was still angry today, but more objective. She had hidden some things from Nick too, like Billy's harassment. Nick knew now that the calls had stopped and that she had seen Billy around town, in parking lots, at Target, and in Home Goods. She had thought he was lurking, but they could have just crossed paths. Billy would catch her eye, smirk, wink, or make a dismissive gesture with his hand. She was reluctant to call it stalking. He was still around and still angry, that's all. It was an awkward situation—how *should* he behave if they ran into each other?

She now knew Nick had had his own encounters, and Billy's suspicious behavior increased the possibility he was behind the threatening letter and the wolf attack. Was he unstable—and therefore unpredictable and dangerous?

Perhaps more of this was her fault than she wanted to admit. Nick said he would have handled it differently if she had told him. He asked her, while they tried to figure out what was happening, to stay in the house with the doors locked—to not even go out to get the mail—and to keep her cell phone in her pocket at all times. She patted her pocket. It was there.

She searched the street and surrounding homes from the window next to her chair. No suspicious cars, no Billy, nothing unusual. She leaned back and closed her eyes.

It all started with that damn book! she thought. She wished now that they had never begun the thing, but they were all so enthusiastic. It was important! It would be a shame, *criminal*—not to publish it. How dare someone try to frighten them?

But frightened she was.

Perhaps she could take the first step to patch things up with Nick—show her support—if she could take some positive action about the threats. What could she do?

She could sit at her computer, like Frannie, who was already doing that.

She could search her mind for suspects and motives, and she *would* do that.

She could call her mother, see if any rumors were circulating back home, ask if her women friends had mentioned anything. And she would do that, too.

She could talk to Billy, pin him down—surely he wouldn't hurt her—and she was the *only* one he might talk to. But what if he *was* dangerous? Nick insisted she avoid Billy. She probably couldn't find him anyway....

She'd think about it some more first. A lot depended on what Nick did when he got home tonight. There was a lot to worry about.

~ ~ ~

That evening, while putting Rose to bed, Dawn knew she was working herself up but couldn't control it. She went over and over the reasons that justified her feelings.

Once again, Nick acted like there was nothing wrong. He avoided her eyes and nodded when Dawn told him her mother didn't know much about Billy, only that he left some time ago. Nick played with Rose and ate dinner. What did she expect? Maybe he didn't want to talk until after Rose went to sleep. That made sense. But she had hoped for more warmth.

Rose seemed to sense something wrong and wouldn't fall asleep. Dawn read the same story over and over. Her voice was taking on a sharp edge before Rose's eyes closed and her breathing became regular. Dawn went into the bathroom, washed her face, and patted her eyes with cold water before going downstairs. She wished she could just climb into bed and cry it out. Instead she went downstairs, her stomach churning.

Nick was sitting on the sofa in front of the television. He looked up. "Sit down and watch—you've got to see this. This guy is amazing."

Instead Dawn walked into the kitchen and made a glass of warm milk. She went back into the family room and sat in a chair, waiting for Nick to realize she was upset. But he continued to watch the program and after a while said, "Did you hear what he said? What do you think?"

Dawn stood up and threw her glass of milk on the floor. "That's what I think!"

She dropped back into her chair, her face red and tears streaming down her cheeks, and then she stood up again and went into the kitchen for a roll of paper towels.

Nick took the paper towels from her and began to blot at the carpet. Dawn went to the front door and stood staring out the side window panel. After a while Nick came and stood behind her. When he spoke his voice was calm but with an angry edge.

"I guess I did something?"

Her voice shook. "It's the *same* thing. I've been waiting since yesterday to talk about *us*, and you act like it's nothing. It's not *nothing!*"

He grabbed her shoulders and turned her around. "I apologized!" he yelled. "What do you want?"

"Oh, yeah! *You're* sorry—*you're* tired—and you go to bed! That's supposed to make everything all right, after *months*? And tonight all you think about is that damn television program? If we keep shutting each other out every time something happens, how is our marriage supposed to survive?"

"Keep your voice down! You'll wake Rose!"

"How about you keep *your* voice down?"

"What are we fighting about here?" he said, his tone pleading. "I'm trying! I thought I was taking care of you. I don't know what I'm doing wrong!"

"You don't tell me what's important to you, you act like there's nothing wrong, and you make every excuse to not talk about it. But I *feel* it Nick. I feel like I've lost my best friend, the person I love most and depend on!"

She looked at him now, saw tears in his eyes too, and started to feel sorry for him. He *was* trying, she knew. But he was doing it *his* way. Why couldn't he understand?

She put a hand to his cheek but he backed away. "You don't have to do everything yourself Nick," she pleaded. "You have to include me, and, when I talk, you have to consider my point of view or ask questions until you understand. And we have to talk things out *together*, not make our own decisions and that's the end of it. It's not your way or my way, it's *our* way."

He stood for a moment with his hands clenched at his sides. Then his face softened. He took her in his arms and rested his cheek against her hair. She let him hold her, closed her eyes tightly, and buried her face in the warmth of his neck.

His voice breaking, Nick said, "I love you, Dawn."

After another moment, he added, "So much...."

Then a bit louder, "So much that sometimes I can't see straight."

She said nothing, but she gripped him tighter and rubbed her face into that familiar warm spot below his chin.

"I guess I've been fucking up pretty bad, huh?" Nick said.

Dawn pulled her head back and studied his eyes. "It's not just you. I didn't tell you everything either. You should have told me what was going on at work and that you ran into Billy. We used to tell each other these things!"

Nick pulled away, but kept her hand in his and led her to the sofa. He turned off the television and pulled her down with him, her back against his chest, his arms and legs surrounding her, his head nestling the back of her head, her hair against his face. She rubbed her cheek into his shoulder—into its comforting warmth, its firm muscles.

"Let's fix us," he said. "Before another moment goes by. I don't ever want to do anything to lose you."

"I don't either," Dawn said, her voice almost inaudible.

"Things have always been so easy for me," Nick said. "I never had problems like the ones I have at Argonne. I was afraid...afraid to tell you, afraid you'd think less of me. And when you asked for my help, well... I thought I couldn't admit to your fears—it would make the problem even bigger in your mind. I was afraid to do that to you."

"I thought...you didn't act like my fears were important. I was afraid to tell you it upset me. I didn't want you to think I wasn't capable of handling Billy or that he scared me. I felt inadequate, that you thought I was weak and whiney. I didn't want you to think I was like that," Dawn said.

"I didn't want you to think I couldn't handle my work problems or that I couldn't take care of you and Rose. I felt inadequate and that was a new feeling for me. I was ashamed."

"Didn't you tell me Cora said people admire us for our strengths but love us for our weaknesses?"

They talked until the wee hours and slept peacefully in each other's arms that night.

Chapter 21

Frannie shifted in her chair, listening impatiently. As her friends talked, she began to regret urging the others to go first. They were talking about things everyone already knew. She, on the other hand, had *new* information. Information that could place things in a different light.

She had been the last to arrive, and everyone was uptight, talking about whether the wolf had been a murder attempt or a warning that succeeded too well, and then if the second wolf was real or a spirit. Cisco thought they had to wait for the police investigation. Frannie had her own opinions about the police, wondering how effective they could be when they weren't considering Cora's spirit wolf or Mishipeshu, the Water Panther.

The conversation seemed to be going nowhere until Cora said, "After last year's attacks, if nothing else, Cisco, Frannie, and I learned to push our fears aside and use our heads to figure out what's going on—quickly, before worse happens. We can't dwell on fear and forget urgency. Let's figure out what happened and what to do." *Just like Cora to be preachy and bossy*, Frannie thought. But she had to admit Cora got things done, as she herded them into the living room for "serious work."

Frannie thought Cora was surprisingly composed after her encounter, but Frannie knew Cora well enough to know she dealt with stress by activity. Nonetheless, in Frannie's opinion this conversation was still wasting time. But, let them go first—let them get their ideas out of the way. They'd be all the more surprised when it was her turn. She dropped her eyes to her lap with a little smile. *They're going to be blown away!*

Dawn sat quietly in a corner. She didn't contribute except to say she was working on some ideas. Frannie noticed a number of loving looks pass between Dawn and Nick and concluded they had made headway to patch up their differences.

Then Cora, Cisco, and Nick finished talking, and Cora uncrossed her legs, leaned over the cocktail table, and picked up her pen. "Okay," she started. "Who's your most likely suspect and motive? Who wants to go first?"

"What about Frannie?" Cisco asked.

"I have lots to say," Frannie said.

"I noticed," Cora said with a chuckle. Frannie realized they had caught her antsy mannerisms after all. "This will only take a minute—just sum up, if you don't mind?" Cora said.

Frannie made a face, bit her lower lip, dropped her eyes, and nodded good-naturedly. *Let them*, she thought. *I'm on a different page than they are anyway.*

"I hate to say it, but my most likely suspect is Billy," Nick said, pulling on his earlobe. "He threatened us to our face and he's acting suspicious."

"I agree with Nick," Dawn said.

"That's two for Billy," Cora said, making a note.

"What if it's *not* Billy? I don't think we should focus only on him," Cisco said. "Billy knew about the memoir long before we started writing the book. Why didn't he try to stop us before we got this far? Shouldn't we consider something that came up after we started?"

"What?" Cora said, watching Cisco's face.

"Could the motive involve history, something specific to Lemont? Not just a Lemont resident, or Megan." He waved an arm in the air. "It's *possible* they're involved, but don't you think it's more likely someone from the historical society or Isle a la Cache?"

Cisco's jaw was tense and he shifted his eyes uneasily. Frannie noticed he was much more involved than he had been when they were working on the book and concluded he was worried about Cora.

Cora shook her head. "We talked about this Cisco. I can't think of anyone at LAHS that would have a motive, inclination, or the ability to carry out anything like this. We're *booky* types, and we're *old*—for the most part. Not up to wrestling with wolves."

"Unless it was more than one person?" Cisco suggested.

Cora made a face. "No. Don't go there. So Isle a la Cache then? Who—in particular?"

"It could be Brad," Nick said. "He was helpful at first, but lately he's distant and moody. I get a feeling he's disgusted, burned out—maybe regrets he hasn't achieved something important by now. He could want to steal our book."

"Pam is strong—she wouldn't have any trouble handling the wolf, and she's the most knowledgeable about wildlife," Cora put in.

"I don't know—no good reason, but I just don't see Pam trying to commit murder by wolf," Frannie said. "Josh, on the other hand, he's *weird* enough, but I don't think he knows much about what we're doing. He's got his fingers in so many pies—I can't see him having the time or the interest. Did you think he seemed interested in what we were doing?"

"I didn't," said Nick.

Cora scribbled on her pad again. "Okay, so Billy and Brad are our key suspects. If we exclude them, we'll go on to the next most likely." She turned to Frannie and pointed her pen at her. "Your turn," she said.

Frannie tried to keep a serious face but was afraid the others would read a smug, self-pleased attitude instead. "You guys finally tired of rehashing your suspicions and going nowhere, ready to listen to some stuff you don't *already* know?" she began.

"We're properly chastised, Frannie," said Cora.

Frannie made a show of reaching into a tote bag and setting four thick batches of computer printouts on the cocktail table, each held with a bulldog clamp. "Can't hardly get these clamps anymore," she said, as she dealt them out in a row. "All they want to sell now is those binder clips, they call them. Don't even like the word 'clip'—sounds all little and tinny. Not like 'clamp'—all strong and hefty-like. Bulldog *clamp*, that's more like it."

"Frannie," Cora groaned. "We've got to keep moving here—figure out what to do before something else happens."

"Okay, okay," Frannie said, admitting she might be overdoing the drama. She reached back into her bag and drew out a piece of paper, folded in half with handwriting on both sides. "So that-all's what I got, only I don't expect you're going to want to go through *all* of that, but it's there if you want. Here's what's important."

She couldn't help making a show again, unfolding the paper, turning it from side to side, pretending to find something; then she raised her head and made eye contact with each person, dragging out the suspense. She caught Cora looking at the ceiling in exasperation, got the hint, and began firing off points rapidly.

"I didn't run through suspects. You guys were doing that, and you know these people better than me. So instead of getting hung up on the *who*, I asked *why* would someone want to stop our book? This threat and attack—it's a crime, right? So I searched for the most common motives for crime."

She picked up the smallest stack of papers. "That's all in here, my *why* pile. You should know, I threw out a lot. We're not looking for some gangbanger or spy. The most common motives are: *greed*—profit, fame, property; *passion*—anger, revenge, vendetta; or *mental illness*. I figured the most likely reason is we have something—or the book reveals something—valuable that the person would lose if we publish our book. Goes without saying, the guy's probably mental, too."

Frannie was encouraged to see her friends exchanging glances, and Cora was making notes.

"That's logical," Nick said.

"Thank you," Frannie said, nodding.

"So—something valuable. If he stands to lose it when we publish—that means he doesn't *have* it, or it's not secured. Maybe it's the book itself, but I don't think so—the book is important, but it's not likely to make a lot of money. I think our book has some clue, and he's afraid someone else could find whatever he found, so he can't let the book get out. That's what I think."

"We tried to find something in the book. We couldn't," Cisco said.

"Maybe he found something *before* we started the book, but couldn't move it for some reason. Then we came along and all of a sudden he's got a problem," said Dawn.

"That's the idea," Frannie said, glad they were following her. "So, next thing I asked: what place might that be? *Where* do we talk about in the book that's secluded, where people don't go now but might go if they read about it? Four places seemed right to me: where Wawetseka's village was, the bluff and wetlands along the river, the forest and prairie she tracked Penney through, and the island."

"Black Partridge Woods, Keepataw Preserve, Waterfall Glen, and Isle a la Cache, which Wawetseka knew as Petite Tasseau. They're all public places now, but once you're off the main trail they're wild and secluded," Cora said, as if thinking it over.

"Argonne is surrounded by Waterfall Glen. Convenient to someone who works there," said Nick. Frannie supposed he was considering co-workers.

Frannie set down the first batch of papers and picked up the second. "This here's my *where* pile—in here, current and old maps, land records, property owners, everything I could find about those places. It's more than when we did our research before—things might look different now that we have a different *reason* to look, thinking about finding *something* instead of about someone escaping." Nick took the stack from Frannie's hands and thumbed through it.

Frannie let the others exchange a few comments, then she cleared her throat to get their attention again. "Next I wondered *what* might be hidden." She waved a finger in the air. "Don't you go saying this is all far-fetched now. This is all true stuff, I swear!"

She cleared her throat again. "In Wawetseka's day, burying stuff was common. Everybody did it. Indians didn't have much personal stuff. They lived in small houses and moved seasonally. If they wanted to keep something, they buried it instead of taking it with them. Same with white people, small cabins, they're alone and can get robbed any time. They travel, there's bandits—they leave valuables home, bury them until they need them. They don't go checking, that'd call attention to the stuff."

"Attention to what?" Cisco asked.

"I'm getting there. So I think whatever it is, it's something *big*, not something you can carry easy. Otherwise, why wouldn't whoever found it just take it home? Next, we know Wawetseka knew some pirates. And those pirates disappeared. Where'd they go? Or one of them other guys —Penney—he could have buried something too, and nobody knows about it to this day.

"So I think we got something valuable and something big, and that something is hidden or buried, that's what I think. But how're we going to *find* something like that?"

She gazed around the room. Nick and Dawn seemed interested. Cisco was biting his lip and shaking his head. Cora avoided her gaze and examined her notepad. Frannie thought she might be losing them, but she blinked, sniffled, and went on.

"So, what might the treasure be? It doesn't have to be old, it could have been hidden any time, but it's in some place we mention in the book. But if it *was* old, when Wawetseka lived there, what was it? And who put it there, or knew about it? If anyone back then knew about it, it was probably someone we wrote about. Otherwise why does someone want to stop us?"

"Treasure!" Cisco scoffed. "Come on, Frannie."

"Hold on. So, who?" Frannie said. "If Wawetseka knew, why wouldn't she have mentioned it in her memoir, unless she *wanted* it to stay hidden. Poji, Nagmo, and Shawnash weren't much interested in valuables either. So that left the white guys. I found some of them online.

"Leckey, he never moved from the station, stayed right there with his family. If he dug up a treasure, he never spent it, so not Leckey. I didn't find anything about Villeaux, so we can't eliminate him. But I think he would have told his daughter, she would have taken it, and there would have been some trace of her if she got wealthy of a sudden. It's more likely to be someone who couldn't go back to get it."

"Logical, so far, *if* it involved someone from the past," said Nick.

"Peniston Wayne was acting suspicious when he left, but if he knew, he would of gone back, but he didn't. Before the end of 1817 he moved across the Mississippi, with no time to come look for a treasure, and he never came back."

"What about Penney," Cora asked.

"Penney was hung, one of the first murder trials in the state of Illinois. Findel gathered his pirate band and went to Southern Illinois at Cave-in-Rock, then went along the Ohio and Mississippi Rivers, and even joined up with Lafitte for a while. Both of those dudes, Findel and Lafitte, could of known there was treasure and never got back to get it."

"And Pascal," Nick said.

"Wait till you hear this!" Frannie said. "I wondered if Pascal was a real priest, so I checked the Jesuit files. There *was* a Father Andri Pascal, but he was killed in Michigan in 1816 on his way to start a mission on the Illinois River, robbed and killed by *pirates*. I assume the Pascal in our story was part of the pirate band and took the priest's identity."

"Maybe the real priest wanted to build a mission where the treasure was, and they had to stop him," Dawn proposed.

"I checked into Forsyth, too," Frannie said. "He left a lot of letters and documents, but there's no mention of him being wealthy. With all the connections he had, good and bad, don't you think he would of taken a treasure if he knew about it? He was more involved in business and politics anyway."

"What about Reddick?" Cisco asked.

"Reddick, now, I thought he was a possibility, 'cause we never knew why he attacked Simon. I found an old letter from his wife, Amethyst, and she tells her sister that he ran off and left her with three young children. I figure if he knew about the treasure he would have taken it and showed up somewhere, so I don't think he was involved either. She said it was good he left, since he was crazy jealous and always accusing men of being with her. Maybe that's why he drug her out to the frontier, to get her away from men. I'm thinking it was something like that made him punch Simon Taylor."

"Let's move on here, Frannie. The third stack?" Cora asked, pointing at the stack on the table.

"Is my *who* pile—everything I found about those people."

"And the fourth?" Nick asked.

"Treasure. The *what* pile. I got to tell you all, reading about treasures was some fun. There's more than you'd think out there. This here," she pointed at the last stack, "is stuff that could be around *here*, not Lake Michigan shipwrecks or more recent stuff."

"Is any of it relevant?" Nick asked.

"Sure is. First of all, if we're suspecting people from Argonne, the historical society, or Isle a la Cache, fossil skeletons have been found in wetlands throughout Illinois. It could happen—someone might of made a major find, like a mastodon or a woolly mammoth. Mammoths are more valuable, did you all know that?"

Cora nodded. "Cisco and I talked about that. Big animals like that often died in rivers, and remains are found around swamps—both in the valley. But wouldn't someone notice an excavation like that?"

"You'd think, unless it's someplace nobody goes. But there's other possibilities. Like the Shawnee silver mines." She picked up the fourth stack of paper, flipped to a page she had marked, and read from it: " 'As long as recorded history it has been well documented that the Shawnee had an extensive source of silver, and they were known for the silver jewelry pieces they traded. When they were forced to relocate to the west, neither the mines nor their large supply of silver jewelry was ever found.' I'm not making this up. It's all in here." She waved the stack she held in her hand. "People are still trying to find this."

"Did the silver disappear before or after Wawetseka captured Penney?" Nick asked.

"Thirty or forty years before. Yeah, and the mines were supposed to be in Ohio or Kentucky—but it could of been taken anywhere or hidden any time or been moved more than once. Doesn't mean it's not there now. Wawetseka mentioned Shawnee silver in her memoir—we didn't know what that meant, remember?"

Cisco didn't seem convinced. "How much more of this is there?"

"Well, this one *is* purely guesswork. You know Cahokia, downstate near the Mississippi, where they got those mounds? The people who lived there were real cultured, so you'd think there would have been valuables in those mounds when they opened them up, but no, not a thing. They all just disappeared, back around 1300." Frannie picked up a bottle of water and took a few sips before continuing.

"Here's what's strange—other tribes never talked about them. Wouldn't you think everyone would have known about such an important place? Some people think something awful happened and caused destruction so bad no one wanted to talk about it because they were too scared. If they had any treasure, it would of been easy to paddle on up the rivers to our area—a straight shot and familiar to them—and hide the valuables. It's even easier than where the silver came from. That's what I think."

"It's all interesting, but…," Cisco said, furrowing his brow and reaching to take the stack of papers from Frannie's hands.

"I'm not done yet—still got to tell about *pirate* treasure," Frannie waved a finger. "Remember how Findel was upset when Penney ran off, and we thought maybe one of them was going after more valuables? Findel went upriver, but who's to say he didn't come back or go get his treasure and move it later? Or maybe Penney had it and put it somewhere before Wawetseka caught him? Or when Penney ran from the east he stole stuff and buried it before he set up at the station, and he discovered Findel's valuables because they picked the same spot? Penney kept being missing from the station all the time, remember? Where'd he go?

"And remember that reenactor we saw, the pirate? He said pirates didn't keep goods on them while they worked—they stashed them. Findel maybe was hiding stuff around here for years, such a good hiding place he kept coming back to add stuff. Maybe not just his own stash but something for someone else, like Jean Lafitte."

Cisco rolled his eyes and shook his head. "Lafitte? You did a lot of work here, Frannie, but you weren't kidding about the far-fetched part."

Frannie stuck her chin out. "People still looking for treasures Lafitte's supposed to have buried—well, mostly down south. But who's to say Findel didn't team up with him and take a treasure upriver? It could of happened."

Cisco's expression was doubtful. No one seemed convinced, although they were interested. "I'm not making this stuff up," Frannie said again, pointing at the papers in Cisco's hand. "It's all in there!"

"That's a lot of maybes, Frannie. I think we're getting out of the realm of possibility here," Cisco said. "Why not search for the Holy Grail while we're at it? Or just let the cops do their job?"

"Well maybe you think that's a lot of *maybes* Cisco. Maybe it's even some *new* treasure, nothing that goes way back at all. And the cops don't know what we all know and won't want to know. We got to start somewhere, take it where it goes, doesn't mean we got to *capture* the guy, like Wawetseka. But if there wasn't something valuable and something big, and if it's not *still there* right now, what reason you think somebody's trying to shut down our book?" Her eyes flashed at Cisco.

"Well, I for one think Frannie deserves a big thank-you for all her work," Dawn said.

"Aw, shucks," Frannie said.

"Aw shucks!" Despite the seriousness of the discussion, Cora burst into laughter. "I didn't know that was in your vocabulary, Frannie."

"Everything's in my vocabulary—you ought to know that about me by now, girl," Frannie chuckled.

Chapter 22

Nick believed promptness and regular hours defined successful people. He arrived at his office at 7 A.M. the following morning, as usual. Matt Vaitkus, head of the Department of Environmental Biology who supervised fellows for the department, was waiting.

Vaitkus glanced at the wall clock and said, "Good morning, Nick." Closing the door, Vaitkus motioned Nick to sit at his desk and took the only other chair in the room. His smile appeared forced.

"Morning, Matt," Nick said in a guarded tone. "Is something wrong?" Nick was puzzled. He and Vaitkus worked well together. *So what was the closed door about?* Nothing they were doing was confidential.

"Sorry Nick," Vaitkus said, rubbing a light growth of beard. He cleared his throat. "I'm sure you know the stake we have in you here—the fierce competition for your fellowship." He crossed his legs, thought better of it, and uncrossed them. He avoided Nick's eyes.

Nick nodded, wondering what Vaitkus was leading up to.

"We picked you not only for your academic record, but also our opinion about your work habits. We thought you were a team player who would work well with our staff." He paused, giving Nick a chance to guess where the conversation was going.

Tony! He must have made a complaint, Nick thought.

Nick forced a blank expression onto his face and drew his eyebrows together. "I don't get it. Do you have reason to think I'm not playing well with others?" he said, trying to lighten the mood.

Vaitkus took in a deep breath, unsmiling. He clearly didn't want to be having this conversation. "I've had some complaints about your reluctance to provide timely information—things needed in order to meet deadlines and other urgent matters. I've heard you don't respect people's work and you aren't cooperative."

Nick felt his face getting hot and he took a deep breath too before replying. "Did Tony complain about me—or someone else? Or anyone besides Tony?"

"It's been corroborated," Vaitkus said, shifting his eyes again.

Nick rested his chin on his closed fist. "But it originated with Tony, right?" he said, his mind searching for explanations. He didn't want to sound like a tattling schoolkid. He preferred to settle his own disagreements, but Tony had taken it to another level. How much should he say?

"This is about the Worth filtration stats, right? I gave those to him the day he asked for them. When he asked again, I reminded him of that. He didn't say anything else, so I thought he found them."

"That's not the way he tells it."

"And you believe him?"

"I'm asking *you*. I want to believe you, but he's been here a long time. I'd like you to explain before I start looking into other complaints."

"Other complaints!" Nick was alarmed and even more baffled. "*What* other complaints? Red tape, delays, paperwork, whatever. It happens to everyone—I thought it was how things were done here. I'm not the only one who deals with these things. I don't see how that comes back to me." He stopped, realizing he sounded defensive and argumentative, and he tried to control his reaction.

"It's not that," Vaitkus said. He turned his gaze toward the wall and scratched his head. "You don't want to go there, Nick. Let's just leave it for now. Give him a copy of the report to keep the peace, okay?"

"It's not that simple, Matt. I can print another copy, but he'll never be satisfied with scans of the original graphs and photos that were with the file I gave him. I'd have to go out to Worth and compile them again, and the dates won't correlate. I'll do it if you tell me to, but I have my own time-sensitive things going on, and that will delay information other researchers are waiting for—which is what you said you don't want me to do."

Vaitkus sighed, stood up, and reached for the door. "I'll do my best to make him understand."

"Wait," Nick said. "I'd like to know what *other* complaints you're talking about."

Vaitkus rubbed his forehead and then looked Nick in the eye. "The question has come up about whether or not your qualifications have been overstated."

"Overstated? Why? Don't you think I'm keeping up? Don't you think I'm doing whatever is expected, and then some, as a matter of fact?"

Vaitkus looked away again. "Sometimes, with protected classes, you know...."

"Protected classes? You mean because I'm American Indian?"

"Nick, let's forget it, please. Just try to get along, okay?" Vaitkus turned and left.

Furious, Nick stood with his hands on his desktop. He didn't need this. Tony on his back; trying to get that book off his plate; his friends, and maybe his own family, threatened by some lunatic—at least he and Dawn had put things back together. And now this shit!

His cell phone rang. He reached into his pocket and checked the caller. Their editor. He was probably calling for an update, wanting to know why Nick hadn't answered the simple questions that would clear up the few remaining edits before the book went to print. Nick let the call go to voice mail.

~ ~ ~

Frannie felt at loose ends this morning. As she often did at such times, she put on her comfortable old pink, oversized sweatshirt and pants, which on her worst day she wouldn't wear outside her flat, made a cup of sweet tea, and prepared to spend the day surfing the net and digging into whatever caught her fancy.

She wondered if she had missed something about Lemuel Reddick. She followed a lead to a Lemuel *Riddick* of Michigan City, Indiana, and ran across a story about Jean Baptiste Point du Sable. Du Sable was said to have lived near Michigan City before coming to Illinois, where he built a farm and became known as Chicago's first permanent resident in 1790, a farm he later sold to John Kinzie, Thomas Forsyth's half brother. Frannie remembered Wawetseka's comment about how tangled the relationships between white men seemed to be.

Point du Sable had a friend named Charles Broussard.

Huh! Frannie thought. Broussard was *her* family name. She wondered if he was a relative. She clicked around for a while, grabbing interesting facts here and there. She discovered that free black men were not unique in Colonial America, arriving as immigrants, not on slave ships. They were wage earners: sailors, artisans, and craftsmen. Many left for the frontier to escape white prejudice, among them, perhaps, du Sable.

Frannie had always believed she was descended from a southern slave. She wondered now if she was the descendent of a free black immigrant. Who knew if her own beginnings originated on the East Coast and followed the frontiersmen to the early Midwest? Who knew if she had an ancestor involved with the treasure she still thought was out there? She'd love to see her friends' faces if that turned out to be the case!

She'd have to get one of those genealogy programs.

Her mind drifted to the previous evening, which hadn't been as successful as she had expected. It seemed she was on a road her friends weren't interested in following, but she had learned long ago not to let people's reactions get her down. It wasn't the first time her ideas were called improbable, or even bizarre. She knew everyone didn't get enthused by the same notions that excited her. Time would tell if any of her opinions turned out to be right.

She'd had fun though, sharing her research. Fun—well, maybe that wasn't a good word to use when her friends were in danger. She didn't feel *personally* endangered—except when near the river—and she sincerely wanted to help. If she was more detached than the others, didn't that make her more clearheaded?

The group agreed that Frannie's research and opinions on motives and locations were helpful, but they couldn't go along with her other conclusions. She stuck to her convictions. People still found treasures today. Why couldn't they?

Cora had left last night with Frannie's printouts to review, since she was already familiar with those places, their history, and their present ap-pearance. They all agreed the matter may have started in the past, but the threat was happening now, which pointed to a current issue, so that would be their focus.

Perhaps something valuable was at stake, they conceded, but not buried treasure. As a courtesy, Dawn offered to study the treasure concept and give another opinion.

Her friends might not want to hear any more about her quest for treasure, but Mishipeshu still haunted her—she hadn't exhausted her appetite for information about the Water Panther. She opened her browser, hoping to find something colorful she had missed.

She found what she was searching for when the Water Panther came up in an obscure article that gave little-known details about the explorations of Father Pere Marquette and Louis Jolliet. While traveling south down the Mississippi River, local Indians warned Marquette not to go past present-day Alton, Illinois, because there were monsters there. Ignoring the warnings, they came upon paintings of such monsters on the side of a cliff where it appeared no man could reach. The paintings were said to represent the legendary Piasa Bird, but some experts thought they were of Mishipeshu. Written descriptions of both "beings" were similar, and both legends involved offerings of tobacco sprinkled on the water for safe passage. Marquette didn't continue his travels much farther.

Frannie brought up a map and ran her finger along it, following Marquette's return trip. From just south of Alton he went up the Mississippi to the Illinois River, on the Illinois River past Peoria to the Des Plaines River, then past Wawetseka's village to the Chicago Portage. The Indians who warned Marquette not to continue his trip subsequently made their permanent home in the area that is now Peoria.

Huh! Cool! Frannie thought.

Chapter 23

"As of this morning, they're no longer actively searching for the second wolf, but a BOLO is still out. No one has reported anything, and there doesn't appear to be any further threat. If anything was out there, it's gone now. We can't justify keeping men on it," Rogers said.

Cisco hung up the landline in the family room. Rogers had said he was no longer involved in their "case" but had stayed on top of the investigation out of interest. The authorities were turning up only dead ends.

County Animal Control remained skeptical about the existence of a second wolf, but no one could explain how the wolf in Cisco's kitchen was killed. Cisco wasn't about to suggest the police consider a phantom wolf.

The dead wolf was not rabid and had been killed by the tearing of structures of its neck, as would be rendered in a canine attack, animal unknown.

An officer had visited the wolf ranch and interviewed its owner. He established that the stolen wolf *had* been adequately secured. The man lived on the ranch, and his family verified that he hadn't left the property on the evening of the attack. There was no indication anyone associated with the place put the wolf in Cisco's house.

The owner also insisted the wolf in question was friendly, a crowd favorite that was often used in educational programs. He couldn't understand why the animal would attack, unless sedating drugs, or sedatives in combination with other drugs, had been used. He knew these could cause aggressive behavior as the effects wore off. He had no idea who might have done such a thing, but speculated that the person must have known some veterinary medicine. Nor did he have any idea how the security was breeched, how the thief managed to cut through the cage and carry away a hundred-pound predator, or where a second wolf might have come from...or gone.

"The investigating officer thought the man appeared devastated over the loss of a valuable animal. He saw no reason to suspect collusion in the crime," Rogers had said.

"Were there any drugs in the wolf that cause aggressive behavior? That would mean this was a murder attempt."

"We're not looking into a human murder here—the lab doesn't do tox screens on dead animals. He's already been disposed of," Rogers had said.

So there's no help from that quarter, Cisco concluded.

Nor had Brad at Isle a la Cache been of any help. Based on suspicions Cisco voiced to Rogers, a visit was made to the museum, all three employees had been interviewed, and background checks had been done. Nothing was found to implicate the staff. Brad confirmed that their education included courses in wildlife conservation, environmental studies, and naturalist training, but they were not experts and did not take veterinarian courses. Rogers stated his opinion that anyone with decent computer skills could pretty easily find out whatever information they needed.

"But where would he get the drugs?" Cisco asked.

Rogers had no idea.

So Isle a la Cache seemed to be a dead end too, Cisco decided.

With each elimination, Billy appeared a more likely suspect. According to Rogers, Billy's family said he moved to Illinois over a year ago, but he didn't give a permanent address. Family reached him by phone, but the cell number they gave Lemont Police had not been answered, and the department was unable to discover where Billy was living. He was probably ignoring calls and staying with a friend, but the only people Billy seemed to know in the area were Nick and Dawn. Rogers said tribal police admitted Billy had been involved in some questionable activities, but no arrests, and Rogers was reluctant to reveal anything specific.

"Drunk and disorderly, bar brawls, erratic behavior, anger issues, stuff like that," Rogers had said. "We'll keep looking for him."

In turn Cisco had tried to update Rogers on the previous night's discussion at his home. In the light of day it all seemed vague, speculative, and of little use. Cisco suggested something valuable mentioned in the book could be a motive, but when Rogers asked who, what, when, where, and why, Cisco had no answers and felt foolish. He wasn't going to start talking about mastodons, buried treasure, and pirates if he wanted Rogers to keep returning phone calls.

Cisco closed his eyes and ran his hand over the top of his head, feeling the few straggly hairs that grew here and there through his shiny scalp. For a moment he reminisced about how a thick head of hair used to feel, then sighed and returned to the problem at hand.

Last year two of Cora's friends had been attacked and she had to dig into an old mystery. Once solved, things had returned to normal, but now, once again, they were in danger. He had been reluctant to get involved then and was no less reluctant now. His efforts in the development of the book had been half-hearted, but now that Cora was in danger it was a different matter. He wasn't going to let anyone harm Cora or threaten his home!

He thought the police would soon stop investigating the incident. He didn't care if they punished the person, he just wanted to be sure there would be no more attacks. Was it over? The police didn't seem to think it was a murder attempt—more likely a prank or wild animals behaving badly. Surely no one would try to *kill* anyone over some old memoir. Things like that didn't happen in real life…but Cisco had similar thoughts last year when they were dealing with the Sag Bridge business. Treasure was nonsense and curses were nonsense. But rage, love triangles, and greed—violent crimes *did* happen over those issues. And bizarre as it was, people motivated to violence couldn't be expected to act logically.

If it was Billy…an angry, erratic, violent man with a personal grudge against Nick, and perhaps Dawn, too…what might Billy do next?

Everyone else was busy following information trails instead of confronting the man they suspected. No one seemed to know where Billy was or what he was doing. Could Cisco use a direct approach and track Billy down?

Cisco stuck his head in Cora's office to tell her he was going out for an hour or so. She mumbled an acknowledgment but didn't look up. He picked up the phone downstairs and dialed Nick's work number. It rang and went to voice mail.

"Nick, it's Cisco. I'm going out, but call me on my cell when you get this. It's important."

Chapter 24

Cora filed materials that had accumulated on both sides of her laptop and then sat down to begin work. She still had difficulty finding a place to put her notepad on the ample desktop that surrounded her. Frannie's printouts were scattered over every available inch. No matter how much space she had, Cora seemed to fill it.

Things were calm at the moment, yet she felt apprehensive. What was going to happen next? Nothing, hopefully—but she couldn't shake the premonition of danger. They had to find out what Billy was doing or identify someone else behind the threats and attack.

Was Frannie right? Was something hidden long ago, or recently? Was it still there? If she *was* right, Cora thought Frannie had identified the best possible locations: Keepataw Preserve, Waterfall Glen, Black Partridge Woods, and Isle a la Cache.

She asked herself where she would hide something big, heavy, and valuable, if she lived here two hundred years ago.

She crisscrossed printouts into a single pile and spread out a map that included all four locations, placing a colored paper clip over each spot. Then she downloaded trail maps of Waterfall Glen and Isle a la Cache and printed them. She did not have maps of Keepataw and Black Partridge—she'd have to rely on memory, which was okay. She'd been there recently and they were close, so she could go there if necessary.

She picked up the trail map of Waterfall Glen, a vast, heavily wooded area that circled the extensive grounds of Argonne Laboratory. A creek ran down the bluff. In the mid-1800s the creek had supported a sawmill, although today the creek was shallow and filled with rocks. She tried to imagine someone with a bulky treasure, maneuvering canoes up a stream studded with rocky rapids, lugging bundle after bundle uphill a hundred feet or so, and deep into a forest, excavating a huge hole through roots of closely spaced trees and filling it again, where the treasure remained hidden from surrounding Indian camps, and where it stayed buried under the farm fields that followed and, later still, from the CCC and WPA camps that rebuilt the forest preserves…and nothing, no clue, worked its way to the surface? Doubtful.

She checked the map again. The river had been farther away then, too—almost a mile away—before it was moved to build the sanitary canal. Cora shook her head. Too far, too high, too much work. She set Waterfall Glen aside and moved on to Black Partridge Woods.

The terrain at Black Partridge was similar to Waterfall Glen, so the area had the same positives. The river curved closer to the village here, and the bluff was convoluted with ravines. Cora's first thought was that the ravines provided good seclusion, but digging into rocky walls would have been hard, especially if a large storage space was needed. And the area was subject to erosion, leaving nothing to mark the spot. To carry something large here, men would not only need to contend with the bluff and the ravines, but the wetland that lay between this place and the river. In the early 1800s, if that's when the "treasure" arrived, Wawetseka's village was here, and transport of anything of such magnitude would surely have been witnessed by someone. Cora concluded nothing was buried at Black Partridge Woods.

Keepataw Preserve was closest to the river and the floor of the valley, only slightly above the floodplain. But the floodplain was a problem. It was a great place to consider if they were looking for fossil remains working up from rock through bog, but not so good for treasure. The valley floor here was underwater at times, and floodwater could wash away surface landmarks and quite possibly anything not deeply buried. Once again, Indians had lived on the bluff, so unusual activity was likely to be seen.

Cora removed three of the paper clips from the map. Only Isle a la Cache remained. The longer she examined the map and the orientation of the island in the river, the more logical the place seemed. Something big or heavy, if it arrived at the right time of year, would need no land transport at all—canoes could pull right up to the island. The Indian village Wawetseka had tried to reach when seeking help for Noah had been on the east side of the river, and the island itself blocked sight of the main channel and river traffic from the mainland. Floodplains and the forests behind them protected the island from the opposite bank. Convenient, out-of-sight access.

Cora played the scene in her mind: canoes, unseen from either river-bank, pull up to the island, unload, and pile their valuables on dry land. With the island's clear springs and abundant wildlife, they could take their time, look for hiding places, and mark spots for their return. Why search any farther? Even the name of the place said it all: the island of caches, of hiding places for items of value and for illegal or stolen things.

What if Frannie was right? What if there *was* a treasure of some sort waiting there all these years? She cautioned herself not to get too excited. After this length of time, if it was such a well-known hiding place, why would something still be there? Why wasn't it found by now? Whoever stashed it must have planned to come back for it during their lifetime—and wouldn't landmarks have changed? How much was the *valley* changed when the Des Plaines River was diverted farther upriver during the construction of the Ship Canal, for instance, and what about when the river was dredged? That must have caused changes to the island.

She suddenly remembered where she had read that the island had been occupied. Busy with their book, it had slipped Cora's mind. Pam got away with lying to them about the north side of the island at first because nothing was available about it on a casual Internet search. When Pam had said that, Cora suspected she was wrong, but now she recalled the reason for her suspicion.

A number of years ago she had visited the Romeoville Historical Society, where she ran across an old anniversary book, known mostly to local historians and elderly residents. The book included a map of buildings that had existed on the island in the past, including some on Isle a la Cache north of 135th Street. Cora searched through her research files to find some pages she had copied. Or had she scanned them?

An image of the map in the book formed in her mind now, but Cora was unable to locate her research from the old book. She left everything spread out on her desk and drove to LAHS, which now had a copy of the anniversary book. She borrowed it and returned to her office.

She found what she was looking for in the middle of the book, a map that showed the location of each of twenty-nine buildings that had once been on the island, followed by descriptions, information about the owners, and photos. In the 1980s the island had been purchased by the Forest Preserve District of Will County, she read, to return the island to a wilderness state. All remaining buildings had been torn down, and the current museum building had been constructed.

Cora studied the photos in the book to get some sense of what the island used to be like before it was reclaimed by forest and undergrowth. Although a few homes had housed year-round residents, the area catered largely to recreational activities, with vacation rental cottages, small hotels, hunting and fishing clubs, and bars and cafes.

Cora reasoned that today the south side of the island, with its museum, walking trails, picnic grounds, and Rendezvous, was too public for "buried treasure." Although in the past the entire island was accessible, it was unlikely that someone had recently *found* anything on the south side, as that person could not recover it without being seen. Therefore, she concentrated on the north side of the island.

Where should she look? It would narrow the possibilities if she knew what and when something was put there, but all she could do was study the book and guess. Photos showed that some large trees remained on the island when it was occupied, but the woods had been cleared. Leveling and development of lawns and open areas must have taken place. One of the clubs had a skeet shooting area with a concrete pad and mounds to protect men who operated the trap. With digging going on in the early and mid-1900s, if anything dated from before that time it must have been buried deep, she reasoned.

All this was very interesting, but it happened a hundred years after Wawetseka's story, so what did it have to do with their book? Was something hidden, not in Wawetseka's time, but when the island was occupied? There were buildings on the island as early as the 1890s—and through the heyday of prohibition. In the 1920s the island would have been attractive to mobsters, with its remote cottages, bars, and shooting ranges. Maybe it wasn't a treasure at all, but an archeological find, or even valuable documents.

Was something found during construction but left in place because no one knew it was important? Was something found recently, or *re-found*, under the foundation of a building or some such place? Was it found by someone who feared their book would lead people to the discovery? It had to be something that was hard to remove, to explain the need for time.

Thoughts of Penney running for his life and Findel retrieving stolen goods popped into her mind.

What could a "treasure" be? Wouldn't pirates bury only small, valuable things they could put in containers like sacks, pouches, or pots? Those things wouldn't be too bulky for today's criminal to move.

Cora rolled her head, getting the kinks out, and rubbed her forehead to ease the concentration lines she felt there. She got up and splashed water on her face, then returned to her desk.

No point trying to guess what it was—it could be anything. But she could try to pinpoint where. She had the map and could examine the known buildings, search for foundations, see if anything made sense.

She made a copy of the map so she could mark it as she worked, and she studied each building identified. When she was finished she had chosen four locations for closer inspection.

A businessman named Joshua Cook seemed to have controlled much of the island. In addition to his personal home, he owned a number of rental cottages, a large barn, and an assortment of outbuildings and storage sheds. They were located toward the center of the north half of the island, some distance from the river, on high ground. For no good reason, the barn caught Cora's attention.

In the late 1890s, Sanitary and Ship Canal engineers constructed a headquarters surrounded by cabins for canal workers. After the canal was completed, it became a sporting club. It was the oldest, farthest north, and most remote building.

A church had once been on the western edge of the island. There was a photo, but little additional information, except that it had burned in 1922. Cora had no way of knowing if the foundation was deep or if there had been a basement, but the location near the water was convenient.

The last building she selected was the Island Hotel, one of the first businesses and the last to close, still operating when the Forest Preserve District bought the island. A large building with rooms to rent, a popular restaurant, and a bar, it was located near the present 135th Street. Cora figured a building that size would likely have needed lower level storage.

Photos showed people standing in waist-deep water in front of their homes, with captions indicating the pictures were taken when the river was at flood stage. She almost abandoned her ideas of searching below-ground if the island flooded that easily, as basements would be unlikely. But then she read that the U.S. Army Corps of Engineers had dredged the river around 1940 to decrease flooding and remembered the island had had many changes over time, so she decided anything was possible.

If she wanted to know what was possible today, she had to see the island as it was today. Cora turned to her computer and opened Google Maps. She zoomed in as far as possible to the north side of Isle a la Cache and switched to Earth view. She could follow the edges of the island, but otherwise her screen was filled with impenetrable greenery. "I'll have to go out there," she said aloud.

She had been concentrating so long, she lost track of where Cisco was. She searched the house and called his name, but he didn't answer. She looked in the garage, and his car was gone. Did he tell her he was leaving? She couldn't remember. Sometimes he ran out and forgot to tell her—sometimes he told her but she was so intent she only half heard him.

Outside the window, the sky was gray and trees blew wildly in the yard. She remembered that storms, possibly violent, were predicted for later in the day. News reports had been saying the warm spell was breaking and the arriving cold front could bring severe weather, but in Cora's opinion weathermen were alarmists looking for better television ratings. On the other hand, if they happened to have this one right, it would be impossible to check out the island in rain and mud. Many times storms bypassed the valley, but she couldn't count on that.

The premonition and urgency she felt when she started her investigation this morning was increasing. She'd better hurry if she was going to see anything today. She didn't have time to track down Cisco.

She'd call and see if Frannie was interested in a little "fieldwork."

Chapter 25

Coming back from Michigan, Dawn drove below the speed limit —an unfamiliar car, driving into a weather front, gusts of wind that made it hard to stay in her lane *and* she was deep in thought with tears in her eyes. She couldn't understand why she was tearful, jittery—why she felt like something bad was about to happen. Was she missing her "Baby Princesa" already, only an hour since leaving Rose with her mother for the weekend?

She should have felt better after she and Nick patched up their argument, not sad. But she *was* sad. Maybe she was mentally or physically drained, or maybe hormonal changes from her pregnancy made her emotional. Not to minimize Nick's problems at work and the incident at Cora's house.

Yesterday, when Nick brought home the car he found for her, she called her mother right away. "I'll be able to get around now, take Rosie places, get things done during the day so I don't have to run errands at night. I wish I could feel sure the 'old clunker' is safe, though."

"Why don't you bring it here?" her mother suggested. "I'm sure Dottie's son would go over it, and he won't charge unless it needs parts. We can switch—I'll drive your car and you drive mine until we know yours is good. I'd like to see Rosie anyway—I miss her." And so it was arranged. Rosie would stay with Grandma in Michigan, and Dawn would return home for a relaxed weekend with Nick.

"Do you have a publication date for Nick's book yet?" her mother had asked during their visit.

"There's been a little snag," Dawn fudged. "The publisher had some complaints they want to check into. Has anyone around here objected to what we're doing?" She downplayed the situation, not wanting her mother to worry.

Her mother had a lot of questions, but she hadn't heard any complaints about the book. "I don't know what the publisher was talking about either," Dawn had said.

Now she turned off I-80 and onto I-355, teary-eyed. Her mind told her to feel good, but her emotions seemed to need more time. *Near misses, difficulties, struggles,* she thought, *make love more intense.* She felt like she never loved Nick more acutely—or more painfully—than she did right now. She experienced the same intensity she felt when Nick assured her of his love and held her in his arms—the memory wouldn't leave her. Maybe it was not sadness or premonition that affected her, but a poignancy so powerful that it found release in tears.

She allowed the feelings to take over, and, after giving them the freedom they demanded, gradually the tears went away and she calmed. She concentrated on the road and fought the wheel for a time, until more pleasant thoughts preempted her melancholy.

Her mood slowly lightened. She wondered how she could ever have feared having the baby she carried. She placed her hand on her growing abdomen and rubbed it fondly. "I love you, you silly little guy—or gal!" she said aloud to herself, and she laughed, although the hollow aftermath of her tears remained. Or was that hunger? She laughed again at the little joke.

Maybe Nick had been right all along and she had blown her personal problems out of proportion. She was determined to do what she could now to make Nick's life easier. She couldn't do anything about his problems at work, of course, except to listen and offer advice. But she could try to make his life outside of work easier.

She exited I-355 at 127th Street and looked at the dashboard clock. Just past noon. She knew what she would do. She'd stop at the grocery store and pick up what she needed to make Nick's favorite Crock-pot chili. She had just enough time to put it all together, take a short nap, and then read Frannie's printouts. She'd save time to take a shower, put on something sexy to welcome Nick when he got home, and then devote herself to him. She grinned as she pictured herself wearing that soft-red gown that would look sexy despite her growing belly.

Then without warning the anxiety kicked in again. They still had problems to fix.

They had to find out who was threatening them and be sure nothing more happened. They had to decide what to do with their book. They didn't know how much danger any of them were in, or what to do about it. And they didn't know how much of a concern Billy presented. Despite the fact that the police had found nothing ominous and nothing had happened for four days, they should take advantage of Rose's absence to try to find answers right away.

What was wrong with her? One minute she was down, up the next, seesawing from one extreme to another, planning a cozy evening with Nick, then panicking about Sunday night's scare.

As she turned into the store's parking lot, Billy's dark-blue truck passed by, heading south. He wouldn't have noticed her in her mother's car.

She wondered why he wasn't working. In fact, how *was* he supporting himself? Where did he go when he wasn't bothering her? Where was he going now?

On a whim she turned her car around and followed him, a few cars between them. He wouldn't notice her in the strange car, so it was a good time to see where he lived, where he worked, or where he hung out. She could tell the police and they could talk to him. She had promised Nick she'd be careful, and she would, but this was too good an opportunity to pass up. She could be helpful at last.

Billy headed south on State Street to Archer Avenue, turned right past Kohl's and Target, and made another right turn, heading west on 135th Street toward Romeoville. Fewer cars were on this road and Dawn had to drop back farther, but she would easily see if he turned off.

She followed his truck over the bridges across the Des Plaines River Valley. When Billy neared Isle a la Cache he turned into a lot west of the museum. Dawn went past the next intersection, turned her car around, and headed back. Gusts of wind blew her car between lanes, and dry leaves and paper scuttled across the road. Cora had told her that for some reason storms seemed more violent on this side of the valley.

She pulled into the parking lot in front of the museum. Billy's truck was in the second lot, but he wasn't in the truck. She looked around. If he had gone into the museum, she would have seen him walking toward it. He must have crossed 135th Street, a wide road with fast-moving traffic, and gone into the woods on the north island. She knit her brow. Was he going fishing? Pam said that only fishermen went to that part of the island—Billy had never had much interest in fishing, to her knowledge. This was strange.

She parked her car, turned off the motor, picked up her cell phone, and dialed Nick's number.

"Hi, hon," she said when he answered. "I'm at Isle a la Cache, in the parking lot—listen, this is odd. I followed Billy here—no, no, he didn't see me. I'm in Mom's car—he wouldn't recognize it. He left his truck in the lot and must have gone into the woods on the north island...I have no idea why. I'm just going to stay here and watch, but I think this could be important—well, if you can get away, okay, but I don't think it's necessary— Yeah, I know storms are coming, but I won't be getting out of the car, and I'll go right home. I'm sure he'll want to finish whatever he's doing and leave before then. Pam said there's no shelter out there."

Chapter 26

When Rogers told Cisco that Billy had been stopped for drunkenness and bar fights, Cisco reasoned that Billy probably didn't have a lot of friends in Lemont and hung out in bars. With that in mind, Cisco went to find out. At the end of the 1800s, Lemont had been notorious for its Smokey Row, a collection of as many as a hundred shady establishments, bars, brothels, gambling houses, and the like. Although quite tame in comparison, today a few drinking places remained in its "downtown" or "historic" part of town, where the oldest buildings still stood.

Cisco's first stop was Nick's. Known for its giant hamburgers, the place was busy with customers seated at the long bar and tables. He eased himself onto a barstool and ordered a draft beer.

When the bartender set a glass in front of him, he said, "I've been helping a friend find someone—a friend of his from Michigan who moved to Lemont about a year ago. I thought he might come here."

"That's pretty vague," the personable young woman said, laughing. "What does this guy look like?"

Cisco realized he had no idea what Billy looked like. He stammered a moment, then started listing what he knew, mainly that he was American Indian, in his mid- to late twenties, and he could possibly seem sullen or angry. The woman didn't know anyone like that.

He sipped his beer as she served drinks, brought food orders, and talked and laughed with diners. She returned when Cisco indicated he didn't want another drink. She took the ten-dollar bill he left on the bar, rang up his tab, and placed the change in front of him.

"I asked a few customers. Nobody seems to know anyone like that," she said. "Why do you want to find this guy?"

"They grew up together—heard he lived here now. Thanks for your help." He walked out, leaving the remainder of the ten dollars for the helpful bartender.

Things went no better at the Main Inn where he stopped next. His third stop was Tom's Place, near the I & M Canal. Popular with long-time Lemont residents, Tom's was a friendly neighborhood kind of tavern that looked like it hadn't changed since Smokey Row days and still served Blatz beer on tap. Here Cisco hit pay dirt.

"You must be talking about Billy," the owner, who was tending his own bar, said. "He's from Michigan—bet you didn't know there were reservations that close."

"Tribal land, or communities, I think they say these days," Cisco said. "But yes, Billy—that's his name. So you know him?"

"Yeah. He started coming in some time ago—about a year or so I think. Quiet guy, stops by for a couple of pops, sits near the door. He's pretty much a loner. A few regulars talk to him now and then, nod or clap him on the shoulder, that sort of thing. He doesn't make any trouble. Why are you looking for him?" the chatty owner asked.

"Friend of a friend. They were close when they were kids."

Cisco sipped his beer while the man served other customers.

"I'd really like to help find this guy," Cisco said when the owner returned. "Any idea where he works or where he lives or how I can reach him?"

The man shook his head. "Like I said, he doesn't talk much. Just comes in, usually around dinner time, has a couple, and wanders off."

As Cisco started to leave, a man sitting a few stools away said, "Check the library. He usually comes here from there." Cisco nodded and thanked the man.

On his way to his car, a fierce wind grabbed Cisco's cap. He chased it down the street. He scolded himself for not noticing the weather sooner but knew he had a tendency to lose track of everything else when he was involved. He shouldn't have been surprised, since violent storms often accompanied a breaking weather front.

He drove to the Lemont Public Library. Cora would be a better person to do this, he thought, since she was a Library Trustee. She knew all the staff and they would feel comfortable talking with her. But Cora wasn't here and he was making progress, so he'd wing it.

He stood for a moment in the large, open space near the checkout desk. Who should he talk to? The reference staff supervised computer usage from their desk and saw pretty much everything that went on in the library. Yes, that's the idea.

An attractive woman with short blond hair sat behind the reference desk talking with a man in front of her. The man waved his arm toward the public computers, seeming irritated. Smiling reassuringly, the librarian went to a computer, and the man watched as she frowned and touched some keys.

A middle-aged woman walked to the reference desk and stood, tapping her foot and frowning. This was going to take a while, Cisco guessed, trying not to appear impatient. Just when he was about to seek a different staff member, the librarian was free. He didn't know her name, but she recognized him. "Hi Cisco," she said. "How are you? Can I help you with something?"

"This is a little awkward," he said. The woman leaned forward, and Cisco lowered his voice. "Cora and I are trying to find someone…uh, someone who I heard spends a lot of time here—a friend of a friend." He spoke Cora's name a little louder, to be sure the woman understood one of the trustees was making the request. He went on to tell her what he knew about Billy.

"I know who you mean," she said almost immediately, nodding her head. She glanced around and then said, "Follow me."

Cisco followed her between the rows of books and she turned to him. "We don't usually talk about patrons, but this guy makes us a little nervous. I hope there's no problem."

Cisco laughed uncomfortably. "I don't want to make trouble for him. I'm only trying to get in touch with him."

"Well, just come here any morning. He's here just about every day— in fact I'm surprised I haven't seen him today. He spends hours on our public computers and a lot of time wandering around talking on his cell."

"I don't suppose you have an address for him," he said hopefully.

"He doesn't have a card—not a resident. That's why he uses our resources here instead of checking books out. I tried to get him a card, but we can't issue one without proof of address, and he couldn't provide that."

Cisco let out a slow breath and squeezed his lower lip, disappointed. "I guess there's no job information either, if he's here all day."

She shook her head and shrugged her shoulders.

"Do you have any idea what he *does* on the computer? Is it just e-mailing and surfing the net, or does it seem to have some purpose?"

"I know he has an e-mail address because I helped him set one up. I see him making a lot of notes, and he has asked me to help him find materials on Indian lore, history, artifacts, stuff like that."

Cisco gazed toward a window. "Very interesting," he said after a moment.

"Yes, it is, actually. I'm getting quite an education while I'm helping him. Once he came in looking upset. He rushed in—his face was drained and he had sweat on his forehead and his eyes were wandering all over. I thought something must have happened, and then he asked me to find information about Indian wolf legends and something called a water panther."

Cisco's cell phone rang, and Nick's number appeared on the screen. He accepted the call and said, "Just a minute," into the phone. He grinned at the librarian and stuck his hand out. "Thank you," he said. "That's very helpful. I guess I'd better take this outside."

He walked out of the building and stopped outside the entrance. "Yeah, Nick," he said into the phone. "Sorry, I was in the library—yeah, the public library. I can't believe how windy it is—I'm having trouble hearing you. I found out a lot about your buddy Billy. It seems he's at the library most days. Who would have guessed we'd find him here, right under Cora's nose?"

"Is that why you called, Cisco?"

"I called to tell you what I found out from Rogers, and that I was going to try to find Billy, get your thoughts. When I couldn't reach you I just went anyway, and now—"

"Can you give me the condensed version, Cisco? I appreciate what you're doing, but there's a lot going on today."

"Sure," Cisco said. He quickly summed up what Rogers told him and what he discovered about Billy. "I don't know where he is yet, but he's been looking up wolves and Mishipeshu—as far as I'm concerned, that makes him our guy."

"Where's Cora now?" Nick asked.

"Cora? Home, I guess. She was when I left—pretty intent in her office. She had that glazed look when I told her I was leaving—I'm not sure it registered. Why?" he asked again.

"I just talked to Dawn on the phone. She's at Isle a la Cache and said she followed Billy there. He wandered onto the north side of the island, and she's sitting in her car watching for him to come back. She didn't want me to come—said she won't leave the car and it's her mother's car so he won't see her. But it doesn't feel right. I thought maybe Cora could go…now, after what you told me…something's wrong, Cisco. I feel it. I'm going out there."

Cisco reached his car and eased into the seat, wrestling with the door against the wind. "I'm sure everything's okay, but I'm going too. I'm closer than you, so I'll probably get there first. On my way…"

He ended the call, hit a few more buttons, and dialed Cora. If he got caught talking while driving, he'd just have to accept the consequences.

The call went to voice mail, so he pulled over and texted her. "Nick and I on our way to Isle a la Cache 3 p.m. Join us if you can."

~~~

Dawn had been staring impatiently at Billy's empty truck and the woods across the street for half an hour. If she waited for Billy to return to his truck and drive off, how would she know what he did in there? She *wouldn't* know, unless she saw what he was up to. Should she go in after him and see what he was doing? She felt guilty, as if everyone was doing something to get to the bottom of the threats except her. She wanted to contribute—especially if it turned out to be Billy who was behind the trouble.

She scanned the other side of the road yet again. Where would she enter the woods if she did go? In front of her, 135th Street was a divided, four-lane highway with speeding cars and little to no shoulder. She couldn't see into the woods at all; they were too dense.

Was Nick on his way or not? She should have told him to join her. She dialed his cell number, but he didn't pick up the call. He must be on his way. The wind was increasing, violent gusts rocked her car, and the sky was ominous. A woman approached a car a few places away from Dawn's, battling the wind as she dragged two preschool children, strapped them into car seats, and raced out of the lot. Dawn assumed she wanted to get home before the storm hit.

Even if Billy *was* behind the attack on Cora and Cisco, she just couldn't believe he was a danger to *her*. Nick, maybe—but she was sure Billy cared enough for her that he wouldn't harm her, even if she did follow him and he caught her.

Dawn picked up her cell phone again, checked the time, clicked on the weather app, and scrolled to satellite view. It displayed a large area of storms approaching and alerts that included a tornado watch. Dawn recalled there had been many such warnings this year, all of which resulted in nothing but thunderstorms.

She couldn't sit still, fidgeted in her seat, more and more impatient to know what Billy was doing. She thought she'd miss her opportunity if she waited any longer. She'd just get a little closer—see what she could see on the other side of the road.

When she opened the car door, the wind blew it out of her hand. She got out, steadied herself with the door handle, and wrestled the door closed. She looked around, hesitated, then walked to the side of the road and waited for a car to pass. She dashed to the dividing strip between lanes and waited again. Finally across, she confronted a wide area of reeds, behind which was an impassable boggy area and then forest.

She wondered how Billy had disappeared through this so quickly. He must have gone that way before, she reasoned. She plodded through tall grass along the side of the road. The ground dropped steeply into a ditch and leveled out on the other side, with dense brush and scrub trees beyond. She continued along the road, searching for a place to cross the ditch.

Eventually she came to an area where the grass was matted and a thin path—probably worn by fishermen—led across the ditch and into the brush. It was free of bog there. She clambered down, pushed through some foliage, and was surrounded by dense trees and shrubs that immediately hid the road behind her. After a short distance the path led to a wide grassy area.

Taking high steps through thick grass up to her knees, holding aside occasional overhanging branches of shrubs and saplings, she followed the trail north. She glanced behind her, to both sides, and peered ahead, but saw no one. Wind rushing through the trees soon drowned all sounds of road traffic.

~ ~ ~

Cora, behind the wheel, struggled to get her cell phone out of her pocket and handed it to Frannie. "Call, immediately followed by text—must be Cisco. Here—read me the text."

"Seems like we're having a party. Cisco and Nick are on their way to Isle a la Cache too, for some reason."

Cora switched on the left turn blinker and slowed to a stop to let traffic clear. "*They're* on their way—*we're* here. Does he say why?"

"Sure don't."

As she waited for traffic to clear, the car rocked in the wind. Cora pulled into the lot and parked halfway between the only two cars in the lots. Both were empty she noticed. She reached for the phone and dialed Cisco. "He's probably driving, won't pick up."

But he did pick up. "Where are you?" he said.

"I'm at Isle a la Cache with Frannie."

"In the museum?"

"In the car—we just got here."

"Good. Be sure Dawn stays in her car."

"Dawn? What makes you think Dawn's here? I don't see her or their car."

"Oh—she's driving her mother's car. Check them all."

"There are only two cars here, and they're both empty. What kind of car does her mother have?"

"I haven't got a clue. Just look, would you?"

"What's going on?"

"Billy's out there somewhere, and Dawn's supposed to stay in her car. Do you see his truck?"

"No, there's just—" She saw a dark-blue truck parked in the west lot. "There's a truck parked in the other lot. It's empty too."

"You and Frannie stay put. We'll be right there." Cisco ended the call.

Chapter 27

Dawn crept cautiously, following the trail, stopping every few steps, searching for any sign Billy had gone this way. After about fifty yards, she laughed at herself. Why was she trying to be quiet? The ferocious wind would mask any noise *she* made.

The footing was treacherous; thick grass obscured everything underfoot. She stumbled on holes, rotting logs, tree roots, mud and stones, forcing her to test each step for solid ground to keep from falling or twisting an ankle. This was a bad place to get injured and stranded. She thought it was a deer trail she followed, remembering that deer lived on the island. Trails rambled in multiple directions and sometimes just stopped, forcing her to backtrack or find another, all while fighting the wind. She became disoriented and almost lost track of why she was there at all in her concentration to keep going.

This place was nothing like the forests Dawn was accustomed to, with their well-worn paths through leafy, mossy trees and trunks of various sizes packed tightly together. Instead occasional tall, old trees grew here and there, oaks and maples such as one might see in a lawn, with large overgrown grassy areas and thick clumps of tall shrubs and saplings between them, along with dried stems of wildflowers and weeds. The grass was terrible in its denseness, hiding what lay beneath, pulling at her legs with each step. Stopping to catch her breath, she saw her clothing was covered with masses of burrs. She brushed at them ineffectively; they only caught again on a new spot.

Trees swayed violently overhead. Now and then she came across areas of mud, depressions where nothing, not even grass, grew, and she had to find her way around them. After twenty minutes, she came to a gully that cut across the northern tip of the island. It was filled with mud and puddles of water, too wide to cross. On the other side of the gully more trees grew, but she could see the river beyond them, and knew this was the end of the island.

She leaned against the trunk of a large tree to get her bearings. The river was high, raging around the end of the island and along both sides, reaching over the banks and rushing fiercely downstream. At first she wondered why that would be the case, since the storm hadn't started yet and there had been no rain for weeks. Then she remembered Cora told them the river sometimes warned of rain to come, as floodwaters from storms far north swept downriver before a trailing part of the weather system reached here. There had been fierce rainstorms in southern Wisconsin the previous day.

Dawn believed she had walked through the center of the island, as she hadn't seen the river on either side before she reached the north end. The terrain had climbed slightly but steadily, and the ground was dry where she stood. But where was Billy? He must be near one bank or the other, which made sense if he was fishing—fishing in this weather? She would have to trace the riverbanks. She decided to turn left first, to the west side of the island, working her way back toward the road, staying under the cover of trees, but within sight of the riverbank.

Trunks and tree stumps littered the edges of the island, some trees growing so close they were partly submerged in water. Nests of root systems were exposed and trees were bent precariously over the banks. Scrambling over trunks of dead trees, she began to notice many stumps that were pointed on top. Beaver, she realized, amazed at the thickness of some of the trees they had felled, upward of two feet in diameter.

Although the rushing river and wind roared in her ears and obscured other sounds, she strained to catch road noise or any sight of 135th Street. Attempting to distinguish the chaotic sounds around her, she noticed *another* sound, a high-pitched whine that grew louder as she approached a small rise. With the river on her right, she saw a cloud of debris blowing *upward* from the hill, in the center of a clearing with a few ancient maples. Curious, she headed in that direction and stumbled over a large stone, regularly shaped with squared-off, cut edges. Although worn, it was obviously not naturally occurring. If the island was unoccupied, as Pam had said, why would a cut stone be here?

The grass had been torn away to dimly reveal a rectangular area of such stones, an area she estimated at thirty feet by fifty feet. The ground inside was muddy and covered with patches of dried and rotting vegetation. Near its center was a depression from which the whine and blowing debris were emanating. She guessed what she was seeing was the foundation of a building—a rather substantial building—with wind coming from a hole under the foundation. She wondered why Pam hadn't told them about this and why wind came from underground.

A strong gust from the southwest made her wish she had dressed more warmly or at least put a sweater over her long-sleeved top. She crossed her arms in a futile attempt at warmth, grimacing as the stickers that clung to her sleeves pricked her bare hands. Moisture was in the air—she could smell and feel it.

As she stared at the hole, she saw something move inside it, something dark and round emerging from the ground. A *head* appeared—Billy!

She jumped and turned to run, but it was too late—Billy had seen her. "Stop!" he shouted, as he pulled himself out. "I'm not going to hurt you, Dawn. Don't make me chase you!"

She hesitated. She *didn't* think he would hurt her, but she wanted to avoid another unpleasant conversation. He had caught her following him—a bad way to begin if she intended to coax him to level with her!

She slowed but kept walking. When she glanced back Billy was out of the hole and heading toward her, walking, not running—a good sign.

When she didn't stop, he added, "Please…Dawn. Let me explain. We used to be friends—good friends. Just wait."

Dawn didn't want a confrontation in these circumstances—what if he wasn't as harmless as she believed? But running wouldn't be of any use. She couldn't make much headway in this precarious terrain—he'd easily catch her. She'd been stupid to follow him.

Was Nick on his way? Would anyone know where she was? Should she pretend to be interested in what Billy had to say? She stopped and turned.

"Don't come any closer Billy. I can't imagine why you're climbing out of a hole in the middle of nowhere, but you don't owe me any explanations." She flung an arm into the air. "Just stay where you are." She pretended a bravado she didn't feel.

"What are *you* doing out here? Did you follow me?" He sounded angry, and she backed away a few steps. He put out a hand. "Wait," he said, and rubbed a dirty hand over his face. He examined her eyes. "Of course you followed me. Why else would you be here?"

He drew in a deep breath and plopped down on a tree trunk. Billy was a slight man, but his well-developed arms and shoulders hinted at strength. His shoulder-length, black hair whipped around his face in the wind, creating a wild appearance, his expression desperate.

"I must seem pretty nasty to you, and I guess I deserve that. But I didn't come to Illinois to track you down, Dawn," he said, as if trying to convince himself. "When I got here and found out you and Nick lived here too, I don't know—I guess I just wanted to let you know how much it hurt when you picked Nick over me. It seemed easier here, away from home. At home…people would laugh…."

"You almost wrecked our marriage, Billy! And that crazy business with the wolf!"

"The wolf? No! That wasn't *me!*"

She made a disgusted face. "Yeah. Right. It wasn't you." She folded her arms across her chest, shivering, facing him a short distance from where he sat.

He seemed confused and she guessed he was trying to decide what to tell her. Lies, most likely. He seemed like a boy lost in the woods, about to cry, and she remembered him when he *was* a little boy, hurt, just like this. Her eyes glistened. *How did we ever get to this?* she thought.

"What is all this, Billy? What are you doing here?"

He stared at his shoes.

"Billy—I found you *under the ground!* Why were you in that hole? Whatever you're hiding down there, I *already* know where it is. You might as well tell me the rest."

Dawn didn't know if Nick was on his way—Billy wouldn't know either. Would it do any good to stall him—to get him to confess? *Keep him talking*, she told herself.

He met her eyes briefly, then began rambling. "It's not mine. I'm just helping—we're not doing anything wrong. What's down there just has to stay secret until it's itemized, moved, preserved—we're not ready. It's not easy. We've been working a long time."

"We?"

"I can't say." He faced her, chin in the air.

From the stubborn expression on his face she knew he wasn't going to tell her who he was working with. She said, "How did you get into this then?"

He paused again. "Joe Good," he said at last, resignation in his voice. "You remember Joe? From back home?"

Dawn nodded.

"He was here last summer, over a year ago. He represented the Potawatomi at some annual Rendezvous they have here. Have you heard of it?"

"Yes. We went this year."

"Joe met someone who asked him to work on a secret project. This person wanted a Potawatomi to interpret Indian legends and identify artifacts. Someone who didn't live here, so friends wouldn't ask what he was doing. Someone who had connections with tribal elders. Someone to assist with research, cataloging, and physical parts of the job. Joe didn't want to move here, but when he got back home he told me about it."

He shifted and glanced away. "I was in a bad state, you know? So I agreed to do it, although I didn't really know what I was getting into until too late. I was going to get a share of the profits. It looked like a lot."

Another strong blast of wind hit, colder now, and Dawn shivered again. Billy stood up and moved toward her. When she backed away, he stopped, took off the denim jacket he was wearing, and held it out to Dawn. She hesitated, then took the jacket and put it on, getting some satisfaction from the fact that it would be covered with burrs inside when she returned it to him. He sat again, and she found another log a short distance away.

Dawn's fright was lessening. She may be *kyesh'at*, "a fool," but she'd known Billy most of her life, and found it hard to think he was dangerous. She also didn't think he would tell what was going on to anyone but her.

"So something valuable is in that hole?"

"Yes—I mean sort of. It's actually a cave."

"A cave?"

He intertwined his fingers, put his forehead on them, and rubbed his brow. Then he looked up. "Yeah—I guess I might as well tell you." He paused. "Truth is, I'm not sure about all this anymore, Dawn. I didn't know what I was getting into," he said again. "Unexpected things…I didn't know what to do, and there wasn't anyone I could talk to."

She ignored his confession, if that's what it was. "So—a cave?"

"People used to live on this island, and there was a church here once, on this spot. It burned in the 1920s."

"And something was under it?"

"When they dug the foundation, they cut into a cave that ran between the foundation of the church and the river. The church used the space for storage."

"I guess your friend, or partner, found something valuable. I wouldn't think it was a wealthy church. What was in it?"

"After the church burned down, prohibition money was hidden in the cave."

"Prohibition money?" Dawn was confused.

"This island was a popular sporting area at the time and some mobsters hung out here. They heard about the cave when people talked about the fire and figured it was a good place to hide valuables, so they loaded it up and sealed the entrance. For some reason they never got back to it."

"And how do you know all this?"

"There were ledgers in there, too. Names, dates, amounts, agreements, letters—we took those out already and went through them."

"So what does that have to do with planning and talking to the elders? Why not just take it out?"

"Because that's not all that was found. The mobsters never looked farther into the cave, never imagined anyone else might have had the same idea."

Dawn was incredulous. "*Two* stashes!"

"Two—or you might say three."

"Three!"

"Farther in the cave are multiple chambers, some higher, some lower, all linked together, like a chain of pearls. You could see into the chambers with a flashlight, but it took some doing to break through enough to pass into all of them."

"So that's what you've been doing, getting into the chambers?"

"Part of it, yes. And it seems that back in the early days of the frontier, some robbers used the cave to store their goods while they continued to rob and plunder. We knew it was from the earliest frontier days because pouches were filled with jewelry and pieces of eight."

"Bandits! Wawetseka's river pirates! And maybe they got caught or had a mishap, or whatever, and never came back for it?"

"That's the thought."

"So, I'm still confused as to why your friend wanted a Potawatomi to help?"

"Because the largest number of chambers were packed with huge amounts of silver jewelry and silver ore—tons of it. The jewelry looked like Indian designs, and we guessed it may have been stolen from American Indians. There was also a great quantity of strings of wampum. Even the containers this stuff was stored in might be valuable historic artifacts. To determine what we had, its value, and what to do with it, we needed to authenticate the items and try to find out where they came from."

Dawn gasped. "The Shawnee silver treasure! Like Frannie said!"

"Frannie?" Billy wrinkled his brow.

"Never mind. So the ore would be heavy and hard to move, and it had to come from the 1700s or early 1800s, around Wawetseka's time. And you didn't want people to read the book and come traipsing around here until you found out what you had, got it out, and figured out what to do with it?"

"That's about it."

"How did the silver get here? The Shawnee didn't live here—they lived in Ohio."

"No idea. Maybe they brought it here, maybe someone stole it from them and hid it here, maybe pirates did it—we had a lot to do before we could take time to check into that sort of thing."

"How did you find it?"

"The person who hired me was exploring out here and noticed that whistling coming from the ground, like you just did. Figured a cave was involved, and searched around to see if there were any more. Didn't find more caves, but saw a whirlpool in the river. Researched the history of the island, put the church and the cave near the same spot. Dug around, exposed the church foundation, and then discovered what the mobsters left."

Billy stood up and walked near the cave, waving his arm in its direction.

"Kept thinking about that whirlpool and checking it every now and then, and it was always there." He pointed at a spot in the river, near the bank. "Eventually came to wonder if the cave under the church communicated with a cave in the riverbank, if fluctuations in water level, exposure of cave vents, and air pressure caused the whirlpool and the air currents. The river had a different course before the 1890s and was dredged in the 1940s. Pirates, or anyone, might have entered through the riverbank before the church was built, and the upper level chambers would have kept everything high and dry even when parts of the island flooded."

"So Indians or pirates hid the Shawnee silver, pirates added their own ill-gotten goods and filled up the cave from the river, and the mob filled it up from the other end, and the two never met."

"That's about it."

"But why would you ever do something as crazy as attacking us with a drugged wolf?"

Billy lifted his head and his face grew panicked, his eyes fixed behind her, as a dramatic voice said, "Don't blame buddy Billy for that one, Dawn, my dear. That was *my* plan, and a lot of fun it turned out to be too!"

Chapter 28

Cora leaned against her car for support against the fierce wind, expecting the storm to break at any moment. She, Cisco, and Frannie barely glanced Nick's way when he pulled into the museum parking lot and got out of his car, so heated was their argument about whether to wait for Nick, go after Dawn, or call the police—so difficult to make any decision while struggling against the elements.

"And tell them what, Cora? That Dawn went into the woods in a storm?" Cisco shouted.

"That Billy guy's nuts!" Frannie said. "Who knows what he could do to that poor girl! How're *we* gonna stop him? We need cops!"

"We've got to tell them at least!" Cora insisted.

"How long do you think it will take to convince them to come out here? And how much longer for them to *get* here?" Cisco was waving both arms wildly and yelling so loud Cora thought *Dawn* would hear him, even over the wind.

"Stop!" Nick said. "She's not here?" He glanced frantically around, his panic obvious.

Frannie pointed across the road.

"Do whatever you want," Nick shouted. "I'm going after her!" He took off at a run into the street, recklessly darting in front of a car. The driver swerved, blew his horn, and shook his head. Nick was already lost in the trees.

"Do whatever you want," Cisco told the women, repeating what Nick said. He headed toward the road, waiting for a break in traffic and then eating up the ground in the practiced pace he had never lost from Army boot-camp training some fifty years ago. He disappeared in the woods where they saw Nick go.

"I'm going," Cora said. She slapped at a pocket to be sure she had her cell phone and keys, slammed her car door, and started after Cisco.

"Me, too, but wait," Frannie said, grabbing Cora's arm. She dialed 911 on her cell phone, and simply said, "A woman is lost in the woods on the north side of Isle a la Cache. A storm is starting and she's in danger. She needs help— No, I don't have time to tell you more— I don't *have* more to tell. My name is Frannie Berkowitz— I'm going after her!"

She ended the call and zipped the phone into a jacket pocket. The two women crossed the four-lane road and followed the men through the trees.

Chapter 29

Dawn froze, stunned. The voice was familiar, but she couldn't place it. She didn't want to see—was *afraid* to know who it belonged to. For the first time she felt real terror. It wasn't Billy who was dangerous, but whoever was behind her.

When she decided to follow Billy, she felt confident in her ability to confront him, but it hadn't occurred to her that anyone else could be on the island. Then she had been so intent on what Billy was telling her that she failed to consider the din of the impending storm that obscured any sounds of approach.

She gathered her courage and forced herself to turn around. Immediately a flash of lightning and a tremendous explosion of thunder shook the ground. She flinched. Something crashed, and a branch tore from a nearby tree with an avalanche of smaller debris.

Josh stood behind her, leaning against a big old maple, insolent, one leg crossed over the other, light reddish-brown hair falling over his forehead—a face she had once considered boyishly attractive, a face now wearing a smirk and a pointed beard, probably grown for an acting role. His appearance now suggested evil—the image of a fox jumped into her mind. She shivered and her hands began to shake. She tried to hide her fear by folding her arms across her chest and staring into his eyes while she frantically tried to figure out what to do.

When he said nothing, she spoke. "You're Billy's partner? You found this cave?"

He bowed and made a grand sweep of his arm, sleek, smooth, cynical

—a gesture she remembered him making when playing the part of a river pirate at Rendezvous last June. "At your service."

They stared at each other, waiting as another roar of thunder rumbled to a stop. Josh studied her with a calculating, smug look on his face. Dawn struggled to pretend defiance and hide the fear that consumed her.

Her mind worked furiously. How long had he been there? How much did he hear? It probably made little difference, as he must realize she now knew what he had been so desperate to hide. What would he do? What should *she* do? Would she be able to stall him, in the hope that Nick would get there, like she had been doing with Billy? She could *play* Billy, but didn't know this man well enough for that—although she intuitively knew Josh had a quick intelligence and would not be easily manipulated.

Could she convince him she, Nick and their friends would do what he wanted, that they would say nothing and let him carry out his plans? He and Billy hadn't done anything illegal, only found valuables—valuables whose ownership was unclear—and kept the discovery secret.

Except for stealing a wolf and attacking Cora and Cisco, that is. Indicating desperation, greed, and a deranged mind, this was a man with the physical strength to heft the dead weight of a wolf through a window—a man who would do anything to protect his secrets, heedless of the lives of anyone in his way.

"How about if I call the others? We can talk this out. We can find a way to make everyone happy. We can delay the book until you finish whatever you're doing...."

He lowered his chin and raised his eyes, as if peering over glasses. "You've got to be kidding. Why would I do that? Get more people involved? Nah! Not good, my dear." He made a snorting sound.

Another flash of lightning blinded Dawn, another roar of thunder followed, and continuous gusts of wind blew first from one direction, then from another.

The man radiated arrogance and, incredibly, seemed to be enjoying himself, as if Dawn were an audience of one. Could she use that against him?

"Why did you set that wolf against Cora and Cisco instead of Nick and me?"

"Ha!" he said, yelling against the din. "Nick already ignored my warning, but from what Pam said it was pretty clear that you'd all just spin your wheels without Cora driving everyone. She was *writing* the damn book, and without her I'd have secured my discovery long before the rest of you ever got anything ready to publish. She's the one I had to scare off."

"Cora doesn't scare easy."

"I found that out. With that trick Frannie played and all of you freaking out about a curse, I figured if I made you think something bizarre was going on, you might not look for a real person—the cops wouldn't take it serious and you'd be sent off in another direction. Seemed like a good idea at the time."

Dawn thought the man sounded like he was *bragging* about what he had done! And he was right about the police. When Cisco gave them his note they *did* think it was a prank. "How did you know so much about what we were doing? You were rarely around when we were."

"Pam was, though. She thought the book was a lark, was happy to fill me in. I didn't miss much."

"Did she know about this place too?"

"Nah. She never came over here—didn't see any reason to."

"Why did you?"

"My thesis, darling, on the history of the island—the whole island, not half of it. As you see…," he swept his arm back and forth, "this place isn't like anywhere else."

"And then you found the cave."

"As you well know now." He glared at Billy. Josh *had* overheard much of their conversation. "Enough of this." He moved away from the tree and took a few steps toward Dawn.

"Wait," she said hurriedly, jumping to her feet. "What was wrong with our book? Wawetseka didn't say anything about a cave."

He laughed rudely. "I couldn't be sure of that, could I? Everything was going so well until you guys showed up. The more I found out about your story, the more convinced I became that people would start roaming out here after they read your book."

Once again, Josh seemed to be boasting. Dawn had a momentary thought: she imagined Hardy Findel to be just like this man—the role of a pirate at Rendezvous suited him well. She inched away, hoping he wouldn't notice.

"First I figured we'd just hurry up and finish securing the contents of the cave—it would take a long time to get a book in print. But then that damn Cora kept driving you all, and it became pretty clear it would be done before I was ready. When I found out about the pirates and figured out who the priest in the cave was, I had no choice. I had to turn up the heat."

"The priest in the cave?"

"The body we found in the cave—you know, the missionary."

Dawn was baffled. Josh looked at Billy. "You didn't tell her about the missionary?"

Billy shook his head. He had worked his way toward the edge of the clearing. He looked panicked, his eyes wandering, indecisive.

"There's a skeleton in the cave and a metal crucifix, about twelve inches tall, the sort of thing priests hold up while speaking, not like something to wear or hang on a wall. Clothing and other indications the man was a missionary. I knew then the cave was tied to Wawetseka's story in some way and others could figure it out too. Plus, what was I going to do about the body? No way I could solve all these issues before the book was out."

The lightning and thunder were almost nonstop now. Josh's hair whipped around his face, his clothing flapping crazily. He moved forward suddenly and grabbed Dawn's arm.

"Enough of this crap. I know you're only trying to stall me. Thanks for the opportunity to finally tell someone my accomplishments—it was fun for a minute or two, but in the final analysis it's useless for you, my dear. No one will find us out here, and it's time to take care of you."

"Billy!" Dawn cried. She had no one else to turn to. She pulled frantically, trying to get away from Josh's powerful grip.

"Be careful, Josh!" Billy said. "What are you doing?"

Josh looked past them to where the river rushed by. "What a shame that current is stronger than you, darling. Should we test it? That might be fun. What a shame you got caught out here in a storm, poor baby, slipped in the mud, fell in the water, and got washed away. What a shame no one was here to see it happen. What a *crying* shame."

As if on stage, Josh dropped the edges of his mouth and made an exaggerated face of sadness and wiped imaginary tears from his eyes with his forefinger.

"Josh, you can't do this!" Billy cried.

"Can't? *Can't?* Of course I can, and *you're* involved my friend. Who's to say you didn't steal and plant that wolf? Indians without paying jobs do that kind of thing, not responsible sorts like doctoral candidates. Who do you think they're going to believe?"

"I don't care! I was afraid it'd wind up like this." Billy crossed the clearing and grabbed Dawn's other arm, trying to pull her away from Josh. "You're insane! Leave her alone!"

Josh laughed. "I'll be real gentle with her, Billy—up to the time she hits the river."

With an abrupt movement, he dropped Dawn's arm, swung his fist, and connected with the side of Billy's head, knocking him to the ground. Billy lay dazed. Josh laughed, kicked him again on the same side of the head, and said, "Don't interfere!" Then he kicked him in the ribs and dug his heel viciously into Billy's stomach. "You'll do what I tell you to do!" Josh said. Billy lay writhing, gasping, unable to get up.

With Josh's attention on Billy, Dawn backed away and was halfway across the clearing, but Josh caught her in a few steps. "Not so fast, my dear."

Dragging Dawn, Josh hovered over Billy for a moment and said, "I'll be back for you." He put a forefinger to his chin, and an evil grin spread over his face. "I have a better idea. Let's change the script a little, set a new stage. A text is found from her phone to yours—it seems two love-birds found each other again and met. But alas, Billy's poor lover slipped in the river and he jumped in to save her. This wild river will finish the convincing."

The velocity of the wind suddenly increased, knocking Dawn and Josh off their feet. They struggled to stand, leaning into the gale to keep from falling again, and Josh grabbed Dawn once more. "Perfect!" he said. "The weather is playing right into my hands! Who wouldn't be swept away in a storm like this?" He laughed demonically.

Billy struggled to his hands and knees. Josh kicked him in the ribs again, and when Billy fell on his side Josh drove the toe of his boot into Billy's head. Billy, unconscious, lay still.

Josh dragged Dawn toward the river, struggling against the force of the wind. As he reached the bank the sky blackened and became dark as night, interrupted by bolts of lightning and deafening claps of thunder. Cold rain and hail descended in a deluge. Dawn threw her free arm over her forehead, trying to see through the dark, the rain, and the hail that stung her face. The wind blew fiercely one direction and then another, seeming to lift her and suck her upward. She could barely see Josh as he still pulled her relentlessly. Then she felt a jolt, and, probably because he held her wet, slippery wrist instead of grasping her sleeve, she slipped free and fell backward on the ground.

An awful, frightful roar, like a gigantic engine in a closed room, deafened her. The rain slackened for just a moment, silent, as if in a vacuum, and in front of her Josh stood at the edge of the river, windmilling his arms, off-balance from the release of her weight and the ferocious blasts assaulting him, cringing as if startled, flung with his back against a tree—and the tree, struck by some monumental force, bent with sluggish reluctance toward the river, its roots heaving upward as it collapsed into the rushing current, Josh fighting to combat the wind and free his legs from entangling roots, like a nest of vipers, to no avail—tree and man toppling into the river, turning, crashing through every obstacle in its path with immense force, yet with all the rushing wind and downburst, strobe-like in the relentless lightning, moving ever so *slowly* downstream.

Chapter 30

THE sea of grass was bewildering—it had looked so dense from across the road. Now that Cora stood in it, the trees seemed sparse, yet she couldn't see twenty feet through the thickets. She spun around—Nick and Cisco were nowhere in sight. Where did they go? She spotted an indistinct trail and set out. With her first step she stumbled over a thick tree trunk buried in the grass. "Be careful!" she shouted, although Frannie was only a step behind her. "There's stuff under this grass you can't see—could be swamp—God only knows!"

Cora plunged on, terrified, frantic to catch the men. Cisco and Nick were sure to be a match for Billy, but what if Dawn was hurt? She and Frannie fought increasing wind, uncertain footing, and grass that wrapped and clung to their legs, making it difficult to put one foot in front of the other without falling. Cora held an arm across her forehead to protect her face from branches and other debris that flew around them. She felt as if she were walking into a wind tunnel, her steps robotic and involuntary, and she suffered a momentary loss of reality. With that sense of disorientation she experienced other times when she had been in imminent danger, trauma, or disaster, Cora felt as if she were watching a movie instead of living the experience.

Barely able to make out the thin trail that took them north through the center of the island, Cora didn't know if they were going the same way Dawn, then Nick, then Cisco, had gone. They came to a gully and could go no farther but saw the north end of the island just beyond. Cora thought that was where the canal headquarters had been. The river rushed madly around them, dizzying, proving to Cora once again that rain as far north as Wisconsin swelled the river even when rain had not yet fallen here. Unable to continue, she spun around and randomly chose to follow the river on the west side of the island, staying within the woods for whatever minimal protection the trees afforded from the elements.

Suddenly they rushed into an open expanse that resembled a neglected lawn with only a few, large old trees. As they reached it, the sky blackened, the downpour burst, and the force of the wind threatened to pull them off their feet and made it impossible to stand. They lowered themselves to the ground, and from that position, not far from where they sat, through flashes of lightning and torrential rain, Cora saw Cisco near the far edge of the clearing, bending over something on the ground. She turned her head toward the river and saw Dawn fall to the ground and lay crumpled near the riverbank. A tremendous crash shook the ground, and she saw Nick struggling clumsily across the clearing toward Dawn. Then her eyes became fixed on a tree at the river's edge.

~~~

The massive tree, caught in the ferocious mainstream current, bore Josh, his arms flailing wildly, tangled in its roots. It rolled and Josh disappeared under the surface of the water, the tree sliding slowly downriver. Dawn watched, helpless, as Josh remained submerged under the tree. Stunned, she felt enormous relief to be free from Josh, but at the same time she instinctively, frantically, felt compelled to save him. She slapped at her pocket, where she kept her cell phone, but the pocket was empty. Panic returned—did she lose it?

Tears streaming down her face, unnoticed in the driving rain, against all logic a giggle bubbled up from her throat and her chest heaved with uncontrolled laughter. After what she had just been through, how could she panic at the possible loss of a cell phone, such a small thing? And she wore Billy's jacket, not her own. She couldn't stop. Inappropriately her laughter went on and on. And then somehow Nick was there, and he threw himself on the ground and embraced her, and she let out a cry, something halfway between agony and joy if there was such a thing, but she felt both things, and so there must be. She buried her face against Nick's chest and clung to him as if only the clinging could keep her alive.

Nick held the shaking, sobbing Dawn tightly in his arms, helpless and stunned by what he had just witnessed.

Chapter 31

After it was over, after the storm diminished to a steady rain, after the wind decreased to a mild roar, after the thunder and lightning stopped, after the police arrived and they told their stories, after the EMTs took Billy to the ambulance that waited on 135th Street, after the proper authorities were notified to search for Josh, after dim daylight returned but the day was almost done, they were finally allowed to leave.

It had taken hours. They were exhausted and groggy, yet in the aftermath of tragedy wide-awake.

"Come to our house," Cora said. "We have towels, robes. We'll get fast food and hot coffee—take showers, dry our wet clothes, get warm. And we'll talk. We should be together." Emotionally overwrought, realizing they needed what professionals would call "debriefing," they accepted Cora's offer.

Cisco picked up sandwiches from McDonalds, and they ate in awkward silence except for occasional polite exchanges.

"I didn't realize I was hungry."

"Does anyone want some of my fries?"

"Is this one mine?"

"Do you have ketchup?"

When they finished, like the last time they met, they avoided the family room, where the presence of a television, even turned off, was a distraction. They gathered once again in the living room. Every light in the room and in the adjacent dining room was on in an effort to dispel the dark, chill, and gloom just outside the windows, a chill and gloom that permeated the deepest level of their psyches.

No one seemed to be able to get warm, so Cisco turned the heat up to eighty degrees and passed out afghans. They selected a chair or the sofa and tried to get comfortable. Cora looked around the room. Everyone was solemn and stunned, processing their own thoughts silently, glances roaming, occasional small smiles of acknowledgement. No one seemed to want to talk.

Cisco wore jeans and a sweatshirt, and Cora was in sweats too. Their guests, however, their clothes in the dryer, wore an assortment of robes. Nick had on an old silk, patterned robe that once belonged to Cisco's father and had never left the closet. Frannie, uncharacteristically quiet, adjusted the belt on a long terry-cloth robe every few minutes, trying to keep it closed. Dawn was draped with a long poncho.

Nick stood up to move to a seat at Dawn's side. Cora began to giggle and couldn't stop. Finally she was able to stumble through an explanation. "It's that robe, Nick. I'm sorry, it's just—it's too short, and silk paisley doesn't go with the ponytail. And the legs, the short socks—I'm sorry, really...." She broke into uncontrolled giggles again, wiping tears on her sleeve.

By now everyone was snickering, and Nick broke into guffaws. "Frannie, you keep looking the other way and hoping no one notices when you're trying to keep that robe shut over your chest. You might as well give up. We all see you!"

Frannie looked sheepish for a moment, then pulled her afghan up to her neck and folded her hands over her lap, laughing loudly.

The ice was finally broken. Once the laughter died down they began to discuss the day's events.

"I wonder what Josh was doing out on that part of the island to begin with, before he found the cave. He had to be doing more than fishing," Cora said.

"He was writing a paper, for his degree, on the history of the island," Dawn said.

Cora furrowed her brow. "How do you know that?"

"He told me, when I was trying to distract him. He couldn't stop bragging once he got started, dramatic, onstage, just like he was acting a role." Dawn filled them in on what she had learned from Billy and Josh: how Josh found the cave over a year ago and got Billy to help him; how when they showed up to plan the book he realized it would destroy his plans; what he found in the cave and a description of that; and why he drugged and stole the wolf and put it in Cora's house.

Cora nodded her head frequently and when Dawn was finished she said, "After Billy regained consciousness, I sat with him and asked him questions to help him stay calm until the paramedics got there." She smiled at Dawn. "He told me some of the story. Probably been holding it in for quite a while."

Nick shook his head, his expression sad. "Poor Billy. Watching his friends marry and go on to successful careers, feeling inadequate and miserable at home, thinking he's finally found something worthwhile and distracting, but instead he gets drawn into Josh's schemes. Out of the frying pan, into the fire. He didn't have anything to do with the wolf, right?"

Dawn nodded. "That was Josh. Billy tried to save me. And paid a price for it."

"He knew about the attack, though," Cisco said.

"What was he going to do? It was over and done when he found out about it," Cora said.

"He'd only get in trouble himself if he told anyone." Dawn sounded defensive.

"Didn't he think Josh might do something even worse?" Frannie asked.

"Maybe he planned to keep an eye on Josh so he *wouldn't* do anything else. Or try on his own to get us to stop publication," Dawn said, her voice quivering.

"Why are you defending him?" Frannie asked.

Cora said in a quiet voice, "We had Billy all wrong. He wasn't stalking Dawn, like we thought. He didn't know what we were doing directly, only what Josh passed along, but Billy seems to be a common-sense guy. Josh would have complained and boasted to the only person in on the secret, and Billy saw Josh getting more and more irrational. Eventually he realized Josh would go to any lengths to prevent the publication of our book. That put his friends in danger. Billy was in too deep, but when he realized what Josh was doing, he kept an eye on Dawn to be sure nothing happened to her or Rose."

"He told you that?" Dawn asked.

Cora nodded. Dawn started to cry.

Nick, sitting on the sofa with his arm around Dawn, both of them under the same thick fleece throw, turned Dawn's face toward him and brushed his fingers down her cheek, looking into her eyes. "He was angry and his back was against the wall. I feel like a traitor. He never meant us any harm—quite the opposite."

"What do you think will happen now?" Dawn asked.

"I don't think he did anything illegal. The worst he did was not tell what he knew about the wolf. And nobody got hurt as a result," Cora said.

"Unless you count the wolf," Frannie pointed out.

"Or Josh," Cisco said.

"Still, you can't blame Billy for that. He had quite a dilemma, it seems," Cora insisted. "Do you think Wawetseka knew about the treasure?"

"No way to tell, but I doubt it," Nick said. "We don't know it was Findel that stored his cache in the cave—anyone could have. She didn't write her story until years later. Either she didn't know, she forgot, or she purposely didn't say."

"You think Noah knew about it? Wawetseka said he kept coming back to 'visit.' Poji didn't trust him to begin with. Maybe there was a reason. Maybe he wasn't really finding his brother's killer and helping Wawetseka, but involved in some way, maybe even in cahoots with Penney, and then he was forced to stop when he was injured. That could be why he came back to visit for years," Cisco said.

"If that was why, he never moved the 'treasure,'" Nick said, making air quotes. "Guess we'll never know."

"I can't believe we never guessed Josh was behind all this, seeing that it was a pirate treasure and he played a pirate at Rendezvous. Seems he had more to do with pirates than just playing one on TV. How'd we miss that?" Frannie said.

"You know I'm never one to talk about coincidences, but there's one that's hard to ignore. In Wawetseka's story and today's catastrophe, both of the people who died were tangled up in tree roots and washed down the river. That's freaking me out," Cisco said.

"You're right about that!" Frannie said. "But what I want to know is what are we going to do about the treasure now?"

"What do you think it's worth? Silver isn't worth all that much these days," Nick said.

"Maybe not per ounce but the amount Billy said is down there could be worth millions," Cisco said.

"And perhaps even more as artifacts. If you ever watch *Antiques Roadshow* you know antique jewelry values go up and down all the time," Cora said.

"It was never ours to decide. Let Billy handle it. He's probably telling the story to the police now. Thank God he'll be okay," said Cisco.

"If they don't handle it, why don't we tell the history department at Lewis University and let them straighten out the inventory and where it should go?" Cora suggested. "I don't know about you, but I've had about enough of handling other people's valuables. We've got a book to finish."

"I'll call Rogers tomorrow," Cisco said. "Maybe he can meet us and we can figure things out."

"Before you go setting anything up, maybe we ought to get our story straight—talk about why we didn't tell the police what we *really* saw," Cora said.

Cora watched the group sneak peeks at each other awkwardly, guiltily, brief flickering glances she thought were aimed at determining what others were thinking before revealing their own thoughts.

"That clearing must have been where an old church once was. How did you guys get there?" Cora asked. "We didn't pass you the way we went."

"Cisco caught up to me and we followed the river on the west side of the island. It probably wasn't the best way to go, since you left after we did and got there at the same time," Nick said.

"It would have been the shortest way, as it turned out, if it hadn't been for all those inlets and downed trees we had to work our way around. They really slowed us down," Cisco said.

"My first thought was that I was so glad to see Cisco and Nick, and then Dawn. After that, there was a lot of confusion, because of the storm. Like we told the cops, we couldn't see clearly through the rain and wind," Cora went on.

"We *did* all see it, but they wouldn't have believed us anyway," Nick finally said.

Cora nodded. "You're right. They didn't believe about my wolf last year, they sure don't want to hear about it again."

"Your wolf?" Dawn said, a puzzled look on her face. "What do you mean?"

"The spirit wolf, you know?"

Dawn shook her head, looking bewildered.

Cora stared at Dawn, wondering how she could have missed the wolf. "Like in our kitchen, she saved us again, *you* this time. She ran in, jumped on Josh. That's why he let go of you, why you fell on the ground, why he fell back and landed at the base of that tree before it tore loose and carried him away. You must have seen her!"

Dawn continued to shake her head. "No. That's not what I saw."

Cora glanced at the others. All avoided her eyes, shaking their heads. "None of you?"

No one spoke.

Cora turned to Dawn again. "What *did* you see?"

"Just the river and the tree. After I broke loose, Josh stumbled over some shrub or debris, I think—and then I saw a flash and heard a loud crash, like an explosion. The river surged up over the banks and tore at the base of the tree. The tree was already leaning out over the river, and Josh was all tangled in it and couldn't get away." Dawn's lower lip trembled and tears came to her eyes. "It was awful. He was getting thrown around and his arm came out, like he was waving to me, and he reached for me Nick, like he wanted me to save him! I was so glad he let go of me...but...I still wanted to help him, only...I...I just lay there and did nothing." She began to weep and buried her face on Nick's chest.

"Shhh," Nick said. "You couldn't have done anything, Dawn. We were all there. None of us could have saved him."

"Maybe...maybe he isn't dead," Dawn said.

"He *has* to be dead," Cisco said. "The tree rolled with him tangled in it, rolled him under the water, banged him around good. I don't see how he could survive, but they're looking for him. Maybe he got lucky, but I don't know how." He stood up and went to the kitchen and returned with a cup in his hand. He stood behind Cora, put his free hand on her shoulder, and gave a gentle squeeze. She reached up and placed her hand over his. After a moment, he pulled his hand away and sat again. Cora noticed his throw, one she had crocheted, in a pile at his feet, and she smiled.

Dawn, composed now, sat quietly with her head against Nick's shoulder, his arm encircling her. Nick looked around the room before speaking.

"Josh could have been dead *before* the tree fell." He looked down at the floor for a moment as if reluctant to go on, then lifted his head and met Cisco's eyes.

"When I got to the clearing I saw Billy before I saw Dawn or Josh, and I was standing near him when it happened. I thought it was lightning at first, that struck the tree—but it went on and on, like a vibrating or pulsing thing, a flashing, flickering bolt, greenish—like lightning but not like lightning—it ran between Billy and Josh and the tree for—I don't know—maybe five seconds? Like a force connected them somehow. Whatever it was, it pinned Josh against the tree, and when it stopped there was a black cloud behind the tree, and the tree fell into the cloud, then into the water, and Josh with it."

He stopped and Cora thought he seemed confused as he looked at Cisco. "Dawn was on the ground and I ran to her, while Cisco stayed with Billy. I'm sure I didn't imagine it. You must have seen it, Cisco. You were right there too."

It wasn't like Nick to be fanciful. Cora was surprised by his version of events, but before she could question him she saw Cisco shaking his head. "Josh let go of Dawn and it was like a magnet pulled him against the tree, not like he was blown there—his arms were in front of him. I didn't see anything touch Billy. I saw a flash and heard a roar and something like an explosion. The ground shook and then I *did* see the dark cloud though, like a huge black cone in the sky. I was sure it was a tornado that just grabbed the tree and pulled it. I saw the tree lift upward, and Josh with it." He began to wave his arms in the air, demonstrating the direction of the tree, of the wind, of Josh. He spilled some coffee on his jeans when he did this, and he rubbed at it.

"It didn't just sway toward the river, it was lifted and *thrown* into the river, and I swear it was a tornado—just pulled that tree right out of the ground and threw it in the water. The directions didn't make sense. The wind was blowing right in my face, so strong, but between blinks I saw the tree and wondered how it could come down falling *into* the wind instead of *with* the wind—and why did Josh get pulled against the wind too? It had to be a tornado. A bolt of lightning struck the tree, and a tornado sucked them both up and threw Josh and the tree in the river. That's what happened."

"No," said Frannie, just that one word.

Cora noted the dazed, dreamlike expression on her friend's face. Dawn pulled away from Nick and leaned forward to see what Frannie had to say, the afghan dropping off their shoulders and onto her lap. Frannie, who always had a funny remark, an odd comment, or a silly interpretation, caught their attention with her hushed demeanor.

"You're all wrong," she said. "It wasn't any of those things. It was the Water Panther, that Mishipeshu guy."

Cisco looked as if he was going to laugh, but stopped when he saw Frannie's face.

"That big black cloud you thought you saw, Nick—what you thought was a tornado, Cisco—it wasn't any of those things," she said again.

Frannie made eye contact with each person before she continued. "While you was all explaining what you thought you saw, I was thinking how this could be. I didn't want to say, because I know you all think I get crazy ideas, but this whole business started some kind of way and ended some kind of way with *Indian* stuff. In late October, almost two hundred years ago, a snowstorm helped Wawetseka do what she had to do. Now this time it's a *rainstorm*, same time of year, same crazy Midwest weather never changed in two hundred years, snowstorm in October, rainstorm in October, either way it happens. And *this* rainstorm, it helped do what had to be done, which is save Dawn from Josh."

Frannie seemed awed by her own story. "Some of this treasure, it's been here this whole time, from Wawetseka to now, and no one ever found it because it's been protected. It's Indian stuff, and it's Mishipeshu is doing what he's always done—rising from the depths of the river, taking on anyone who dares to disturb the treasures buried nearby it was *his* duty to protect. We never gave him credit in our book, and maybe that would have been the right thing to do. But the Indians, they knew he had to be involved and kept telling us so."

She folded her arms across her chest and slowly nodded her head up and down. "And this time I saw him. Uh, huh! Those pictures we had of him? They didn't hardly give him justice. He's a real big guy, could be fifty or a hundred feet all told, I guess, big like the first time I saw him at Rendezvous. He's got a long, scaly tail with sharp points on the end; a head like a big cat with sharp fangs and these huge whisker-like things around his face, whiskers maybe five feet long; and legs too, with sharp claws. And he's black as can be, with spiky fins on his back. That wasn't no black cloud, Nick, and that wasn't no tornado, Cisco. It was Mishipeshu, raising himself up from the depths of the river and tearing that big old tree out of the ground along with the guy who wanted to steal what was his to protect.

"The whole time you was helping Billy and Dawn, I was watching this guy, and I got me a good look, even through that storm. No doubt about it at all. That's the story, and you'll never convince me otherwise."

The others blinked, not sure what to think, but not laughing this time. No, not laughing.

Afterword

Northern Illinois, 1817—what a fertile field for the setting of a murder mystery! The War of 1812 had been over for two years, and the Northwest Territory was attracting settlers. The area consisted of the land between Pennsylvania and the Mississippi River, north of the Ohio River. This area would eventually become the states of Ohio, Indiana, Illinois, Michigan, Wisconsin, and the eastern part of Minnesota.

Ohio and Indiana had already been granted statehood by 1817. Illinois was preparing to be next, but still fell under the Northwest Ordinance. Recorded history of day-to-day life is sketchy since most people in the region, more numerous than textbooks would suggest, were too busy to leave written records. Thus, the writer is free to make educated choices about how a murderer might have been identified and punished.

Readers often ask which parts of my story are history and which are fictional. My research was extensive, so I will confine myself to the specific elements that I think will generate the most questions.

My story depended upon the existence of both Native Americans and people of European descent. It took some digging to establish that such a situation was plausible where I was setting the action. Most written history of the northern part of Illinois generally begins in the 1830s, after the Indian population left the state and land became available for purchase by settlers. Although 1817 may have been too early for permanent non-native settlement that did not mean there were no visitors. When I found evidence that a fur station existed in 1816 roughly at State and Main Streets in Lemont, I was convinced I was on the right track.

I had established that by 1816 much of northern Illinois had already been "sold" by Indian tribes in exchange for annuities, although native bands had retained the right to fish and hunt there. The treaty in 1816 was signed by three historic persons who appear in the story: **William Clark**, after the Lewis and Clark Expedition, served as Governor of the Missouri Territory from 1813 to 1820 and became Superintendent of Indian Affairs in 1822. **Thomas Forsyth** traded with Indians in the Illinois Territory as early as 1798, and in 1802 opened a trading post at what is now Chicago with his half-brother, John Kinzie. Forsyth later moved to Peoria Lake and established regular communication between Fort Clark and Fort Dearborn before and after the War of 1812. **Black Partridge** was a major Potawatomi chief who lived near present-day Lemont, probably very near the woods that bear his name, and where the fictional character of Wawetseka lived. After saving the Kinzie family from the battle at **Fort Dearborn** in 1812, Black Partridge left the area to relocate with some of his village to **Fort Clark** (Peoria). Some of his people remained near Lemont until their relocation occurred around 1830.

The treaty signed in 1816 was misleading, but it was based on a decision to extend the border of Illinois farther north to ensure the I&M Canal would be entirely within the state when statehood was granted. It made sense that before the treaty the region was already explored for purchase and canal construction; otherwise, how could be border be established?

In 1817, an act of Congress excluded all foreign companies from fur trading in the U.S., making the American Fur Company, owned by John Astor, the only legal fur operation in the Great Lakes Region. The fictional character, Davey Leckey, would have been in authority over trade operations as well as local Indian matters.

Fort Dearborn had been rebuilt by 1817, and ships on the Great Lakes brought supplies, transported furs, and carried military, government, settlers, and priests from Canada and eastern states. Essentially a trade post, there was no delivery to points west of Fort Dearborn, so mail, messages, annuities, Indian agents and businessmen came there. Although Northern Illinois was not yet populated with settlers, ships would not have been bringing supplies or mail if there was no white population that needed them. Knowing this, I felt I could then populate my story with both Native Americans and white people, both groups living under the criminal justice system that existed under the Northwest Ordinance.

Insofar as possible I have tried to present the history of the period accurately. Where contradictions occurred or details were unavailable, some interpretation was required. Any errors are solely mine.

All the major characters in the book are fictional. Some historic figures are mentioned in addition to the three listed above. Among those are **Father Jacques Marquette, John Baptiste Pointe du Sable, John Kinzie, William Henry Harrison, Charles Jouette, Major Daniel Baker,** and **Chiefs Keepataw, Tecumseh,** and **Black Hawk.** Wherever these characters interact with fictional characters, the events and conversations are fictional. The descriptions of their history are factual.

Father Jacques Marquette did travel the Des Plaines River and the **Chicago Portage**, and envisioned the construction of the Illinois and Michigan Canal. He did see the "Piasa Bird" painted on a bluff along the Mississippi River, and there is some speculation that the paintings are of **Mishipeshu.** Mishipeshu is a *Manitou*, or mythological being of Indian lore.

Black Hawk did write an autobiography in an attempt to clarify the Black Hawk War that occurred in 1832. The war never reached the Lemont area.

Tecumseh, who was killed during the War of 1812, had predicted the New Madrid earthquakes and the appearance of Haley's Comet with amazing accuracy, and used these predictions to recruit followers.

Major **Indian villages** existed roughly at the places Cora described in chapter 8. Others were located at Mount Forest Island, where St. James at Sag Bridge is today (Rte. 83, Archer Avenue, and 107th Streets); on the north bluff of the Des Plaines River Valley west of Lemont Road; and on the south side of the valley near 135th Street. These areas have been the subject of archeologic digs that revealed extensive artifacts. In 1897 a large collection of Indian bones was disinterred at Sag Bridge (now part of Lemont), followed by a rash of ghost sightings. Residents demanded the bones be reburied. Some were, but some were sent to Chicago's Field Museum.

Fort Clark was established at what is **Peoria** today. There were many large Indian villages in the area, and as early as 1691, when Henri Tonti built a second fort there, a French settlement grew up around the fort, said to be the earliest European settlement in Illinois.

The descriptions of **Fort Dearborn** are historical and accurate. **Major Daniel Baker** was the commander in 1817, and he did assign his men to dig out a sand bar that was preventing ships from getting closer to the fort. **John Kinzie**'s home was located across from the fort. It was originally the home of **John Baptiste Point du Sable** and was a substantial home and farm.

The **Chicago Portage** was described based on historical data and personal visits, as well as interviews with members of the **Friends of the Chicago Portage**. Many changes have occurred over the years. Wawetseka's trips through the area may not be geographically correct in every detail, but they represent essentially what traversing the portage would have been like during her time. For more information, visit chicagoportage.org. The site has extensive and fascinating information.

Galena, Illinois was not settled until 1821, but the Indians had long dug lead (galena) from mines there. The French were mining the ore as early as 1690, and by 1816 American businessmen were shipping ore down the Mississippi River. The concept of Jim Penney getting lead from Galena is a bit of a stretch. Although the Lemont area does have rich beds of sand and lead is used in the process of making glass, this may not have led to the riches Penney expected. It *was* a condition of land ownership to clear a certain amount of land and build a cabin that included at least one window, so window glass was important and expensive for settlers.

The **Des Plaines River** where it passed Lemont was moved to a new riverbed during construction of the Chicago Sanitary Canal in the 1890s. Although it no longer has the original picturesque islands and meandering stream through the valley, much of the river is still lined with flood pools and swamps, particularly on its north side, and it still overflows its banks at flood stage.

Today **Argonne Laboratory** sits atop the north bluff of the Des Plaines River in Lemont and is surrounded by **Waterfall Glen Forest Preserve**, which has many fine walking trails, including an overlook of the Des Plaines River Valley. You can also visit **Keepataw Preserve** and **Black Partridge Woods** along Bluff Road west of Lemont Road.

As of this writing, a privately-owned **wolf ranch** is operating in Lockport, Illinois. It has been established for educational purposes, and the animals are well-treated and secure. The events involving the ranch in this story could not happen and are pure fiction.

Isle a la Cache Museum exists. So do *Island Rendezvous* and *Living History Demonstrations* that take place there. The descriptions are based on personal explorations of the island and my concept of how it would have appeared in Wawetseka's day. The springs mentioned did exist, along with others in Willow Springs and Hickory Hills. Spring water can still be drawn at Isle a la Cache. The history of the buildings on the island, including the popularity of sporting clubs and likely visits by Chicago mobsters, were based on fact, but when I visited, I could find no remaining evidence of them. There are no elevated areas as described at the end of the story, nor is the island likely to support caves, although limestone quarries are present throughout the valley between Lemont and Joliet, Illinois.

Women voyageurs often traveled with the men and also followed armies in the War of 1812 and Indian wars. These "camp followers" cooked, sewed, nursed, and guarded supplies, among other tasks, and provided companionship. Some were wives or daughters of the men they followed, but all were put to work.

The canoes used in the story are **bark canoes**. Indians and other travelers also used flat-bottomed pirogues and dugouts, but bark canoes were used wherever the need to portage (carry the canoe across unnavigable areas) was expected, as log canoes were too heavy. Bark canoes weighed only thirty to forty pounds, were very fragile, and needed to be repaired daily. For this reason, they were unloaded while still in the water, then carried and reloaded in the water, as dragging would have damaged them.

The information Frannie relates in chapter 17 about the **Shawnee silver mine, Cahokia**, and the pirate **Lafitte** is found on a variety of websites. The stories she relates are likely to be a combination of truth and legend. The possibility of Jean Lafitte or the Shawnee burying a treasure (should such treasure exist) as far away as northern Illinois is within the realm of possibility. Piracy, both on the rivers and on land, was common during Wawetseka's time. It is said that over a million dollars of stolen loot, gold, cash, and counterfeit bills changed hands near Cave-In-Rock, Illinois, between 1790 and 1830 alone, much of which was buried and still remains to be found. **Pieces of Eight** (Spanish dollar) were the standard of currency on which the original United States dollar was based and remained legal tender until 1857.

The **pawpaw tree** and its fruit exist in the forests along the Des Plaines River to this day. The exact locations and ripening times for the fruit are approximate and could have been as described in Wawetseka's story.

The snake that bit Poji was a **cottonmouth**. Unlike many other snakes, they can be found year-round, and on sunny days they may bask on logs, rocks, or branches at the water's edge. They seldom attack unless stepped on or picked up. They no longer inhabit northern Illinois.

The animals in the story are known breeds that could have been in the area in 1817. Cat is a **Maine Coon Cat**, and Dog a **Newfoundland**. Both are interesting breeds with interesting histories. "Newfies" were known to accompany explorers and voyageurs. Seaman, a Newfoundland, was owned by Meriwether Lewis and accompanied the Lewis and Clark Expedition.

The weather patterns described in the story actually occur, and a severe snow storm could have occurred in late October in 1817, as well as a hot spell and a tornado in 2013. On October 12, 2006 three inches of snow was measured at O'Hare Airport in Chicago.

For further information, there are many historical articles on my blog, available on my website at patcamallierebooks.com. You can sign up there to receive blog posts and updates about my books. If your question is not answered, feel free to send it to me at the same website, or email me at pat@patcamallierebooks.com. I love to hear from readers.

Acknowledgements

"How long have you lived with your characters?" was the question Jay Amberg, my publisher, asked when I told him I was ready to send him *The Mystery at Black Partridge Woods*. I gave what I thought was the right answer—a long time. The characters had been in my mind even before I wrote my first book.

Jay's question haunted me throughout the subsequent editing process. At every step, aspects of each personality became increasingly familiar, bringing new life with every reread, sometimes only a single word choice, sometimes whole chapters to further flesh out dimensions that were sketchy. It is not the initial conception, but the *living with each person*, that brings the characters to life, and the team of writer, publisher, editor, and designer that asks the right questions, the ones that challenge the writer to discover aspects and qualities that enrich the story.

For this, I am eternally grateful to Amika Press: to Jay Amberg, publisher; John Manos, editor; Ann Wambach, copyeditor; and Sarah Koz, designer. They inspired my efforts, "got" the story I wanted to tell, helped me visualize as well as pare out the superfluous bits, and directed my efforts into a polished product.

I am grateful to those who generously commented on the early drafts of this story: Clare Dempsey, Dorothy Bogan, Gail Ahrens, Barb Mulligan, and Carolyn Jamieson. Special thanks to Ruth Hull Chatlien, author of *The Ambitious Madame Bonaparte*, who in addition to critical opinions on my entire manuscript was available at a moment's notice for grammatical and other advice. Thanks to all of you for your interest, sharp eyes, and reassurance.

I couldn't do without my writer's groups: the Lemont Library Writers' Club, the Downers Grove Writers Workshop, and Sisters in Crime Chicagoland. Thanks to each and every one of you for your support and advice.

Thanks to those who were there when I needed historical background and for fact checking: Dr. Eileen McMahon, Professor of History, Lewis University, Romeoville, Illinois; Gary Mechanic, Friends of the Chicago Portage; Gregory Smith, Operations Director, Lemont Police Department; Daryl Morrison, Head, Department of Special Collections, UCDavis University Library; Gwenith Podeschi, Abraham Lincoln Presidential Library, Springfield, Illinois; staff of Isle a la Cache Museum, Romeoville, Illinois; and staff and volunteers of the Lemont Area Historical Society.

Special thanks to Richard Hoyt Lee and Ingrid Kallick. Richard, not only for his interest and friendship, but for being available for impromptu photo shoots. His talent graces the cover of this book. And to Ingrid for the fantastic art creations that illustrate the map and lend an added dimension of mystery to my story.

To my family, who patiently put up with my absences, my excited (but not so fascinating to them!) ramblings about all things historical or literary, and whose encouragement, support and efforts in the background make it possible for me to write. Chris, John, Bob, Clare, Dolly, Collin, Aidan, and Mia: I love you all more than words can say.

Book Discussion Questions

Historic Period

1 Wawetseka was torn between traditional Native American culture, what she learned at a Jesuit mission, and her life with a mixed-blood family. Do you think she embraced or disdained non-native culture? How did her experiences as a young woman affect how she went about saving Nagmo?

2 How did Wawetseka change during her story? What qualities did you see in her from the beginning that foreshadowed her ability to succeed at what she set out to do?

3 In the final chapter of *Wawetseka's Tale* she says, "What was normal for a woman who was educated beyond her family and friends, who has experienced such adventures, who must now live away from those she loves and forget her past? How does a woman do that?" Discuss her dilemma. Why do you think she decided to remain at her traditional home instead of relocating with the majority of her people?

4 Wawetseka did not know, or did not say, what message Simon brought to Fort Dearborn. What do you think it might have been?

5 Why do you think Simon approached Findel at Fort Dearborn to discuss his problem, rather than taking it to the military commander or some other authority?

6 Why do you think Penney interrupted his escape to stop at Isle a la Cache? Convenience? Weather? Hiding? Something he, or someone else, left there?

Contemporary Period

1 Why did each of the present-day characters decide to write a book, despite other pressing issues in their lives? Do you think they would make the same decision if they had it to do over again?

2 Why do you think the writer added Mishipeshu to the story? Why do you suppose Frannie thought the Water Panther could be a real threat? Why did Nick discount it?

3 Why did Dawn decide to follow Billy alone instead of waiting to confront him with others present?

4 If mobsters had never used the cave, would the other treasures have been found?

5 Discuss how your feelings about Billy changed during the story. How well did he handle his dilemma when he realized Dawn and Nick were in danger? What should he have done?

6 Was the wolf attack an intentional murder attempt or an accidental result of sedating it for transport?

7 Do you think there is any possibility Josh survived?

8 In the final chapter each character gives a different version of the climactic scene. Which do you think happened? Why?

Bridges and Parallels

1 There are many parallels between the present-day and 1817 characters: Dawn and Wabmimi, Frannie and Shawnash, Nick and Nagmo, Cisco and Poji. How are these characters alike? How are they different? What similarities are there in their stories and the challenges they face?

2 Except for the Author's Note, Cora wrote *Wawetseka's Tale*. What effect did that have on the first-person characterization of Wawetseka? What were the likenesses and differences between Wawetseka and Cora?

3 Did you trust or suspect Noah? Did you see any parallels between Noah and Billy? In what ways are these characters and their stories alike?

4 In chapter 4 many reenactors are introduced at Rendezvous. Did you recognize any of the reenactors when you read *Wawetseka's Tale?*

5 Do you think M'ewé was a real wolf or a spirit? Do you think Cora's wolf-protector was M'ewé or some other spirit?

6 Nagmo and Wabmimi, Nick and Dawn, Cora and Cisco all have difficulties early in their marriage. Discuss the parallels.

7 Geographic features of the setting and violent weather affected both the historic and present-day parts of the story. Did the setting enhance your enjoyment of the story? Compare and contrast how the weather affected the historic and present-day stories.

8 An arm beckons from the water when Wawetseka first sees the body and again at the end of the present-day story. Comment on the significance of this detail.

About the Author

Pat Camalliere is the author of *The Mystery at Sag Bridge*, a popular, five-star-rated historical mystery novel. She lives with her husband in Lemont, Illinois, a suburb of Chicago. She serves on the boards of the Lemont Historical Society and Lemont Public Library District and is a member of Sisters in Crime. She speaks locally on a variety of topics and writes a blog that features unique history stories. Visit her website at patcamallierebooks.com.